# DEADLY PURSUIT

BRIAN HARPER

A SIGNET BOOK

SIGNET
Published by the Penguin Group
Penguin Books USA Inc., 375 Hudson Street,
New York, New York 10014, U.S.A.
Penguin Books Ltd, 27 Wrights Lane,
London W8 5TZ, England
Penguin Books Australia Ltd, Ringwood,
Victoria, Australia
Penguin Books Canada Ltd, 10 Alcorn Avenue,
Toronto, Ontario, Canada M4V 3B2
Penguin Books (N.Z.) Ltd, 182–190 Wairau Road,
Auckland 10, New Zealand

Penguin Books Ltd, Registered Offices:
Harmondsworth, Middlesex, England

First published by Signet, an imprint of Dutton Signet,
a division of Penguin Books USA Inc.

First Printing, July, 1995
10 9 8 7 6 5 4 3 2 1



REGISTERED TRADEMARK—MARCA REGISTRADA

Printed in the United States of America



PUBLISHER'S NOTE
This is a work of fiction. Names, characters, places, and incidents either are the product of the author's imagination or are used fictitiously, and any resemblance to actual persons, living or dead, events, or locales is entirely coincidental.

# NIGHT TERROR . . .

Kirstie turned. Ran.

The flashlight's glare had temporarily wiped out her night vision, and she nearly blundered off the trail as she sprinted headlong for the garden gate. No need to look over her shoulder; she could gauge Jack's distance by the brightness of the beam tracking her.

The gate flew up fast and slammed into her midsection. She flung it wide, ran through, then shut it, and gambled a precious second fumbling with the latch. It snicked into place, and then she was running again.

Hope lifted her. The flashlight no longer had her pinned in its beam. She seemed to have outdistanced her pursuer.

As she passed the wicker lounge chair, she tipped it on its side, blocking the portico. Anything to slow Jack down and give her time to get out the front door, to the dock, the boats—

Just inside the patio doorway, she whirled, intending to close and lock the French doors.

She froze. Hope died. A new surge of terror grabbed her by the throat.

He was there.

# DEADLY PURSUIT

## ACKNOWLEDGMENTS

Sincere thanks are due to my agent, Jane Dystel of Jane Dystel Literary Management in New York, for guiding my career wisely over several years; my editor at Dutton Signet, Joseph Pittman, for his enthusiasm, strong support, and sound judgment; Michaela Hamilton and Elaine Koster, also of Dutton Signet, for helping to shape all four of my books, as well as a successful marketing strategy; the marketing and sales personnel; and my friend Russ Dvonch, who provided me with detailed maps of the Florida Keys.

—Brian Harper

# 1

Leaning forward, resting his elbow on the long mahogany bar, he gave the woman a look at his white smile.

"You don't mean that?" he asked quietly.

"But I do. I envy you, living in L.A. That's a real city. You can *do* things."

"Phoenix isn't a real city?"

"Well, sure it is, but . . ." She giggled. "*You* know."

He liked her laugh. He liked everything about her. She was exactly his type. Blue eyes, smooth skin lightly dusted with freckles, blond hair. About twenty-seven, he'd guess; eight years younger than himself. The tight blue dress showed a lot of leg and cleavage and, when she bent toward him, offered a glimpse of her white breasts.

She'd been sitting alone at the bar when he alighted beside her an hour ago. He'd bought her four cocktails so far. She was drinking vodka, straight, and though she held her liquor surprisingly well, the drinks were having an unmistakable effect.

"Personally," he said, "I like your town." He sipped the slush of gin and ice in the bottom of his glass. "Nice and clean. Feels safe."

"If you lived here, you'd know different."

"It's not safe?"

"Not *hardly*." Her sudden intensity brought out a Southern dialect only partly scrubbed away by years spent far from home. "Why, my girlfriend Erin, she was out walking two-three weeks ago, just after dark, and these Mexicans—not that I've got anything against them in general . . ."

"What did they do to her?"

"Stole her purse. Yanked it right off her arm and started running."

He grunted disapproval.

"Nobody's safe anymore." She tipped her glass to her mouth, and he watched the lazy swallowing motion of her throat. "Here—or anywhere."

His gaze drifted away from her to take in the rest of the bar. The place was crowded, doing good business on a Friday night, even at this post-midnight hour. Two overworked waitresses, bearing trays laden with fresh drinks and dirty glasses, maneuvered through the crush of people in the dim ambient light. Cigarette smoke soured the air, diffused by the ceiling fans and the humming air conditioner.

He returned his eyes to her face. "Sorry to hear about your friend. Even so, Phoenix is considerably safer than L.A."

"Safer maybe—but a lot more boring."

"I'm sure you know ways to have a good time."

A grin flickered at the corner of her mouth. "I might."

She studied him. He endured her frank inspection without flinching. He knew he made a good impression, sitting relaxed at the bar in his conservative brown suit and open-collared shirt.

He pictured himself as she was seeing him: the sharp planes of his face, the crisp white line of a vaguely wolfish smile, hazel eyes that squinted coolly in a way that was both promise and warning.

These were assets he knew well, assets he'd exploited throughout his life—ever since high school, when in his senior year he had been voted Prom King, Class Stud, and Most Likely to Succeed. He knew the rare secret of appealing to both sexes. Men found him instantly likable and unthreatening; women found him sexy.

"You planning to be in town long?" she asked, still watching him, appraising his face as he had appraised hers.

"Only for the weekend."

"Business?"

"Pleasure."

She hooted. "Honey, *nobody* comes to Phoenix in August for fun."

"I do."

"It's hotter'n Hades in the daytime. Doesn't cool down much at night, either."

"I like my nights hot."

She looked down at her hands, thinking about that. Slowly her gaze traveled up the length of her glass, then higher, and met his eyes. "Sometimes . . . so do I."

He let her words hang in the space between them, gathering weight.

"You live around here?" he asked, his voice just loud enough to be heard above the background clamor.

"Mile away."

"Alone?"

"My roommate's out of town for the weekend. Getting banged by her boyfriend in Santa Fe."

"Doesn't seem fair she should have all the luck."

"Maybe she won't."

He touched her hand, let his index finger slide slowly over her knuckles, then gently caressed her thin and delicate wrist. "You're a very beautiful lady."

The compliment, and his slow stroking, lifted a blush to her cheeks. "You L.A. guys . . ."

"What about us?"

"You know."

He traced faint whitish lines in the smooth skin of her forearm, watched them fade like contrails in a cloudless sky. "We're operators? Hustlers? Is that it?"

She wouldn't look at him. "Sure."

"You're right." He teased the sleeve of her blouse. "We have to be. The women there—they're jaded. Tough. Not friendly. Not . . . trusting."

She answered with a soundless laugh.

"What?" he asked.

"Like I should trust you?"

"Why not?"

"I don't even know your name."

"It's Mike. Mike Allen. How about you?"

"Veronica Tyler. Folks call me Ronni."

"That's cute. *You're* cute."

"Actually . . . so are you. Mike."

"You don't want me to be lonely tonight, in a strange city all by myself, do you, Ronni?"

"If I walked away, you wouldn't be lonely for long. You'd charm some other sweet young thing."

"I don't want some other sweet young thing."

She took his hand. "That's good, mister. 'Cause you're getting me."

He paid for the drinks, adding a standard tip. He let Ronni Tyler lead him out of the bar.

They emerged into the balmy night. Downtown Phoenix rose on their left, bright and stark, the tall buildings aglow. Traffic hissed past on Second Street. Somewhere a car radio howled a Garth Brooks tune.

"How'd you get here?" Ronni asked.

"Delta shuttle from LAX."

She blinked at the answer until it made sense to her. "No, silly, I mean, how'd you get to the bar?"

"Took a cab. My motel's in Scottsdale."

"My place is closer."

"You've got a car?"

"Heck, yes. I'm a regular career woman, you know?" Unsteadily she guided him down the street. "Eight to four, Monday through Friday, First Interstate Bank." She pronounced it *Innersate.* "I'm an assistant manager."

"That's good. Real good."

"Oh, yeah, fantastic. What're you, some hotshot movie exec or something?"

"Nothing like that. I'm in sales."

"Sales?" She made a breathy sound, not quite a hiccup. "Should've figured."

They reached a blue Toyota Paseo parked at the curb. She let him in on the passenger side, then climbed behind the wheel.

"Sure you're all right to drive?" he asked.

"I'm okay. It's only a mile from here, like I said."

She started the engine and eased into traffic. He noted with some relief that she had used her directional signal. Apparently she really was sober enough.

"You're not from around here originally," he observed, just to make conversation.

"No. From South Carolina. Little town called Bennett."

"Nice?"

"If it was, I guess I wouldn't be in Phoenix, would I?"

"Point taken."

She turned onto Jefferson Street. "No, honestly, it's not so bad. Nice country. But there's no work to find, and no young people. No life, you know? That's what I'm always looking for. Life."

The car hummed a tuneless air, strip malls and billboards swept past, downtown receded.

After exactly a mile the Paseo hooked left onto a residential street lined with apartment complexes and elm trees. Ronni Tyler swung the Toyota into the parking lot of a five-story building identified by a lighted sign as Saguaro Terraces.

"Well," she said, "here we are."

"Nice place."

She eased into her assigned space in a crowded carport and shut off the engine. "Yeah, I'm pretty happy with it. Everything's first-class, you know? Pool, spa, clubhouse, the works." *Works* came out badly slurred. "Even got a security guard in the lobby."

"Security guard? He on duty now?"

"Always is. I mean, not the same guy all the time . . ."

She was fumbling with the latch on the driver's-side door. He stopped her. "Wait."

"What for?"

"I want to kiss you."

"Right this second?"

"I've held off long enough."

His mouth found hers. He shut his eyes and kissed her hard and thought about the guard.

It was a problem. An obstacle. He couldn't be seen entering with her. Leaving the bar together hadn't worried him too much; the place was crowded, and as best he could tell, no one knew her there. But the security guard, who saw her every night, might very well take note of any new man she was with. Some of these guys were ex-cops; they had a memory for faces.

She broke away from him with a gasp. "God, you're really turned on, aren't you?"

"I'm just getting warmed up."

The words were automatic. He was thinking fast. Take her to his motel? He could get her into his room without being seen. But how to convince her to go there, when they were already parked at her place?

"Well, in that case"—she reached for the door latch again—"let's not waste any more time."

Her head was turned, the side of her neck exposed, and he knew what he had to do.

They didn't need to go to her apartment or to his motel room or anywhere. Here in the carport would be fine. Just fine.

His hand reached into his jacket pocket and brought out a plastic syringe.

"These seats recline?" he asked softly.

She popped the latch, and her door swung open. The ceiling light winked on. "Huh?"

"Do the front seats recline?"

"Sure, honey." Another giggle. "But you don't wanna do it here, do you?"

"As a matter of fact," he said quietly, "I do." He gripped the syringe with four fingers, laid his thumb on the plunger. "Good night, Meredith."

Ronni turned toward him, her blue eyes bright and unsuspecting.

"Meredith? My name's not—"

She had time to blink, perhaps to detect a flash of motion on the periphery of her vision, and then the needle punched through the soft skin under her jaw, biting deep and squirting venom, cruel as an adder's kiss.

# 2

The island bloomed like a second sunrise on the horizon, and Steve Gardner smiled.

*Still looks the same,* he thought with a rush of nostalgic yearning. *Unspoiled. Perfect.*

He turned to Kirstie, standing beside him on the motel balcony, her face colored by the pink blush of morning. Her blond hair, recently permed, was losing its curls in a fresh easterly breeze. The flaps of her blouse collar beat like wings against her smooth, tanned throat.

"That's it." Steve pointed. "Pelican Key."

She caught his excitement and reflected it in her smile. "Looks beautiful. Like paradise."

Padding at their feet, Anastasia let out a soft whine. Steve scratched the borzoi's angular snout.

"That's how I always thought of it," he said softly. "Paradise. The kind of place that never changes. The rest of the world can go downhill, straight to hell—but there'll always be Pelican Key, pristine and uncorrupted."

"I don't think there's too much corruption in Danbury."

She made an effort at levity, but he caught the familiar undertone of irritation in her voice.

"No," he said briskly. "Of course not."

Conversation ended then, leaving a silence between

them. There had been too many silences in recent months.

*My fault,* Steve told himself. *Always is, right? My fault—and my guilt.*

The thought was a clinging cobweb. He brushed it away.

He knew he couldn't make his wife see what the island meant to him. Whenever he tried, the words came out sounding like a criticism of their home, their marriage, all the pieces of the life they'd built together. Better, safer, to say nothing at all.

Back inside the room, he repacked his razor, toothbrush, comb, and the few other items he'd used that morning, then methodically checked the nightstand and bureau drawers, though he knew neither he nor Kirstie had even opened them. They had spent less than ten hours in the motel, just enough time to grab some desperately needed sleep after the thirty-six-hour drive from Danbury, Connecticut, to Upper Matecumbe Key.

Kirstie used the john, and Steve did the same, and Anastasia barked and they both silenced her, fearful of disturbing the neighbors at this early hour, and finally they were ready to check out.

Trundling and lugging suitcases, they made their way down to their Grand Am and loaded the trunk. Steve wandered over to the office and paid the bill. The off-season rate was pleasingly low.

Not that the place was likely to win four diamonds in the AAA guidebook anytime soon. There were better motels on the key, but two people who meant to keep a Russian wolfhound in the room with them could hardly insist on elegance.

On his way back to the car, Steve took a short detour to look at the saltwater swimming pool—shallow now, at low tide—and beyond it, the tiny square of pitiful manmade beach that was the establishment's pride. Sand beaches were rare in the Keys. The coral reef that paralleled the chain of islands on their seaward side, all the way from Key Largo to Key West, stopped the wave action that normally deposited drifts of sand on coastal platforms. For the most part the shoreline consisted of coral and limestone ledges, mangrove forest, and mud flats.

He had no real interest in the pool or the trucked-in sand, of course. What he wanted was one more sight of Pelican Key.

There it was—a faint green line on the blue waters, tremulous as a daydream, elusive as hope.

He and Kirstie ate breakfast at a fast-food place, buying an extra sausage-and-egg sandwich for Anastasia to consume in the car. After that, a trip to a local market, where they stocked up on groceries and other supplies.

He paid for the items and wheeled the cart outside. Kirstie was waiting for him near a pair of vending machines, a newspaper in her hand. "Got you a *Miami Herald.*"

Steve's heart constricted with a brief squeeze of fear. "I don't want it."

"You always read the paper. Two or three of them a day, lately."

"Not today. Not on this trip. We're on vacation, remember?"

"What does that have to do with anything?"

"We're taking a break from . . . from the world."

A frown briefly clouded her face. Then she shrugged. "Well, okay. But since I already bought this one, we might as well take it with us." She placed it in the cart. "I can do the crossword—"

"I said, I don't *want* the goddamn thing." He

grabbed the paper and wedged it roughly in the mouth of a trash can.

She stared at him, eyes narrowed, then turned and walked quickly through the parking lot, toward Anastasia yelping in the car. The cart wheels squeaked as he followed.

Hell. He shouldn't have done that. But he had to establish the trip's ground rules sometime. For the next two weeks, no newspapers, no TV, no radio. No contact with anything outside Pelican Key.

The island was his haven. He meant to keep it secure.

At eight o'clock, precisely on schedule, the Grand Am eased to a stop outside the gated entrance to a marina in Islamorada. Steve leaned out the window, and the security guard swung down from his seat in the guardhouse.

"We're here to meet a captain named Pice," Steve said.

The guard grinned. "Going to Pelican Key, are you?"

"That's right."

"Bring mosquito spray?"

"Sure did."

"You'll be okay, then." The guard thumbed the button to lift the gate. "Captain Pice is on his boat—that's the *Black Caesar,* a thirty-foot sportfisher moored in Basin C."

"Mosquitoes," Kirstie said flatly as Steve drove through. "I don't recall any mention of that particular selling point in the brochure."

Steve forced a smile. "They won't bother you as long as you make them keep their distance."

"How do you do that?"

"Beats me."

The joke registered. She rewarded him with a brief softening of her features.

They found Pice on the deck of the *Black Caesar,* fussing with the contents of a stowage cabinet. He greeted them in a booming voice like a cannon shot.

"You must be the Gardners. Right on time, too."

Steve shook the captain's hand. Creased and leathery, like a well-worn glove.

Somehow Pice managed to compress his entire biography into a few introductory sentences as he walked back to the car with them to help unload their supplies. His full name was Chester Edmund Pice, and he'd lived in the Keys all his life, thereby qualifying as a bona fide Conch. His boat, as they had surely observed, was the *Black Caesar,* so christened in honor of a half-historical, half-legendary buccaneering companion of Blackbeard.

"But old Caesar, now, not only his *beard* was black," Pice explained with a lion cough of laughter. "*He* was black, every bit as black as yours truly. He made piracy an equal-opportunity profession."

Pice himself, he assured them, had never run the Jolly Roger up his mast. For more than forty years he'd fished the Florida Straits, before deciding to give the fish a break and himself a rest. Semi-retired now at sixty-five, he'd made an arrangement with the Larson family to ferry vacationers to and from Pelican Key.

"I'll get you there," he promised cheerfully while helping the Gardners load their luggage and groceries aboard his boat. "And I'll be back to pick you up in two weeks."

Steve handed him a small traveling case of Kirstie's. "There's supposed to be a motorboat at the island for everyday use."

"Sure is. Little wooden-hulled job with an Evinrude outboard. Nothing fancy, but she'll get you back and forth to town. You won't use her much, though. You won't care to leave Pelican Key. It casts a spell on you. Half a month there, in blessed isolation—why, it's as good as a miracle cure."

He hefted their heaviest suitcase without strain and went on speaking as if he were empty-handed.

"Believe me, I know. I see them all the time—people like you. They show up worn out and frazzled and cranky, with the world's weight bearing them down, and when I retrieve 'em a couple weeks later, they're like members of a whole new species."

Kirstie was amused. "We're not usually quite so worn out. It's just that we're a little tired after the drive—"

"Oh, I didn't mean to imply that *you* look frazzled, ma'am," Pice said hastily, worried that he'd given offense. "You're a vision of loveliness and youth." He winked at her. "But your hubby, now, *he* could use a rest."

Kirstie nodded, meeting Steve's eyes. "Definitely."

Steve could hardly dispute the point. "That's why I'm here," he said mildly. "And I know I picked the right place, because I used to visit Pelican Key fairly regularly."

Pice put down the suitcase on the gangplank and studied him with a squinty pirate's eye. "Did you, now? Paying a call on Mr. Larson?"

"No, this was seventeen years ago or more. Back when I was in high school. Before Mr. Larson lived there."

"Before . . . ? Son, in those days Pelican Key was uninhabited."

"I know it."

"So who exactly were you visiting?"

"Nobody."

"You'll have to explain that."

"My best friend's dad had a boat docked up north. Every summer the three of us would cruise south to Islamorada. Then my friend's dad would canvass the local bars, while the two of us boys rented a dinghy with a outboard motor and went exploring. Somehow we always ended up at Pelican Key. Probably we weren't supposed to be there; Larson owned it even then, of course, though he hadn't started the restoration work yet. Anyway, nobody ever stopped us."

"What did two boys encounter on Pelican Key that was so fascinating?"

"Everything. The old plantation house, the reef, the boardwalk through the mangrove swamp . . . Is the boardwalk still there?"

"Fully repaired, and good as new."

"Glad to hear it. It's important to me—the whole island, I mean. We had some great times on Pelican Key." Steve felt wistful sadness welling in him. "Some great times."

"Now he's bent on recapturing his lost youth," Kirstie said, aiming for a tone of playful banter, but just missing.

Steve felt a flush of embarrassment. "That's not it. Or not . . . not exactly."

"Then what, exactly?" she pressed. "What are you really trying to find?"

"Nothing. I mean . . . Pelican Key is a special place, that's all. I wanted to see it again." His answer sounded lame even to him.

Pice cut in with a diplomat's poise. "This friend of yours—what was his name, anyhow? Maybe I knew him."

"I doubt it. He was a kid like me."

"His pappy, then. You said he liked to hoist a glass. I've been known to frequent the local groggeries myself on rare occasions."

"Albert Dance was his name. His son was Jack."

"No, doesn't ring a bell. Unusual name, Dance. I'm sure I'd remember it. Was this the marina where you tied up?"

"As a matter of fact, it was."

"There might be some folks here who'd know you."

"I imagine so. Mickey Cotter, for one. He was a security guard at the time."

"And he still is. He's an old man now—older than me, if you young folks can imagine such a thing—but he keeps on working. Mans the guardhouse from midnight to seven."

Steve was pleased to hear that. "Well, if you see him, let him know that Steve Gardner is here for a visit. He might not recall the name, but he'll remember Mr. Dance's boat. Twenty-five-foot flybridge cruiser called the *Light Fantastic.* Mickey has a memory for boats."

"That he does." Pice smiled. "You know, it's comical. Here I've been sounding off about Pelican Key like you're a pair of ordinary tourists, and you know the island better than I do."

"Steve knows it," Kirstie said. "I don't. I've never even been to Florida before."

Pice picked up the suitcase again. "Well, you beautify the landscape, ma'am. Believe me, you do."

He boarded the boat, lugging the suitcase and whistling.

"What do you think?" Steve asked Kirstie once Pice was out of earshot.

She smiled. "I think he *is* Black Caesar, reincarnated. All he's missing is a peg leg and a parrot on his shoulder."

"You never know. He just might have that parrot around someplace." He took her hand. "Our captain is right about one thing. You *do* beautify the landscape."

"Oh, stop," she whispered, turning away.

The trip got under way a few minutes later. Anastasia stretched out in the cockpit, Pice took the helm seat on the flying bridge, and Kirstie settled into the bench behind him. Steve remained on the dock long enough to cast off the bow and stern lines, then jumped aboard.

Pice started the twin diesel engines, engaged the astern gears with a double clunk, and carefully throttled back, easing the boat out of its berth. When the bow was clear of the dock, he swung toward the channel, shifted to the ahead gears, and nursed the paired throttle levers forward. The *Black Caesar* chugged into the entrance channel at a cautious speed.

Steve climbed the ladder to the flying bridge and sat down beside Kirstie.

"Seasick yet?" he inquired.

She showed him her tongue. "Does it look green?"

"No more than usual."

They passed between the buoys marking the harbor entrance. Pice headed southwest, past Shell Key, then motored under a bridge festooned with fishing lines into Hawk Channel, the waterway between the Keys and the reef.

They were running east now, toward the sun. Pelican Key was ahead somewhere in the brassy glare.

Steve was too fidgety to stay seated. He rose, bracing himself against a stainless-steel safety rail, and drew deep breaths of the briny sea air, swallowing it like food.

From this vantage point he could look down unobtrusively over Pice's shoulder and read the tachometers and oil-pressure gauges on the control console. He watched the tach needles climb to 2,000 rpm as

Pice opened the port and starboard throttles a little wider. A light spray misted the windshield; the wipers beat briefly to clean it.

Ahead, a boiling cloud of gulls flocked over a fishing boat as it steamed toward the Gulf Stream beyond the reef. To the south lay Indian Key; at their backs, Upper Matecumbe. Both receded, leaving Pelican Key to its—how had Pice put it—its "blessed isolation."

That isolation was perhaps part of the reason why the place had never been developed into a resort hotel complex or a tournament golf course. Route 1, the elevated highway that played connect-the-dots with most of the islands, had missed Pelican Key by three miles. Henry Flagler's railroad, built years earlier and demolished in the hurricane of '35, had come no closer. No bridge or causeway linked Upper Matecumbe to Pelican Key. The only access to it was by boat, helicopter, or seaplane.

Nobody had ever much desired to go there anyway. Compared with most other local islands, Pelican Key was small—only three-quarters of a mile long and a quarter-mile wide—and a good part of its hundred and twenty acres was taken up by mangrove swamp. Hardly a developer's dream.

A lime plantation had operated on Pelican Key during the early years of this century; the Depression had shut it down. After that, the island had remained unwanted until Donald Larson bought it in 1946. Larson was a young man who'd already made a great deal of money in aviation and was destined to make much more. His dream was to restore the plantation house, a victim of time and storms, and retire to it someday.

Someday hadn't come until 1980, when Larson, no longer young, had finally begun the renovations planned decades earlier. In the interim he'd fought a fierce, protracted battle with the state government, which had wanted to purchase Pelican Key and preserve it as a park.

Larson had held on to the property and forestalled an eminent-domain ruling only by guaranteeing that no further development would be attempted there, either in his lifetime or afterward. The house and other features already present would be repaired, modernized, and maintained; otherwise, Pelican Key would remain as the coral polyps and red mangrove had made it.

He'd been true to his word. And from 1981 to 1992 he'd lived in the big limestone house on the island's south end, enjoying, no doubt, his blessed isolation.

When he died, his heirs had faced the dilemma of what to do with Pelican Key. A considerable tax write-off could be realized by donating it to the state of Florida. But some residue of the elder Larson's stubborn pride and sentimental attachment to the island had prevented such a move.

Instead the estate continued to maintain the house and pay the property taxes, offsetting part of the costs by renting out Pelican Key to vacationers as a private retreat, on a monthly basis in season, with biweekly deals available during the hot, wet summer months.

Steve had found out about the vacation rentals in March. The need to return to the island had been driving him like a quiet frenzy ever since.

"I see it," Kirstie said suddenly, leaning forward.

Steve craned his neck, following her gaze, and picked out a smear of tropical verdure against the blinding sun.

Close now. Unexpectedly close, appearing out of the dazzle like a vision in a dream.

Down in the cockpit, Anastasia barked, as if in confirmation of the sighting.

"There's the house." Pice pointed. "See the windows shining like coins?"

Steve nodded eagerly. "Yes. I see." A broad tile roof was visible now, partly screened by branches. "Larson must have gone all out on the restoration. The place was a ruin when Jack and I used to come here."

"Could you go inside?" Kirstie asked.

"Oh, sure. Found a dead coral snake in a bathtub once. Must have crawled in there for some reason and died."

Her nose wrinkled prettily. "Remind me not to bathe for the next two weeks."

"Don't worry. It's a big bathtub. Plenty of room for you *and* a snake."

The rap of her knuckles on his arm was meant to be playful, but hurt anyway.

The *Black Caesar* motored closer. Pice glanced back at them with a grin. "What do you say we circle her once, just to say hello?"

He was already steering the boat northeast. The mangrove fringe on the island's western side blurred past—dense clumps of twisted trees, foreboding and mysterious, the eldritch landscape of another world.

At the north end, there was a small cove, a semicircle of shallow water, mirror-lustrous, bordered by mangroves and stands of hardwood trees.

"That's where we used to beach the dinghy," Steve said, remembering. "There's a Calusa Indian midden not far inland—you know, a shell mound. The salt ponds are nearby, too."

Kirstie studied him. "How much time did you and Jack spend here, anyway?"

"Oh, about four days a summer, three summers in all. Maybe twelve days, total." He shook his head. "Doesn't seem like much, does it?"

"I don't know. I've had love affairs that were briefer."

"None recently, I hope."

"Wouldn't you like to know."

They were cruising along the seaward side now, past a narrow beach composed of broken bits of coral, pebbly and coarse, over a solid coral foundation. Palms and the imported Australian pines called casuarinas fringed the beach, swaying gently as if to unheard music.

Near the southern tip of the key, the motorboat Pice had promised came into view, bobbing in the shallows. It was moored to a small dock at the end of a pathway twisting down from the house between landscaped beds of poinsettias and yellow jasmine.

The dock was new to Steve. It hadn't been there when he and Jack explored the key. Neither had the path, for that matter, nor the flower beds. A lot had changed. But the important things had remained untouched, unsullied—a small but precious part of his life that had never been tainted.

The boat glided toward the dock. Anastasia was barking again. Pelican Key waited, silent and calm.

Abruptly, Kirstie turned to him, her face almost solemn. "Steve. I . . . I hope this works out for you. For both of us."

"What does?"

"The trip. The time we spend here. I hope you find . . . whatever it is you're looking for."

The words touched him in a tender place. He reached out, stroked her hair, soft and golden, and she did not pull away.

"I don't need anything more than what I have right now," he whispered.

It was the right thing to say. But he no longer knew if it was true—or if it could be true for him, ever again.

# 3

At eight-fifteen on Saturday morning, a tenant of Saguaro Terraces was unlocking his Jeep Cherokee in the carport when he noticed the ceiling light in a Toyota Paseo glowing dimly, the passenger-side door slightly ajar.

He found a young woman lying in the driver's seat, which had been levered back to a nearly horizontal position. Her dress had been lifted above her hips, her panties shredded.

"Miss?"

He rapped on the windshield and, when that failed to rouse her, reached through the open window and shook her gently.

She listed sideways in her seat, her pretty face turning toward him as her head rolled. Through a net of blond hair, her eyes stared at him and through him, their blue gaze fixed on death.

After that, things happened very fast.

Phoenix P.D. was on the scene by 8:27. A senior homicide investigator, Detective Robert Ashe, arrived soon afterward. Examining the body with gloved hands, he found the needle mark at the side of the throat.

Ashe was a twenty-year veteran, eligible for a full pension and thinking seriously about taking it, but he was still conscientious enough to read the bulletins that crossed his desk. He recognized the pattern.

"Better call the feds," he told the watch commander.

It was nine-fifteen by then, and already Phoenix was getting hot.

Two special agents from the Denver field office of the Federal Bureau of Investigation were on the ground at Sky Harbor Airport three hours later. A Phoenix agent met them at the flight gate and introduced himself as Ramon Peña.

"I'm Peter Lovejoy." The tall, pale Denver agent shook Peña's hand and sneezed. "Don't worry. Nothing catching, as far as I know. Only allergies."

Tension and fatigue were recorded on Lovejoy's thin face. His high forehead was prematurely lined, his eyes tired and angry. It was obvious that the long investigation had worn him down.

"You'll like Phoenix," Peña said, trying for a light note. "Whole environment is hypoallergenic."

Lovejoy's partner smiled. "Don't count on it. Peter's nose has the extraordinary ability to sniff out individual pollen grains five hundred miles away."

She said it with affection, but Lovejoy looked nettled anyway. "Possibly a slight exaggeration," he muttered, then blew wetly into a crumpled Kleenex.

Peña wasn't looking at him. The woman held his attention now. She was slender and poised, her skin the color of dark rum, her brown hair close-cropped in a skull-tight Afro. The sculptured planes of her face captured a regal quality that made him think of carved likenesses on ancient monuments.

He supposed she must be worn out, too, and as frustrated as her partner, but she didn't show it. Though she wore the Bureau's trademark navy blue jacket, white shirt, and beige slacks, she conveyed the austere glamour of a model on a fashion runway.

"I'm Tamara Moore," she said as they started hiking down the concourse.

"Tamara, huh? Nice name."

"I've been told it means 'date palm.' "

"A date palm in the desert. You'll fit right in."

Moore smiled, and Lovejoy sneezed again.

Guiding the government sedan onto I-17 with the air conditioner on high, Peña asked how long they'd been after Mister Twister.

"Eight months," Lovejoy answered. "Since he did a girl in Denver."

"How'd the Denver office get involved in a homicide?"

"The victim's body was dumped on Trail Ridge road in the Rocky Mountain National Forest. Federal jurisdiction."

"And you tied it to some earlier murders?"

"Yes." Lovejoy honked into a tissue. "In our judgment, there appeared to be two relevant unsolved homicides, one in San Antonio, the other in Albuquerque. Each case had been handled locally, and nobody had made the connection."

"What *is* the connection? What pattern do you look for?"

"Within certain broad parameters, he follows the same M.O. each time. Bar pickup, lethal injection in the neck. Always on a weekend—Friday or Saturday night. And always the same victim profile: attractive woman, mid-twenties to mid-thirties, blue eyes, blond hair, fair complexion, slender build. That would appear to be his type."

Peña caught a strong whiff of the bureaucrat's cover-your-ass mentality in Lovejoy's answers. "In our judgment . . . within certain parameters . . . that would appear to be . . ."

*This guy will go far,* he thought with a mixture of amusement and bitterness. "So there've been three victims since?"

This time Moore answered. "Not counting the latest one. Las Vegas, Dallas, San Diego. Add Phoenix to the list, and you've got seven in all."

"He keeps busy, doesn't he?"

"Too damn busy. Murder is a compulsion for him. He won't stop till he's caught or killed."

No equivocations or qualifications for her. She was a straight-shooter.

"Guess you've got a lot of people working this thing," Peña said.

"Over sixty law enforcement agents full-time. It's a multijurisdictional task force, and somehow we wound up in charge. Well, actually Peter did."

Lovejoy shrugged. "It appears I had the seniority, so the Denver SAC made me task force leader. But from my perspective, Tamara and I are functioning as equals. We share the work and the responsibility."

*And the blame if anything goes wrong,* Peña thought. Aloud, he said, "I'm surprised the Denver SAC didn't take over the task force himself." A special-agent-in-charge normally grabbed the high-profile assignments for himself.

"He might have wanted to." With effort Lovejoy stifled a sneeze. "Initially they seem to have unloaded the case on a couple of street agents—that is to say, us—because they thought it was just another random homicide that would never be solved. Once we detected what appeared to be a pattern, we were in too deep to be pulled off."

"Lucky you." Peña had one more question. "Where did his name come from? Mister Twister?"

"Not our idea," Moore said. "Officially he's the Trail Ridge Killer. But that's not sexy enough for the media. There's a line in a song—something about a Mister Twister. How loving him is like embracing a whirlwind; he destroys everything he touches. Must have struck someone as an appropriate image, and it just caught on."

"Well," Peña said as he found the Central Avenue off-ramp, "this guy's sure as hell been cutting a swath of destruction across the great Southwest. And we usually don't get twisters around here."

On Veronica Tyler's neck, near the puncture wound, the M.E. had found a few droplets of clear fluid that must have spurted from the syringe. Serological analysis identified it as a 9.25% solution of hydrogen chloride in water, with traces of n-alkyl dimethyl benzyl ammonium chloride and n-alkyl dimethyl ethylbenzyl ammonium chloride.

"The same stuff used in the other six killings," Moore said, putting down a faxed copy of the serology report. She had just looked at the crime-scene photos of Veronica Tyler, and for some reason she found it difficult to hold her voice steady. "The details of the injection were never made public in any of the cases. This is the real thing—no copycat."

Nobody had expected a copycat anyway. The murder was right on schedule for Mister Twister. Seven victims in fourteen months. A new corpse every eight or nine weeks. Always on a weekend. Reliable as clockwork.

Detective Ashe studied the report, smoothing out the flimsy fax paper with one hand. "Hydrogen chloride. Is that like hydrochloric acid?"

"In a more diluted form."

"Something he mixes up himself?"

Moore shook her head. "It's toilet-bowl cleaner. A commercially available brand. Highly corrosive. He shoots it into the carotid artery, straight to the brain."

"I guess that's one way to think clean thoughts," cracked a homicide cop, and the other detectives in the squad room, men in rumpled brown suits and loosened neckties, laughed nervously.

The Phoenix SAC, a silver-haired man named Gifford, shifted in his seat. "Is this brand distributed nationally?"

Lovejoy nodded. "Unfortunately, yes. There appears to be no hope of tracking the purchase. The manufacturer reports moving thirty thousand units a day."

"What about the syringe? You can't just walk into a store and buy one, can you?"

"Under normal circumstances, no. Syringes are prescription items. There was some preliminary speculation that our man could be a doctor, but the M.E.'s who've done the postmortems don't think so. He appears to show no unusual skill or knowledge in the placement of the needle. Possibly he's an orderly or he works at a medical-supply firm."

"Of course," Moore added, "anybody can obtain needles on the street." She'd seen enough of that in her childhood years.

Gifford frowned. "Dead end." He seemed about to say something more when Ashe's phone shrilled.

The desk sergeant transferring the call said there was a guy on the line who seemed to know something about the Tyler case. Ashe put him on the speakerphone.

"Detective? Name's Wallace Stargill. Call me Wally." His voice, coming over the cheap speaker, had a hollow sound. "I tend bar over at the Lazy Eight on Second Street. Think I saw that girl in here last night."

By this time Veronica Tyler's family had been notified of her death, and her most recent photo had been released to the local media.

"Okay, Wally," Ashe said, nicely composed. "You pretty sure it was her?"

"Yeah, damn sure."

"Was she with anyone?"

"This guy. I mean, she was by herself at first, and then he sat down next to her. Seemed to be coming on pretty strong."

"Can you describe him?"

"Not too good. It was crowded in there. The girl I noticed; she was a looker. As for the guy—I don't know. He was dressed nice, I remember that."

"Where are you now?"

"At the bar. I'm just opening up. Saw the report on TV while I was getting the kitchen ready for Julio."

"Who's Julio?"

"Substitute dishwasher. Our regular guy, Pedro, came down with the flu last night and had to go home early. Got a mess of dirty glasses here."

Moore was out of her seat. "Tell him not to wash anything. We'll be right over."

The bar had a friendless, disconsolate quality in daytime. Upended chairs rested on rows of tables. Sunlight struggled through high, frosted windows. The smell of stale booze hung over the place like the odor of disinfectant in a morgue.

There was a kitchen at the rear where the overworked waitresses had deposited trays of used glasses. "Slow nights, I wash 'em myself," Wally Stargill said to the small mob of agents and cops crowding in for a look. He was a tall, laconic man, his fleshy forearms crossed awkwardly over a spreading gut. "But Fridays and Saturdays are crazy here."

"Crazy," Gifford echoed, perhaps thinking of Veronica Tyler with an ampul of toilet cleaner in her neck.

Moore asked if the victim and the man who'd picked her up had left before or after Pedro went home.

"After."

"So the glasses they used weren't washed?"

"Probably not, unless I cleaned them in the sink under the bar. Like I said, I do that when we're not too busy. Last night I doubt I got a chance."

Moore pointed at the rows of glasses. Only Lovejoy knew her well enough to see that she was worked up. "He handled one of those."

Ashe frowned. "What are you going to do? Print them all?"

"Right."

"You serious?"

"Sure am."

"There must be three hundred glasses here."

"Then we'll print three hundred glasses."

Lovejoy cleared his throat, a tentative sound. "There might conceivably be a way to narrow it down." He turned to the bartender. "You happen to recall what the man was drinking?"

Stargill thought for a moment. "Beefeater on the rocks."

"You're certain?"

"Oh, yeah." A sheepish smile. "I never forget a drink."

"So it was a lowball glass," Gifford said.

"That's how we serve 'em."

Lovejoy coughed again. "As best I can judge, there would appear to be no more than thirty or forty of those."

"All of a sudden this sounds a lot more practical,"

Ashe said. "Got to warn you, though, our lab is pretty backed up. Staff cutbacks. You know the story."

"Possibly we can requisition some help, expedite the process." Lovejoy sneezed. "Damn. I hate this climate."

"You hate all climates," Moore said briskly. "Come on, let's talk to I.D. Wally, may we use your phone?"

Identification Division flew in the Latent Fingerprints section chief, Paul Collins, to assist the Phoenix P.D. crime lab in the tedious procedure.

Collins, an East Coast native who thought of Arizona as cow country and the local constabulary as rubes, was pleasantly astonished to find an argon laser at his disposal, along with cyanoacrylate fuming cabinets, iodine fume guns, and gentian violet baths. By the end of the assignment, he was humming "My Darling Clementine" and considering retirement in the Grand Canyon State.

One hundred forty-six latents were recovered. It took three days to run cold searches on them all, using a modem link between the Phoenix P.D. computer and the FBI's FINDER system, a database of eighty-three million prints. FINDER did the gross preliminary work, but the final, subtle matching had to be done by visual comparison, a time-consuming process.

Lovejoy and Moore stayed busy while the print searches progressed. Lovejoy flew home to brief the Denver SAC and wound up in a conference call with a deputy director and the Behavioral Science section chief. He appeased the media with a thirty-minute briefing in which he conveyed the impression of speaking substantively while actually saying nothing at all. He made no mention of the massive fingerprinting procedure already well underway.

Moore read a transcript of the news conference and

felt a familiar blend of irritation and bemusement. She knew that Peter was good at what he did, a competent agent and a decent man, but he was too willing to play the game on others' terms, to stifle his own personality in a numbing quest for blandness. Fundamentally he was weak, crippled by insecurity; and a hard life had taught her to despise softness of any kind.

In Phoenix she kept the other members of the task force updated by phone, fax, and E-mail. She was dealing with police departments in three cities, sheriff's offices in three counties, and the FBI field office in each of the states where a killing had occurred. The logistics were maddening.

Most of the effort was wasted anyhow. So far there was little news to report, as she informed Lovejoy when he called. "Ashe's people interviewed the two waitresses at the bar; they don't remember Veronica or her date. Her car has been dusted. Smooth glove prints on the passenger-side door handle."

"It would appear he wore gloves, as usual." Exhaustion dragged Lovejoy's voice down.

"Of course he did. There *were* some viable latents in the car that don't belong to the deceased. For elimination purposes Phoenix P.D. is printing Veronica's friends, neighbors, coworkers, anyone who might have ridden with her. But we both know he doesn't leave prints."

"How about the autopsy protocols?"

"Just delivered. No sign of anal or oral intercourse, but penile-vaginal contact is certain. Penetration was postmortem and rough. No semen was found; he's careful, used a condom."

"As usual," Lovejoy said again. "He doesn't seem to give us much to go on, does he?"

"You got that right."

"Well"—Lovejoy tried to sound hopeful—"possibly the bar angle will pan out."

"Speaking of which, Wally Stargill spent two hours with an Identikit artist and gave us a vague but not totally useless sketch."

"I know. I received the fax. But Drury wants to keep it out of the media for now. If the prints don't come through, we'll probably have to release it. Until then, the policy is to indicate no hint of any progress, nothing to make him cut and run. Have to go, my other line's buzzing. I expect to be back in Phoenix tomorrow, first thing in the a.m."

"Stay healthy."

Lovejoy sneezed. "Easy for you to say."

Each night Tamara caught a few hours of troubled sleep in her hotel room. When bad dreams woke her—dreams of a man with a honey-smooth voice and a vial of poison in his pocket—she would stand on the balcony, gazing at the downtown skyline under a canopy of stars.

There had been no stars above the Oakland slums where she'd been raised. No men with poison either—at least not Mister Twister's kind of poison. Other varieties were easy enough to come by. She had seen friends try some and get hooked, had seen conscientious students become burnouts and bums. Every day meant running a gauntlet of proffered drugs. It took a heroic effort just to stay clean.

Her looks hadn't helped. The other girls had envied her, called her Miss America and Charlie's Angel; but Tamara had passed many angry hours wishing she had been born plain. Her face and figure made her an irresistible object of seduction for every strutting gang-banger, every pimp or aspiring pimp plying fantasies of a modeling career, and every one of her mother's boyfriends—men who could barely wait for Doreen

Moore to leave the room before hitting on her daughter.

At night, through the cellophane-thin bedroom wall, she would hear her mom and her current paramour shaking the mattress springs and grunting; and she would wonder if the man was thinking of sweet little Tamara as he did it, if it was her breasts he imagined himself kissing, her legs that were spread for him in invitation. Even the thought of it would leave her dizzy with nausea.

She had survived, though. Had fought off the pushers and pimps and priapic older men, had been graduated as class valedictorian, had gone to U.C. Irvine on a full scholarship, and had ended up somehow at the FBI Academy in Quantico, Virginia, learning to be a G-man or a G-woman or whatever the hell she was.

Tamara sighed. The dry, balmy night air brushed her cheeks and reminded her of how far she'd come from Oakland. No chill morning fog creeping in off the bay to carpet the littered streets in a shimmering ground cover, not here. This was the desert, an environment alien to her, a Martian waste of leafless plants and chalk-dry riverbeds, flat and arid and brutally hot. Not her sort of place, but there were some who loved it.

Had Ronni Tyler been one of them? Had she awakened at night to study the stars, or risen before dawn to watch the pink glow of sunrise brighten the encircling mountains?

Ronni's roommate, interviewed by the police and FBI on the day of her return from Santa Fe, had said something funny about her friend. "Ronni—cripes, she was just a small-town girl at heart, but she didn't know it. She kept looking for something more, something bigger, better, than what she had. That was the thing with her. There always had to be something better . . . somewhere."

Tamara had known the same need. Huddled under her blankets in her mom's apartment in the projects, listening to the rattle and squeak of the bed next door, she had made herself believe that there was something better somewhere. That there had to be.

She had found it, too. An exciting life, a job that challenged and satisfied.

But Ronni Tyler hadn't made it that far. Now she never would.

Alone on the balcony, unseen in the dark, Tamara cried a little, in memory of a woman she had never met, in mourning for a stranger.

She cried, and the thirsty air licked the dampness from her cheeks.

"Collins just called," Lovejoy reported as Moore walked into their borrowed office on the morning of the fourth day. They were encamped in a hastily furnished storage room in the FBI's Phoenix field office. Photos of the President and the Director gazed down on them, one smiling, the other stern.

She tossed her purse on the chipped Formica desk top and tried her best to be calm. "Search over?"

"It appears to be. As of approximately an hour ago."

"Results?"

"From what I understand, there were thirteen hits." Lovejoy consulted his scrawled notes. "Four are women. Of the nine men, six would seem to be disqualified because of age, race, or body build. In all probability, the bartender's description rules them out."

"The remaining three?" She heard the excitement

in her voice, straining against the short leash of her self-control.

"Michael Benjamin Garrett, resident of Scottsdale, one arrest for reckless driving."

She shook her head. "Unlikely, since he's a local. Our man travels."

"Noted. Paul Thomas Squire, Chicago, two arrests on battery charges."

"Interesting."

Could it be him? Could Paul Thomas Squire be Mister Twister? Could the nightmare have ended at last?

"They were bar fights," Lovejoy said slowly. "He would appear to be a brawler."

Her brief enthusiasm failed. "That's not how I see our guy. Not how Behavioral Science profiled him, either. He's slick, polished, not some bruiser spoiling for a fight."

"I'm somewhat inclined to agree. Still, we'll have Chicago check him out."

"Sure." Moore had already dismissed Squire from her mind. "Who's last?"

"John Edward Dance. L.A. No violent crimes on his rap sheet, just three arrests for fraud."

"What kind of fraud?"

"Telemarketing, some kind of home-equity con, and a bank-examiner scam. He did time for the last one. Beat the rap on the other two. He—"

Moore shut her eyes, drew a sharp breath, felt the sudden violent trembling of her body.

"That's him," she whispered.

"Do you think so?" Lovejoy frowned at his notes. "I don't know. There's no sexual assault, no indication of homicidal tendencies."

He was missing the point. Good Lord, how could he be so close to it and not *see*?

"Peter, the man is a con artist." She rushed the

words out, impatient to give form to her thoughts. "Don't you get it? He's a smooth talker. A manipulator. A Don Juan. The kind of guy who'd be good at picking up women in bars."

"A lady-killer," Lovejoy said thoughtfully. "Perhaps . . . literally."

"No perhaps. No doubt about it." Moore paced the narrow office, tremors shaking her thin shoulders. "He cons women the same way he cons the marks in his bunco games. Charm and phony self-confidence. A pose that a girl like Ronni Tyler would fall for. He sells himself. He's good at it. That's how he gets people to empty their bank accounts for him. And it's how he gets beautiful blondes to take him home."

"You appear to be awfully certain about this."

"Damn straight I am." She heard herself laughing, a wild, ecstatic sound. "Come on, Peter! Get pumped, will you? Mister Twister is history. We got him. We *nailed* the son of a bitch!"

# 4

The morning sun splashed wide bands of orange light across Wilshire Boulevard, fifteen stories below Jack Dance's feet.

Standing at the corner windows of his high-rise apartment, he surveyed the glittering tide of traffic flowing past Westwood Village toward the on-ramp of the 405. Beyond the distant marquees of the Bruin and Village theaters rose the Santa Monica Mountains, pasted on the sky like billows of frozen smoke, purple and gently rounded.

Jack loved Los Angeles. Yes, loved it, despite the grit and ugliness now visible nearly everywhere, despite the muttering legions of shopping-cart people who'd turned the city into a vast open-air mental ward, despite the gang graffiti on alley walls and the taggers' slogans defacing every other billboard, despite the traffic snarls and freeway closures and unpatched potholes pockmarking the streets. Hell, despite *everything.*

He loved L.A. because it was his type of place: phony, just as he was; crass and exploitative, sure; obsessed with flesh and money; selfish in the most thoughtlessly amoral sense; often cruel, otherwise indifferent; a city that preyed on vain hopes and foolish delusions and the desperate yearnings of the unfulfilled.

He checked his watch—time to go—and drew the curtains, shutting out the sun.

Before leaving, he went into the bedroom. Sheila was still asleep, naturally. She had kicked the covers off, exposing her long, suntanned legs and tight white buns.

Jack approached the bed and leaned close. Her brown hair, prematurely accented with streaks of gray, lay across her bronzed back in a luxuriant mess. He poked her shoulder, not gently.

"Hey."

She stirred, eyelashes fluttering, then rolled on her side and blinked at him. Her eyes were gray-green, very lovely and very safe.

"Fuck . . ." The word slid out of her like a groan.

Jack grinned. "Hello, sleepyhead. I'm off to work. Figured it was time for you to rise and shine."

"Shut up. Just shut the fuck up. Oh, Christ, I hate mornings."

"Hey, hey, that's not the right attitude. You've got places to go, people to see." Jack enjoyed baiting her, contrasting her inertia with his leaping energy, his caffeine-and-adrenaline rush. "Up and at 'em. There's a great big world out there, and it's waiting for *you.*"

"Eat shit." She dragged the back of her hand across her face. "Give me a cigarette."

"I don't smoke."

"One of *my* cigarettes."

"Get it yourself."

"Goddamn you, Jack."

He bent and kissed her roughly on the mouth. "Love you, too," he breathed in her ear.

She pushed him away, then scowled with a sudden thought. "What day is it?"

"Thursday."

"Oh, hell. What did you wake me up for, you stupid shit? You know I've got Thursdays off."

"But you don't want to waste the whole morning, do you?"

"Like fuck I don't." She flung herself on her pillow and shut her eyes. "You asshole."

"Spoken like an angel."

"Get out of here." Already her voice was a murmur. "Leave me alone."

"Your wish is my command, O beautiful one."

"Bite it," she murmured, drifting away.

He left the room, chuckling.

Jack's relationship with Sheila Tate, whom he'd met in a singles bar last March and had dated intermittently ever since, was perhaps not a model of romantic bliss. It was more like an exercise in undisguised mutual contempt. He despised her because she was, at heart, a whore, using sex to gain gifts and favors and money. She despised him because he knew what she was and continued seeing her. She interpreted this behavior as weakness. In that conclusion, however, she was mistaken.

He persisted in the affair, such as it was, solely for convenience. Masturbation had never done much to relieve his hormonal urges. He needed flesh and hair to sink his fingers into, needed the smell of a woman's sweat.

And for him, Sheila was the ideal woman. She made no demands on him, expressed no curiosity about those weekends when he was out of town, performed whatever sex acts he requested, and expected nothing in return except presents of jewelry, electronic toys, and cash.

Above all, she was safe, because she was not his type.

Once, last May, Sheila had frightened him by remarking idly that she might try dyeing her hair blond. Jack had argued strenuously against it, the pitch of his voice rising as he insisted she would be crazy to become a blonde, absolutely *crazy*.

He must have been persuasive. Or perhaps she had simply lost interest in the notion. Either way, she hadn't done it; but for weeks afterward he had been terrified that she would walk into his apartment one evening, the transformation accomplished.

He was by no means certain he could control himself in those circumstances. And if he killed her . . .

Disaster. The police would be all over him like flies.

Still, it hadn't happened, and he no longer feared that it would.

She wouldn't look good as a blonde, anyway.

Whistling, Jack left the apartment. He pressed the call button, then stood waiting for the elevator, appraising himself in the polished metal doors.

The slate blue Brooks Brothers suit had been a good choice, he decided. He always dressed conservatively, his attire selected purely for the benefit of his associates at work. He'd found that presenting a businesslike demeanor promoted professionalism and efficiency, admirable qualities even in his field.

The elevator dropped him to the underground garage, where his red Nissan Z waited in its assigned space. The license plate read DEFY F8.

*Defy Fate.* Jack liked the sentiment. To his way of thinking, Fate was just one more mark to be conned.

He slipped behind the wheel and eased out of his space, thumbing the remote control to lift the automatic gate. Wilshire Boulevard swept him to the freeway on-ramp. He gunned the engine and hurtled onto the northbound 405.

Traffic was surprisingly light. Slicing deftly from lane to lane, he fed a disc into the CD player and cranked up the volume. Springsteen poured out of the four coaxial speakers, howling "Thunder Road" in his raspy, street-worn voice.

Jack rapped his knuckles on the steering wheel and sang along.

Bruce was an old story to him. Jack had listened to his LPs as a high-school student in Montclair, New Jersey, twenty years ago, long before the *Born in the USA* album made the Boss a national celebrity. He liked the anger and violence of the early Springsteen, the scrawny kid wounded by the world and snarling back at it in furious despair.

On a humid August night in 1978, he'd listened to Springsteen for hours, huddled in his bedroom in his parents' house, headphones bracketing his ears, till he'd gotten up the nerve for his first kill.

He had been eighteen then. At the time he hadn't thought of it as a *first* kill. It was the only murder he was contemplating, the one he had fantasized and rehearsed for seven long years.

Meredith had deserved it, too. That bitch.

A chill moved through him as he remembered the ecstatic pleasure of slamming her head into the concrete rim of the swimming pool, then holding her, unconscious, under the surface till her lungs were waterlogged sacs.

Afterward, he'd been free of any impulse to kill for a long time. Having exacted his revenge, he felt liberated, unencumbered by the past.

Except that he exhibited a curious reluctance to date women who reminded him of her. He preferred brunettes and redheads. He stayed away from blondes, most particularly blue-eyed, fair-skinned blondes.

He made it through his twenties without violence. But in his early thirties he did a thirteen-month stretch at Lompoc for a bank-examiner scam. His confinement gave him time to think, too much time, and the frustration of enforced abstinence from sex seemed to draw other, darker needs to his surface.

It was then that the *feelings* started.

He knew no word to describe them more exactly than that: *feelings*. Not sexual urges, not homicidal impulses, not sadistic tendencies—yet a little of all these, mixed with something else, something indefinable.

He had always been smooth with women. He could have a one-night stand whenever he liked. But it seemed that ordinary sex just wasn't enough anymore.

He kept remembering the reflexive muscular twitches of Meredith's body as he held her submerged, the pops and jerks of her shoulders, the sudden heaving of her chest as she inhaled water. And once she was dead, the wet blond hair wrapping her face like ribbons of kelp, the glazed emptiness in her eyes when he peeled back the lids.

It had been the supreme moment of his life, more satisfying than any con. And he wanted another triumph like it. And another. And another.

But he was determined to do it right. He'd made a small but potentially serious mistake in carrying out Meredith's execution. The cops had been suspicious, and he'd spent some sleepless nights before her death was finally ruled an accident.

This time there would be no sloppy screw-ups. Thirteen months in a cell had been long enough; he would never go back.

He delayed his plans until he settled on the perfect strategy—the killing of strangers in random cities far from home—and the ideal method.

His discovery of the method was pure luck. During a routine medical checkup, the nurse left him alone in the examination room for a few minutes. Restless, he looked through the drawers and found a box of unused disposable syringes. One of them went in his coat pocket, never to be missed.

Being plastic, with only a thin steel needle at its core, it could be hidden in his suit jacket and carried through an airport metal detector without triggering the alarm. It was quick and sure, bloodless and silent, and above all, intensely satisfying. He loved watching the women's convulsions, their rolling eyes and flapping limbs.

Ronni Tyler's death throes had been particularly gratifying. He had kissed her when she was finally dead, murmuring in her ear: "I hope it was good for you, too."

The 405 rocketed him to the eastbound 101, where traffic was heavier and progress slow. He had nearly finished the Springsteen CD by the time he reached the strip mall in the North Hollywood district of L.A. at 9:25.

Of the eight business establishments in the modest L-shaped complex, Consolidated Silver & Gold Investors, Inc., had the largest office but the smallest sign. It was not meant to attract customers off the street.

A clamor of voices calling out buy and sell orders assaulted him as he stepped into the boiler room. The impression of frantic activity, like everything else about the operation, was a scam, a cheat; there was no mob of traders here, merely a tape loop playing sounds of a busy commodities exchange over four speakers bolted to the walls. A corny ruse, but it kept his salesmen wired while they worked the phones, and it served well as background noise during the pitch.

Jack paused just inside the doorway and surveyed his kingdom. Gray short-nap carpet, painted plywood walls, extension cords stretched along the baseboards. Half a dozen cheap metal desks and swivel chairs, flanked by wastebaskets filled with old newspapers and takeout food containers. The wide front windows had been covered with Venetian blinds, now partially open to let in stripes of sun that complemented the frosty glare of fluorescent panels.

Three of his four men—he only hired men; women couldn't sell; it was an article of faith with him—were already on the phones, pressing hard for the first deal of the day. They greeted him with smiles and waves, and kept talking. The smiles were genuine; his men respected him and liked him. Behind his back, but sometimes within earshot, they called him The Master.

Jack poured himself a mug of coffee, then sat at his desk, in a rear corner, away from the glare of the windows. He wondered, not for the first time, what his men would think of him if they knew how he spent his weekends.

Perhaps they would despise him for it. But he didn't think so. There was an undercurrent of boiling violence beneath the average scam artist's smooth exterior.

He would never know for certain, but he liked to believe that if his men did learn the truth about him, they would respect The Master that much more.

# 5

Jack Dance's arrival at his place of business was observed and recorded by four FBI technicians in a green van parked across the street. Video and still cameras captured his brief walk to the office door. The same cameras, their telephoto lenses focused on the front windows, caught glimpses of him through gaps in the venetian blinds. Only once he sat at his desk, away from the windows, was he lost to sight.

"He's in there," the camera operator said. "If he follows his routine, he won't come out till noon."

The communications technician radioed a transmission on a VHF band. The signal was unscrambled, necessitating a coded message.

"Weather Central, this is Tracking Post A. Storm front has moved in."

Peter Lovejoy's voice crackled over the technician's earplug: "Continue monitoring the system's progress. We're placing additional resources at your disposal."

Jack's first call of the day was to a Mr. Pavel Zykmund of Downey. Mr. Zykmund's name had come from a mailing list, one of several Jack had purchased from publishers of religious magazines and investment newsletters with conservative leanings. He'd found that people with an apocalyptic outlook and a distrust of paper money were more likely to put their faith in precious metals as a hedge against society's collapse.

A gruff male voice edged with a strong Eastern European accent answered on the fourth ring. "Service." Electric tools whirred in the background.

"Pavel?"

"This is me."

"Hey, Pavel, how you doing? This is Dave Michaels over at Consolidated."

"Consolidated?"

"Consolidated Silver and Gold Investors. Listen, man, I'm sorry it's been so long since I talked with you, but I've gotten kind of backlogged here. You know how it is."

Dance had never spoken with Zykmund before. Faking a previous relationship was the first key part of the pitch.

In the alley behind the strip mall, a red Camaro eased to a stop near a trash bin. Two men in dark business suits emerged. They were Dallas P.D. homicide detectives, and they had been members of the Trail Ridge task force ever since a twenty-two-year-old legal secretary named Dorothy Beerbaum had turned up dead on the Trinity River greenbelt with a puncture wound in her neck.

Both caps were carrying Smith .38 Chief's Specials, drawn, cocked, and locked. They approached the back door of CSGI and waited, hugging the wall to minimize the risk of being seen from a rear window.

Zykmund wasn't buying it, not right off.

"Excuse me?" he said with evident impatience. "I'm afraid I do not recall you or your company, Mr. . . . ?"

"Michaels. Dave Michaels, of Consolidated Silver and Gold. Come on, Pavel, has it been that long? Let me check my records. . . . Holy smoke, you won't believe this. It's been *six months* since I called. No wonder you don't remember me."

"Mr. Michaels, I am busy man."

Precisely what Jack was counting on. A busy man could never keep track of all his phone calls and business contacts.

"Call me Dave," Jack said. "Look, I know it was a while ago, but you remember what we talked about last time? I was trying to get you into silver at five dollars an ounce. You weren't able to do business with me at that time, which is a shame, because today silver's at six dollars and twenty-seven cents. If you'd gone with me when I asked you to, Pavel, you could have made yourself a twenty-five percent profit."

"Twenty-five percent," Pavel murmured, and Jack smiled.

Late last night, the street directly outside the strip mall had been lined with orange cones and signs warning Tow Away Zone. No vehicles had parked at the curb, leaving plenty of open space for the blue Honda Civic that pulled up now.

At the wheel was a detective from the San Antonio Police Department, who had worked the case involving Jack Dance's first known victim, a biochemistry graduate student at UTSA killed in her apartment fourteen months earlier.

Seated next to him was the sheriff of San Bernalillo County, New Mexico. Dance's second victim had been found in an arroyo near the Rio Puerco.

Overhead, an FBI surveillance chopper swung into view, executing loops over the arrest site.

"I've got something for you now, Pavel, that's even better than the deal you passed up. Not silver this time. Gold."

"I know very little about such things. . . ."

"Let me ask you a question. You're a businessman, as I recall."

"I run auto-body shop."

"Right." That explained the power tools still screaming on the other end of the line. "So you must follow financial developments pretty closely. Did you read the business section of the *L.A. Times* today? Interest rates are about to climb. That means inflation, my friend. And when inflation takes off, so does gold."

"I do not think I can afford—"

"Sure you can. That's the beauty of our system here at CSGI. We understand the needs of smaller investors like yourself. Which is why we permit you to purchase quantities of gold as modest as three troy ounces. At three-eighteen per ounce, that works out to only nine-fifty-four total."

"Nine hundred fifty-four dollars? Is too much."

"But all you have to pay is four-seventy-seven. You put down just half the price up front, with a fifty percent balloon payment required only when and if you choose to take physical possession of the metal. In other words, you can lock in the total price right now, no matter high how the market eventually goes. See what I'm saying, Pavel? You just can't lose."

A Saturn coupe parked behind the blue Honda. San Diego P.D. and the sheriff's department of Clark County, Nevada, were represented inside.

"For half price . . . I get all the gold?"

"What you get is a half interest in your share, plus the guarantee of making an outright purchase at any time in the future. When you're ready to take delivery, just pay another four-seventy-seven, and the gold will be delivered to your door by our bonded messenger."

The bonded messenger, a slack-jawed kid draped over a folding chair and thumbing through a gore-movie magazine, glanced up briefly, registering some reference to himself, then resumed reading.

"And you keep gold for me until I want it?"

"Not us personally. The gold is stored in a Credit Suisse bank vault in Zurich, Switzerland, for maximum peace of mind. Even in an international crisis—and you know that's always a possibility, the way the world is going today—your investment will be safe and sound."

"I see. . . ."

Jack knew he would reel this one in. He could sense it. He needed patience, nothing more. Patience and confidence.

The scam was a simple pyramid scheme. Some gold and silver bullion actually was stored in a Credit Suisse vault—Jack had documents to prove it—but not nearly enough to cover all the "certificates of ownership" purchased by CSGI's clients. Buyers who wanted to make the balloon payment and take delivery of the metal were encouraged instead to "increase their leverage" by putting the money into a down payment on a new certificate.

Some especially gullible marks had gradually invested $50,000 or more in worthless paper titles to nonexistent metal. They couldn't have made the balloon payments now if they'd wanted to. Their life savings were gone.

Detective Ashe of Phoenix P.D. parked in the strip-mall lot, outside the dry-cleaning establishment next to CSGI. He spoke four words into the transmitter on his Telex headset: "Unit Six in position."

A second car joined Ashe's Pontiac. It contained a Detective 2 and two D-1's from LAPD's Homicide

Special Section and the assistant special-agent-in-charge of the FBI field office in Westwood.

The L.A. cops carried 9mm Berettas, and the assistant SAC, Patterson, used a .38 Smith. There had been some friendly discussion earlier about the relative merits of the two guns.

Nobody said anything now as the LAPD men checked their clips and Patterson inspected the Smith's cylinder and speedloader.

"So what do you say, Pavel? Can I messenger over a contract for three troy ounces?"

"Well . . . I do not know. I must talk it over with my wife."

Jack snorted. "Your wife?" Incredulity raised the pitch of his voice. "You need to get permission from your wife?"

"Not permission. We always discuss money things. She is very good with money."

"Yeah, you make it, and she spends it. So your old lady's got you on an allowance, huh?"

Pavel was wounded. "Is no allowance."

"Well, call it whatever you want. Sounds pretty sad, though—a working man from the old country, letting his better half walk all over him."

"She does not—it is not like that—"

"Right, right. Look, I guess I was wrong about you, Pavel. You're not serious about investing. Maybe it's your wife I should have been talking to all along. Sorry to waste your time."

"Wait." A pause. "How much is silver now?"

He was still thinking about that twenty-five-percent profit he'd missed out on. Beautiful.

"Six-twenty-seven," Jack said. "Up from five dollars even."

"And . . . gold?"

"Three hundred eighteen an ounce—and getting ready to take off."

"Big increase?"

"We're looking at a major run-up here, Pavel. Check the *Times* if you don't believe me."

"As much as twenty-five percent?"

"I wouldn't be surprised. This is one hot opportunity. Speaking of which, I've got other clients who need to know about this, so . . ."

"I'll do it."

Jack leaned back in his chair and found life good.

The final car to swing into the parking lot was driven by Peter Lovejoy, with Tamara Moore at his side.

"Weather Central in position," Lovejoy reported.

Moore licked her lips. "When do we take him?"

"In one minute." He checked his watch, then spoke into his transmitter. "All units. Downpour at nine-forty-eight. Sixty seconds from now."

For the first time Tamara could remember, Peter seemed to have forgotten his allergies.

"Glad to hear you say that, Pavel. You're making a real smart move. Okay, I'll have our bonded courier at your place of business within the hour. The contract explains everything. If you have any questions, call me. Let me give you my number and confirm your address. . . ."

Thirty seconds later, Dance was off the phone and chuckling. Four hundred and seventy-five dollars—a nice round five hundred, with the five-percent "transaction fee" tacked on—easy money. But even that was hardly anything. It was the next call to Mr. Pavel Zykmund, and the next, and the next, that would bring in the real rewards.

Welcome to America, Pavel, old pal. And hold on to your wallet.

9:48.

"Go," Lovejoy said, throwing open his car door.

Then he and Moore were sprinting toward the entrance of CSGI, the three L.A. cops and Assistant SAC Patterson right behind.

Jack sauntered up to the desk of one of his salesmen, a bright young guy named Ted Stuckleberry, who did business as Ted Stone. "Guess what, Ted-o? There's life in the old man yet."

Ted liked to hear Jack's stories. "Never doubted it, boss. Give me the gory details."

"No big thing, really. I just closed some pussy-whipped Lower Slobenia garage mechanic for five Ben Franklins."

"First sale of the day. You . . ." Ted's voice trailed off as he looked past Jack, through the blinds. "Hey. What the *fuck*?"

Jack turned. Stared.

Half a dozen dark-suited figures were crossing the parking lot at a run.

They had guns.

His blood chilled.

"Jesus," he hissed.

A hundred times since moving into this office, he had shaped and reshaped an escape scenario in his mind. That thinking galvanized him now.

He ducked away from the window and spun toward the far corner of the room.

# 6

The front door was unlocked. Lovejoy flung it wide and entered, his Smith sweeping the four salesmen at their desks and the messenger with a lurid magazine in his lap.

*"Freeze, FBI!"* Lovejoy shouted as his colleagues fanned out, covering the room. "Put your hands up!"

Moore was scanning the faces and frowning hard. "Where's Dance? Where's *Dance*?"

"Where's your fucking boss?" Patterson yelled at the salesmen.

One of them showed an insolent smile. "Haven't seen him."

Lovejoy talked into his Telex headset. "Outside posts, stay alert. Jack isn't home."

As he completed the transmission, the two Dallas detectives charged in from the rear.

"Any way he could've gotten past you?" Lovejoy demanded.

"No chance," the first cop said. "Nothing back there but a toilet and a closet, and we checked them both."

"Peter." Moore pointed at the far corner. A door under a red Exit sign. It had been shut hastily, but the latch had not caught. As they watched, the door drifted slowly ajar, revealing a staircase: metal treads and railings.

"Shit." Lovejoy had studied blueprints of the strip-mall complex. The staircase led to a second-floor storage room. Dance must be up there already.

Dead end, though. The room was windowless. There were no exits. Still, he could make a stand. If he had a weapon, he could fire on the arrest team from the top of the stairs. Everyone was wearing vests, but the Kevlar offered no protection to the head and limbs.

An assault was no good, then. This was a job for somebody with a bullhorn.

Moore was thinking the same thing. "Think he's gone barricade?"

"It, uh, it appears . . ." Lovejoy tried to control the breathless shaking of his voice. "It appears we'll have to play it that way." He turned to Patterson. "Better get SWAT in here. We'll need a negotiator and containment. In the meantime, LAPD can evacuate the building. That is . . . if you think that's the best option."

Patterson nodded. "It's our only option." He hurried off to give the orders.

"This isn't a disaster, Peter." Moore patted his shoulder. "He's ours. Either he gives himself up, or SWAT takes him out."

"In all probability, you're right." Lovejoy sighed. "But in this instance the probabilities may not apply."

Jack had never expected to face arrest again. The precious-metals scam was too subtle, almost borderline legal, not the kind of thing the authorities would come down on.

They had, though. They meant to put him out of business. That was the reason for the bust. It had to be. The law couldn't have found out about his other activities. He'd handled the murders with meticulous care, leaving no clues. There was no chance he could have been linked to even one of the homicides.

No, it was only a fraud charge. But that was bad enough. It could put him in jail.

He had sworn he would never go back. And because he'd meant it, he had taken precautions to ensure that he could extricate himself even from a tricky situation like this.

Alone in the low-ceilinged storage room with the door locked, Jack groped along the side wall till he found a vertical crack in the whitewashed plasterboard. He pushed at the edges of the crack. A three-foot-square section of the wall yielded to the gentle pressure of his fingertips, loosening, and tipped free.

Jack slipped through the gap, then replaced the panel, taking care to wedge it precisely back into position. He was in another storeroom, above the temporary-employment agency next door to CSGI. The room was crowded with empty cartons that had once contained word processing equipment and telephone gear.

Behind one of the cartons, months ago, he had hidden a large plastic bag. It was still there, thank God.

Inside was an olive green jumpsuit with a homemade insignia stitched onto the chest. The suit was a reasonably close facsimile of the outfits worn by the exterminators who visited the complex on an irregular basis, spraying for cockroaches and ants.

Jack slipped into the costume, easily donning it over his suit. He rummaged in the bag and produced a matching green cap, then a spray gun with a long nozzle and a bulky canister.

Carrying the tool, he eased open the storeroom door and peered down the stairwell. Empty.

Quickly he descended. He could hear the commanding tones of an authoritative voice from the offices outside. A cop.

He caught the word "evacuate."

Despite himself, despite everything, Jack smiled. He

had known they would do that. Once they believed he was holed up in a locked room, the next step was to clear out the building.

He waited until sounds of confusion, of hurried footsteps and mingled voices, bled through the hollow door to the stairwell. Then he took a breath of courage and emerged into the office.

For a few precious seconds nobody saw him. The trainees and job applicants were shutting off their computers and gathering up their personal items, the supervisors doing the same as they told everyone to hurry up, get moving, come on. From the rear of the building half a dozen other employees were herded forward by two plainclothes cops with stern faces.

Jack shuffled through the room and blundered into the crowd, mumbling in Spanish. He knew enough of the language to get by.

"Move along, folks," one of the cops snapped, then saw Jack and frowned. "Where'd *he* come from?"

Jack kept his head low, the bill of his cap covering much of his face. He gestured as if confused, a steady stream of Spanish flowing from him like a derelict's vapid muttering.

"He's one of the bug people," a helpful employee said. "You know, Rid-a-Pest."

"Didn't know they came on Thursdays," someone else put in, but the words were lost in the babble of voices.

*"Policia,"* the second cop said to him, flashing his badge. *"Siga. Siga todo derecho."* Walk straight ahead.

Jack stumbled in a half circle. The cop shoved him.

*"¡Dese prisa!"* Hurry up!

Nodding his head mechanically, Jack got into step with the rest of the crowd.

The scene outside was a circus. Employees, cops, and curious passersby milled everywhere. Jack made his way through the throng of people, not looking back.

A black SWAT war wagon screamed into the mall as he reached the sidewalk. Overhead, an aerial-surveillance unit chopped the air with its rotor.

He kept walking, heading west, putting distance between himself and the territory that would be the focus of the aerial observer's scrutiny.

After three blocks he veered onto a side street, then entered an alley. He discarded the spray gun and cap, stripped off the uniform, smoothed his jacket and pants. He was a businessman again, in a blue Brooks Brothers suit.

He breathed deeply, then exhaled. Again. Again. Gradually his heartbeat returned to nearly normal.

Three blocks farther west, an RTD bus groaned to a stop, collecting passengers. Jack joined the line.

He looked eastward as he boarded. The helicopter was a gnat in the distance, still buzzing the arrest site, glinting silver in the sun.

It was standard procedure for the SWAT snipers, politely called containment officers, to station themselves as close as possible to the barricaded suspect without giving their presence away.

Two of them were deployed in the stairwell, flanking the negotiator, who used a bullhorn to address the closed door at the top of the stairs. There was no phone in the storeroom and no window through which a field phone could be tossed. The suspect would have to shout through the door when he was ready to talk. So far he hadn't made a peep.

In the boiler room of Consolidated Silver & Gold, a technician on a ladder was holding a stethoscope to the ceiling, listening for footsteps upstairs. He'd heard none.

Another technician, accompanied by two SWAT commandos with shotguns, entered the storeroom above the employment agency. The storeroom shared a common wall with the room in which the suspect was holed up. The technician quietly attached an electronic eavesdropping device to the wall, then slipped on headphones.

No sounds at all. The equipment was sufficiently sensitive to pick up a person's breathing in close quarters. There ought to be something.

Frowning, he removed the device and moved a few feet down the wall. The two snipers covered him. The thin plasterboard offered no protection against a gun on the other side. If the suspect heard someone moving there, he might open fire. A bullet would punch through the layers of felt and gypsum like a knife through paper.

The technician started to reattach the bug, pressing the suction pads into place. Then he paused.

The wall had moved.

No, not the whole wall. Only a piece of it. A loose section.

His flashlight beam revealed a movable panel, three feet square.

Patterson, Lovejoy, Moore, and the SWAT commander were in the storeroom ninety seconds later. They looked at the secret panel, still in place, and spoke in whispers.

"He slipped out that way," Moore said.

Patterson shook his head. "Then where is he? We checked downstairs."

Lovejoy spoke up. "I would say . . . as a provisional hypothesis . . . he could have blended in somehow with the civilians we evacuated."

"Impossible," Patterson hissed. "Every member of the task force was looking for him."

"It's conceivable he changed clothes, disguised himself." Lovejoy shrugged, a heavy, hopeless gesture, then added with a faint note of optimism, "Unless he's still inside."

"Want us to go in?" the commander asked.

Lovejoy looked at Patterson. The assistant SAC called it. "Go in."

Instructions were relayed via radio headsets. The negotiator cleared out of the stairwell. The two snipers stationed there moved quickly up the stairs.

In the adjacent storage room, the other two containment officers covered the panel, ready to blast it if it moved.

At the top of the stairs, the first sniper shot the storeroom door open, and then he and his partner were inside, scanning the dark, windowless chamber.

Empty.

Nothing to see, not even cartons of junk.

They flicked on the overhead light. White walls and cheap short-nap carpet.

Lovejoy and the others waited tensely in the parking lot, outside the kill zone.

There was still a possibility Dance was in there. Maybe he'd given up, shot himself. Maybe he was dead.

*Please, Jesus, let him be dead.*

Lovejoy realized he was praying. Catholicism had a way of coming back to you at times like this.

Over his earphone, the SWAT commander's voice: "We're in."

"And?"

"He's gone."

Moore slumped her shoulders. Patterson pulled off his headset and swore.

"Understood," Lovejoy said.

He turned to the assistant SAC and spoke rapidly, squeezing all emotion out of his voice.

"All right. We'd better have LAPD broadcast an alert and deploy any unit they can spare to cruise the area. There's a chance he's still in the vicinity. West L.A. Division ought to stake out his apartment building in case he's stupid enough to return. Admittedly, that kind of blunder seems unlikely. Another thing: From what I understand, his girlfriend works at Bullock's in Westwood. It would appear advisable to have a street agent take her into protective custody."

Patterson nodded. "I'll alert security at all the local airports, the bus station, the train station."

"Rental car companies," Moore said. "And his bank—he may try to withdraw funds, close out his accounts."

"Got it." Patterson moved off to speak with the LAPD Valley Bureau commander, who had just arrived on the scene.

Lovejoy waited till the assistant SAC was gone before permitting any crackup of his surface calm. Then he lowered his head, wrestling with the urge to scream.

"Fuck. We blew it. *Blew* it."

A wet sneeze shook him. Suddenly his allergies were back, as if in punishment for failure.

"We'll get him, Peter," Moore said gently.

"That's what we thought this morning."

"Next time—"

"Next time may be too late. I mean . . . he's done seven already. Who'll be number eight?"

Moore took his hand, squeezed it tight. She had no answer.

Jack sat in a window seat at the back of the bus, watching the smoggy wasteland of the San Fernando

Valley shudder past. He felt calm and confident and wonderfully self-possessed.

He had beaten them. Beaten them all. Cheated the law of its prize.

Across the aisle, a little boy was practicing coin tricks while his Latino nanny looked on.

The boy smiled at Jack. "I can do magic."

Jack nodded. "So can I."

"Really?"

"Let me show you."

He took out a quarter and passed it deftly from hand to hand, then palmed it. A simple illusion he'd learned years ago while running a street-corner shell game.

"Wow," the boy said. "You made it disappear."

"I can do better magic than that. I can make myself disappear." He lowered his voice to a stage whisper. "In fact, I just did."

He couldn't stay invisible for long, though—not in this city. He had to get out. And he knew where to go.

Jack checked his watch. Ten o'clock. He could make it to LAX by eleven-thirty at the latest. There had to be a noon flight to Miami. He would land by nine P.M. Eastern time.

From there it was less than a two-hour drive to Islamorada . . . and Pelican Key.

# 7

Night sounds, drifting like echoes of dreams through the heavy tropical air.

From the mangrove swamp, the choral croaks of rain frogs, excited by the afternoon's brief downpour. Out on the tidal flats, the cries of night herons, feeding. *Kee-o, kee-o, keer:* the song of a redheaded woodpecker nesting amid the forest's mossy conifers. Everywhere, the background buzz of cicadas, an endless static sizzle.

The rippling shallows around the dock, dimly visible through gaps in the garden foliage, coruscated lazily in the starlight. The sparkle on the horizon marked Upper Matecumbe Key and the flow of traffic on Route 1.

There were nights when faint noises could be heard from passing boats, someone's laughter or the tinny nocturnes of a radio wafted across the water by a westerly breeze, but not tonight. Tonight, Pelican Key listened only to itself.

"It really is perfect here." Kirstie Gardner reached down to rub Anastasia's smooth neck, and the dog eased out a sigh. "Like another world."

Steve kicked off his loafers and curled his toes, reclining in the wicker lounge chair.

"I didn't exaggerate, did I?" he asked quietly. "There's something special about this place."

"It's the colors, I think. They're more intense than in real life." Kirstie laughed. "Listen to me. Real life. As if this isn't real."

"I know what you mean, though. The water—it's not like water anywhere else. Stripes of color. Turquoise and teal. It ripples like a flag."

"And the sunsets. The one tonight—I'll bet they don't have them like that even in Arizona."

"The wildflowers . . . the birds . . . even the insects are colorful. Those big red and gold spiders are really something."

Kirstie shuddered. "Yeah. They're something, all right." She waved off a whining mosquito. "Frankly, the bugs I could do without. They're the one imperfection. The flaw in paradise."

"The serpent in the garden," Steve said lightly, then frowned. She saw the faraway look in his eyes she knew too well, the look that said he was drifting off into private thoughts. She spoke briskly, hoping to pull him back.

"That's right. There's always something around to foul up Eden." The mosquito buzzed her again, and she annihilated it with a handclap. "But these darn bugs are worse than any serpent. There are more of them, and they're annoying. In fact, they're downright rude. The serpent, at least, was polite."

Steve blinked, coming out of himself. "Was he?"

"Oh, I'm sure he was. Very smooth, very charming. Good-looking, too."

"'A good-looking snake?"

"He'd make you think so. Maybe by hypnosis. You'd trust him implicitly, though you couldn't say why."

"Eve was the one who trusted him. Maybe he's only good at deceiving women."

Kirstie smiled, pleased that he was playing along.

"Back then, maybe. Women have a lot more savvy now. Today it would be Adam who'd pick the apple."

"No snake could tempt me with any lousy apple. I can't be bought that cheap."

"What would tempt you?" she asked half seriously. "What would constitute an irresistible offer?"

Steve closed his eyes. A long moment passed before he answered. "Maybe . . . to be young again. Young forever."

"You're thirty-five. Not exactly Methuselah."

"I mean fifteen, sixteen. You know what we were saying about colors? That's the way I felt back then. Not just about Pelican Key. About everything. The whole world was more . . . I don't know, more vibrant. More vivid."

"And now it's gone gray?"

"I didn't say that."

"Young people have problems, you know. Growing up is no picnic."

"I realize that. But when you're a kid, your problems are outside you. Not . . . not within you."

"What's within you that's so terrible?"

"Nothing. Forget it."

Kirstie sighed. How many times had he ended a dialogue that way? *It's nothing. Just forget it.* As if she could forget. As if what troubled him was no more than an upset stomach or a passing headache.

She wanted to help her husband get over this mid-life crisis he was having, or whatever it was that had him in a vise. But he wouldn't let her help. Wouldn't talk to her at all.

Of course, he had always been emotionally muted, somewhat distant and remote. For most of their marriage she hadn't minded. Perhaps she'd even seen such qualities as signs of strength, of masculine reserve. The exquisitely sensitive, encounter-group type of male had never interested her; she met enough of them at the PBS affiliate where she worked.

But reserve was one thing; a total shutdown of communication was another. For months Steve had been moody almost to the point of clinical depression. And he refused to open up about it. Refused to let her share his pain.

She had hoped that visiting the island would revive his spirits. Apparently not.

"You didn't find it, did you?" she asked quietly. "What you came here looking for?"

"I've had a great time."

"But you didn't find it."

He shrugged and smiled. "Maybe because I don't know what I'm trying to find."

"I don't, either." The words came out harsher than she'd intended.

Steve looked away. "Well," he said with forced levity, "we've got one more full day on Pelican Key before old Peg-leg Pice picks us up. Maybe I'll find it tomorrow. If I do, I'll let you know."

Kirstie refused to match his bantering tone. "Be sure you do."

After that, no more words for a while. They listened to the night beyond the patio. A vireo trilled a courtship melody—a whisper song, it was called, in recognition of its delicate airiness. The female of the species must love being seduced so gracefully. Kirstie smiled at the thought.

She had learned the names and habits of many tropical birds in the thirteen days since Pice had left them on the island, after unloading their luggage and supplies and showing them around. The house, he'd explained, was equipped with dual generators that supplied electricity for appliances and hot water; a two-way radio would keep them in contact with the outside world. The UHF emergency frequency was 243.0; VHF, 121.5.

"If there's any problem and for some reason you can't use the motorboat, just get on the air and let 'em know about it in Islamorada. A boat can be here faster than a frog can jump." He'd smiled, showing a cracked tooth like a paint chip. "Don't worry, though. Nothing will happen—except you'll have a great time. And in two weeks I'll be back to collect you, and you'll hate me for it."

His prediction had proved accurate, for the most part. Despite Steve's continuing remoteness, Kirstie had enjoyed their stay on Pelican Key, and she believed her husband had also. She was almost sorry to see the vacation end.

They had left the island only twice, taking the motorboat over to Upper Matecumbe Key to replenish their supply of food and other necessities. Not all their meals had come from the grocery store, though. The garden supplied fruit and vegetables: oranges, limes, grapefruit, breadfruit, sapodilla plums; tomatoes, asparagus, eggplant. Once, they'd dined on fresh snapper, caught by Steve as he lounged on the dock with a fishing pole. Baked, lightly seasoned, and brushed with lemon juice, it was the best thing she'd ever tasted.

Fishing and gardening were only two of many diversions offered by Pelican Key. They had motored out to the reef and snorkeled among the coral gardens, spying on schools of parrotbills and beau gregories in their wonderland of spiral towers, rococo ridges, and white sand holes. They had played Frisbee with Anastasia on the beach, explored the dense hardwood forest, waded in the tree-shadowed cove, made love in a madly swaying hammock on the porch.

Some of their leisure had been enjoyed indoors. The

bedroom featured a well-stocked bookcase. Kirstie had read Robert Graves's spellbinding *I, Claudius* and was halfway through the sequel, *Claudius the God.* There was a TV also, but at Steve's insistence they hadn't turned it on even once. Hadn't listened to the radio either, except for daily monitoring of the NOAA weather frequency, a necessary precaution in hurricane season.

So far the weather had been clear, with occasional thundershowers to relieve the heat. Still, even the possibility of a hurricane had made real to Kirstie the isolation of this place, so unnatural to her after the hectic suburban life she was accustomed to, the balancing of careers and quality time, the whole dizzy yuppie scramble. It was good to get away from all that for a while—and good to know that it would be there when they returned.

Kirstie wondered if Steve would agree with the second part of that thought. Was he ready to head home the day after tomorrow, to go back to the life of a corporate attorney while his wife resumed scrounging for contributions to PBS?

She watched her husband, his face limned by starlight and the pale glow from the kitchen window. Wire-frame glasses shielded his gray, thoughtful eyes. His short brown hair was in need of combing. He was thin, almost skinny, not very muscular; work left him no time for an exercise program, but at least he didn't smoke, thank God.

A rumpled T-shirt and cut-off jeans were his only attire. He hated dressing up, felt imprisoned by a jacket and tie. But then lately he seemed to feel imprisoned by a lot of things.

He was staring past the rhododendrons and the trellises of bougainvillea, out to the sea. That distant gaze was the same one she had seen so often in recent months, as he looked past her, always past her, out a dew-frosted window or upward at the purple bellies of rain-pregnant clouds.

For a long while nothing had seemed to interest him. Then in March, he'd chanced to see an ad for Pelican Key in a travel magazine. Until then he hadn't known that the elder Larson had died, or that the island was now available as a getaway spot.

Immediately he had latched on to the idea of going there. His determination to do so had become an obsession. Coming up with the money had meant taking a knife to their savings, and Kirstie had resisted until she saw that he would not be denied.

Still, it was not the island as such that mattered to him or occupied his thoughts; she knew that. It was youth, or innocence, or some other intangible thing he felt he'd lost.

She wished she could help him. But she didn't know how.

Anastasia yawned and stretched supine on the patio tiles, her left ear ticking irritably at a mosquito. Kirstie smiled down at her, enjoying the beauty of the animal, the lean limbs and supple angularity of a purebred Russian wolfhound. The dog was three years old, milk white, her long hair the color and texture of fine silk. A bushy tail fanned out behind her like a silvery spray of moon rays.

Poor Ana was exhausted now, after her earlier encounter with the frog. She had discovered it in the garden shortly after sunset. Its madcap hopping had first perplexed her, then driven her frantic with frustration as the frog eluded her pursuit. Finally she'd hounded the frog into the trees on the verge of the garden, where with a final buoyant leap it had vanished into a deep thicket of anemone.

"I still can't get over how *new* this place looks,"

Steve said suddenly, and she knew his mind had been leafing through a scrapbook of memories again. "When we used to come here, it was like an ancient ruin. Literally uninhabitable. The garden was completely overgrown, and the orchard was a jungle."

"Orchard?" She'd explored the entire island a dozen times and had seen no evidence of one.

"Oh, it's long gone now. Swallowed by the forest, I guess. But back in the twenties this was a lime-tree plantation. Where we're staying was the owner's place. Those ramshackle row houses about a hundred yards from here—they were the workers' quarters. I'm surprised Larson didn't have them bulldozed."

Kirstie had never asked him about the island's history; vaguely she'd assumed he wouldn't know much about it. But she should have known better, shouldn't she? In many ways this was the most important place in the world to him.

"Why was the plantation abandoned?" she asked, stroking Anastasia's back with her bare foot.

"The Depression shut it down, and the big hurricane drove off whoever was still here in 1935."

"Hurricane?"

"It was a monster. Roared out of the Atlantic on Labor Day morning. There was a train running on the old railroad tracks, picking up evacuees. When the hurricane made landfall at Upper Matecumbe, it just knocked that train off the tracks. Eight hundred people died."

"Eight hundred." Kirstie drew a breath.

"They were still finding skeletons in the jungle years later. . . . Sorry. I shouldn't have mentioned that."

"It's all right. I'm just as glad I didn't know it before we got here, though." She shook her head. "That's a terrible story."

"It's not the only one. I don't know, maybe this

part of the Keys is cursed. Sometimes I almost think so. Take the name Matecumbe. Nobody's certain what it means, but a good guess is that it's a corruption of the Spanish words *mata hombre.*"

"Kill man," she translated uneasily.

"The Indian name was Cuchiyaga, which means essentially the same thing. Then there's Indian Key, south of here. The Spaniards called it Matanzas: 'slaughter.' Legend has it that hundreds of French sailors were massacred by Calusa Indians on that island after their ships foundered on the reef. May not be true, but there *was* a Seminole raid on the settlement there in the mid-eighteen hundreds. Some of the settlers made the mistake of hiding in wells. The Indians found them and poured in boiling water."

"My God . . . Who told you all this, anyway?"

"Jack Dance. I thought he was making up stories, but later I researched the area's history on my own. It was all true."

"Were horror stories a principle topic of conversation with him?"

"Not often. His sexual conquests were more frequent seeds of discussion."

"Yours, too, I guess."

"I didn't have much to say on that subject at the time. Certainly not compared with Jack. He was a ladies' man, even at that age. . . ." He looked away, and his words trailed off.

"Have many people died on Pelican Key?" Kirstie asked, unwilling to let him slip into memories and silence again.

"Not as far as I know. But they've had other kinds of bad luck. Remember those salt ponds near the cove?"

"Sure."

"Somebody tried using them for salt manufacture

about 1800. Went bust a few years later. Before that, the island was inhabited by the Calusas. Now they're extinct. All that's left of them is their burial grounds and garbage dumps." He shrugged. "No one prospers here."

Kirstie frowned, rebelling against this grim inventory. "You did," she said. "You prospered."

"Me? How?"

"You got yourself some good memories. That's a kind of treasure. Isn't it?"

He almost delivered some humorous response, then paused.

"I hadn't thought of it that way," he said slowly.

"The island may not have been lucky for other people, but it's been lucky for you."

"Yes. Yes, I guess it has."

She saw him smiling calmly, easily, like a man at peace, but the smile did not reach his eyes.

# 8

Mile marker 103.

Jack was fifty miles out of Miami, heading south on U.S. 1, driving a stolen Sunbird. The engine hummed and the tires hissed on the pavement, and the endless stretches of the Overseas Highway blurred past.

Through the open window on the driver's side, warm moist air blew in like wet kisses. Jack tasted salt on his lips and smiled. He'd always loved water, any sort of water. Maybe that was why he'd chosen to drown his first victim so many years ago.

Another green-and-white mile marker slid by. 102. The miles ended at zero in Key West, but he wasn't going that far.

Far enough, though. Far enough from L.A. and the life he'd led.

He had left it all behind, all the nice things he'd accumulated since his release from prison. His Sony Trinitron. His compact-disc player and mountain of CDs. His expensive wardrobe. His corner apartment with its great view. His car.

Oh, yes, and Sheila, too. Well, that was no great loss.

The feds must be crawling all over his apartment by now, but he wasn't worried. The only item that could link him with the murders was the syringe, and it would never be found. The law would continue to see him as merely a con artist, a white-collar criminal, hardly a top priority. In a few weeks he would be forgotten. Then he could execute the final stages of his plan.

It had worked beautifully so far.

In Encino, roughly midway between his home and office, he kept a storage locker, which he'd visited after getting off the bus. He removed two shopping bags, then shut himself in a men's-room stall at Burger King. The first bag contained blue jeans, a denim shirt, and a knapsack; he changed clothes, placing his folded suit in the pack.

The second bag held eyeglasses, a can of mousse, and a thick envelope. He donned the glasses, slicked back his hair, and distributed the envelope's contents among his wallet and various pockets: ten thousand dollars in twenties, fifties, and hundreds.

When he emerged from the rest room, he was no longer an executive in a business suit; he was a bespectacled youngish man in blue denim, toting a backpack.

A cab took him to LAX, where he bought a one-way coach ticket at the American Airlines counter, paying cash.

His flight was uneventful. The plane touched down at Miami International at 9:47 P.M. Eastern time. He roamed the long-term parking area until he found a Pontiac Sunbird hardtop sedan with an unlocked rear door. Somebody in a hurry had gotten careless.

His Swiss Army knife came in handy when he slipped behind the wheel. An amusingly boyish possession, a relic of his days of camping out on Pelican Key with Steve Gardner, yet practical, too. The knife was innocuous enough to get through airport security, yet potentially useful should one of his victims ward off the needle jab. He had practiced extracting the two-inch spear blade with his thumbnail until he could release it switchblade-fast.

He didn't need the blade now. Instead he used the built-in screwdriver to pry off the ignition switch, then hot-wired the ignition.

In Florida City, he stopped at a supermarket. His purchases totaled $128. Canned goods predominated: vegetables, fruit, tuna, sardines. Bread, peanut butter, honey. Chocolate chip cookies. Bottled water. No booze—he needed to keep his head clear—and nothing perishable.

The housewares aisle provided him with rubber gloves, paper towels, plastic utensils, and a manual can opener. In the hardware section he picked up wire cutters, a flashlight, and batteries.

After leaving the supermarket he prowled the streets of Florida City in search of a late-model Pontiac Sunbird parked outside. On Tower Road he found one. He removed the vehicle's front license plate and placed it on the rear of his stolen Sunbird, discarding the hot car's two original plates.

Then he headed south on U.S. 1, driving just within the speed limit. The highway took him through a few miles of flat, dreary land at the edge of the Everglades, then out over the water and into the Florida Keys.

Now it was shortly past midnight; he'd been on the road a little more than an hour.

A new mile marker expanded in his headlights. 98.

Restless, he turned on the radio. He dialed past melancholy country songs and twittering chamber music till he found some raucous rock 'n' roll. The lightning chord changes and racing drums acted on his system like a shot of caffeine. He laid his foot on the gas, then remembered the danger of being stopped by the highway patrol and hastily applied the brakes.

The song ended in a cacophony of percussive clatter

and synthesized wails. He left the radio tuned to that station as a news update came on.

A fire in Fort Lauderdale. Multiple-vehicle collision on Route 95. New developments in the investigation of a scandal involving the state legislature. Nationally, a manhunt was under way for John Edward Dance. . . .

"Jesus," Jack whispered, and turned up the volume.

". . . evaded arrest in Los Angeles and is now believed to be on the run. Dance, thirty-five, is described by authorities as a slick and experienced con artist who once served time for fraud. He is now wanted on charges of multiple homicide—"

All the breath went out of him. He was cold everywhere. A high, tuneless singing rose in his ears.

". . . so-called Mister Twister crime spree, the serial murders of women in several southwestern states . . ."

They knew. Somehow they *knew.*

". . . request anyone with any knowledge of Dance's whereabouts to contact . . ."

He had believed he was wanted only for fraud. He had been wrong. Totally wrong.

The newscaster moved on to a sports update. Jack clicked off the radio with a jerk of his wrist.

This new development changed everything. It meant a larger, more intensive manhunt than he'd anticipated. Saturation news coverage. His picture on TV and in the papers coast to coast.

Mile marker 92 appeared in his headlights. Ten miles to Islamorada.

Jack breathed in the damp salt air and tightened his grip on the wheel.

Gates were lowered across the entrance to the marina, their orange tiger stripes lit by harsh floodlights. Inside the guardhouse the dim figure of a man was visible, silhouetted against the bluish flicker of a black-and-white TV.

Jack steered the Sunbird past the driveway and parked thirty yards down the road, on the gravel shoulder. He killed his headlights and engine, then got out. Two quick steps brought him up short against a ten-foot hurricane fence, overgrown with virgin's bower and buttercup.

From the trunk he removed the three bulging paper bags of groceries and his knapsack. He rummaged in the bags till he found the things he needed; wire cutters, batteries, flashlight, towels, gloves.

Six Duracells went in the flash, which then went in Jack's pocket. All the other items except the wire cutters found a temporary home on the Sunbird's passenger seat.

Then he set to work. The fence was a challenge, the eighteen-gauge galvanized steel strands tough to defeat. Even so, within five minutes he'd cut a breach big enough to slip through. He deposited the grocery bags and knapsack on the other side, concealing them in a thicket of columbine, and returned to the car.

Half a mile away, there was a failed restaurant, the windows boarded up, the cinder-block walls webbed with graffiti. Jack drove around to the rear and parked out of sight of the road.

Wearing the rubber gloves, he tore paper towels off the roll and thoroughly wiped any surfaces he might have touched—steering wheel, dashboard, door handles, trunk lid, license-plate frames. Next he unscrewed the license plate. It belonged to the other Sunbird, the one in Florida City; if the law had tracked his movements as far as the supermarket, someone might make the connection.

The vehicle identification number came off next. He nearly broke the jackknife's screwdriver while levering the plaque free of the dash. Then he cleaned out the glove compartment, taking the registration slip and other paperwork that could have established the vehicle's ownership.

Hefting a rock, he shattered the Sunbird's windshield. Slashed the tires. Jimmied loose the hubcaps and discarded them in the weeds. Peeled the molding off the passenger-side doors. Poured handfuls of dirt over the car till it was a brown-streaked horror.

An abandoned wreck behind a condemned building. Not the sort of thing likely to be noticed or attended to by anyone in authority anytime soon.

Walking back to the marina, he dropped the license plate, VIN plaque, gloves, towels, and glove-compartment wastepaper in a trash bin.

He struggled through the gap in the fence again, retrieved his groceries and pack, and made his way down onto the dock, wary of a security patrol. None was evident. There might be people living aboard some of the vessels, but even if they glimpsed him through a porthole, all they would see was a man lugging groceries to his boat at bedtime.

From somewhere out on the water, laughter and a murmur of voices rose over a rippling undercurrent of salsa. Somebody was throwing a party.

He headed in the opposite direction, toward silence and solitude, scanning the dock slips as he walked.

In a berth at the north end of the marina, he found what he needed. A rigid-hulled inflatable tender, eight feet long, equipped with a Yamaha outboard. The little boat floated on the water, shrouded in canvas, tied to the stern of a cabin cruiser. It reminded him, with an unaccustomed nostalgic pang, of the motorboats he and Steve had rented here, so many years ago.

Jack reached out and pulled the tender close to the dock, then worked the canvas free. The boat was a nice one—Hypalon skin, wooden hull, aluminum oars. The outboard had been tilted forward to raise the propeller out of the water; the blades looked clean.

Quickly he loaded his supplies on board, stepped in, and cut the mooring line, slicing it close to the cruiser's gunwale and tossing the short end on deck, out of sight. He coiled the longer end at the stern of the runabout, then rowed out of the slip, through the narrow basin, into the main channel.

The night was warm, the air stroked by a gentle breeze out of the south that raised a light chop on the water. Jack let the boat drift for a few minutes, until he was sure no other vessels were approaching, then pulled the starter rope. The engine came alive on the first try. Steering with the throttle arm, he motored at less than five knots down the right side of the channel, keeping the centerline buoys to port.

Ahead was the harbor entrance. He opened the throttle slightly, accelerating to eight knots, and passed between the starboard and port buoys.

Then he was out of the harbor, riding the shallow bay. He turned south and throttled forward, increasing his speed to fifteen knots. Visualizing a chart of the area, he mentally plotted a course for Pelican Key.

Though there was no moon, the sky was clear, the stars shining with the hard brilliance of gems. Jack could distinguish the dark shape of Shell Key as he motored past. Ahead, the bridge over Tea Table Key Channel arched its long back like the mounted skeleton of a dinosaur. He nosed into the channel, leaving the bay for swifter waters.

As he guided the dinghy east, he reviewed and expanded on his plans. As far as he knew, Pelican Key was still uninhabited. He could stay there for weeks—months, if necessary—motoring to Upper or Lower Matecumbe Key occasionally to replenish his supplies.

There was a chance, of course, that old Donald Larson or his family actually had taken up residence on the island after all these years. In that case Jack would have to move on. The Keys covered a lot of territory. He could find someplace else to hide.

A more immediate worry was that Steve Gardner or some other friend from his high-school years would mention Pelican Key to the authorities. He found it unlikely that the police would pay much attention; roughing it overnight in the wild as a teenager was one thing, but surviving alone on a tropical island at the age of thirty-five, not for hours but for weeks, was something else.

Even so, some local cops might be sent over to nose around. Jack was confident that he knew Pelican Key well enough to stay out of their sight for however long they lingered there. The island offered many places of concealment. They would depart empty-handed and report a dead end.

When he finally left Pelican Key, perhaps in late September, the government heat would have died down somewhat, and he would have had time to cultivate a tan and a beard, grow his hair long, and bulk up his muscles with rigorous workouts. The alterations in his appearance should keep him safe from recognition.

In Islamorada he would board a bus to Miami. From there it was only a short hop to the Bahamas. Plenty of banking, finance, and investment activity in Nassau, much of it occupying the gray areas at the edges of the law. Many opportunities for scams.

A good life in other respects also, from what he'd heard. Casinos, powerboating, sportfishing, tennis in the tropical sun. Conch fritters and boiled grouper spiced with red-hot peppers and washed down with dark rum at a tiki-bar. Lithe brown girls who could be had for less than Sheila's extravagant tastes had cost him—girls who were safe to flirt and consort with, because they were not at all his type.

And when he needed one of his type again, when the feelings became too strong to ignore . . .

Well, there were plenty of American, Canadian, and British women in the Bahamas, both tourists and residents, many of them fair-skinned, blue-eyed, and blond. They would be no more difficult to pick up on a Friday night than Ronni Tyler had been.

And the Bahamas—think of it—a chain of seven hundred islands, the majority uninhabited. There was no need for the bodies ever to be found.

Yes, a good life. And all he needed to make it happen was a permanent change of identity. That particular detail would be arranged in the coming month.

Jack opened the throttle another notch. The engine burred like a lawn mower. Spray measled his face, moistened his hair. He thought about Teddy Lunt.

Teddy Lunt was a chirpy little bald guy he had met in prison—another hustler like himself, only Lunt's game was phony ID, a growth industry in California, with its proliferation of illegal immigrants. Not all of the illegals were impoverished *campesinos*; some had money, enough to pay for specialized services of the sort Teddy provided.

For five thousand dollars Lunt could supply anyone with a new identity—driver's license, passport, Social Security card, birth certificate, the works—quality paper, backed up by official entries in government files. The hacker's art of obtaining access to encrypted computer data was one of several skills Teddy had mastered.

Lunt was out now, relocated in San Diego, supposedly reformed. Jack knew his address. And he knew that con men were never reformed. They simply switched to subtler scams, such as his own precious metals swindle. Teddy was still in business. Jack was counting on that.

*I'll rent a post office box in Islamorada,* he mused. *Then send Teddy my driver's license—he can use the photo for the new license and passport—along with whatever cash I can spare. Probably about twenty-five hundred. He'll know I'm good for the rest.*

Once Lunt sent the papers, Jack could travel to the Bahamas under his new name; no visa was required for U.S. citizens traveling as tourists. After establishing himself in some pseudo-legitimate enterprise, he would apply for a green card, or whatever they called it over there; if the bureaucracy gave him any hassles, perhaps Teddy could doctor up the requisite Bahamian papers as well.

It would work. It had to.

Jack maintained an easterly course, navigating by landmarks familiar from his boyhood: the lights of the Matecumbe Keys due west, the beacon of the Alligator Reef lighthouse to the south. From time to time he made small corrections to adjust for the gentle push of the southerly breeze. There was a natural inclination to steer away from a wind on the beam; he nudged the nose of the dinghy a few degrees starboard to compensate.

Dead ahead, the stars nearest the horizon began winking out, swallowed by a deeper darkness. The black, ragged line of Pelican Key resolved itself out of the gloom.

Jack relaxed, seeing it. "My private island," he breathed.

He felt his mouth smile.

# 9

Wetness. Wetness on his hand.

Steve Gardner surfaced from sleep and felt a soft tongue licking his knuckles. Anastasia, whining softly.

"What is it, Ana?" he whispered. "You need to go outside?"

The dog sniffed the air and growled.

*No,* he realized. *That's not it. She's worked up about something.*

Apprehension slapped him fully awake. He listened to the house. Heard nothing but Kirstie's soft, regular breathing and Ana's warning growls.

Soundlessly he slipped out of bed, careful not to wake Kirstie. The room was a cage of stifling heat, the claustrophobic stuffiness only marginally relieved by the warm breeze through the windows. His underpants stuck to his groin and thighs in clinging patches; his torso was slick with droplets of perspiration.

He reached under the bed and withdrew a gun.

It was a 9mm Beretta 92SB pistol, which he had purchased at a gun show two years ago, after a rash of burglaries in their Danbury neighborhood. The blue-black barrel gleamed in the pale starlight.

He checked the clip to confirm that it was fully loaded. Sixteen 9mm Parabellum jacketed hollowpoints lay stacked on top of the magazine spring like sardines in a can.

Anastasia let out a louder sound, half cough, half bark. Kirstie stirred, murmured briefly in her sleep, but did not wake.

"Come on, girl," Steve breathed.

He left the room, Anastasia padding after him.

The house seemed larger at night. It covered twenty-five hundred square feet, all on ground level; there was no cellar, no second story. The architecture was of the Spanish Colonial Revival style: thick walls, lead-framed windows, a great deal of hand-painted ceramic tile. Though much of the original decor had been ruined by the hurricane of '35 and by subsequent years of neglect, Larson's carefully supervised renovations had restored it.

Steve started with the guest bedroom, satisfied himself that it was empty, then checked out the bathroom, a nest of bright turquoise tile in floral patterns. Nothing.

He proceeded down the long, tiled loggia that connected the two bedrooms and bath with the rest of the house. To his left was a wall of carved cedar, the recessed display cabinets holding terra-cotta curios. On his right, a row of French doors framed a corner of the patio and garden.

He paused at one of the doors and peered through a filigree of decorative ironwork. A blue tile fountain—two dolphins with interlocked tails—spat an arc of salt water into a star-shaped pool. He saw no crouching shadow figures, no hint of movement.

At the end of the loggia were doorways to the entrance hall and the living room. He went into the foyer first, passing under the skylight, through a glittery fall of starshine.

Anastasia scooted ahead of him and sniffed at the front door. Steve tensed. Somebody outside?

Gingerly he tested the door. It felt secure, unviolated. He nudged Ana back, then unlocked the door and pushed it open.

The hammock on the front porch swung lazily in a fresh breeze. The flagstone court beyond the steps was as vacant and still as the surface of the moon. The gate was closed.

"Nobody there," he reassured the dog as he shut and locked the door.

The living room was next. He stopped in the doorway and scanned its wide expanse. Starlight filtered through tall, arched windows, gleaming on the mahogany furnishings, the miniature schooner on the mantel, the ceramic vases squatting like trolls in the corners.

Nothing out of the ordinary, as far as he could tell. Still, a person could be concealed behind the sofa or one of the leather armchairs.

He considered flicking on the lights. Caution stopped him. Illumination would make him a better target.

In darkness he circled the room, the gun held at waist height, cocked, a pound or two of pressure on the trigger. The large antique globe creaked, spinning a few degrees, when he brushed against it. No one lurked in any of the possible hiding places.

Anastasia preceded him into the dining room. A wrought-iron chandelier, unlit now, hung over a long mahogany table flanked by hand-carved chairs. He found no intruders huddled under the table or behind the floral-print curtains drawn over the French doors.

He and Ana slipped through a side doorway into the quaint, 1920s-style kitchen, largely restored to its original appearance, replete with bottle-glass windows and inlaid wall tiles in a pelican design. A pile of crockery was soaking in the sink; along the counter scuttled a large shiny palmetto bug.

Steve crept forward, past the antique stove, toward

the door at the rear of the kitchen. The tile floor was cold against the soles of his bare feet. Anastasia's toenails clicked softly.

He reached for the doorknob, and then there was a hand on his arm.

His heart kicked. He shook free of the hand, pivoted, the gun rising—

And saw Kirstie in her nightgown, drawing back with a gasp as she saw the pistol, her eyes very big.

Anastasia woofed.

"Jesus," Steve hissed, fear receding and leaving him limp. "Never sneak up on a nervous man with a loaded gun."

"Sorry." Her voice was a frightened whisper. "I woke up and you weren't there. What the hell's going on?"

"Ana's antsy about something. As if we've got company. But I haven't found any sign of trouble."

"Have you looked everywhere?"

"Just about. But I'd better be thorough."

He drew a couple of shallow breaths to calm himself, then opened the door and entered a small, musty chamber, a maid's room in an earlier day. Unoccupied now, it was unfurnished save for a chair, a table, and the two-way radio. Through the walls thrummed the pulse of two diesel generators, which Steve fed with fuel oil on a daily basis; they were housed in a shed directly outside.

"Looks okay," he told Kirstie after checking the window for signs of intrusion.

"How about the patio?"

"That's the only place I haven't looked."

He returned to the dining room, Ana and Kirstie following, and opened one of the French doors, then passed through the pergola, breathing the thick, humid air. Around him lay white wicker lounge chairs, gleaming like bone in the colorless starlight. They made him think of the skeletons of some large inhuman vertebrates, picked clean.

Turning in a slow circle, he took in the rear of the house with its whitewashed facade and red-tiled roof—the low coral wall, draped with chalice vine, enclosing the patio and garden—the trellises of bougainvillea and neatly tended beds of pink primrose and aster, hemmed in by stands of royal poinciana, gumbo-limbo, and woman's tongue tree.

He checked the garden gate, which was locked, then poked around meaninglessly in the trees until he started to feel silly. "False alarm," he said finally.

Kirstie nodded. "Must have been. Funny, though. Ana doesn't usually get spooked in the middle of the night."

"Well, she did, this time." Steve petted the borzoi. "What was it, sweetie? Bad dream?"

Anastasia whined.

Kirstie had a thought. "Bet she's still hung up over that frog she chased. It drove her crazy."

"Sure. You're right. That's probably all it was." Steve smiled, taking his wife's hand. "A frog in the garden. Not a serpent."

He kept his words light. But he couldn't shake the uneasiness that had been with him since Anastasia's lapping tongue pulled him out of sleep.

As he led Kirstie back to the patio, he found himself looking at the chain of lights that marked Upper Matecumbe Key.

Matecumbe. A corruption of *mata hombre.* Kill man.

The thought haunted him, and it was a long time before he finally drifted back to sleep.

# 10

"I still can't believe it. Can't frigging believe it."

"It must have been a shock."

"Oh, fuck, yeah. I mean, when I heard his name on KFWB, it was like whoa, hold on, you know what I mean?"

"Of course."

"I'm driving home from the movies, and all of a sudden they're talking about him, about Jack, and I'm like . . . holy *shit.* You know?"

"I know."

Tamara Moore kept her voice neutral, her face carefully blank save for a practiced hint of sympathy in the eyes. She had been listening to Sheila Tate ramble on for forty-five tedious minutes, and despite the possible importance of the interview, she was thoroughly bored.

Sheila, as the FBI surveillance team had already known, had been carrying on a romantic relationship with Jack Dance, spending the night with him on an irregular basis. As soon as the task force realized that Dance had disappeared, Lovejoy had suggested taking the woman to the field office for her own protection. It was possible Jack would go after her, intending to kill her or take her hostage or try some other crazy, desperate move.

Unfortunately, Sheila Tate had proved impossible

to find. The surveillance unit had followed Jack when he left for work; no one had bothered to put a tail on his girlfriend. It was assumed she would be working at Bullock's, as usual; but as it turned out, Thursday was her day off.

A stakeout car had waited outside her apartment in Santa Monica all day and into the night. She hadn't shown up. The task force had been beginning to worry that Jack had found her somehow, perhaps added her to his list of victims, when at ten o'clock the watch commander at LAPD's West L.A. divisional station had called with word that Sheila was there.

Apparently she'd spent the day in Malibu, working hard on her tan, then visited Century City to shop, eat, and take in a movie. She hadn't heard any news until she'd been driving home. Then, panicked, she'd detoured to the police station, afraid to go home while Jack was still at large.

Two LAPD detectives had interviewed Sheila long enough to learn the essentials of her story, then had delivered her to the FBI field office in Westwood. Lovejoy had asked Moore to talk with her privately in a conference room.

Rigid in a straight-backed chair, Moore studied Sheila Tate, sprawled bonelessly on the couch. She was twenty-eight years old, slender and hard-bodied like so many southern California women, with a lustrous suntan and waves of chestnut hair laced with oddly alluring threads of gray. She should have been beautiful, but wasn't. Her looks were spoiled by her mouth, a sneering, angry mouth well suited to the frequent profanities it uttered.

"Did he really kill all those women?" she asked for the tenth time. Her lower lip still trembled slightly with the aftereffects of shock.

"We believe so."

"Shit. It might've been me next, huh? He might've done me?"

"Well, fortunately he didn't."

"Could have, though. Jesus hung-up Christ, what a wacko. Crazy as the Dahmer guy, and I was practically shacking up with him. Who would've known?"

"Sheila, did Jack ever discuss what he did or where he went on the weekends when he was out of town?"

"Nah, and I never asked. Figured he was bopping somebody else on the side."

"That didn't bother you?"

"Not as long as he made nice with me. He was generous, you know? Real loose with his money."

"Do you remember seeing any syringes around the apartment?"

"Needles? No way. Jack isn't a user. He doesn't even drink much."

"Any items that might have come from other women—a ring, a bracelet, even a lock of hair or a button from a blouse?"

"Nothing like that. Why? Did he keep, like, souvenirs?"

"I'm not at liberty to say."

The lip was quivering again. "He didn't have pieces of them stashed in a drawer someplace, did he?"

"Don't worry about it."

The truth was that searches of Dance's apartment, office, and car had so far failed to turn up any trophies or syringes. Conclusive evidence linking Dance to the murders continued to elude the task force. His fingerprints on the drinking glass at the Phoenix bar were not enough.

After the print run, it had been hoped that a surreptitious inquiry into Dance's credit-card accounts and bank statements would yield a record of airline-ticket purchases that could be matched to Mister Twister's weekend outings. But there was no record of any such purchases. He must have paid cash.

Then it had occurred to someone that Dance was unlikely to have left his Nissan Z in an LAX parking lot, notorious for poor security. LAPD detectives had made the rounds of the privately operated parking lots near the airport and had found the one Jack used. He had paid cash there, too, but that precaution hadn't helped him; it was standard procedure at the establishment to log in every vehicle, recording the license number, make, and model. The Nissan had been left there each weekend when Mister Twister was at work.

The coincidence of dates still wasn't sufficient to ensure a conviction. But it had persuaded a judge to sign the arrest and search warrants early this morning.

Now the arrest had been bungled, and the searches had come up empty. If Dance could not be definitely tied to the homicides, he might end up being prosecuted only on multiple counts of telemarketing fraud. After the publicity given to the manhunt, such a reversal would constitute a disaster.

"Was there anything in the apartment that was off limits to you?" Moore asked. "Any room he didn't want you to enter? Any drawers you weren't supposed to open?"

"No way. He couldn't boss me around like that. What do you think, he had me tied around his little finger like some fucking bimbo?"

"Did you ever see him hide anything or cover up something he was looking at?"

"Uh-uh."

"Did he have a scrapbook, photo album, Polaroids?"

"Not that I ever saw."

"Did he act strange at times?"

"Strange, how?"

"Secretive. Defensive. Paranoid."

"That's not the way . . ." Her lashes batted, and a small crease of concentration appeared above the bridge of her nose. "Well, there was one kind of weird thing."

"Tell me."

"Well, see, one time I walked in on him when he wasn't expecting me. He's on the phone. Sees me and goes ballistic. Says I should ring the goddamn doorbell next time. I say, then what'd you give me a goddamn key for?" She shrugged. "Doesn't sound like shit, but man, it felt really bizarre. I mean, he never gave a crap whether I rang the doorbell any other time."

"Which room was he in?"

"Uh . . . the bedroom."

"Who was he talking to?"

"I don't know. He must have hung up right after."

A knock on the door, and Peter Lovejoy stuck his head in.

"I just got off the phone with Drury." Deputy associate director. "He seems to want us on a plane to Miami ASAP."

"I'm not finished here."

"How about letting Baxter take the rest of Miss Tate's statement?" Linda Baxter was a street agent in the L.A. office.

"Right." Moore smiled at Sheila. "Got to run. Sorry."

"Is Jack in Miami? Is that why you're going there?"

"We don't know where he is," Moore said, rising. She left before Sheila could press her with another question.

Lovejoy was already heading for the elevator, wiping his runny nose. Moore caught up with him in the hallway. "My things are at the hotel."

"Mine, too. We'll pick them up on the way." He checked his watch. "It's eleven-forty. Delta has a red-eye to Atlanta at twelve-fifteen. We can connect with an eight-twenty flight to Miami and get in at ten A.M. Eastern time."

"Can we stop off at Dance's apartment first?"

"Why? The girlfriend tell you something?"

"She may have."

The apartment building was only a few blocks east of the FBI office. Moore watched the Wilshire corridor blur past. It reminded her of Phoenix at night. Tall modern buildings, elegant landscaping, many lights. Wealth built beauty; she'd always known that.

And the absence of wealth . . . She knew about that, too. The Oakland projects. The urine-stained stairwells, the caged light bulbs, the concrete walls of her mother's apartment, beading with sweat on summer afternoons.

The worst part of poverty was the grinding ugliness of it. That feeling of never being clean. She wondered if Sheila Tate had ever known that feeling, or ever would.

Dismissing those thoughts, she turned to Lovejoy at the wheel. "How positive are we that Jack flew to Miami?"

"I would estimate . . . eighty percent. Miami P.D. got the flight attendants out of bed to look at his mug shot. One of them is almost certain she remembers him."

"Wearing glasses?"

"Right. And blue jeans. Just like Mr. Markham said."

Hugh Markham represented a lucky break for the task force, and a bad break for Jack Dance. Sixty-eight years old, a retired bus driver, he ate lunch at a Burger King in Encino every day, usually lingering over the *LA Times*. Said his wife was grateful to have him out of the house for a while.

Markham was a people-watcher. In thirty years of driving for RTD, he had seen a parade of characters pass in and out of the bus's folding doors. He noticed things.

He had been watching when a man in a blue business suit, carrying two shopping bags, entered the restaurant via a side door and disappeared immediately into a rest room. For a few minutes Markham tried idly to guess what line of work the man was in. It was a game of his.

Then it occurred to him that the man was taking a long time to come out. He found this mildly interesting. He went on watching the rest-room door over the top of his newspaper.

Five minutes. Ten.

Finally the door opened, and someone emerged. But it couldn't be the same man. The outfit was different, the hair was different, the shopping bags were gone.

No, it was him, all right. He'd undergone a complete transformation. Left without ordering any food, too. Very odd.

When he told his wife about it, she made him watch the local news, waiting for an update on the day's big story, the manhunt for Jack Dance. "Was that the man you saw?" she asked when Jack's picture appeared on the screen.

Hugh Markham said it was. Twenty minutes later, he was saying the same thing to a West Valley cop.

Markham had a good memory for details. He ticked off the specifics of Jack's new look: moussed hair, glasses, denim shirt, blue jeans, knapsack.

A sketch artist altered the mug shot accordingly. Police circulated copies of it in the vicinity of the Burger King. A taxi driver stationed outside a hotel two blocks away recalled driving Jack to LAX. The American Airlines terminal.

The ticket clerks had already gone home for the day. LAPD tracked them down and showed them the picture. One clerk remembered selling that man a one-way ticket to Miami.

"From what I understand, Miami P.D. is still trying to find someone who might have observed him in the terminal," Lovejoy said. "So far they've apparently had no luck. Of course, it's late there—three A.M. approximately—and they can't roust all the employees."

"If the flight attendant can't make a definite ID, how do we know Jack was ever on the plane? He might have bought the ticket just to throw us off. He could still be in L.A."

Lovejoy nodded. "I raised that possibility with Drury, strictly on a conjectural basis." *Strictly to cover your rear,* Moore corrected silently with a brief smile. "But it appears unlikely. If Jack were trying to divert us, he would most probably have charged the plane fare on one of his credit cards. That way we'd be certain to know about it."

"True."

"Anyway, Miami appears to be our best lead, and Drury wants us to follow up."

"Why can't the Miami field office handle it?"

"They will. But we'll supervise."

"Drury say anything about the, uh, problems with the arrest?"

"Oh, yes." Lovejoy showed her a tight, nervous smile, and for the first time she realized how scared he was. "Yes, he said a great deal."

Moore looked away. She'd had no opportunity to consider any implications of the botched raid this morning other than Jack Dance's continued elusiveness. Now she saw the matter from a different perspective: Peter Lovejoy's career. He was the task force leader. He would take the heat for the screwup that had allowed Jack to evade capture.

Every facet of Lovejoy's life, every detail of his daily routine, even his mannerisms and vocabulary, had been carefully selected to protect him from the ultimate catastrophe of a career meltdown. Tonight he was facing that nightmare—perhaps already had faced it, in his talk with the deputy director.

She glanced at his face in profile, read no expression there. His hands gripped the wheel a little tighter than usual. That was all.

He was taking it well. Better than she would have expected. She wondered if she had underestimated him. She hoped so.

The whine of electric saws was the first thing she and Lovejoy heard as they emerged from the elevator on the penthouse floor of Jack's high-rise. The search team, having finished with the Nissan and the CSGI office, had returned to the apartment, where they were methodically tearing apart walls. Complaints from the neighbors about the noise had been ignored.

The wholesale dismantling of an apartment was perhaps outside the strict parameters of a legal search. But the task force was convinced that Dance had hidden the syringe somewhere. It had not turned up in any of the obvious places. And, after all, the suspect had already demonstrated a fondness for secret panels.

Passing under the yellow crime-scene ribbon strung across Dance's doorway, Moore followed Lovejoy inside.

The living room was three times the size of her entire apartment in Denver, lavish and plush, the giant windows framing a CinemaScope view. It must have been spectacular once, before the thick pile carpet had been torn free of the tacks, the paintings taken off the walls, the sofa cushions unzipped and emptied of stuffing, the drapes removed, the wall fixtures unscrewed.

Now it was a scene of orderly wreckage and controlled destruction, unoccupied save for the Justice Department attorney in charge of evidence recovery. He lounged on what remained of Dance's sofa, listening to Jay Leno over the high-pitched howls of power tools.

In the bedroom two FBI men, Tobin and Mays, were cutting neat vertical slices in the plasterboard. They shut off their saws and raised their goggles when Lovejoy and Moore entered.

"What's up?" Tobin asked. Five o'clock shadow darkened his cheeks and gave him a slightly disreputable appearance that was not improved by an overlay of plaster dust and sweat.

"I need to look at something," Moore said, moving toward the nightstand.

"Nothing in the drawers. Believe me, we checked. Took out all his papers and knickknacks, even X-rayed some of them with the portable fluoroscope."

"I'm not interested in the drawers." She lifted the telephone handset off its cradle, studied it.

Sheila had said Jack was on the phone. But apparently she hadn't heard him talking. She had merely seen him with the phone in his hand.

The handset was thin and lightweight. She saw no sign of tampering. But the cradle . . .

Heavy. Thick. She turned it over. The bottom plate was attached with two small screws.

Squinting at the screws, she saw abrasions on the minuscule grooves of the heads.

"This phone has been taken apart," she said quietly. "More than once, I'd say."

"Well, what do you know," Tobin breathed.

Mays got a small Phillips screwdriver and carefully removed the screws, then lifted off the plate.

Inside the cradle, in a narrow cavity between the plate and the guts of the phone, was a single plastic syringe.

"Physical evidence." Lovejoy showed Moore a broad smile, his first since the raid. "Thank God."

"We would have found it eventually," Mays said with a note of defensiveness.

Lovejoy ignored that. "You'd better get the syringe over to the LAPD lab and see if they can find enough fluid in it for serological analysis. Also, see about matching the needle to the puncture wounds in the victims' necks. And find out if there's any sort of brand name on this thing, some way of tracing its origin and distribution, determining how he got hold of it."

Tobin already knew the procedure. "Right. Right."

"And get Justice in here to preserve chain of evidence." Lovejoy moved toward the bedroom doorway. "And check the other phones—Jack's office phones, too—in case he tried the same gimmick twice. And—"

Moore, smiling, gave him a gentle shove from behind.

"*And* we need to get going, Peter. We've got a plane to catch."

# 11

Jack Dance woke at dawn and rubbed his aching neck. Sleeping curled up in the runabout had left him sore and stiff.

He had beached the dinghy in the cove, on the seaweed-strewn mud flat, and camouflaged it with palm fronds. He didn't want it to be spotted from the air in daylight.

Throughout the night, biting insects had harassed him without mercy. Only after arriving at the island had he realized that he'd forgotten to purchase bug spray. Sleep had been fitful, his fragmentary dreams disturbing.

Breakfast was a can of pears. He consumed the entire contents, including the heavy syrup. The thick, sugary liquid made his gut roll.

Jack sighed. Yesterday's euphoria, born of plotting strategy and taking action, had faded. He pictured his apartment in Westwood—the well-stocked refrigerator, the comfortable chairs, the thick-pile carpet, the king-size bed. It made a disheartening contrast with his present circumstances.

Yes, he'd had quite a fall. Less than twenty-four hours earlier, he had gazed down on Los Angeles from a height, a monarch surveying his dominion. Now he was a sweaty, muddy, ravenous thing, a hunted creature seeking refuge in the wild, master of nothing, not even of ticks and sandflies.

He would rise again, though. He swore he would.

First light was breaking, a soft luster brightening the sky. Time to reacquaint himself with the island. Seventeen years had passed since his last visit here, with Steve Gardner, in the summer after their high-school graduation.

Leaving the cove, he immediately found the boardwalk that ran through the mangrove swamp. Sure, he remembered this. He and Steve had traversed the walkway many times. It was a haphazard, crooked thing, twisting and bending like a malformed spine. At its far end, as he recalled, was a forest trail.

He started off down the boardwalk, moving slowly, wary of potential weak spots in the old wood. But the structure seemed sturdy enough. Remarkably well preserved, in fact. In better condition than his memory would have led him to expect.

The swamp folded over him like a nightmare, surrounding him with rank smells and contorted shadows and sinuous shapes that glided through the murk. Clumps of mangroves, their skirts of aerial roots exposed now, at low tide, formed a labyrinth of twisted trunks and branches. In the narrow channels meandering among the trees, the water had the dark gloss of an oil slick, its surface puckered and dimpled with random bubbles.

This was a prehistoric world, fetid and lush, crowded with mysterious life. Jack almost expected to see *Tyrannosaurus* come sloshing into view with a bellows blast of breath and a jet-plane roar. A peculiar thought, unusually imaginative for him.

He kept walking. As he did, he ran his hand along the boardwalk's wooden railing, studied the planks passing by under his feet. He began to feel the first stir of misgivings.

He'd counted on having Pelican Key all to himself. But the boardwalk's condition was too good, too perfect. It had not been left to rot. It had been repaired—even partly rebuilt, he believed. There were sections were the wood looked new and the nail heads gleamed.

Jack frowned. Was the key occupied? Had old Donald Larson finally restored the old plantation house and taken up residence there, as he'd promised to do?

"Shit," he muttered. If he wasn't alone, he would have to leave in a hurry, before he was discovered.

No point in jumping to conclusions. Maybe the island was inhabited only in the winter months. In that case he could stay until at least the end of September. By then Teddy Lunt should have come through with the documents.

To find out, one way or the other, he would have to take a look at the house and determine if it was presently in use.

He could hardly walk up to the door and knock. But from a vantage point on the beach, he could scope out the place with little risk of being seen. He quickened his steps.

In less than ten minutes, the boardwalk delivered him to the hardwood forest at the center of the island. He hurried along the trail toward the red radiance of the sunrise, intermittently visible through breaks in the foliage.

His shoes crunched on the dry, crumbly soil, frightening small lizards out of his way. Walls of dense shrubbery and trees enclosed the path, forming a tunnel of green. Somewhere a parrot squawked.

The tropical hammock was a showcase of the superabundance of life, nature's insane fecundity. Things grew everywhere here, even on other things. A palette of varicolored lichens smeared the bark of mastics, gumbo-limbos, and banyans, paint splotches dabbed on by some frenetic, freewheeling artist. Orchids, wild pine, and resurrection fern ornamented other trees, bright as Christmas bows. A tall mahogany tottered, its trunk wrapped in the twisted roots of a strangler fig, slowly smothering in that octopus embrace.

Jack walked on, blinking at the steadily growing brightness of the day. A rabbit flitted through the underbrush and vanished beneath the yellow blossoms of a Jerusalem thorn. Something splashed in an unseen pond. The recesses of the forest seemed impossibly remote, lost in shadows and mist, partitioned by screens of foliage and ropy webs of medicine vine.

The end of the trail was just ahead. He could smell the fresh salt breeze.

The brush thinned. Dark loam gave way to white coral sand. Past a scrim of ferns and waving sawgrass in red bloom, he saw the crimson thread of the horizon. The sky blushed. The sea flamed.

On the fringe of the forest, he halted abruptly. He shaded his eyes, blinked, then leaned against the rough bole of a date palm and stared out into the blinding light.

"Oh," he said very simply, the word hushed and almost reverent.

For a moment—just one moment—Jack Dance forgot who he was and what he did for fun. He forgot the syringe and his victims' convulsions and his sweaty exercise afterward with their undressed bodies.

In that moment he was not a killer. He was only a man gazing transfixed at the woman on the beach.

She wore sandals and shorts and a yellow tank top. Her hair was golden, her skin sun-bronzed. Her slender body was limned in fire against the red dazzle of the sun.

She ambled lazily along the irregular line of seaweed that marked high tide, her head thrown back, arms loose at her sides. Plovers scattered before her, comical in their helter-skelter distress.

An enchanting picture. So perfect it might have been posed. The woman belonged on a postcard or a calendar. Anyone looking at her would smile, just as Jack was smiling now, not in lust but in simple aesthetic appreciation.

She knelt to examine something on the beach. A shell. It gleamed in her hand. She put it back, reached for another, and then her gaze lifted and, across a span of thirty feet, she met his eyes.

Slowly she stood. She watched him.

Jack saw the sudden tightness in her mouth, the unnatural stiffness of her body. He saw fear. And seeing it, he remembered himself.

His interlude of rapt contemplation ended instantly, as if a switch had been thrown. No more time for that. There was a job to do.

He stepped out of the brush into the loose pebbly sand and started toward her, still smiling, but his smile held a different meaning now.

From this distance he could not quite distinguish the color of her eyes. He hoped they were blue.

Even if they were not, he would enjoy watching her face when he took out his pocketknife and buried the spear blade in her throat.

# 12

Rigid, breath stopped, Kirstie stared at the man as he emerged from the shadows of the trees.

He was tall—taller than Steve—and about the same age, thirty-five. He wore a denim shirt, blue jeans, black shoes. His careless posture and casual way of walking implied an ample fund of confidence, frequently tapped, instantly replenished.

The man moved toward her, crossing the bleached moonscape of coral sand, his long, sinuous shadow sliding at his heels.

She was abruptly conscious of how alone she was. This walk on the beach was her morning ritual; sometimes Steve joined her, but most often not. Today he'd mumbled something about catching up with her as she slipped out of bed. Most likely he had just rolled over and gone back to sleep.

She looked toward the house. Beyond the trees, at the southern tip of the island, the red-tiled roof glowed like a carpet of embers. The dock stood on the reflected image of itself, a many-legged insect balanced on the surface tension of a pond.

Would Steve hear her if she screamed for help? She didn't think so. The distance was too great, and the breeze, blowing out of the south, would throw her shouts back in her face.

As calmly as possible she faced the man, her head lifted, shoulders squared.

"This is private property," she said as he came nearer.

He smiled, a clean white smile full of friendliness but empty of affection. "I'm aware of that."

He closed to within six feet of her and stopped. For a beat of time they watched each other without speaking.

Overhead soared a brown pelican, the island's namesake, showing the white belly and brown wings characteristic of a young bird in its first year of life. It wheeled toward the sea in search of food, dipped and rose, then dipped again, dark against the blaze of sun.

*Hunter and prey,* Kirstie thought. The words touched her with their chill.

"If you know it," she said slowly, "what are you doing here?"

"Visiting."

"It's not allowed."

"I'm not bothering anyone."

"You're bothering me."

"I would think you'd be lonely. You *are* alone, aren't you?"

The question pulled her stomach into a tight, acid knot.

She forced herself to keep her eyes focused on his face. A handsome face, in its way. Sharp-featured, faintly cruel. Stubble dusted his cheeks. The breeze flicked listlessly at his unkempt brown hair.

He stared back without blinking, a cool, flinty gaze that raised prickles of gooseflesh on her arms. His hazel eyes sparkled, but not with merriment. With mockery perhaps. Or malice.

"No," she answered evenly. "I'm not alone. My husband is with me. And . . . some friends."

"How many friends?"

"You have to go."

"There are no friends, are there?"

"I want you to leave. Right now."

"No husband, either, I'll bet. You *are* alone."

"If you don't go—"

He took a step nearer. She wanted to retreat, but if she gave ground, the man would only be emboldened.

"You have pretty eyes," he said suddenly. "Blue eyes. Deep blue. They match the water."

Her pulse beat in the veins of her wrists. There was a greasy coldness in her belly. Her mouth was very dry.

"I want you off this island." Her words came slowly, paste squeezed from a tube. "Now. Immediately. Or my husband and I will radio the police."

He moved forward again, and this time she did step back, unwilling to let him invade her personal space. A splash of cool tidal water lapped her ankles.

"The police?" He frowned. "That's not very nice. I have a feeling you and I aren't hitting it off too well."

"How perceptive."

"I'm a surprisingly sensitive fellow."

"If you're so goddamn sensitive, you ought to know when you aren't wanted."

"I have gotten that message, actually."

"Then you're going?"

"In a minute. First there's just one little thing I have to do. . . ."

His hand moved toward his pants pocket, and suddenly Kirstie felt sure she had to run or scream or do *something*, dammit, because this man was not normal, this man was not *safe*.

An explosion of barking split the air.

She jerked her head sideways and saw Anastasia blunder out of the brush onto the beach, loping this way.

Tension hissed out of her body, leaving her muscles slack. She could breathe again.

"My husband is here," she said, struggling to hide her relief. "Maybe you'll listen to him, if not to me."

The man made no reply, simply gazed past the dog at Steve, following Anastasia across the sand.

He had tossed on a pair of long pants, a cotton shirt, and the battered Nike running shoes he refused to throw away. His glasses glinted, the lenses screening his eyes.

Kirstie wished he looked bigger, more imposing. The man before her was muscular and fit. He could take Steve in a fight. But not with Anastasia to help. Thank God they'd bought a big dog.

Steve hurried toward them, urgency conveyed in his long, ungainly strides. As he drew closer, Kirstie was surprised to read more puzzlement than concern in his expression.

He stopped two yards away. For a long moment no one spoke. Anastasia was silent, watchful. The breeze died off, even the air around them holding its breath.

Then slowly, hesitantly, Steve smiled. "Jack? Jack Dance?"

The other man extended his hand. "Steve Gardner. Jesus Christ, it *is* you."

Kirstie watched, speechless, as they locked grasps in a violent handshake.

*This* was Jack Dance? Steve's high-school friend? His companion on the Florida trips that had always ended on Pelican Key?

But that was two decades ago. What the hell was he doing here now?

Steve voiced the same question, his smile still fixed

on his mouth—a giddy, sunstruck smile, curiously unreal.

"Just visiting," Jack answered. "Got bitten by the nostalgia bug, I guess. Developed a sudden hankering to see the place again. Relive some old memories. Know how that is?"

Steve nodded slowly. "Oh, yeah. I know how that is."

"So you live here? You bought the island?"

"Not exactly. We're like you—just visiting. The Larson heirs are renting out the plantation house to vacationers."

"Must have fixed up the house pretty nice, huh?"

"You'll have to see it. I'll give you a guided tour."

"Got the whole island to yourselves?"

"Absolutely. Total privacy."

"Sounds great."

"It *is* great." Steve shrugged. "Look, you've got to spend the day with us. Lunch and dinner. We'll explore the island, just like in the old days."

Kirstie bit down hard and said nothing.

"Terrific, Steve." Jack patted Anastasia's head, and the dog tentatively licked his fingers. "I'd love to."

"You've met Kirstie, obviously."

"Of course." Jack spoke in a courtly tone quite different from his earlier mocking insolence. "She's something special. I'm jealous."

"You should be. But don't get any ideas. She's mine."

"Then I'll just have to content myself with this elegant creature's affections." Jack stroked the dog's silken fur.

"Her name's Anastasia," Steve said. "We call her Ana."

"Beautiful animal. Reminds me of my dad's Doberman."

"How *is* the skipper?"

"Passed away four years ago. Heart failure."

"Oh. Sorry to hear that."

"It was quick, at least. He didn't suffer."

Jack scavenged a stick of driftwood and tossed it high in the air. It twirled like a boomerang and landed in a puff of coral sand. Anastasia ran to retrieve it, tail swishing joyously.

A sense of unreality stole over Kirstie as she watched. A couple of minutes ago she'd been confronting Jack Dance alone, trying to find the strength either to scream or flee. Now here he was, accepting the stick from Ana, then kneeling to let her lick his face, her tongue slopping across his mouth in a slobbery kiss.

Kirstie found herself studying Jack's clothes. They were creased, slightly soiled, as if they'd been slept in.

She remembered Anastasia's jittery nerves last night. Perhaps a bad dream hadn't been the cause, after all. Perhaps she'd heard Dance's arrival.

Had he beached the boat in darkness? Had he spent the night on the island?

The thought traced a slow shiver along her spine.

"How did you get here, Jack?" she asked in a neutral tone.

"Rented a dinghy with an outboard motor."

"This morning?"

"Just showed up."

"Funny. I've been awake for a little while. I didn't hear a boat."

Jack shrugged. "The way the wind's blowing, the sound wouldn't have reached you."

"If you tied up at the dock," she said, pressing slightly, "you must have seen the house. I'm surprised you didn't notice that it had been repaired."

He showed her a bland smile. "I didn't use the

dock. Didn't see the south end of the island at all. I approached from the north and beached the dinghy at the cove. That's where Steve and I used to come ashore."

Kirstie wouldn't let it go. "Pretty early in the morning to rent a boat." She watched his eyes. "It must have been tough to find anyplace open before dawn."

She detected no flicker of uncertainty when he answered. "I rented it last night. Figured I'd get an early start this morning. A friend at the marina arranged it."

"Mickey Cotter?" Steve asked.

"That's right. Good old Mickey."

"Didn't he tell you I was out here?"

This time there was hesitation, and Kirstie was sure Dance had been caught in a lie. But all he said was: "No, never mentioned it."

Steve sighed. "Maybe Pice forgot to let him know."

"Who's Pice?"

"Boat captain who ferried us to the island. He's got a thirty-foot sportfisher called the *Black Caesar*. Picking us up first thing tomorrow."

"You're going home then?"

"Afraid so."

"I nearly missed you. Glad I didn't."

"So am I. Come on back to the house and we'll have breakfast. We've got a refrigerator full of groceries we need to use up."

They headed off together, Anastasia trailing Jack and woofing happily, Kirstie taking up the rear.

Ahead loomed the line of trees bordering the beach, furnace red in the intense daylight. The palms threw feathery shadows on the hardwood stands behind them. The casuarinas were graceful sculptures in bold relief.

At the end of the beach Kirstie paused to look back. The sun was a full circle now, stamped on the sky like a target, burning a fiery path through the shallows to the shore. As she watched, the pelican dived into the glitter and bobbed up with a catch in its pouch. It floated on the surface, head lowered, as if in thankful prayer for the gift of food.

The same thought recurred to her: *Hunter and prey.*

She turned away with a jerk of her head and followed Steve and Jack into the forest.

Close-packed trees and shrubs swallowed them like the walls of a cave. Flies buzzed like miniature dive bombers. Green darners chased mosquitoes in the tremulous young light.

Jack twisted a cane free of a blackberry bush, then produced a pocketknife and deftly sliced off leaves, stems, and thorns. Kirstie thought of Jack's hand reaching for his pocket as they faced each other on the beach. A tremor passed through her as she watched the slim, clever blade coruscate in a patch of sun.

He threw the twig to Anastasia, continuing their game. The dog snatched it up and scampered away. Jack followed at a jog trot, laughing.

Kirstie touched Steve's arm to hold him back.

"How could you invite him to stay all day without asking me?" she hissed.

"I didn't have much choice. He's an old friend."

"So I gathered. Tom Sawyer, reunited with Huck Finn."

"It's not like that," Steve said quietly, as his eyes took on that unfocused gaze she knew too well.

She wouldn't let him drift away. "When he was alone with me," she whispered insistently, careful not to let Jack overhear, "he seemed . . . weird. Dangerous."

"Dangerous?" Steve frowned. "How?"

"The things he said."

"Like what?"

She replayed their conversation in her mind. Suddenly the encounter struck her as frustratingly innocuous. There had been no open threats, nothing blatantly improper, only an intuitive sense of jeopardy, impossible to justify with a bare recital of the words exchanged.

She tried, anyway. "He kept asking if I was alone. When I told him to get off the island, he ignored me."

"Did he say he wouldn't leave?"

"Well . . . not exactly. But I didn't feel safe with him. And I still don't."

Steve smiled. "Look, there's nothing to worry about. He's just a high-school friend who happened to turn up. Anyway, I'm here to protect you. Okay?"

He moved on, rejoining Jack, without waiting for an answer. Kirstie stared after him.

She'd barely heard what her husband had said. Her whole attention had been focused on his face.

His mouth had been smiling. But his eyes had captured some other emotion, something she could not define. Grief, perhaps, or guilt. Or . . . fear.

She wasn't sure what she had seen or what it meant. But somehow it scared her, scared her worse than the knife in Jack Dance's pocket.

Kirstie felt herself trembling as she continued down the trail.

# 13

Delta flight 627 out of Atlanta touched down at Miami International at 9:57 A.M. Lovejoy and Moore hustled their carry-on bags out of the overhead bins and got off fast.

An Airphone call to the Miami office shortly before landing had established that no one would be meeting them at the gate. The field office's resources were entirely consumed by the hunt for Mister Twister.

"At least there isn't any shortage of cabs in this town," Lovejoy said as he and Moore hurried down the concourse. "But before we leave the airport, it might be advisable to pay a call on security."

William Proster had been chief of security at Miami International for seventeen years. He offered his visitors a donut (declined) and a seat (accepted). The radio chatter of patrol units crackled and buzzed over the squawkbox on his desk.

"I understand you're still not a hundred percent sure your boy actually deplaned here," Proster said, dunking a cruller in a mug of coffee. "So I came in early today and watched some TV."

He chewed the donut, waiting for the obvious question. Moore obliged. "TV?"

"Well, nothing that'll give Phil and Oprah a run for their money." Proster chuckled at his witticism. "We've got dozens of video cameras set up in strategic locations. Any arriving passenger would have to walk right past some of them to exit the terminal. This morning I screened the sections of the tapes recorded in the relevant time frame."

"Did you see him?" Lovejoy asked.

"I can't say for a certainty." The soggy cruller vanished in two last bites. "But maybe yes. At least, there's one fellow who's dressed right—jeans, casual shirt, knapsack. 'Course, a million joes dress like that. The face . . ." Proster sighed. "To me it's a blur. Why don't you take a look-see for yourselves?"

He escorted them to the video surveillance center, where rows of color monitors lined the walls from floor to ceiling, showing overhead views of the concourses and baggage-claim areas. Flocks of miniaturized travelers hurried past in real time, exiting from one monitor only to enter another a moment later. Two security guards nursed coffees and watched the screens.

The tape from last night was already cued up on a video deck in the corner. "This camera is stationed on the American Airlines concourse," Proster said, "near the security checkpoint." He punched Play, and a hazy image of what might have been Jack Dance passed across the upper right-hand corner of the picture tube. A digital display in a corner of the frame marked the time at 10:04 P.M.

"Again," Lovejoy said.

Proster rewound the tape a couple of feet and replayed it.

Lovejoy shook his head. "I'm not sure." He looked at Moore. "You?"

"I think it's Jack. But I can't be positive. The image is too hard to read."

"We picked up the same man on a couple of other cameras, but in those instances he's pretty much lost in the crowd or in shadow. This is the best look at him we got."

"It's not enough to confirm his arrival," Moore said.

Proster nodded. "True enough. However, I'd bet my winnings from a good night of five-hand stud that this fellow"—he tapped the picture tube, where the frozen image lay like a painting behind glass—"*is* your boy, and here's why. Two cars were stolen from long-term parking yesterday. Now admittedly this is Miami, where grand theft auto is not exactly unheard of, but even so . . ."

Lovejoy was taking notes. "What kind of cars?"

"One was a '93 Dodge Dynasty LE sedan, silver exterior, gray interior. Owner went off on a day trip, got back at eleven P.M. and discovered it missing. With the other car we got a little bit lucky. The owner expected to be away till Sunday night, but his seminar got canceled, so he came back from Houston only a few hours after he left. His car was gone. Must've disappeared between four and midnight."

"Make and model?"

"Pontiac Sunbird. Four-door hardtop. 1992. White exterior, blue interior."

"Plates?"

Proster rattled off both license numbers without consulting any notes.

"Miami P.D. put out APB's?"

"You betcha. Statewide. But I wouldn't hold my breath. Lots of cars go to the chop shop in the Sunshine State."

Lovejoy was still looking at the fuzzed image on the monitor. "Would it be possible for us to borrow that tape?"

"Think if you ogle it long enough, you can convince yourself it's him?"

"Not exactly. There might be a whole new way of seeing it."

Moore asked him what he'd meant once they were back in the concourse.

"Well, I'm not personally familiar with the technology, but from what I understand, certain computer programs can do video enhancements of single frames. Improve the resolution, bring out more detail."

"Good thought. We can messenger the tape up to D.C. Have the Headquarters lab take care of it."

Lovejoy pursed his lips. "Yes. That would be one possible approach. But we might have to wait awhile for the results."

"What's the alternative?"

"Perhaps . . . local talent." Lovejoy stopped by a bank of pay phones, found the Yellow Pages, and flipped to a section marked Television Production Services. "One of these outfits may be able to digitize and enhance the image while we wait."

A couple of quick phone calls, and they had an appointment at a video-production house called Sorcerer's Apprentice on Flagler Street in downtown Miami.

A revolving door ejected them into the scorching dragon's breath of the day. The air was humid and thick, the heat stifling. Lovejoy sneezed twice before climbing into the first taxi in the queue.

"I hate this climate," he said as he dabbed his nose. His standard complaint.

"You hate all climates." Her standard response.

Lovejoy gave the video firm's address to the driver.

As the cab pulled away, Moore said thoughtfully, "You know, taking this tape to an outside agency for analysis isn't exactly going by the rules and regs."

"Well, sometimes it may be necessary to . . . slightly . . . bend the rules."

She had never expected to hear Peter Lovejoy say that.

Sorcerer's Apprentice was an unprepossessing warren of offices in a rundown brownstone. The receptionist introduced them to a technician named Davis, a youngish man, bearded and pony-tailed and amazingly pale for south Florida. He wore a loose T-shirt that growled HATE THE STATE.

The slogan led Moore to expect a hostile reaction when she and Lovejoy identified themselves as federal agents, but Davis merely nodded, listened patiently to their request, and said, "Okay. Come on."

He led them down the hall to a narrow room cluttered with electronic gear. Lovejoy surrendered the tape, and Davis popped it into a camcorder plugged into a connection box at the back of a Quadra 950 computer, then ran the video in a full-motion display.

"Huh," he said, sitting comfortably at the console. "Pretty bleary, all right."

"Can you enhance it?" Lovejoy asked.

"You can always tweak an image. But in this case, maybe not enough. Let me grab a frame and see."

He ran the video in slow motion, then frame by frame, till he found the most promising image. A double click on the mouse made a dialog box appear; he selected "Capture to RAM" in response to a prompt.

"You want just his face?"

Lovejoy said yes.

Davis cropped and resized the frame, enlarging the man's face to fill most of the screen. He activated a pull-down menu, clicked on one of the options, and increased the contrast.

"Looking a little better already. Now let's sharpen it up, improve the edge definition."

He clicked on another menu option, then went on

clicking as the blurred picture came into progressively crisper focus in a rapid series of adjustments.

"That's as clear as I can get it," he said finally.

"Quite possibly clear enough," Lovejoy muttered. "At least, my preliminary reaction is that, personally, I think we've got a match."

Moore thought so, too, but wanted to be sure. From her briefcase she removed a copy of Jack Dance's mug shots, modified by a sketch artist to incorporate his disguise. She compared the profile view with the face on the monitor.

Same hair. Same glasses. Same nose and jaw.

"It's him," she said. "We've confirmed him in Miami."

Davis leaned back in his swivel chair. "Want a hard copy of this frame?"

Lovejoy nodded. "If possible." Half a minute later a laser printout was in his hand. "Thanks. You've been a considerable help. What do we owe you?"

"No charge. Glad to be of service to the authorities." He saw Moore's raised eyebrow and added, "Oh, don't mind the T-shirt. A holdover from my Murray Rothbard phase. I used to think anarchy was cool."

"What happened?" she asked, amused.

"I got mugged." Davis pivoted in his chair and tapped the screen. "This is the serial killer, isn't it? Saw his picture in this morning's *Herald.*"

Lovejoy coughed into his fist. "Actually, the Bureau is involved in a large number of manhunt operations at any given point in time, only a few of which make the headlines. It's hardly prudent to jump to conclusions concerning any particular—"

"It's the same man," Moore cut in, impatient with her partner's evasions. "But we'd appreciate it if you didn't spread the story around. We don't want this to get on the news. It's best if he doesn't know how close we are."

"How close *are* you?"

"Well . . . we know he's in Florida."

Davis grunted. "Florida's a big place."

"He's correct, you know," Lovejoy said as he and Moore pulled away in a second cab. "Florida *is* a big place."

"We need another break, that's all."

"In my estimation, we've already gotten more breaks than we had any right to expect."

Moore had no answer to that. They were silent during the rest of the ride to the field office.

# 14

"Terrific lunch." Jack polished his mouth with a paper napkin. "Steve, you're a lucky man. Not only is your wife beautiful, she's also a hell of a cook."

Kirstie showed him a cool smile. "Cheeseburgers aren't exactly gourmet fare."

She was seated across the patio from Jack, her tray balanced in her lap, her suntanned legs stretched lazily along the chaise longue. Sometime earlier she had kicked off her sandals; her bare toes wiggled. Jack thought she had cute feet.

"Ordinary cheeseburgers—no." He enjoyed taunting her with his phony courtesy, his lying compliments. "But yours are something special. What's that sauce you put on them?"

"Ketchup."

"Oh, come on, there was more to it than that. Some secret ingredient. Am I right?"

Her shoulders lifted. "Dash of Tabasco."

"The master stroke."

She looked away, a muscle in her cheek ticking angrily.

"I think you're embarrassing her," Steve said through a mouthful of potato chips. "She's not accustomed to such rave reviews."

"Well, she should be. Treat her right, Stevie, or you never know. I just might steal her away."

Kirstie turned in his direction again. Her eyes were two blue slits.

She was not embarrassed, of course. Jack knew that. She hated him, feared him, and she wanted him off the island, out of her life. Well, he could hardly blame her.

The sun beat down. Flies buzzed, droning their insect songs. Anastasia, curled at Jack's feet, burred in deep sleep.

Jack was glad they'd chosen to eat outdoors. The house was stifling, claustrophobic. It felt like a cage. Memories jumped at him from every corner—good memories, but tough to face now, as he pondered the problem of what to do about the Gardners.

The patio felt safer. Here he could smell the flowers and smile at the blue sky. Surrounded by beautiful distractions, he hardly even had to look at Steve . . . or at Steve's wife.

But it was hard not to look at Kirstie. She was perfect. She was exactly his type.

He studied her as she finished her sandwich. A slender woman, not fashion-model tall, but perfectly proportioned. The teasing breeze had thrown her hair into lovely disarray. It tumbled across her shoulders—thin, gently rounded shoulders naked save for the tank top's straps, the smooth skin dusted with soft freckles.

He liked the graceful curve where her neck met her collarbone, liked the way her skin stretched tight over the bone, liked the thinness and fragility of the clavicle itself, delicate as a wishbone, so easily snapped. And below it, above the yellow tank top, a vee of tanned cleavage that drew his gaze inexorably downward to her small, firm breasts, the nipples poking pertly at the thin fabric. . . .

A slow shudder passed through him like a current of electricity, leaving a tingling numbness in his extremities. Abruptly he was hot and dizzy.

"If you don't mind"—he heard a cheerful, buoyant voice, realized it was his own—"I think I'll avail myself of the facilities."

Gently he dislodged his feet from under Anastasia without waking her, then rose from the patio chair. He did not look at Kirstie again.

Leaving the patio, he hurried down the hall to the bathroom and shut the door. The latch slipped into place with a soft snick.

He lowered his head, exhaling a fluttery breath. All morning he'd fought to suppress the impulses raging in him like fever. He'd endured breakfast with the Gardners, then Steve's endless guided tour of the house, then meaningless chitchat about old times, and finally lunch.

The interludes with Steve hadn't been so bad. Almost pleasant, in fact. It was good to recall old times, the summer days on the island, the invigorating sense of freedom and expanding horizons he had known in his youth. Steve was one of the few friends Jack had ever known in his active, extroverted, yet ultimately unsocial existence.

Which made it all the more difficult to contemplate what he might have to do.

He didn't want to . . . *hurt* Steve. Didn't want their friendship to end . . . that way.

But he wasn't sure he had any choice.

Turning in slow circles, looking blankly at the room around him, he considered his situation.

At breakfast Steve had told him that he and Kirstie hadn't watched television, listened to the radio, or read a newspaper in two weeks. For the moment, then, he was safe; the Gardners suspected nothing. But once they left the island, they would learn he was a fugitive. They would call the police, report that he'd been on Pelican Key only a short time earlier. The search would narrow, the net tighten. There was little chance he could get away.

Unless he had transportation. Something faster than the little runabout, and with a longer range. Something like the thirty-foot sportfisher that would arrive at the island tomorrow, piloted by a man named Pice.

Steve had mentioned the boat while they were talking on the beach. The *Black Caesar.*

Jack stopped turning. Motionless, intrigued, he focused his gaze inward on the slowly materializing outline of a plan.

A vessel thirty feet long would carry a fair quantity of fuel. Probably one hundred fifty gallons. At its maximum cruising speed, say thirty knots, it would burn roughly ten gallons per hour, allowing for a range of four hundred fifty miles.

The boat could get him to Andros Island, at the edge of the Bahamian archipelago, in seven hours. From there he could proceed southeast around Snap Point and lose himself among the seven hundred islands in the chain.

He would take the runabout with him. Having hidden the *Black Caesar* in some isolated cove, he could use the tender to make short excursions to more populous areas. He would put a new name on the sportfisher, maybe repaint the brightwork and make other alterations. Meanwhile he'd drop a note in the mail to Teddy Lunt and set the wheels in motion for the creation of his new identity.

Slowly Jack nodded.

Yes, it really could work. Everything he'd planned to do on Pelican Key, he could accomplish just as easily in the Bahamas—if he had the boat.

But to get it, he first had to put Steve and Kirstie out of the way.

His mind recoiled from the most obvious solution.

Killing Kirstie would be no hardship; quite the contrary. But Steve Gardner, good old Stevie, once his best friend . . .

Desperately he groped for an alternative.

Knock him out? Strike a blow to his skull from behind? Unconscious, he could be bound with the mooring line from the runabout or with some other rope.

Jack studied the idea for long moment, then reluctantly discarded it.

Too risky. In the movies it looked easy, but in real life it was hard to drop a man with a single blow. And if Steve failed to go down, Jack would have to fight him. Jack was in better condition, but that might not matter. In prison he had seen scrawny, underfed cons defeat bruisers twice their size. Adrenaline could do astonishing things for a man.

No, half measures were inadequate. Evasions were pointless. There was only one sure way to incapacitate his friend, and that was to use the knife.

One quick thrust, and Steve's throat would open up like a torn paper bag.

Jack bent forward at the waist and pressed his palms to the wall above the commode, his fingertips squeezed white against the smooth ceramic squares. He stared at the tiles, at the complicated pattern of inlaid pieces, but he was not seeing the pictures they made, was not seeing anything in this room.

It was the future he saw, the future that had been sealed by fate, as firmly as if by an oracle's prophesy, since the moment when he and Steve shook hands on the beach at sunrise.

He didn't want to do it. But he had no choice.

Unless . . .

"I can run," he whispered. "Run right now."

If he left the island immediately, headed south in

the runabout, then went to ground somewhere in the Lower Keys . . .

The Gardners might not hear of the manhunt until they returned to Islamorada tomorrow afternoon. He would have a twenty-four-hour head start.

But suppose they learned the news sooner. Suppose his abrupt departure raised suspicions in their minds. He would lose his small but crucial advantage.

And there was one other consideration not to be neglected.

Kirstie.

If he left now, he would never have her.

Jack pivoted away from the wall, faced his reflection in the mirror above the basin. Asked himself if his need for Kirsten Gardner outweighed his friendship with Steve. Was his obsession that strong? His compulsions so irresistible?

He was mildly shocked to hear the answer.

*Yes.*

He looked away. His face in the silvered glass was too hard to watch.

All right, then. He would do it. Kill them both. Steve first, Kirstie later. Find a way to separate them, then feed his knife their blood.

Jack relieved himself, washed and dried his hands, and ran the damp towel over his face. Finally he felt calm and composed once more.

The Gardners were carrying their trays inside when he returned to the patio. He picked up his own tray and followed them into the kitchen.

"Hey, Steve," he said casually, "you have any snorkeling gear around?"

"Sure. Kirstie and I have been out to the reef twice."

"I'd like to try that. Go skin-diving on the reef again—like we used to do. You up for it?"

"Sounds great."

"Kirstie, how about you?"

She ran the plates under a stream of hot water. "I'd rather not."

*Good.* Jack had been hoping she would say no.

"Let me get the gear," Steve said. "Have you got a bathing suit?" Jack shook his head. "You can borrow one of mine. I'll be right back."

He disappeared down the hall in the direction of the bedroom. Jack, left alone with Kirstie, felt the familiar itch in his palms.

She leaned over the counter, toweling off the plates, her back to him. He took a step toward her, put insouciant friendliness in his voice.

"Want some help with that?"

"No, thank you."

"I can wash the glasses."

"I'll do it."

"You're sure?"

"Very."

The plate in her hand squeaked. She was rubbing hard.

"You don't like me," he said softly, "do you?"

"Whatever gave you that idea?"

"If you got to know me, you'd feel different."

She turned. Gave him a hard, level stare. "No, I wouldn't."

Blue eyes. So deeply, consummately blue. They stabbed the hot, impulsive part of him like ice picks.

He was conscious of the knife in his pocket, the blade that would snap free at the prick of his thumbnail, the wicked triangular point. . . .

One second. That was all it would take to pin her against the counter, slam the spear blade into her soft throat.

*No. Don't. Keep it together.*

"Are you . . . feeling all right?" she asked slowly, watching his face.

He needed to get away from her. Right now. He took a faltering step toward the doorway.

"Just a little gas." He managed a smile. "Must've been that Tabasco sauce."

He left her. Went through the dining room, out the French doors, onto the patio. Inhaled the calming fragrance of roses.

Anastasia, stirring from sleep, trotted over and licked his hand. He scratched her ears.

"Good girl. That's a good, good girl."

The dog mewed softly, and Jack thought of Ronni Tyler in her death throes, whimpering with her last hissing exhalation of breath.

It would be better with Kirstie. The best so far. Even without the syringe, it would be perfect.

*Soon,* he promised himself. *Very soon.*

He let his mouth relax into a smile.

# 15

Kirstie intercepted Steve on his way out of the bedroom. He had changed into a bathing suit and was toting a bulky carrying case loaded with two sets of snorkel tubes, face masks, and swim fins.

"Don't go with him," she said urgently.

He stopped in the middle of the loggia and set down the case. "What?"

"Out to the reef. Don't go."

"Why not?"

She couldn't say, exactly. There were no words for it. In the kitchen a few minutes earlier, Jack had acted odd again, vaguely menacing—yet when she replayed the incident in her mind, she could find nothing definite to object to.

He had asked if she wanted help with the dishes. Had said he wanted to be liked. A perfectly innocent exchange. Hardly one that should have left her frightened and unsettled.

Yet it had. It had.

"I've got a bad feeling, that's all." Even in her own ears the answer sounded lame.

Steve smiled. "Like a man-eating shark is gonna get me?"

"Not a shark. A snake."

She turned toward the French doors. Through the

sun-streaked glass, Jack was visible in a far corner of the patio, petting the dog.

Steve followed her gaze. His eyes narrowed as he understood.

"Jack . . . ? Oh, come on."

The doors were shut, and Kirstie was sure Jack couldn't hear their conversation, but she pitched her voice low anyway. "He scared me on the beach. He still scares me."

"I've known him for years—"

"No. You *knew* him—years ago. That's different. You haven't seen him since high school."

"He hasn't changed."

"Everybody changes."

"I don't notice any difference."

"Because he's hiding it."

Steve studied the floor. "What are you saying?" he asked slowly. "That he's a psychopath? That he's luring me to the reef so he can drown me?"

Kirstie felt her scalp prickle. "I don't know. Maybe."

"Listen to yourself."

"No—*you* listen to me." She took his hand. "I'm asking you not to go. Whether it makes any sense or not . . . that's what I want."

He lifted his head and stared at her for a long moment, then let his gaze travel through the French doors, to rest on Jack again.

"I already promised," he said softly.

"So break your promise. People do it all the time."

"Not me."

Something snapped inside her. "Jesus Christ, when did you get to be so goddamn righteous?"

"Calm down. He'll hear you."

She almost screamed at him that she didn't care what Jack Dance heard. Then self-possession took hold of her, and she bit back the words. She stood unmoving until she could speak quietly, reasonably.

"You won't even humor me a little?" she said at last.

He wouldn't meet her eyes. "Not when I think you're being irrational."

"Then will you at least do one thing for me?" He waited. "Take the gun."

"The *gun*?"

"Just stick it in your bag. Where you can reach it—if you have to."

Steve shook his head disbelievingly, then crossed the narrow space between them and embraced her.

"Kirstie . . . Jack's an old friend."

"I don't want you to be alone with him."

"It'll be all right."

"You won't take the gun?"

"Forget the gun. Everything will be fine." He brushed a wisp of hair off her forehead and smiled. "I'll be back in an hour. Still in one piece. I guarantee it."

Useless to argue. She yielded.

"Of course you will," she breathed, the words toneless, a memorized lesson. "Don't mind me. I'm paranoid."

Abruptly he pulled her closer, his mouth meeting hers with surprising urgency. His sudden need, the driving intensity of his desire—she found it shocking, disorienting.

Then he drew back, and Kirstie caught her breath. She searched for something to say.

"What . . . what was that all about?"

"Do I need a reason to kiss you?"

"No. No, of course not, but . . ." Watching his eyes, she felt her mouth slide into a faltering smile. "Oh, look at you. You got your glasses all smudged up."

"It doesn't matter—"

"Sure it does. Let me have them."

She fogged the lenses with her breath and carefully polished them with a soft tissue.

"You know you can't see without your glasses," she said weakly. Some species of emotion she couldn't quite identify quavered in her voice and made it ragged. "You're . . . practically helpless."

A violent tremor passed through her hands, and the glasses nearly dropped from her grasp.

"You okay?" Steve asked.

"Just a little worked up, I guess."

He slipped the glasses back on. He had trouble snugging the stems behind his ears.

Kirstie frowned. "Your hands are shaking, too."

"It was that amorous interlude we just shared," he said lightly, then planted a quick social kiss on her cheek, merely an affectionate peck. "Left me kind of unglued."

He picked up the carrying case and headed off before she could say anything more.

# 16

Jack's anxiety had passed, leaving him composed and controlled, by the time Steve stepped onto the patio.

"Ready to go?" Steve asked brightly.

"Sure. As soon as I climb into my suit. Your suit, I mean."

"I left one in the bathroom, on the towel rack."

"Be right with you."

Jack pulled on a pair of red-white-and-blue trunks, concealing the knife, with the blade safely retracted, under the elastic waistband.

It was the same knife he had brought with him to the island on those summer days nearly two decades ago, and now it would slash Steve's throat. The thought made his stomach clench.

He cooled his face with a damp towel again, then emerged from the bathroom and found the Gardners waiting wordlessly in the foyer. The tension between them was obvious. Kirstie must have been trying to warn her husband not to go, but he hadn't listened. Part of Jack—a very small part—almost wished he had.

"Suit fit all right?" Steve asked.

"Perfect."

"All set, then." A clap of hands. "On the attack—Jack!"

Jack's smile covered his wince as he echoed the clap. "Ready to go—Steve-o!"

It was a ritual from their high-school days, pleasantly goofy then, painful now. It brought back memories of better times. Unwanted memories.

He followed Steve and Kirstie out the door, then along the flagstone path to the dock. Together he and Steve climbed down the ladder and boarded the motorboat. Kirstie threw off the mooring line.

"Have a good time," she called, her voice neutral, eyes guarded. She fixed her gaze on Steve and added, "Be careful."

Steve returned the stare complacently. "Always am." He settled into the stern and fumbled with the starter cord, smiling at Jack. "Great day, isn't it? Just like summertime when we were seventeen."

Jack looked at the blue sweep of sky, the turquoise water, the dancing spangles of sun. His answer, low and bitter, was swallowed by a ripping cough of sound as the outboard motor revved to life.

"Yeah, Steve-o. It's a perfect day."

He touched his waistband, felt the shape of the knife.

Throttling back, Steve guided the boat away from the dock, heading east, toward the reef.

Jack looked back once and saw Kirstie still standing at the end of the dock, her hair blown in the wind, her arm cutting the sky in a long, sweeping wave.

# 17

Anastasia was waiting by the front door when Kirstie stepped back inside the house. The dog whined.

"You miss your buddy Jack?" Kirstie snapped. "Well, I don't."

Then she sighed. Kneeling, she stroked Ana's silky coat. "Sorry, girl. Mommy's a little worked up right now. And the thing of it is, she's not even sure why."

Steve was probably right: she was being irrational. She'd taken an instant, visceral dislike to Jack Dance and had allowed it to color all her subsequent impressions.

Most likely he really was nothing worse than a creep. Not the devil incarnate, just your garden-variety . . . snake.

"But how come he had to spoil *our* paradise?" she wondered aloud.

Ana had no answer.

The house seemed disturbingly empty with Steve gone. Empty and quiet. Unwanted phrases slipped through Kirstie's mind: quiet as the dead, lonely as a cemetery, silent as a grave.

She wandered the rooms restlessly, finding no joy in the bars of sun slanting through the arched windows in the living room or the French doors of the loggia. The cheery tinkle of the fountain in the patio seemed irritating, extraneous, an artificial merriment, like a music box's tinny rhapsody or the rippling chatter of wind chimes.

She looked for more dishes to wash, but there were none in the kitchen sink. She poured a glass of water and left the water running, pointlessly, wastefully, until she realized she had left it on just to hear the noise it made. Then with a jerk of her wrist she closed the tap.

Back in the living room she confronted the television set, which had remained off throughout the past two weeks. She had considered it a victory of sorts not to have turned on the set even once, to have lived for half a month without the canned idiocy that was too much a part of modern life.

But now she needed it. The TV was company, and a distraction; she wanted both.

She found the remote control, figured out how to work it. The TV popped on with a buzz and crackle. She flipped through channels, passing game shows and soap operas, before settling on a noontime Miami newscast.

Ana stretched out before the flickering picture tube as if lying by a fire. Kirstie was too fidgety to relax. She circled the room, idly rearranging things—the schooner on the mantel, the potted fern in a corner, the globe near the couch—while the newscasters alternated glibly between happy talk and sober seriousness.

The world, it appeared, had survived her two weeks of neglect. Nothing had changed. The same dreary procession of disasters and senseless tragedies still filled the airwaves.

On the screen, a video graphic reading FIRE; cut to a burned-out housing project on Tenth Street, someone's mother shrieking in Spanish as a small body was wrapped in sheets and carted away.

Back to the news desk. Another graphic: CARJACKING. Cut to the scene of a fatal struggle over an automobile, the victim's remains already gone by the time cameras arrived, the lenses focusing greedily on a smear of blood discoloring the curb.

The news desk again. Graphic: MURDER.

"Nationally," the female anchor said, "the manhunt continues for a serial killer now officially linked to the deaths of seven women in six western and southwestern states—"

This wasn't helping. Wasn't helping at all.

Kirstie clicked the remote, and the TV shut off.

"I guess listening to the news isn't exactly the best way to calm your nerves," she remarked to the room.

Ana cocked her head and panted.

The heat was starting to get to her, or maybe it was tension. Either way she was sweating too much; she felt sticky, grimy. A shower would cool her off.

She went down the loggia, into the bathroom, and found Jack's clothes neatly folded on the rim of the tub. Lifting them in her arms, she carried them into the master bedroom. As she laid them on the bed, something small and green slipped out of the back pocket of the jeans and fluttered to the floor.

She picked it up. A folded bill—no, many bills. Five twenties, four fifties, four hundreds. Seven hundred and twenty dollars in all. A fair amount of cash to be toting around. It struck her as vaguely suspicious.

Oh, come on. Plenty of people carried more money than this, even when they weren't on vacation.

Still, she couldn't help wondering what else Jack had in his pockets. Something incriminating? Proof that her distrust of him was justified? Vindication of her warnings to Steve?

Doubtful. But not entirely impossible.

The only way to find out, of course, was to look and see.

She recoiled from the thought. Search his clothes

like a thief? She wasn't some crooked chambermaid. She was Jack's hostess. He was her guest.

But an uninvited guest. An unwelcome guest.

Even so, Miss Manners definitely would not approve.

Well . . . fuck her.

Harassed by guilt, yet feeling a certain sneaking pleasure despite herself, Kirstie unfolded Jack's blue jeans, then emptied the pockets one at a time.

In the other back pocket, a wallet. She examined its contents. California driver's license. An additional $213 in bills of various denominations. Three major credit cards, all in Jack's name.

Nothing dramatic there. She replaced the wallet and inspected his side pockets. Car and house keys. Antacid tablets in a blister pack. Folded tissues. Loose change.

That was all.

Kirstie released a breath. Disappointment competed with relief. His belongings were thoroughly dull. Not much different from what Steve would carry in his own pockets. No cocaine, no amphetamines, no phony ID or stolen credit cards, no straight razor crusted with blood—

She blinked.

And no knife.

But Jack had carried a knife. She'd seen it. He'd removed it from his pants pocket, stripped a blackberry-bush cane of its thorns, stems, and leaves to make a stick for Ana to fetch.

She checked all the pants pockets again, then searched Jack's shirt.

Nothing.

He must have taken it—taken it with him—on the boat.

She hadn't seen the knife when Jack left. And

Steve's bathing suit, the one Jack borrowed, had no pockets.

He'd hidden it somehow. Hidden it on his person.

And now he was out there with Steve, the two of them alone together.

She heard a sudden rapid clacking noise and realized it was her teeth, chattering idiotically.

"Jesus, why didn't you take the gun? Why were you so stubborn?"

She was addressing her husband, who was not here, who might never be here again.

The room was hot. Of course it was. This was Florida. Everything was hot. But the heat seemed suddenly more intense, stifling, overwhelming—she pressed her hand to her forehead, felt a rush of lightheadedness, a curious weakness in her knees.

*Your head. Lower your head.*

She leaned over the bed, her head down, until the faintness passed and her heart was not racing in her chest. With effort she cleared her mind of panic and forced herself to think, to be calm, to be reasonable.

What exactly was she afraid of? Did she honestly think Jack would . . . *kill* Steve?

Crazy.

Even if he had taken the knife, so what? Skin-divers routinely carried knives, which came in handy for digging up artifacts found on the sea bottom, cutting free of entangling boat lines or seaweed, even killing a moray eel if by chance one should bite down on a groping hand.

There were many possible reasons why Jack had thought it best to take the knife with him. The intention to commit some irrational act of violence was the least likely explanation. Of course it was.

But if all that was so unarguably true, so faultlessly logical, then why couldn't she stop shaking? Why couldn't she control the tremors shuddering like miniature earthquakes through her body?

She knew the answer. Knew it before she even raised the question.

She feared Jack, that was why. She sensed danger in him.

People made jokes about feminine intuition, but Kirstie had always believed in it. Women *were* more intuitive than men, better at reading emotions and gauging a person's inner state. Perhaps biology had equipped members of her sex with some neurological hard wiring that made them more adept at interpreting feelings, relationships, nonverbal communication—the soft, fuzzy parts of life that most men scorned.

There was nothing soft and fuzzy about Jack Dance. Outwardly he was a smiling, affable rogue. But inside . . .

Inside there was something hard and angry and pitiless, something that hungered for power, reveled in pain.

She had never sensed a similar hardness in her husband. And while ordinarily she would be grateful for that, now it made her afraid.

All right, what to do? She could radio for help. Call the police. But by the time she explained the situation, it might be too late. Besides, she had nothing concrete to report. Her fears could easily be dismissed as the products of a hysterical fantasy, as perhaps they were.

But perhaps not. And if not, then Steve was in danger, might already be under attack, might even be dead, and there was nothing she could do, no way to reach him, no way to help—

Wait.

The boat Jack said he'd rented. The dinghy.

He'd beached it at the cove.

The cove was at the other end of the island, but Pelican Key was small, the distance short. She could get there in ten minutes—fifteen at the most.

She'd never operated a boat, any kind of boat, but she'd seen Steve do so when he steered the motorboat to shore. It looked simple enough.

And for her own protection she would do what Steve had refused to do. She would take the gun.

The thought banished the last wisps of fog clouding her brain. She ran around to the other side of the bed, knelt, raised the bed skirt, groped eagerly for the pistol.

It wasn't there.

But it had to be. Steve kept it under the bed, where he could grab it in an emergency, as he'd done last night.

She searched the floor desperately for over a minute before concluding that the gun really was gone.

"Steve changed his mind," she whispered. "He took it, after all. Thank God."

But how could he have done that? When she'd spoken with him in the hall, he'd dismissed the idea. And he hadn't gone back into the bedroom afterward.

Jack had been in here, though. He had changed into his borrowed bathing suit while she and Steve waited in the foyer.

Had he looked beneath the bed for some reason, found the gun, taken it? No, that made no sense. Besides, he couldn't have concealed the Beretta in the swimsuit. Too bulky.

So where *was* the goddamn thing?

Well, maybe Steve hadn't replaced the Beretta in its usual spot after the false alarm last night. Maybe he'd hidden it in a drawer or something. Or packed it this morning for the trip home.

Wherever it was, she would have to go without it.

She couldn't waste precious minutes on an exhaustive search.

Too much time had passed as it was. Nearly a half hour since the boat's departure. Anything could have happened by now.

Anything.

She was running as she headed out the bedroom door.

# 18

Jack swam just under the surface, head down, legs flexing and thrusting in a series of scissor kicks. The oval lens of his face mask framed the reef passing slowly below.

Lavender sea fans undulated in the drift and drag of the current, sensuous as swaying palms. Rainbow parrotfish nibbled at coral towers, consuming the living polyps within. A squadron of inch-long neon gobies darted among the colonnades and galleries of coral, streaking under archways and congregating on terraces, then capriciously reversing course to retrace the route they'd traveled.

The clarity of the water was astonishing. *Clearer than the air in L.A.,* Jack thought half seriously.

Mesmerized by the stream of hallucinatory images gliding past, he had almost forgotten what he'd come here to do.

Almost.

But the intention was still there, still beating inside him, hard and steady, like a second pulse.

He focused his attention on Steve, swimming a few yards ahead, fins pedaling at a steady rate of twenty beats per minute. The proper rhythm for a flutter kick, Jack knew. He had taught Steve to swim and dive in these waters many years ago.

The memory stung him, painful as fire coral, but the

hurt did not penetrate as deeply as it once would have. He was adjusting to the reality of what he had to do, coming to terms with it, suppressing his last twinges of conscience. He wasn't sure whether to be pleased or dismayed at that development.

It didn't matter either way. His feelings were irrelevant. There was a job to do.

He peeled back the waistband of his swimsuit, touched metal. The knife was still in place. Good.

For the past twenty minutes he had awaited an opportunity to use it. But Steve, swimming steadily, had remained always out of reach.

Not for much longer, though. Jack would have his chance soon. He could feel it.

Steve circled a tall coral tower that broke the surface, forming one tooth in a ridge of jagged dentures above the waterline. Jack followed, breathing through his mouthpiece, aware of the slight tightness in his chest and diaphragm exerted by hydrostatic pressure even here, one foot below the surface.

Below, a moon jelly lazily passed over an alien landscape strewn with greenish brain-coral boulders and staghorn coral trees, scaring grunts and sharpnose puffers out of its path. Battlements of coral fortresses flickered madly with the racing shadows of a school of silver pilchards, like a wild rush of warriors storming the walls.

Steve's kicking slowed. He pivoted to face Jack and pointed down. Waited for Jack's nod, then took a breath and dived.

Jack lingered on the surface a moment longer, inhaling and exhaling deeply—four breaths—five—reducing the carbon dioxide in his lungs to extend his time on the bottom.

He needed extra time, extra stamina. Because he

was going to do it now. Four fathoms down, or deeper, he would strike.

One thrust of the knife, and Steve's throat would open up, black blood curling upward like smoke. Even if the wound wasn't fatal, Steve's ensuing panic and disorientation would kill him. He would never make his way to the surface in time.

Jack inhaled once more and held his breath. Body arrowed downward, legs briefly thrust into the air, he pulled himself completely under the water with a power stroke, then let his arms trail at his sides as he kicked hard, driving himself lower.

He passed palaces and labyrinths of coral, spires and canyons, archways like stone rainbows, garishly varicolored. Hydrostatic pressure increased markedly in seconds. His sinuses closed up, and his ears hurt; he swallowed several times to equalize the pressure between his eustachian tubes and the water outside his eardrums.

Steve dropped still lower. Jack struggled to close the gap between them. The damn fins were slowing him down. He was wearing Kirstie's gear, and her flippers were small and flexible, designed for novices; they lacked the speed and maneuverability afforded by the rigid fins Steve wore.

At a depth of thirty feet lay a grove of gently waving gorgonians, a miniature forest of bright yellow branches, threaded with the sleek, nimble forms of half a dozen bluehead wrasses. Steve perched on a coral ledge and examined the sea fans in the strong sunlight that filtered through the crystalline water like a luminescent mist. The blueheads scattered, seeds flung by an anxious hand, melting into shadows.

Jack alighted on the ledge also. Steve glanced at him, pointed to the gorgonians in lazy slow motion, then returned his gaze to the coral colonies, intrigued by their vivid colors, their languid undulating dance.

Steve himself would be dancing soon. A frenetic tarantella of muscle spasms and thrashing limbs.

Jack reached for the knife. Took a step closer . . .

Abruptly Steve turned. Tapped his throat once. Ascended, swimming swiftly toward the glitter of refracted light on the surface.

He needed to take a breath. Damn.

Jack felt a faint burning sensation in his own lungs. He rose also. His ears gurgled as the pressure eased. His sinuses opened again, and the dull pain above and below his eyes faded.

He broke water a few yards from Steve, removed his mouthpiece, and gulped air. The motorboat lay fifty feet away, wheeling slowly, tracing a large circle with the anchor line as its radius.

"Had enough?" Steve asked, treading water. His oversize mask, large enough to accommodate his eyeglasses, looked vaguely comical, an adult's gear worn by a child.

Jack considered his reply. He could try to prolong the dive, hope for a second chance, but he didn't think he'd get it.

The boat, then. He would have to do it on the boat.

"Yeah, I'm pretty beat," he said, putting exhaustion in his voice. "Guess I'm not used to this Jacques Cousteau stuff anymore."

"You're not the only one." Steve's fatigue sounded genuine. He was out of shape; Jack could see that. No definition to the abdominal muscles. Flabby pecs. Bony shoulders.

He'd gone soft. Easy prey.

Jack replaced his mouthpiece, cleared his snorkel tube with a snort, and swam back to the motorboat. Before boarding, he and Steve removed fins, snorkels, and masks and placed them inside the boat. Together they climbed over the gunwale.

Steve sat cross-legged in the stern. "Might as well stow your gear."

Jack, squatting in the bow, handed over his equipment one item at a time. Steve put it in the vinyl case at his feet, then began packing his own gear, head lowered, the sunburnt nape of his neck exposed.

Jack felt his heart speed up. Felt the familiar tension in his body, the song of rushing blood in his ears, the electric tingle in his fingertips.

He could reach Steve in a single step. Lunge forward, plant the deadly blade between his shoulders.

The muscles of his calves and thighs tensed, coiled springs wound tighter, ever tighter. He knew how the lioness feels as she hunkers down on the windswept veldt, scenting antelope at a water hole. Like her, he was a predatory animal, preparing to pounce and claw.

His hand slipped under the waistband of his swimsuit and withdrew the knife. Slowly he extracted the spear blade. It gleamed like a viper's fang.

Steve, preoccupied with stuffing his flippers into the crowded case, still had not looked up.

Jack pursed his lips. A last twitch of irresolution stirred in him, a final tick of conscience. He hardened himself against it.

This was for survival. And survival justified . . . anything.

Do it.

Goddammit, do it *now*.

He sprang upright. The boat rocked. A lurching step carried him forward, the knife in his fist poised to descend in a looping thrust, and then with shocking suddenness Steve recoiled, his hands clearing the bag, left hand empty, the right gripping something small and shiny and blue-black.

A gun.

Jack froze, holding the knife awkwardly at chest height, the blade aimed downward, pointing like an arrow at the hull.

Steve lifted the pistol a little higher. The muzzle was a small black hole, an unwinking eye, staring coolly up at Jack from three feet away. Steve's own eyes, gray and darkly thoughtful, hazy behind the sunstruck lenses of his glasses, did the same.

Jack took a long moment to speak. When he did, his voice was a hoarse rasp, sandpaper on old wood.

"Stevie . . . ?"

Steve's face showed no expression, no life. He might have been a mannequin, save for the jewel of sweat tracking slowly down his temple like a raindrop on a windowpane.

"Sorry, Jack," he said softly, in the flat, pitiless voice of an executioner. "I've been one step ahead of you the whole time."

# 19

Jack heard the words, understood their meaning, but could not make them real.

"Put down the knife," Steve continued in the same unflinching hangman's tone.

Jack had forgotten he was holding it. Fingers splayed, he let it drop to the floorboards. It made a soft, distant thump.

"Now sit."

He retreated a step and seated himself on the sailing thwart. He waited.

"You goddamn asshole," Steve said quietly.

There was pain in his voice now, pain that gave the lie to the emotionless expression he still wore.

Jack tried striking a light note. "Hey, Steve-o. I thought we were friends."

"Is that why you were about to stab me?"

"Stab you? Hell, is that what you thought?" A sharp, forced laugh. "I saw some gulfweed tangled in the anchor line. Figured I'd cut it free." He pointed. "Look for yourself."

"Shut up, Jack."

"I'm serious—"

"Shut up."

Jack fell silent.

The boat bobbed slowly on the turquoise water. Pelican Key was a green smear in the distance. Jack smelled salt and moisture, felt the noon heat on his skin.

Sun and air. How much longer would he know these things? There was little daylight in a cell, and prison air stank of sweat and disinfectant. He could see what shape the rest of his life would take, a dismal, ugly prospect, hardly better than death.

Still, he might have a chance. Steve must have sensed the danger Jack posed, must have brought along the gun for that reason. But he couldn't know the full story: the seven murders, the nationwide manhunt.

It might be possible to talk Steve into forgetting this incident in exchange for Jack's immediate departure. Later the Gardners would hear the news and realize they'd let a multiple murderer escape—but by then he would be long gone.

His spirits rallied slightly. He had limitless confidence in his ability to manipulate and deceive. He'd built his life on it. And with it, he could save his life now. All he had to do—

"They're after you," Steve said, the words cutting like a razor into Jack's thoughts. "Aren't they?"

"Who?"

"The police."

Panic clutched his heart like a fist. "After me? For what?"

"For killing all those women."

All the breath went out of him, and with it, all hope. No possibility of a getaway now, no chance to stay on the run. Steve already knew . . . *everything*.

It took Jack a long moment to speak. When he did, the false levity was gone from his voice. "You told me you hadn't turned on the radio or TV in two weeks. Hadn't seen a newspaper in days."

"I haven't."

That made no sense. Jack shook his head. His eyes asked an unvoiced question.

"There was plenty about it in the news before Kirstie and I came to Pelican Key. You've been making headlines for months."

"Not me. It was all Mister Twister. Never Jack Dance."

"But I knew it was you. At least"—Steve dropped his gaze—"I was pretty sure I did."

"That's impossible. You couldn't."

"They showed pictures of the victims, Jack. Some of them looked almost exactly like Meredith."

Meredith. Finally he understood.

His voice was a whisper. "I see."

"You've been killing her over and over again. Christ, you're so sick."

"I prefer to think of myself as unconventional," Jack said dryly. Distantly he was pleased with himself for finding some faint humor even in this most extreme crisis of his life. "So you deduced everything from a few photos? You should have been a detective."

"There was a little more to it than that. All the murders took place out West; I knew you'd moved to L.A. years ago. The girls were picked up in bars; that sounded like you. You always were a ladies' man."

"And you always were jealous."

"Not anymore."

Bitterness flavored the words. Steve's face was no longer empty of expression; his pinched lips and narrowed eyes conveyed an unmistakable impression of disgust.

"Besides," he went on acidly, "there were limitations to your sexual prowess, weren't there? You never dated blondes. I remember your once saying you had a problem with blond women. That was how you put it: a problem. I've thought about that a lot in the past six months. Looks like you've still got the same problem, Jack. Looks like killing Meredith didn't get it out of your system."

Killing Meredith. Steve was right, of course. But how had he known?

"I thought you believed Meredith's death was a diving accident," Jack said slowly. "I thought that was what everyone believed."

"It's what I *wanted* to believe. Up until a couple of minutes ago, I was still capable of persuading myself that it might have happened that way. If you hadn't tipped your hand, I never could have been sure."

Steve reached down and retrieved the knife. He studied it, the blade turning slowly, a pirouetting dancer.

"I recognize this. You used to bring it with you on our boat trips."

Jack swallowed. "Yeah," he said, his voice unexpectedly thick.

"And now you were going to plant it in my back. Nice." He put the knife on the seat beside him and lifted the gun a little. The blued barrel gleamed like the cresting fin of an albacore. "How about Kirstie? What did you have in mind for her?"

"I don't know."

"I think you do."

A beat of silence. The sun, hanging at its zenith, set the sky aflame. Jack wondered, in an oddly impersonal way, if he was about to die here, in this boat that rocked so gently, gently, a cradle on the water.

"You going to shoot me, Stevie? That the idea?"

"I ought to. I really ought to. My wife fits the pattern, doesn't she? Blond, blue-eyed, fair-skinned. She's another Meredith. That's how you see her, right?"

"I really hadn't thought about it—"

"Drop the pose. She explained how you acted on the beach. I had to tell her it was only her imagination. I still wasn't certain about this—any of this. Now I am."

The gun trembled. Jack could almost feel Steve's trigger finger slowly drawing down.

"You would have killed her," Steve breathed, "if I hadn't come along. Wouldn't you?"

A truthful answer might prove fatal, but instinctively Jack knew there was more certain danger in a lie.

"Yes," he said, and tensed himself for the crack of the pistol's report.

Nothing.

The gun didn't fire, the world didn't go away.

Steve merely nodded and went on nodding, as if in confirmation not only of Jack's words but of every evil he had ever known.

"You would have left her floating in the shallows," he said, voice hushed. "Facedown like Meredith. You bastard." He glanced at the knife. "Was this what you were going to use?"

"Yes."

"Cut her throat?"

"Yes."

"You motherfucker. You piece of shit."

Jack sat motionless, untouched by the insults. Bullets could wound, kill. Words left no mark.

"Is that how you murdered your other victims? With the knife?"

"No. A needle. An injection."

"Meredith, too?"

"That was different. Cruder. I was only a kid then."

"Yeah, sure, you were just the boy next door." Steve frowned, the disgust on his face deepening, becoming open revulsion. "Literally, in fact. You did live next door to the Turners."

"Yeah."

"But you didn't kill Meredith at home. You went to the bathing pavilion. Why?"

"I wanted it to look like an accident. I knew she always stayed late after locking up. She would practice her breaststroke, execute some dives. She took that lifeguard job seriously, I guess. Anyway, I hid in the bathroom till the other bathers were gone, then crept up from behind while she was swimming laps. Slammed her head against the side of the pool. Held her under till she drowned. Easy."

"You sound real remorseful."

"I don't pretend to be. That bitch deserved it."

"Why?"

"There's a reason."

"You always hated her. Never made any secret of it. But you wouldn't say why."

"It's not important."

"It was important enough to kill her for." Jack said nothing. "Did she turn you down? Is that it? Was she immune to the patented Dance charm?"

"No—shit—nothing like that, Stevie." Jack sighed. "Just drop it, okay? It doesn't matter now."

"Maybe it doesn't. But it sure did matter back then. That must have been why the cops got interested in you—because everybody knew how much you'd hated her, how you'd always referred to her as a bitch, a cunt, every ugly word you could think of."

"All of them entirely appropriate."

"You think you're so goddamn smart. So fucking superior. But if you are, how come you never anticipated that you'd become the most obvious suspect? How come you didn't prepare an alibi in advance?"

Irrationally, Jack bristled, his criminal competence

challenged. "I assumed the coroner would say she'd struck her head on the bottom of the pool after a dive. Which is what he did say—eventually." His shoulders moved in a shrug. "I didn't mess up so bad. In the end, things worked out exactly the way I'd planned."

"Oh, sure. Everything worked out great, just great—thanks to your quick thinking. Did you come up with that story of yours on the spur of the moment?"

"More or less. I worked it out on my way over to your place. It sounded plausible. You knew Lisa and I had a little thing going."

"That part was true, I suppose."

"Yeah," Jack said, mildly surprised to taste the bittersweet flavor of nostalgia in the words. "It was true."

Lisa Giovanni had been a married woman of thirty-three, recently separated from her husband. She'd liked sharing her bed with an eighteen-year-old lover, tanned, muscular, virile; and Jack in turn had enjoyed her small, firm breasts and slender legs and silky dark hair, her finely chiseled Italian features, the perfume that wound around her like a flower's fragrance.

Their trysts had been secret, of course. A scandal if the relationship should come out. Only Steve had known.

So it had been easy enough to formulate the lie and sell it.

"The cops are going to want to know where I was the night Meredith drowned," Jack had said, pacing Steve's bedroom on that humid August evening, while Steve listened, first puzzled, then concerned, then afraid. "They're desperate for somebody to pin it on. Here's the thing: I've got an alibi, but I can't use it. 'Cause I was with Lisa. She gave me the world tour, as usual. But if I mention her name, it'll be all over town in two days."

"What can I do about it?"

"Tell the cops we were together that night. Doing something—I don't know—maybe we took a drive. A long drive, say, down to Asbury and back. We've done that before."

"Lying to the police—"

"It's not a real lie. I've *got* an alibi. Just can't use it, that's all. Come on, Stevie, you don't want this thing between Lisa and me to come out, do you? My folks'll fucking *kill* me."

It had taken some time and some talk, but Steve had agreed to go along. No other suspects had emerged, and finally the coroner had been persuaded to close the case. End of story, or so Jack had supposed.

"You already admitted you believed me at the time," Jack said now. The wind kicked up; the boat rode gentle swells. "What changed your mind?"

"A rumor I heard around town a few weeks later. Story was that Mrs. Giovanni had been trying to get back with her husband. They'd spent a weekend together in Cape May—the same weekend Meredith died."

"Oh, Christ. You mean the little guinea bitch was two-timing me?"

"Apparently. Of course, it was only gossip. Might not have been true. Or maybe whoever started the rumor got the details wrong. Even so, I started to think I'd better go to the police. But if I did, it would look really bad for you—and I still didn't believe you could have killed Meredith."

"So you went off to college," Jack said slowly, as faint hope stirred in him, revived by the beginnings of an idea, "and forgot about it."

"Tried to."

"Never said a word—for all these years."

"All these years."

Jack smiled then. Smiled like a jackal on a fly-blown mound.

"We *are* friends," he said with rising confidence. "We really are. Better friends than I knew."

"No."

"You kept my secret."

"Wrong. I kept . . . *my* secret."

Jack understood. And suddenly he knew he could master this situation. He could turn things to his advantage. He could take control.

"Yes, Stevie," he said softly. "That's right. It was *your* secret, as much as mine. You lied to the police in a homicide investigation. You were an accomplice after the fact."

"In a sense."

"Not 'in a sense.' That's the way it was."

"You could say so."

"Anybody would say so."

"I didn't know your story about Lisa Giovanni was a lie—"

"But you knew the alibi you gave the cops was a lie."

"You asked me to do it."

"And you agreed."

Steve closed his eyes, conceding the point. "Yes."

"And later," Jack went on, pressing harder, "after you heard the gossip, you began to suspect the truth. Began to realize what you'd done."

"Maybe so. On . . . on some level."

"On a pretty conscious level, I'd say. At first, anyway. But you didn't want to think about it. So you buried it. Buried it deep."

"Not deep enough."

"No. Of course not. Never deep enough." Jack leaned forward, stronger now, taking charge. "Guilt's like toxic waste. No matter how deep a hole you hide it in, it always leaks out somehow. And pollutes everything around it. Isn't that right, Stevie? Isn't it?"

Steve said nothing this time, nothing at all—and that was good.

# 20

Kirstie ran along the boardwalk, the tattoo of her sandals on the planks thumping in rapid counterpoint to the beat of her pulse.

Her fear had been steadily swelling, battening on itself, as she traversed the island. A sense of desperate urgency possessed her, yet a corner of her mind stood back from her escalating panic, appraising it with cool skepticism, reminding herself that her terror had no logical basis, no solid foundation at all.

The swamp matched her mood. Past the railing of the boardwalk lay clumps of mangroves divided by narrow channels of brackish water. Things flitted among the trees' twisted prop roots and gnarled branches; ribbons of glossy darkness slid soundlessly through the ooze. But no detail was visible, nothing specific, only a teasing impression of movement, as indistinct and ephemeral as the vague forebodings that shadowed her awareness.

She was certain of only one thing. She wished Jack Dance had not come here. She wished he had stayed a hundred miles—a thousand—from Pelican Key.

The boardwalk completed its zigzag course and deposited her on the marly loam near the cove. She emerged onto the mud flats, out of breath and flushed from running.

She scanned the area, looking for Jack's dinghy. It

wasn't there. She saw nothing but mud and seaweed and a few reddish egrets harassing the minnows in tidal pools.

Had Jack lied about beaching the boat here? Had he come ashore someplace else?

Then her drifting gaze fell on a mound of palm fronds a few yards away. Something grayish and rough-textured, like whale skin, was concealed beneath.

The runabout. Thank God.

She approached the boat. At first she assumed the fronds had been blown over it by some freakish breath of wind, but as she got closer, she saw how carefully the leaves had been arranged.

Camouflage. Jack had hidden the dinghy. But why?

Kneeling, she brushed the fronds away. Inside the boat she found a suit jacket and pants, expensive items, badly soiled and wrinkled.

She remembered wondering if Jack had slept on the island last night. Now she was certain of it.

In the bow were three bulging grocery bags stuffed with canned goods and other nonperishable supplies. Near them, a manual can opener and an emptied can of peaches.

"He came here last night," Kirstie whispered. "Brought enough food for a week. Slept till dawn. Woke up, had breakfast, then went for a walk—and found me."

And he had left the boat hidden. Had not wanted it to be seen.

A flurry of splashes and beating wings. In one of the tidal pools, an egret chased down a minnow and snatched it up greedily.

*Hunter and prey.*

The thought shocked her into action.

She sledded the dinghy through the mud and

launched it in the shallows. Climbing aboard, she paddled with her hands till she was out far enough to lower the outboard motor.

She jerked the starter cord. The motor sputtered and died.

A second try. Still nothing.

Oh, hell, was it out of gas? She should have brought a can with her.

She searched Jack's supplies and found no extra fuel. Dammit. Goddammit to hell.

Panic surged again, threatening to overwhelm her. She forced it down, made herself test the motor once more.

*Don't yank the cord this time, just give it a good firm pull. Easy. Easy . . .*

The motor coughed, rattled, nearly faltered . . . then caught.

Relief weakened her. She eased the throttle arm forward, and the dinghy headed out of the cove toward open water—and the reef.

# 21

"Think about it, Stevie," Jack said smoothly, while Steve listened, hating him. "If not for your little lie and subsequent silence, I would have been arrested seventeen years ago, and none of those other women would be dead now."

Steve knew what Jack was doing, of course. Trying to manipulate him by preying on his conscience. Jack was a master at exploiting weaknesses to gain control. Throughout their friendship he had always been the leader, the dominant personality. Even as a teenager Steve had been conscious of the subordinate role he played; and though sometimes it galled him, he'd been willing to go along. He'd taken a kind of comfort in surrendering his independence, allowing himself to be pushed and pulled by a force stronger than himself.

But not this time. He wasn't a kid anymore.

"I don't want to hear it," Steve said brusquely.

Jack merely smiled. "Of course you don't. Truth hurts. Especially this sort of truth. Seven women have died since Meredith. Seven women you helped to kill."

Steve blinked. "Six. There've been six."

"You're behind the curve, pal. Another young lady was found dead in Phoenix two weeks ago, on Saturday morning. Veronica Tyler, but everybody called her Ronni. I didn't, though. Not when I put that needle in her neck. I called her . . . Meredith."

Steve gripped the transom with his free hand. The sudden pounding of his heart was like the onset of an anxiety attack. Fear always came on like this whenever he learned of another victim.

"Jesus," he heard himself breathe. "Oh, Jesus."

Jack watched him coolly. "Guess you were already on the island by then, huh? Voluntarily out of contact with the outside world?"

"We arrived that day. First thing in the morning."

"Just as well. Hearing about poor Ronni might have spoiled your vacation. I figure you came here to get away from it all, anyway."

That was true, but not the whole truth. Yes, he had fastened on the idea of revisiting Pelican Key as a way to escape from the news reports, the mounting body count. But he had also felt an almost mystical yearning for the island. It stood in his mind as a symbol of the most precious part of his life, his years of innocence, the time before Meredith's drowning and Jack's false alibi and the beginning of guilt.

Irrationally he had hoped that by returning to Pelican Key he could erase that guilt, wash himself clean of sin, find renewal and redemption.

He'd been wrong. He had escaped from nothing.

And now Jack Dance was here, facing him across five feet of creaking wood, and there could be no escape, not ever.

A plane hummed past, low over the northeast horizon, wings glinting silver in the sun. Steve followed it with his eyes, wishing he were on it, flying away from this place, from his own past, from himself.

"You've thought a lot about those women I killed, haven't you?" Jack asked. "You've been torturing yourself for six months."

Torture. Yes. That was the right word. And with every new victim, the wheel of the rack had turned a little more.

"What's it done to you, Stevie? How's your sleep been? Your work? Your marriage?"

He didn't want to answer. But something inside him, the timid, obedient part of himself that had always responded to Jack's greater strength, made him speak.

"It's been hell," he whispered, surprised by the croaking rasp of his own voice. "I kept wanting to call the police, but I wasn't certain it was you—wasn't totally certain even about Meredith, let alone the others. And if I told, I'd be incriminating myself. Even if you were innocent of the murders, I'd be guilty of providing a false alibi."

"That's true," Jack said, and again Steve saw through his technique, saw how he reinforced the idea of guilt, guilt, guilt, like a dramatist obsessively emphasizing a favorite theme. A transparent ploy, yet it was working, wasn't it? Despite Steve's best efforts to resist manipulation, it was working.

"So I would wait and hope they'd catch the guy and he would be someone, anyone, other than you. I kept expecting to hear about a break in the case. It was making me crazy. But nothing ever happened except the FBI and the cops would say they were pursuing various leads . . . and every two months or so, another woman would die."

The horizons wheeled slowly, the boat as their axis. Steve imagined himself on a slow-motion carousel, turning, turning. There was something dreamlike and fascinating in the lazy spinning of the world.

"Does Kirstie know any of this?" Jack asked.

"Not a thing. She thinks I'm going through some

sort of midlife crisis. Probably thinks our marriage is coming apart. Shit, maybe it is. I don't know."

"Tough to hold all that inside you for so long," Jack said with a pale imitation of sympathy.

"Yeah. And there was one other thing. Not just the guilt. Fear. Of you."

"Me? Why?"

"I'm the only one who knew your alibi was phony. Suppose you decided I was dangerous to you. That I might make the connection with Mister Twister and go to the authorities. Suppose you decided to launch a preemptive strike."

Yards away, the water blurred into bubbles and ripples as a school of baitfish, jumping madly, fled some unseen pursuer.

"Sounds like you were getting a little paranoid," Jack said. "Coming after you never even entered my mind."

Steve thought that was probably true. Jack could never have seen pitiful, hero-worshiping Stevie as a threat.

Still, he hadn't been sure. And last night, when Anastasia woke him with her growling, he had been almost certain Jack had tracked him down. Searching the house, the Beretta cocked and ready, he had expected to find Jack folded batlike inside every patch of shadow.

"You looked happy enough to see me on the beach," Jack said.

Happy? Steve nearly smiled at that. He had been stunned, staggered, his worst fear realized. Yet at some deeper level he had not been surprised at all. It was as if Jack's arrival had been predestined, as if the two of them were chess figures moved by unseen hands into opposition with each other.

"I tried to act natural," Steve answered, wishing he

could make himself stop talking. "After all, I still didn't know why the hell you were here. Then you asked if Kirstie and I had watched TV or listened to the radio since we came to the island. And I started to think there might be something in the news about you. That break in the case I'd been waiting for." Steve gazed at him over the shiny gun barrel. "They identified you, didn't they?"

"I'm on the run."

"Well, you picked the wrong place to hide out."

"I'm not so certain of that." Jack leaned back against the gunwale, arms folded across his chest. "Think for a minute, Stevie. Just think about what you've gotten yourself into. The feds know who I am. And they're after me. It's a coast-to-coast manhunt. Now, don't you think they're going to look into my background? I'll bet they've got cops or field agents in New Jersey interviewing our high-school friends and neighbors right now. How long will it take before somebody mentions Meredith Turner's death?"

Steve's chest tightened. He began to see where Jack was leading. "Not long," he said softly.

"A day or two at most. Then they'll make the same connection you did: blond hair, blue eyes, looks a lot like the girls I've done on my weekend escapades. So they'll look at the police report, and guess what they'll find. Jack Dance was eliminated from consideration as a suspect—because his best friend, Steven Gardner, provided him with an alibi. Now, given my subsequent behavior, how credible is that alibi going to be?"

"What's your point?" Steve asked, though he already knew it.

"The point is, friend of mine, that pretty soon Uncle Sam will know that you lied to cover for me. Which makes you my partner in crime. An accessory to murder. That's a felony offense, and there's no statute of limitations on it. And in a well-publicized case like this, they'll have no choice but to prosecute. It'll be an easy conviction. They'll put you away."

"You can't threaten me."

"Not a threat. A simple fact. A small army of nice men in dark suits will be hunting you, Steverino, right along with yours truly. They're going to be real interested in talking to you. And you're not going to have a hell of a lot to say."

Steve couldn't argue. What Jack said was true.

Years ago, while home from college on summer break, he had consulted the New Jersey Penal Code in a public library. Continuing doubts about what really happened to Meredith Turner had driven him to consider confessing the fabrication of Jack's alibi. After reading two or three sections of the code, he had changed his mind.

The words of the relevant passages were still imprinted on his memory, as they had been for more than fifteen years: "Every person who, after a felony has been committed, harbors, conceals, or aids a principal in such felony, with the intent that said principal may avoid or escape from arrest, trial, conviction, or punishment, is an accessory to such felony. . . .

"An affirmative falsehood to a public investigator, made with intent to shield the perpetrator of a felony, may constitute aid or concealment. . . .

"An accessory is punishable by a fine not exceeding ten thousand dollars ($10,000), or by imprisonment in the state prison or a county jail not exceeding five years. . . ."

He knew he could not be tried for having failed to come forward with his suspicions regarding the subsequent homicides; the law could not punish him for a sin of omission. But a judge could impose the maximum sentence for his actual crime—and, under the circumstances, almost certainly would.

A five-year sentence could be served in two years, perhaps less with good behavior.

But even two years would be a long, hard stretch of time. Steve knew about that, too. Pete Creston had told stories. . . .

Angrily he brushed aside those thoughts. Dammit, Jack's maneuvers were having their intended effect. He was getting rattled, finding it harder to think straight with fear chewing through him.

He focused his mind, saw a flaw in the line of argument being presented to him, seized on it.

"You're not helping yourself, Jack. If the false alibi is going to come out no matter what, then I'm screwed whether or not I hand you over. So I might as well do it."

Jack was unfazed. "Only if you're a fool. You think by turning me in you can make amends for the past? People won't see you as the guy who nabbed Mister Twister. They'll see you as the guy who kept mum while one girl after the next was getting whacked. They'll scream for your head, Stevie. And they'll get it."

"I'm not saying I can make amends. I'm just saying it's too late for me now. You said so yourself."

"That's not quite what I said. And you'd better hope it's not too late. Because a year or two in prison, Stevie—well, you don't want to know about it."

*I already do,* Steve thought. He said nothing.

"It won't be one of those country-club places, either. I guarantee it. When I said the public will want blood, I was serious. You'll be in a maximum-security institution, and your fellow prisoners will be hardened cons. I know what it's like. Did some time in Lompoc not long ago—fraud charges, not homicide. And even though I'm a pretty big guy, good negotiator, accustomed to dealing with criminal types . . . it was the roughest year of my life."

Steve tried not to listen. But in his thoughts he heard Pete Creston, and that was worse.

"Look at you," Jack went on remorselessly. "Scrawny yuppie type, wears glasses, can't do more than three chin-ups without passing out. They'll eat you alive. Some of those big motherfuckers will want to marry you right off. Guys'll be fighting over which one gets to go in first, if you catch my drift. I knew a con once, had all his teeth knocked out so the shower brigade could use him better for the kind of games they liked. Teeth got in the way, you see. But a guy who's all gums—well, using him is just like putting it between Becky Lou's thighs back home. . . ."

Pete had related anecdotes of the same kind, in countless luncheons, over plates of fettucine Alfredo and broiled salmon, and Steve had listened, thinking all the time of Meredith, of his own clawing guilt.

"That's how it'll be if they like you," Jack said with a smile like a mouthful of razors. "But if you get on their bad side—watch out. Amazing how creative these sons of bitches can be. I saw one poor schmuck get killed with a plastic spoon. Can you imagine that? Fucking plastic, like something you'd get at McDonald's with a frozen-yogurt cup. They jammed the handle through his left eye, into his brain. . . ."

In Pete's story it had been a screwdriver stolen from shop class—or maybe a bolt removed from a cot. Steve couldn't remember the details anymore.

Pete Creston was an attorney like Steve himself, but unlike Steve, his specialty was criminal law. His everyday dealings with ex-cons had supplied him with a fund of nightmare fables about life in the joint. For years he had passed along each tidbit, relishing new variations on old horrors. Steve had never stopped him, despite the anxiety the stories produced, the nightmares they left him with. In some perverse way he had felt that by punishing himself, he was atoning for the lie he'd told.

Now the lunchtime stories ran through his mind in lurid counterpoint to Jack's monologue.

"Two guys in my cell block were diagnosed with AIDS while I was there. They didn't test HIV positive when they checked in. Guess they picked it up somehow. Nobody inquired into it too closely. . . ."

Pete had told him about a prisoner raped anally with a shoe. A *shoe.*

"One asshole used to cry in his pillow all night. He knew they were going to get him, just didn't know when. Waiting for it to happen made him crazy. Finally he tried to kill himself. Chewed open one of his wrists. I mean, literally *chewed* . . ."

A con wrongly branded as a snitch had been ambushed, then beaten so badly his nose was crushed. *Like a snail,* Pete had said, lifting a forkful of ravioli to his lips, *crushed like a snail.* His assailants had gagged him with a torn pair of underpants and watched him suffocate, unable to draw breath through nasal passages blocked by shattered bone.

"They do little things for the fun of it. No malice involved, just restless energy. I remember a guy got hold of a paper clip somehow. He and his pals decided it would be interesting to stick that paper clip up somebody's fingernails. They didn't even hate the guy they picked. He was just available. It was an experiment, you see. They wanted to see how much pain the poor son of a bitch could take. As it turned out, he could take quite a lot—"

"Shut up," Steve said abruptly. "Just shut the fuck up."

"Just trying to be informative, Stevie. Everything I've told you is factual. That's what you've got in store for you. And there's one other thing to consider. Your wife."

"What about her? She's not part of this."

"Oh, but she will be. Imagine how it will be for her, with her husband in prison. Her husband, who'd been profiled in all the news coverage of the Mister Twister case. Her husband the celebrity. What kind of job does she have, anyway?"

"What goddamn difference does it make?"

"Social worker? Parole officer?"

"She's an administrator at a public TV affiliate—"

"Well, in that case I'm sure her business associates will be very understanding of her plight. No doubt they know lots of people whose spouses are doing time as accessories to murder. Then again, maybe not."

"I don't care what her colleagues at the TV station think, for Christ's sake." Steve heard ragged panic in his voice.

"But she may. She may not appreciate the fact that you've made her a pariah among her coworkers—and her neighbors. You said your marriage is already in trouble. How strong will it be after you've been arrested? Convicted? Put away?"

Steve drew a breath. "She'll stand by me."

"So much the worse for her, if she does. For her sake, you should hope she divorces you. It'll look better for her."

"Look better? What's that supposed to mean?"

"Only that there are plenty of people who'll assume she helped you keep your secret all these years. And the longer she sticks with you, the more certain of it they'll be."

"That's ridiculous."

"It *is* pretty hard to believe you could have kept her in the dark about something so important, something that was eating you up inside for so long."

*"She doesn't know anything."*

"I'm not sure the tabloids will see it that way. I mean those supermarket newspapers and syndicated TV shows. They're not known for giving people the benefit of the doubt."

"Nobody pays any attention to that trash."

"You might be surprised. Honestly, Stevie, she'll be better off if she divorces you. It's just about her only hope of salvaging her reputation."

"Maybe . . . maybe that's what she'll do."

"Either way, you've got a lot to look forward to. Your future looks very bright."

Steve shook his head, trying to clear his thoughts. He remembered that error in Jack's logic he'd found, the one Jack had never satisfactorily addressed.

"You might be right," he said slowly. "About all of it. Even . . . even Kirstie. But nothing I do now is going to change it."

"Wrong. There is one way out. For you—and her."

Steve hesitated, almost afraid to ask the obvious question. Jack waited, volunteering nothing, forcing him to make the next move.

"All right," he said at last. "Tell me. What's the way out?"

Jack spread his hands. "Simple. Fly away from all this. And start over—with me."

A long moment passed. Steve felt a bead of sweat course slowly down his cheek to dangle pendulously on his chin.

"What are you talking about?" he asked finally.

"I've got an escape plan. Two men can execute it as easily as one. More easily, in fact."

"Escape with you? Go on the run? You've got to be kidding."

"Being on the run is better than being in the joint. I've done both. I know."

"Sure. So we'll run from state to state till our money is gone, then get nabbed anyway. No, thanks."

"You've got it completely wrong. I told you, I've got a plan. We . . ."

Jack paused, listening.

Steve frowned, hearing the drone of a motor. Drawing nearer. He shaded his eyes from the sun and gazed across the shimmering water.

A gray runabout was speeding directly toward them.

"What the hell is that?" he whispered. "The police?"

Jack shook his head. "It's my boat." His eyes narrowed. "Your wife is piloting it."

Steve's heart kicked. "Why would she be coming out here?"

"Maybe she got worried about you. She doesn't trust me, you know."

"I can't imagine why."

Jack turned to him. "Look, Stevie, if she sees you holding that gun on me, it's all over. She'll radio the Coast Guard as soon as she gets back to the island."

"That's what I was planning to do, anyway."

"Is it? Then why didn't you reject my deal outright? You questioned the practicality of it. You wanted more details. But you didn't say no."

"I'm saying it now."

"Don't be a hero. Give me a chance to explain how we can get away. If you don't buy it, then you can still turn me in—and yourself along with me. Maybe you'll want to do that. But maybe you won't."

Steve hesitated. The boat raced closer. Through a rainbowed mist of spray, Kirstie came into clear view, riding in the stern, her hand on the outboard's throttle stick, blond hair unraveling in the wind.

"Stow the gun," Jack said. "And the knife. Come on, do it."

Steve knew he shouldn't. He had kept too many secrets from his wife. It was time to come clean—with her and with the world.

But the price would be high. Perhaps too high.

If Jack really did have a workable plan . . . if they could escape together . . .

Crazy thought. Of course it was.

Still, there was no harm—was there?—in hearing the rest of what Jack had to say.

And the alternative was the world Pete Creston had described in vivid word pictures that still haunted Steve's bad dreams.

Slowly he placed the Beretta inside the waterproof case, then dropped Jack's knife in with it.

"I'm not agreeing to anything," he said, his voice unexpectedly throaty.

"Of course not, Stevie. Of course not."

As Jack turned away, Steve caught the glint of gleeful malice in his eyes.

# 22

Kirstie killed the outboard and let the dinghy drift in languid slow motion a few yards from the anchored motorboat.

Steve stood and hailed her. "What brings you out here?"

She rose also, planting her sandals wide apart on the wooden floorboards to maintain her balance. "Got a little worried. You two have been gone awhile."

"Not that long." Jack, still seated, trailed a lazy hand in the water. "You're turning paranoid, Mrs. G."

She met his smile with a frozen grin of her own. "Maybe I am."

Relief and anxiety competed for priority in her mind. Steve was unharmed, the gun and knife nowhere in view. Yet she sensed tension between the two men, the false calm of a hushed room ready to explode into violence.

And there was something odd, unsettling, in the way each of them was looking at her—Jack with his vaguely saturnine smirk, Steve with an expression of puzzlement and pain, eyes narrowed in a strangely searching gaze. He seemed to be studying the familiar contours of her face for the answer to some unvoiced question.

"I see you found my inflatable." Jack was still smiling, his eyes dark.

She nodded. "At the cove. Funny thing, though. The boat was all covered with palm fronds."

"Camouflage."

She was surprised to hear him admit it so promptly. "What made you think camouflage was necessary on Pelican Key?"

"You said yourself that the island is private property. I didn't want to get chased off by the owners."

"But you thought Pelican Key was deserted."

"I *assumed* it was. I wasn't sure. Besides, someone could always come along. I was planning to stay a couple of days—as I guess you've figured out."

He inclined his head at the trio of grocery bags in the runabout's bow.

Kirstie didn't know whether his ingenuousness was authentic or merely the studied technique of a skilled liar. She suspected the latter.

"You did bring a lot of stuff with you," she said carefully. "Canned goods, mostly."

"Nonperishable supplies. I had this notion of camping out. For old times' sake."

"But you didn't have a sleeping bag, a camp stove—"

"No, it was a last-minute thing. Sort of half-assed, admittedly. I had no time to get all the items I needed."

The tender bumped up against the motorboat, then ran slowly alongside it, a cat nuzzling a friendly leg. Kirstie smelled wet wood and briny skin dried in the sun. The wind dragged her hair across her face; she brushed it back with the heel of her hand.

Jack's answers weren't entirely satisfactory, but she had failed to catch him in an obvious lie. She decided to drop the subject for now.

"How was the dive?" she asked Steve. "See anything interesting?"

"Nothing too spectacular." His words came slowly, heavy with thought. "We didn't stay out long. Got back on the boat at least twenty minutes ago. And talked."

A change had come over his face, as if, in exploring her features, he had found the solution to the riddle he'd been pondering.

"About high school?" she asked.

He sat down on the transom seat. His right hand dropped to the vinyl case where the snorkeling gear was stowed. He plucked idly at the zipper with thumb and forefinger.

"About all kinds of things. Jack's been telling me some stories. You might find them worth hearing, too."

He unzipped the case a few inches.

"Yes," Jack cut in, a shade too sharply. "I think you would. I was telling your husband about a mutual friend from school. Poor son of a bitch got convicted on a felony charge—accessory to murder."

The words were addressed to Kirstie, but Jack's gaze was fixed on Steve.

Kirstie didn't understand where this was leading. "How awful," she said tentatively. "Is he still in prison?"

Jack kept his eyes on Steve. "Died there."

A gull passed overhead, keening, then flew on, leaving an abrupt and weighty silence. Kirstie became uncomfortably aware of the desolation around them, the bleak stretches of open water broken only by the coral ridge's polished fangs and, in the far distance, the green shimmering mirage of Pelican Key.

"That's too bad," she said. To Steve: "Did you know him well?"

He nodded, eyes hooded. "Better than I wanted to." He fingered the case a moment longer, then zipped it shut once more. "Anyway, it's not a pleasant topic. Sorry I brought it up."

She looked at Jack. "What made you want to talk about something like that?"

"I've got a morbid streak in me. Didn't Stevie tell you?"

"As a matter of fact, he did. You used to entertain him with horror stories about these islands."

"Historical anecdotes, if you please. Though I guess 'horror stories' would be equally accurate. There's no shortage of material to draw on. A lot of people have died in the Keys."

"But none on Pelican Key?"

Jack got up and stretched luxuriously, displaying the ropy sinews of his arms, the bunched muscles of his abdomen. His powerful physique made a clear contrast with Steve's obvious lack of conditioning.

"None," he answered, showing that same ambiguous smile. "At least, not yet."

A tremor passed over Kirstie's shoulders, lifting them in an involuntary shrug. Suddenly she felt the need to get away, though she couldn't quite say why.

"Well," she said lightly, "it looks like my premonition of disaster was a false alarm. Guess I'll be heading back."

Jack stretched again, pectorals flexing. "We'll follow you in."

"Sure you were through diving?"

"Yes," Steve answered. "We're through."

He wasn't looking at her anymore. Wouldn't meet her eyes.

She wondered why that simple fact seemed frightening to her.

Restarting the motor, she angled the dinghy to face Pelican Key. She throttled forward, running at a slow, steady pace.

Sun rays fractured on the shifting surface of the sea, bursting into multicolored fragments like a kaleidoscope's whirling shards. On the eastern horizon, a sportfisher rushed noisily into the deeper blue of the Atlantic, plowing a wide furrow in the water, casting spray like seed.

Kirstie glanced back and saw the motorboat trailing at a distance, Steve at the controls.

Her fears had been groundless, it appeared. Her husband had never been in any danger. He and an old friend had simply been passing the time on a summer afternoon, swimming among the coral towers and talking idly about nothing in particular while they sunbathed on the boat.

An attractive picture. She could almost believe in it.

Almost.

# 23

Jack was feeling pretty good about things.

Seated on the sailing thwart, facing astern, he felt flurries of spray peppering his back as the motorboat plunged landward, each droplet stinging like a fleck of spattered grease.

He didn't mind. The discomfort was minimal compared with the indignities of prison—and prison was a trap he had only narrowly avoided.

For a few tense moments, it had looked as if Steve would draw the gun and confess everything to Kirstie. Luckily his courage had faltered, and now Jack was sure the mark was his.

He'd bitten on the hook. All that was necessary was to reel him in, just as Pavel Zykmund, CSGI's last customer, had been hauled, thrashing and flopping, into the net.

"You almost made a big mistake, Stevie," Jack yelled over the buzz of the Evinrude outboard.

Steve gazed toward the distant runabout and said nothing.

"Fortunately I was here to remind you of the consequences. Did you see your wife's face when I told her about our mutual friend who'd gone to jail? She was shocked, wasn't she? Imagine her looking at you that way."

Steve nudged the throttle arm forward, revving the engine higher. The boat bounced lightly on the water.

"You're better off doing things my way. And she'll be better off, too. You made the right decision."

"I haven't decided anything, Jack." His voice was soft enough to be nearly inaudible. "I said I'd give you a chance to convince me you've got a viable plan. Go ahead."

A setback. The sale was not yet closed. Well, it would be, soon enough.

"No problem." Jack put all his breezy confidence into his tone and body language. "All we need is Captain Pice's boat."

"How are we supposed to get hold of that?"

"It's no more difficult than stealing a car. Which I did last night without breaking a sweat."

"Pice is a big man."

"You've got a gun. Remember?"

Steve smiled, not kindly, and tapped the bundle of gear at his feet. "Don't worry, Jack. I hadn't forgotten. So we hijack the *Black Caesar*. Then what?"

"You said it was a thirty-foot sportfisher, right? A boat like that can take us to the Bahamas in less than a day."

"The Bahamas? Oh, Christ."

"It's the perfect destination. Seven hundred islands, American tourists coming and going all the time. We'll blend right in."

"As soon as somebody recognizes the boat, we're finished."

"We'll rechristen her, paint over the brightwork, make a few other modifications. Has she got a tuna tower?"

"No."

"We can add one. That'll change her appearance dramatically."

"A new tower won't come cheap. And we can't exactly charge it to our credit cards. What do we do for money?"

"I brought ten thousand dollars with me. Twenties, fifties, hundreds. Stashed most of it in those grocery bags on the runabout after I came ashore, except for a few bills I stuck in my pants pocket in case I got separated from the boat somehow. Believe me, we won't run short of cash for a good long while."

"We'll need more than money. In a foreign country we've got to have passports, visas—"

"A guy I know can supply us with whatever documents we require. We'll change our names, alter our appearances, start new lives."

"As beachcombers."

"As anything we want. There's business in the Caribbean, lots of it. Me, I'm planning to stay in the investments game. You're a lawyer; my friend can get you a law degree in your new identity from any university you want. Quality paper, the kind that will check out. Then just type up a résumé and name your price. Rake in the bucks, pay no U.S. taxes, and spend your weekends lying on the beach."

"It'll never work. We'll get caught. And instead of two years in prison, I'll get twenty."

Despite the constant rebuffs, Jack could sense Steve's sales resistance weakening as one objection after another was knocked down.

"We won't get caught," he answered soothingly. "Hey, you think I'm an amateur at this? Yesterday morning the FBI raided my place of business in L.A. Surrounded the building, thought they had me. And I walked right out."

"How'd you manage that?"

"Same way I'm going to manage this. By outthinking them. They're looking everywhere in the whole country for me. They don't know where I am or what I'll do next. They're boobs, pal of mine. I can run rings around them. Already have. And if I can outmaneuver the feds, how hard can it be to do the two-step around the Bahamian police?" Jack chuckled. "It's almost not enough of a challenge."

Puddled water shivered on the floorboards, silver in the sun, like spilled mercury. It was cold against Jack's bare feet. Steve's too, most likely, but Jack didn't think Steve noticed anymore.

"How long have you been planning all this?" Steve asked slowly.

"Years. Which is why I've had ample opportunity to work all the bugs out. It's glitch-free, foolproof." Sell it now. Sell hard. "And you can do it with me—if you've got the nerve. It's your choice. Lie on the beach . . . or rot in a cell."

"I'd rather rot than lie anywhere—with you."

"You don't have to stay with me. Once we've established our new identities, we'll split up. The Bahamas covers a lot of territory. We'll never have to see each other."

"And you'll go on killing."

"Maybe. But you won't have to know about it."

The words touched Steve like a spark. He gave a violent shake of the head. "No way, Jack. I won't be a party to that. No goddamn way."

"People die all the time, pal. It's a hard world."

"No way," Steve said again, and Jack saw that he had come up against an apparently immovable obstacle to the closing of the deal.

Well, he had an ace up his sleeve.

"Okay." Jack moved his shoulders in a lazy shrug. "It's prison, then."

"I can handle it." Steve swallowed, trying hard to be brave. "It's only . . . a couple of years."

"More than that."

"Not necessarily."

"Oh, yes, Stevie. Much more. You're looking at life imprisonment."

"Come off it. I looked it up in the Penal Code, remember? I know the maximum sentence for being an accessory after the fact."

"Sure. But what's the sentence for homicide?"

"I'm not guilty of homicide."

"I say you are."

Jack watched Steve's face as the meaning of his last words registered.

"You can't get away with that," Steve said finally.

"Can't I? I say you were with me the night Meredith died. You helped me sneak into the pavilion. You distracted the bitch while I crept up behind her. And afterward you masturbated into her mouth."

"No one will believe—"

"Everyone will believe it. Why else would you lie about my alibi? Out of friendship? Pretty lame, Steve. The real reason you covered for me was that if I went down, I was taking you with me."

"It'll be your word against mine. You're a fucking multiple murderer, for Christ's sake. I'm . . ." His voice trailed off.

Jack smiled. "Yes, Stevie? What are you, exactly? I'll tell you what you are. You're a frightened yuppie lawyer who's concealed a homicide for seventeen years. And you know what else you are? You're my best friend. We've stayed in touch—secretly—all this time, and after each murder I call you from a pay phone and describe it in detail, and you listen and beat yourself off. That's our pattern, Stevie, our symbiotic relationship. I kill, and you're my audience."

"That's crazy." Strong words, but the panicky darting of his eyes betrayed how he really felt. "You can never prove any of it."

"Prove? Maybe not. But consider this. Why did I come to Pelican Key to hide out at the very time you happened to be here? Coincidence? Hardly. I *knew* you were vacationing on the island, and I came to you for help. I figured you'd have to help me, because we've always been in this thing together."

Steve was looking for a way out, looking hard. "Then . . . then why did I turn you in?"

"Attack of conscience. You couldn't live with your guilt any longer. That much is true, isn't it?"

"Yes. And there's something else that's true, Jack." Steve grabbed at the bundle of gear with a jerky thrust of his hand. "I've still got the gun."

"I'm very much aware of that."

"What's to prevent me from blowing a hole in you right now? Then you can't tell any of these lies."

Jack kept his voice calm. "No. But you'll have to explain why you killed an unarmed man if you had nothing to hide."

"You attacked me. It was self-defense—"

"You're a bad liar, Steve-o. The FBI will break your story in twenty minutes. Then they'll start to wonder what motive you had for shutting me up, and why I came to Pelican Key in the first place. Pretty soon they'll draw the same conclusions I already sketched out for you."

Steve clutched the bag as if grasping a last hope. "Why didn't you say all this in the beginning?"

"I hoped it wouldn't be necessary to threaten you. I wanted us to be friends again. Friends and willing partners. Now I guess I'll have to settle for our being reluctant allies."

"I . . . I should kill you. Dammit, I really should."

"Go ahead. But if you do—you kill yourself."

Steve's hand lingered a moment longer on the zipper of the vinyl bag, then slowly released it.

"All right," he whispered in the voice of a beaten man. "All right, goddamn you. I'll do it your way. I'll go along."

As always upon the consummation of a sale, Jack took a deep, contented breath and found life good.

Ahead, Kirstie steered the dinghy south, piloting it toward the dock. Steve swung to port and followed. The eastern shore of Pelican Key passed by, palm trees and casuarinas and the white beach where Jack remembered encountering Kirstie early this morning.

Hell, he wished he'd killed her then. It would have been so good, having her on the coral sand, in the warm shallows, before the newly risen sun.

Steve seemed to read his thoughts.

"She can't get hurt," he said, not needing to identify whom he meant.

The words were spoken with firmness; that much, at least, was not negotiable.

"Of course not," Jack answered easily.

"I mean it. I'm serious."

"It's not a problem. Don't worry about it."

"If you even touch her—"

"I won't."

"If you do"—Steve tightened his hold on the throttle stick, squeezing it in a rigid death grip that bled his knuckles white—"I'll use that gun. I swear to Christ I will."

"Look, chill out, as we used to say in the Big Orange. I'm not after your wife. Not anymore." Jack managed an insouciant shrug. "Plenty more like her on the islands, anyway."

Steve winced. "No. No more like her." He looked away, toward the turquoise water blurring past, catching and reflecting the light in a shifting scintillant display. "It'll be hard . . . giving her up. Never thought I'd . . . have to do that."

"Sure it'll be hard. But it would be harder still to face her from the wrong side of a visitor's cubicle in a penitentiary for the next forty years."

Steve didn't answer. He appeared to be realizing that his life—his safe, comfortable, respectably ordinary life—had ended today.

"All right." Jack spoke briskly, confidently; he was now in full and unquestioned command of the situation. "Here's the plan. We'll reveal nothing to your wife. Are there any sleeping pills in the house?"

Steve shook free of his thoughts. "Yes. I've had some rough nights since I started worrying about all this. Kirstie doesn't know I take them."

"Good. Very good. Tonight, after dinner, you'll mix a few of those pills into her coffee. Once she's asleep, she can be tied up. We'll lock the dog in the guest bedroom. Then tomorrow we deal with Pice."

"Deal with him how?"

"We won't inflict any permanent injury. Just overpower the man and restrain him. By the time anyone arrives at the island looking for him, we'll be in the Bahamas."

Steve lowered his head. "When Kirstie wakes up . . . when she finds out what I've done . . ."

"She'll cry. She'll scream. But she'll survive, buddy. People do. And so will we."

Some residue of Steve's earlier contempt surfaced briefly in his features. "That's all that matters to you, isn't it? Your own survival?"

"Sure. And the same is true for you. Otherwise, why haven't you shot us both?" He showed Steve a knowing, benevolent smile. "Don't feel bad, Stevie. Nobody's a hero, except in the movies. You should have learned that lesson by now."

Steve said nothing to that. He was staring past Jack, at the runabout now easing up to the dock, at Kirstie as she stopped the motor and reached for the ladder, her movements swift and unconsciously graceful, pleasing to watch.

Jack enjoyed the sight for a moment, as he had enjoyed observing her stroll on the beach. Then he turned back to Steve, some smart and thoughtless remark riding on his lips.

The comment died unspoken. Even Jack, not the most sensitive of men, knew enough to keep silent now.

Behind the sunstruck lenses of his glasses, Steve's eyes ran wet with tears.

# 24

Albert Dance, father of Jack, had died four years ago, at the age of sixty-six. Social Security records listed his last address as a retirement community in Fort Lauderdale.

Briefly, Lovejoy had allowed himself to speculate that Jack had visited his father often. Being familiar with Fort Lauderdale, he'd gone to ground there.

A phone conversation with the director of the retirement home killed that slight hope. Jack, she reported, had never come to see his father. Not once.

"Do you happen to know who administered Mr. Dance's estate?" Lovejoy asked. There was a chance Jack had inherited a house or condo, perhaps in Florida: another possible hideout.

"As I recall, it was his lawyer. We've probably still got his address on file."

Lovejoy's pen scribbled busily, recording a street and number in Pompano Beach, a suburb of Fort Lauderdale.

Dennis Gibson, the attorney in question, answered his own phone on the third ring. Yes, he remembered Al Dance. Yes, he'd probated the estate. Lovejoy arranged to meet with him in a half hour.

"Think this will pan out?" Moore asked from the passenger seat of their borrowed motor-pool sedan, speeding north on Interstate 95.

"In all probability, no." Lovejoy shrugged. "But it would appear to be slightly more productive than chewing our nails."

"Jack could be anywhere by now. Could have boarded another plane and left the country."

"From what we understand, he doesn't have a passport."

"You don't need a passport to enter Mexico or Canada."

"I know."

"Or Bermuda, the Bahamas . . ."

"I know."

"Besides," Moore said, "he might have a phony passport. The rest of his escape was planned well enough. He's got connections. He could have bought whatever paper he might need."

"Well, what the fuck do you want me to do about it?"

Moore puffed up her cheeks and let the air out in a hiss. She was silent.

Lovejoy didn't speak until they were rolling down Thirty-sixth Street in Pompano Beach. Then he said, "Sorry."

"Don't worry about it."

"I'm overtired, that's all."

"We both are."

"And I'm . . ."

"Worried."

"Yes."

"Of course. This isn't exactly going to put you on the fast track, is it?"

He blinked at her. "What?"

"Your career. Drury must have told you—"

"Is that what you think I'm concerned about?"

"Well . . . yeah."

He shook his head. "I haven't had time to even consider it."

"You haven't?"

Her startled tone amused him. "I see. You think that's all I would ever have time for. Peter Lovejoy, the ladder climber, the bureaucrat's bureaucrat."

"No. That's not how I—"

"Sure it is. And ordinarily it would be true, too. On any other case I'd be primarily engaged in my normal cover-your-ass mode of operation. Which has worked quite well for me so far, I might add. Why do you think they made me task force leader? It wasn't just seniority. I know how to play the game."

"But not now?"

"Not now. This is different. This is Mister Twister. This is someone who kills for pleasure. Even animals don't do that." He turned to her. "What worries me is that he's still on the loose. And . . ." He swallowed. "And it's my fault."

"If I'd been supervising the raid," she said with unaccustomed gentleness, "I would have handled it the same way."

"Possibly. But you weren't. I was. The failure was my responsibility. And if he kills again, while he's on the run—that will be my responsibility, too."

"You're being way too hard on yourself."

Lovejoy chuckled, a dry sound, without humor. "Guess it would be a fair statement that I was raised that way. Catholic school. Those nuns . . . Well, based on my experience, I would say that they really drill it into you. The four R's. Religion being the fourth. I thought I was a lapsed Catholic till yesterday, during the raid. Then I found myself praying."

"My knowledge of Catholicism is fairly limited," Moore said. "But doesn't it involve forgiveness?"

"Yes. But also punishment."

"You've punished yourself enough."

"Have I? I doubt that's what the nuns would have said. Not under these circumstances."

"What circumstances?"

"Jack Dance is the devil. And I let him get away."

The door to Dennis Gibson's office was open, his secretary apparently out to lunch.

"Come in, come in," Gibson said, rising from behind a clutter of legal documents on his desk. His face was a study in gradations of monochrome tones: jet black hair, gray steel-rimmed glasses, white beard. "You must be the feds."

Morse smiled. "That's us."

Lovejoy was all business. "We don't want to take up too much of your time, Mr. Gibson."

"I've got plenty of time to talk about Jack Dance."

Lovejoy and Moore seated themselves in response to the lawyer's gesture of invitation.

"I take it you've heard the news," Lovejoy said.

"Yes, I heard. Wasn't as surprised as you might think, either. I knew that guy had a screw loose."

"What makes you say that?"

"Let me start at the beginning."

He told his story quickly and well, with the practiced conciseness of someone trained to summarize complicated material.

A widower of many years, Albert Dance had taken early retirement in 1985, sold his split-level in New Jersey, and moved south to the Gold Coast. For six years Gibson had handled his affairs and investments.

"And in all that time," Gibson said, "his son Jack—his only child, only close living relative—never visited him, never wrote or called. Albert didn't even know Jack's phone number or address after a certain point."

He paused to sip his coffee and, with a touch of

embarrassment at his belated hospitality, offered his guests the same refreshment. They declined.

"Well, anyway, a heart attack killed Al in '91. Completely unexpected; he'd seemed to be in excellent health for his age. He died intestate, unfortunately. I'd pressed him to make out a will, but he never seemed to get around to it. The court appointed me administrator of his estate. Jack, as Al's sole issue, was entitled to everything. I had to track down his address in L.A., then call to inform him that his father was dead. His reply: 'So?' That's it. He was interested in the estate, though. His father didn't matter to him, but money did."

"How large an inheritance are we talking about?" Moore asked.

"Three hundred thousand dollars, most of it in mutual funds and tax-free bonds. Jack instructed me to convert everything to cash, sell the furniture and family heirlooms at auction, and transfer the funds to his bank account. His *checking* account. The assets of a lifetime, and he meant to spend it all. But that wasn't the worst part."

Lovejoy leaned forward. "Then what was?"

"In going through his father's effects, I'd found scrapbooks, photo albums. Pictures of his father in the Army, of his mother as a small girl. His parents' wedding portraits. Vacation snapshots. I told Jack I'd send the items to him. He said not to bother. 'Just throw all that shit out'—those, I believe, were his exact words." Gibson shook his head. "No human feelings whatsoever. A true sociopath. It's not a long step from there to serial murder, is it?"

"No," Lovejoy said quietly. "Not necessarily a very long step at all. So you're saying that all the assets you transferred were liquid? No house, no condo, not even a time-share?"

"Nothing like that. Albert was only renting his apartment in the retirement complex. He owned no real estate."

Lovejoy moved to rise. "Very well, Mr. Gibson. Thank you for your time."

"Those scrapbooks and things," Moore said without getting up. "Did you comply with Jack's instructions?"

Gibson smiled. "Couldn't bring myself to do it. I thought that would make me as bad as Jack."

"What did you do with them?"

"Kept them. Here, with my files."

"May we see them?"

"I don't see why not. Though I can't imagine what you'd find in there to concern you."

"Vacation snapshots. We're interested in places Jack would know about. Places he might go."

Gibson rummaged in a file cabinet and returned with four thick, leather-bound albums. Lovejoy and Moore took two apiece.

Then silence, broken only by the flipping of cellophane sheets and stiff cardboard pages.

"Here's something." Moore angled the scrapbook in her hands to show Lovejoy a collage of postcards. Mangrove islets, blue herons, hooked marlin: the Florida Keys.

"Perhaps you should check the postmarks."

Moore peeled back the page's acetate cover and removed the cards. "Islamorada. All of them. But the dates are different. The years, I mean. 1976, '77, '78 . . ." She looked up. "August. Every time."

"It's August now." Lovejoy felt his fingertips tingle.

Moore was reading the scribbled messages on the cards. "Jack went along on each trip. His father keeps referring to him. 'Jack and Steve and I took the boat out yesterday. . . .' Wonder who this Steve was."

"Personally, I'm more interested in the boat," Lovejoy said.

"Oh, I can tell you about that," Gibson broke in. "Al owned it for years, then finally sold it shortly before his retirement. Had some good times on that boat. I can't recall the name. . . ."

Lovejoy, studying the photo album in his hands, plucked a snapshot from its cellophane pocket and held it up. "By any chance, would this help?"

A man in his late forties—an older, heftier version of Jack Dance—posed on the deck of a flybridge cruiser. On the hull, part of the name was readable: LIGHT FAN.

"Yes," Gibson said. "I remember now. The *Light Fantastic*. But Al never mentioned any trips to the Keys. Guess he didn't want to bring up anything that would remind him of Jack."

"Do you know who bought the boat? Where it's berthed now?"

"No, I didn't handle that transaction. But I can give you the name of a tax attorney Al had retained in New Jersey prior to relocating. He might know."

Gibson went back to his file cabinet. Lovejoy and Moore continued to turn pages.

"Look at this." Lovejoy tossed a snapshot into Moore's lap.

At the end of a pier, near a disdainful pelican roosting on a post, stood a teenage Jack Dance: long-haired, muscular, shirtless, smiling a smile of easy confidence, eyes concealed behind mirrored sunglasses.

"He could be any kid," Moore whispered, then lifted her eyebrows, surprised at herself. "For some reason I wouldn't have expected that."

Standing at Jack's side was another boy of the same age. He wore a New York Giants T-shirt, loose on his gangly frame, and prescription eyeglasses, the thick lenses shrinking his eyes. His hair was cut shorter than Jack's, his smile less natural, suggesting the self-conscious embarrassment of someone nervous around cameras.

"Steve?" Moore wondered.

"Could be. But it's not advisable to jump to conclusions."

Gibson gave Lovejoy a slip of paper filled out in his neat hand. "This is the lawyer Al used. Wallace Hardy of Montclair, New Jersey. May have retired by now. Unfortunately, I have only his business address and phone number, so you may have trouble tracking him down."

Lovejoy smiled. "I'm told that's what they pay us for."

Back in the sedan, rushing south on 95, Moore used the car phone to dial Hardy's number. She got a video-rental store. New Jersey information listed no Wallace Hardy in Montclair.

"The best option, in my judgment, is to let the New Jersey field office handle it," Lovejoy said. "In all likelihood, they'll find him if he's still alive."

"Think Jack bought that boat from his father?"

"Improbable, given the fact that the two of them were obviously estranged. Then again, Albert sold the boat before he ever met Gibson. There's at least a small chance that he and Jack were still on friendly terms at that time."

"If he did get hold of the *Light Fantastic,* and had it berthed in south Florida—"

"It could explain why he came here. But all of this is strictly hypothetical. With luck, New Jersey will be able to give us some facts."

"I'll call them."

"They can reach us at the car-phone number when they have to. I don't plan on going back to the office."

Moore looked at him. "Islamorada?"

Lovejoy nodded, eyes on the road. "Islamorada."

# 25

Funny how it felt to have your world collapse.

Steve lay in bed, fully clothed, stretched supine on the taut bedspread; he hadn't bothered to climb under the covers. With empty eyes he gazed at the ceiling, whitewashed with afternoon sun rays, speckled with the gently waving shadows of palm fronds.

Somewhere, either in the room or just beyond the open window, a solitary insect droned. It sounded like the hum of a distant lawn mower in his Connecticut neighborhood, a Saturday morning sound.

He wished he were in Connecticut. Wished he had never come to Pelican Key.

At dawn he had been a man with a wife, a job, a home, even a dog. And with a guilty secret, too; but he'd carried that guilt so long, he was wearily familiar with it. It was a pain he'd grown accustomed to, a dull ache from an old wound.

Now, only a few hours later, he had lost everything. Everything except the guilt, which was of a new and different order, not familiar anymore.

His life had taken on an unreal quality, a strange remoteness. Since returning from the reef, he'd found himself touching things—doorknobs, countertops—merely to feel the small shock of contact with something solid and firm.

In a dream there was no sensation of touch. So this was not a dream.

A sigh shivered through him. He thought about the gun. About using it. First on Jack. Then on himself.

It would be the best thing.

But he didn't have the courage. And Jack knew it.

*When you lied for him last time,* he told himself as the palm shadows rustled in a breath of breeze, *when you backed up his phony alibi, it wasn't for friendship or loyalty or any other noble bullshit.*

*You did it out of fear. Fear of Jack.*

He didn't even know what he had thought Jack might do. Nothing specific, really. The mere prospect of disobeying and displeasing him had seemed as awful in its implications as angering some cruel, dark, tribal god.

Was that what Jack had been to him? And what, in some irrational way, he still was?

A god?

*My private god*, Steve thought. *My personal deity.*

His eyes squeezed shut. He moaned.

"Steve?"

Blinking alert, he saw Kirstie standing in the doorway.

"Steve, are you all right?"

"Sure." Vaguely he was pleased to hear that his voice sounded normal. "Just resting."

She approached the bed. He didn't want to look at her, didn't want to see how beautiful she was, couldn't help himself. He took mental snapshots of her features, focusing first on one detail, then on another—the line of her jaw, the bridge of her nose, the sunlit shimmer of her hair—storing up memories for his long exile.

"You never take naps," she said, her mouth pinched in a worried way.

"Guess the diving tired me out."

"You weren't asleep."

"I was just nodding off when you came in."

She sat on the bed, took his hand. Her touch was gentle, her fingers very soft. He remembered kissing her hand on the night he proposed.

"Are you cold?" she asked.

"Cold? No."

"Then why are you wearing your jacket?"

Before lying down, he'd changed back into his long pants and shirt, then donned a blue nylon jacket to conceal the Beretta tucked into his waistband.

"Thought I was getting a little sunburned," he said lamely.

"Indoors?"

He feigned a smile. "You can't be too careful. Where's Jack, anyway?"

"Around." She leaned closer, and he could smell her fragrance—not perfume—salt and perspiration and the indefinable scent of her hair, hair that had been his pillow so many times. "I wanted to talk to you about him."

He waited, gazing up at her, marshaling his strength for more lies. The wash of sunlight on the ceiling haloed her in a golden aureole. Silly thoughts of angels flitted like schoolboy fancies through his mind.

"He took his pocketknife with him to the reef," she said.

"How did you know that?"

"I went through his clothes."

His head lifted. "What?"

"It was wrong, I know, but . . . Well, some money fell out of his pants pocket. Seven hundred dollars in cash. I thought that seemed suspicious. It made me curious."

"What's suspicious about carrying cash on a vacation?"

"Nothing, I guess."

"You think he stole it or something?"

"Of course not."

"Jack Dance, the notorious bank robber, on the run from the law." He laughed, but it came out wrong, not laughter at all. Dry coughing sounds.

"All right," Kirstie snapped, "maybe I was being ridiculous, but I searched his damn pockets and the knife was gone. He took it. Why did he do that?"

"He always carries a knife when he dives. Safety precaution."

"Did you know he had it?"

"Sure. I saw him strip some gulfweed off the anchor line."

Jack's own lie had come out of his mouth. Steve felt slightly sickened, as if the two of them had shared a kiss.

"Oh." Kirstie frowned. "Guess I was wrong, then."

"Were you afraid he was going to . . . attack me?"

"I don't know what I was afraid of."

"Jack's harmless. Stop worrying about him. He's a great guy."

Ribbons of images threaded his thoughts: Meredith Turner as she'd looked in her yearbook portrait, newspaper photos of the women Mister Twister had picked up in bars. *Harmless. A great guy.* His stomach knotted.

"I looked for the gun," Kirstie said quietly. "It wasn't under the bed."

"I already packed it."

"Where?"

"One of the suitcases." He deflected further questions by asking one of his own. "What do you want it for? You planning to shoot Jack the next time he does something *suspicious*?" He put a nasty sarcastic lilt in the last word.

"I just want to feel safe," she answered coldly. "And I don't."

"Because of your overactive imagination."

"Because I don't trust your friend—and because I can't seem to communicate with you."

"We're communicating right now."

"No. We're not." She got up and stood looking down on him. "What's going on here? Why are you acting this way?"

"What way?"

"You're not yourself."

"I told you, I'm just tired, that's all."

"Your behavior is . . . off. Strange."

"Christ, all I'm trying to do is lie down for a while."

Kirstie studied him for a long moment. A glimmer of dampness trembled on one eyelash, her only confession of pain.

"I'll leave you alone, then," she said finally. "Sorry to disturb your rest."

She did not slam the door when she left. The cold snick of the latch bolt was worse. It conveyed the quiet finality of a death rattle.

Steve shut his eyes again.

God, he wanted to be out of here. Wanted this to be over.

He pictured himself on the flying bridge of the *Black Caesar*, speeding recklessly toward the Bahamas in a stinging cloud of spray.

Despite Jack's best salesmanship, the escape plan still struck him as a crazy fantasy. Steve had no confidence it would succeed. But the alternative was prison, and he couldn't face that. Death would be better. He would kill himself before he let a cell door clang shut behind him.

So those were his options now, the total range of possibilities open before him, shaping the rest of his life. A fugitive's hounded existence or a bullet in the head.

Rolling on his side, he curled into a fetal pose, shivering all over, his face buried in his arms.

*He's lying.*

Kirstie strode into the living room, circled it twice, and flopped down on the sofa.

*He's lying.* The words beat in her mind with the repetitious insistence of a song lyric. *He's lying. He's lying.*

A gossamer fall of sunlight burned white stripes on a fern's glossy leaves. Outside, a breeze shivered through the hedges and set the garden gate creaking. Anastasia, sprawled before the cold fireplace, favored her mistress with a cool glance and an interrogative whine.

All right, so he was lying. That much was certain.

But what exactly was he lying about? And why?

A vague scenario took shape in her imagination like the outline of a movie plot. Jack had found the gun. Somehow he was using it to intimidate Steve, forcing him to go along with something Steve didn't like.

Great theory.

Except Jack was absent at the moment. Nothing prevented Steve from hustling Kirstie and Anastasia onto the motorboat and fleeing to Upper Matecumbe Key.

No, whatever he was doing was of his own free will.

Besides, there was no longer any particular reason to suspect Jack of criminal behavior. Had he wanted to hurt Steve, he could have done so at the reef. Could have stabbed him with the knife. Could have killed him.

But he hadn't. Which proved he was no threat, regardless of her intuitive forebodings.

Of course it did. Of course.

She got up, paced. Anastasia watched her, fascinated by her restless prowling.

The living room was normally her favorite spot in the house. Today it was a prison. The decorative ironwork on the windows had become the bars of a cell. The thick, moist air was suffocating; it clogged her lungs.

She found herself drawing rapid, shallow breaths and forced herself to stop. Hyperventilating wouldn't help.

Too much nervous energy. That was her problem. Well, there ought to be some way to work it off.

The garden. She'd amused herself several times in the past two weeks, pulling weeds and trimming shrubbery. The work was by no means necessary—the Larson heirs paid a maintenance crew to attend to the upkeep of house and garden twice monthly—but she'd found it relaxing.

Some relaxation was precisely what she needed right now.

In the kitchen she collected scissors, work gloves, and a small plastic bag for cuttings. She carried the stuff into the garden and set to work, humming to herself.

The tune, she realized with a small shock, was "Stranger in Paradise."

It fit. But who was the real stranger? Jack . . . or Steve?

Jack switched off the radio when he heard Kirstie's footsteps in the kitchen. He sat stiffly in the straight-back chair before the worktable, listening to the rattle of drawers, a hummed melody that diminished with distance, and finally the muffled closing of a French door in the dining room.

Then there was no sound but the throb of the generators through the thin wall and the answering beat of his heart.

He had spent the past fifteen minutes in this narrow hideaway that Steve, in his guided tour, had somewhat incongruously referred to as the maid's room, though there was no maid in residence at the Larson house now. The radio room—that was what it should be called, since the two-way radio on the worktable was the sole object of interest in the place.

Part of his time had been occupied with a small but important operation requiring some minimal mechanical skill. Only when that chore was done had he switched on the radio, dialed the volume low, and found a news channel. Ear pressed to the speaker, he'd waited for an update on the manhunt.

According to leaks from anonymous sources "close to the investigation," the FBI had tracked him at least as far as Miami International Airport. Meanwhile, Sheila had achieved the status of a minor celebrity, peddling her story to a tabloid television show for $25,000.

There'd been more, but he hadn't heard it. He'd been afraid to leave the radio on with Kirstie in the next room. His behavior—sitting alone by the radio with the door shut—would only deepen her suspicions and perhaps prompt her to listen to the news herself.

He wondered what she had been doing in the kitchen . . . and what she was up to now.

Rising, he crossed the room and eased open the door. The kitchen was empty.

He remembered the sound of the French door shutting. She'd gone out onto the patio. Perhaps she was sunbathing.

His blue jeans, which he'd donned again after the trip to the reef, swelled slightly with the beginning of an erection.

Voyeurism was not his usual mode of operation. But he wouldn't mind a glimpse of Mrs. Kirsten Gardner stretched in a lounge chair, wearing a swimsuit, skin oiled with suntan lotion.

Cautiously he passed through the kitchen into the dining room and approached the French doors, their square panes dappled with sun. He peered through the glass and felt a brief stab of disappointment.

She wasn't sunbathing. She knelt in the garden, her back to him, pulling dandelions.

No swimsuit, either. Her outfit was the same one she'd worn all day: sandals, shorts, yellow tank top.

Still, even that attire was revealing enough. Save for the tank top's straps, her shoulders were bare, the upper part of her back exposed. Her muscles flexed as she worked. Firm, well-toned muscles.

He watched as she leaned forward, still humming the same melody he'd heard in the kitchen, and uprooted another weed. He thought of kneading her shoulders, her back.

Her lean, sinuous arms reached for a clump of ragwort. The weed was unexpectedly stubborn. She pulled hard, muscles stiffening. Jack thought of Ronni Tyler in her last living moment, her body snapping taut, head thrown back, arms extended like rigid poles. And years earlier, Meredith thrashing in the pool—her muscles had been well-toned also—she'd reached up for the surface, grasping desperately for life. . . .

A shudder moved through him, the shock wave of some internal explosion, and abruptly he knew what he had to do.

His need was suddenly too strong, the blind, raging need that had been building steadily throughout the day. He had no choice but to satisfy it. Will, self-control, his very sense of self melted away in the furnace heat of the fever within him.

Distantly he recalled Steve's warning, but the memory seemed remote and unreal. Steve wouldn't shoot him. Little Stevie? No way. He didn't have the nerve.

The door opened under his hand as soundlessly as a door in a dream. No creak of hinges. No squeal of wood.

He stepped into the humid air, heavy with flower scents. For a moment he stood in the shadowed coolness of a portico, peering out at the garden like a predator lying in ambush in its den.

Then silently he advanced into the heat, the light.

She was only six feet away. Her suntanned shoulders were dusted with soft brown freckles. The down on her nape shivered in a lazy current of air. She went on sweetly humming, the tune hypnotic and gently sad, haunting as a lullaby.

Regrettably he didn't have his knife. It must still be packed with the snorkeling gear, which Steve had concealed somewhere in the house.

Well, his bare hands would do.

Her neck was thin, delicate.

If he grasped hold of her head from behind, gave it a good sharp twist—

He could almost hear the wet crackle of snapping bone.

With luck he would merely paralyze her when he broke her neck. Then he could finish her more slowly while she watched with wide, helpless, staring eyes. Blue eyes. Meredith's eyes.

He took another step.

A hand closed over his arm from behind.

His heart stuttered, missing a beat. He jerked his head sideways.

Steve was there, his gray eyes cold behind his glasses. Slowly, wordlessly, he nodded toward the house.

Making no noise, the two men retreated, leaving Kirstie to continue her work, unaware.

Steve didn't speak until the French door was shut, and he and Jack were in the living room. Then: "You son of a bitch."

Jack was certain the Beretta was concealed under Steve's jacket. And equally sure Steve was very close to using it.

Maybe he *did* have the nerve.

"Hey, Stevie," he said with a faltering smile, "relax. I didn't . . . *do* anything."

"Only because I stopped you. All of a sudden it occurred to me that it wasn't such a good idea to leave you alone with her."

"You can trust me."

"Like shit I can. Now listen to me, asshole"—Steve jabbed him rudely in the chest, the first time in their long friendship he had ever done so—"you keep your goddamn distance from her. Got that? Keep your fucking distance."

"Sure. Sure. No problem."

"Oh, yes, it *is* a problem. A big problem—for you. Remember what I said on the boat. You so much as touch her, and I'll kill you. I mean it, Jack. I really do."

Jack met Steve's wintry gaze and understood that he was serious, he did mean it, he really would kill to protect or avenge his wife. It was the one hard spot within him, the one place where he was not weak and pliable and yielding.

In that moment Jack knew there would be trouble before the night was over.

Because regardless of what he'd promised, he no longer had any intention of allowing Kirstie Gardner to live.

# 26

The car phone chirped at seven P.M. Moore talked to a field agent in New Jersey while Lovejoy drove.

The *Light Fantastic,* New Jersey reported, had been sold to Albert Dance's next-door neighbors, Jim and Jeanne Turner, in 1985. It was still berthed in Belmar.

Moore lowered the phone long enough to say, "Boat's a dead end."

Lovejoy grunted, unsurprised, and hooked left onto a side street on Plantation Key. To the west, the Everglades lay in purple silhouette against the reddening sun. A solitary bird circled the endless expanse of marshland, a blinking check mark in the sky.

"You interviewed the Turners, then?" Moore asked New Jersey.

"Yeah, we went over there. They remember Jack. Watched him grow up. Their daughter used to babysit for him."

"Would she be worth talking to? Maybe they kept in touch."

"She's dead."

"How'd that happen?"

"Accidental drowning when she was twenty-two. Her folks have got a sort of shrine on the mantel: her picture with flowers and candles all around it. Their only child. You never get over that."

Moore had a thought. "What did this girl look like?"

"Blond, pretty, all-American type . . ." New Jersey caught on. "You think so?"

"Unlikely. Still . . . blue eyes?"

"I didn't notice."

"Could her death have been something other than an accident?"

"Don't know that, either. We'd have to ask the Turners for details—or see if we can dig up the police file."

"File would be better. No use getting the family all upset for no reason. If you get hold of it, fax it to us at the sheriff's substation in Islamorada." She gave him the number and terminated the call.

"I gather you think you can tie Jack to an old homicide," Lovejoy said. He executed a U-turn near a closed-down gas station; a huge fiberglass mermaid loomed over the service island, tail looped in multicolored serpentine coils. It was not the tackiest thing Moore had seen in the Keys.

She shrugged. "It's a long shot, I know."

"Not necessarily. The Behavioral Science profile indicated a high degree of probability that Mister Twister had at least some experience in homicide prior to the first known killing. It's a conclusion that I personally concurred with."

"So I recall. But this Turner girl . . . She used to baby-sit for Jack. If he did kill her when she was twenty-two, he must have been only a teenager."

"I believe it's fair to say that there's no shortage of teenage sociopaths—or even subteens, nowadays—capable of murder."

Moore nodded, remembering Oakland's mean streets. "True."

Something made her shiver—perhaps memories of

adolescent gangbangers, their eyes flat and dead as nailheads, or perhaps merely the chill of the air conditioning.

The sedan was cool, but the humid heat outside still pressed against the windshield, straining to seep through. For most of the afternoon Moore had felt curiously like a space traveler sealed in a capsule, gliding through an alien environment inimical to life. Occasional forays out of the car had meant plunging into a steaming sauna, to emerge bathed in sweat.

There had been little time to concern herself with comfort. The second half of the day had been as busy—and perhaps as fruitless—as the first.

She and Lovejoy had arrived in Islamorada at two-thirty and had promptly learned several discouraging facts.

First, an Islamorada postmark indicated only that Al Dance's cards had been mailed somewhere along the fifteen-mile stretch of real estate running from the town of Plantation to the waterway called Channel Two at the southern tip of Lower Matecumbe Key. The Islamorada post office served the entire area.

Second, even if the search was limited to Islamorada, the town's dramatically reduced summer population meant a large supply of vacant housing. Jack could easily break into any empty cottage and hole up inside.

Third, as an unincorporated part of Monroe County, Islamorada had no police department, and the Monroe County Sheriff's Department, headquartered in Key West, maintained only a substation here.

Fourth, the substation's personnel and resources were too limited to permit the exhaustive search Lovejoy and Moore required.

The upshot: For the past four hours, Lovejoy had driven up and down U.S. 1, through Plantation, Windley, and Upper and Lower Matecumbe Keys, veering onto the parallel Old Overseas Highway at times, exploring short side streets that dead-ended at the water and mangroves, while Moore had studied every passing car, looking for either of the two vehicles lifted from airport parking last night.

She'd spotted two white Sunbird hardtops and one silver Dodge Dynasty LE. None had the right license number, but she and Lovejoy had checked out each in turn, anyway; plates could be switched. In every case the car had proved to be legally registered to its driver.

Along the way they had stopped at all the local marinas. None of the security guards had seen anyone matching Jack's mug shot, and there had been no report of any boat stolen in the last sixteen hours. Of course, boat owners didn't necessarily visit their vessels every day; many were snowbirds spending the summer in Maine or Montana, gone for months.

Hotels and motels had yielded no results, either; likewise for a sample of restaurants and tiki-bars. If Jack was here, he was keeping himself well hidden.

The sole positive development since their arrival had been the disappearance of Peter's sniffles and sneezes. The Keys were virtually allergen-free. Moore had not seen her partner use a Kleenex in hours. He was a new man.

Lovejoy pulled back onto Route 1, heading south. The westering sun blazed through the passenger-side window.

"Dark soon." Moore averted her face from the glare. "What will we do then?"

"Unless some unanticipated circumstances arise . . . we'll continue looking."

"You're sure he's here, aren't you?"

"Sure? No. But I regard it as our most promising hypothesis."

Lovejoy squirted fluid onto the windshield. The wipers ticked briefly, erasing a paste of accumulated bugs.

"Just because he visited this area as a teenager . . ." Moore let her words trail off.

"It was more than a single visit," Lovejoy reminded her in a pedantic tone. "As far as we were able to ascertain, this was the only area in Florida to which they returned on a repeated basis. Four years in a row, apparently."

"Small towns, though. All of them. Hardly more than rest stops on the way to Key West. Even given the number of unoccupied cottages available, it would be tough to lose yourself here for long."

"In my estimation, Jack can manage it."

"How?"

"I told you before. He's the devil." Lovejoy grimaced. "He can do whatever the hell he wants."

Moore glanced reflexively at a white hardtop passing them on the left. A Sunbird? No, it was a Chevy Cavalier, the driver a blond woman tanned nut brown like everyone in the Keys.

A billboard advertising an alligator farm in the Everglades blurred past. The gator's toothy smirk struck Moore as arrogant, cocksure.

She thought of Jack Dance. Was he smiling like that? Was he safely ensconced in a bungalow on Plantation Key—or a hotel room in Dallas, or a cabin in British Columbia—following the news on TV and leering at the hopeless, bumbling efforts of his pursuers?

*When we catch him,* she told herself gamely, *we'll rub that grin off his face.*

The phone chirped again. Moore identified herself and heard the graveyard voice of Deputy Associate Director Drury in reply.

"What are you two doing in Islamorada?"

Drury did not shout. He never shouted, never cursed. His chilly self-control was somehow more unnerving than any angry tirade.

To Lovejoy she mouthed: Drury. "Sir, we have reason to believe the suspect may be here—"

"You're supposed to be in Miami, Agent Moore, supervising the field investigation, not chasing down hunches. Anyway, it looks like your hot lead just turned cold."

"What do you mean?"

"It means the Dodge swiped from Miami International turned up an hour ago in Fort Myers."

"Have you confirmed that Jack stole it?"

"We haven't scrambled a search team yet, can't say if there are prints or not. May not matter; your boy always wears gloves, anyway. Important thing is, Fort Myers P.D. informs us that two locals saw him in a convenience store near the spot where the car was dumped. They're concentrating the search in that vicinity."

Moore tersely relayed the news to Lovejoy.

"Give me the phone." He drove with one hand, cradling the handset against his ear with the other. "Mr. Director, this is Agent Lovejoy. What was he buying at the convenience store?"

A beat. Moore could not hear Drury's answer, only a faint, tinny buzz.

"I would have to say, sir, that I don't think it was Jack," Lovejoy replied at last. "The man is concerned about his health. His kitchen was stocked with low-fat foods. He had a gym membership and used it. Kept himself in shape. In a convenience store he might buy tuna fish or canned fruit or nonfat milk, but not potato chips and a quart of ice cream. Those purchases, in my judgment, are out of character. Sir."

Moore listened, astonished. Was this really Peter, her partner, weak and defensive, mealymouthed and officious? And was he actually holding his own with the deputy associate director? Disputing his superior, standing up for himself?

Incredible. She remembered wondering if she'd underestimated him. Now she knew she had.

Drury buzzed again, briefly. Moore had the impression that he might be on the verge of losing his notorious cool.

Lovejoy remained calm enough. "My understanding, sir, is that there were *two* cars stolen from long-term parking in the appropriate time frame. Why are we assuming that the Dodge is the one he took? From what I gather, Latent Prints hasn't even dusted it yet, and of course we both know that an eyewitness identification is always problematic. It's possible Fort Myers is a blind alley. Islamorada, on the other hand, is where he and his father used to vacation every August. . . . Yes, August. It's my belief that he's come back to a place he's familiar with, a place he associates with safety. . . . I understand, sir. . . . I'm willing to take that chance. . . . Yes, sir. . . . Yes, *sir*."

A click as Drury broke the connection. Lovejoy handed the phone back. Despite the air-conditioned chill, his forehead was suddenly measled with sweat.

"What?" Moore prompted when he remained silent for too long.

"He wants us in Fort Myers. Insists it's the investigation's best lead."

"And?"

"I made no commitment."

"No *commitment*?" Moore was torn between newfound admiration for her partner and trepidation at where his recklessness might lead. "Peter, for God's sake, we can't refuse an order."

"He didn't issue an order. Said he'd let us pursue the Islamorada angle if we choose to. But if it doesn't pan out—well, let's just say he's not in the mood to cut us any slack."

"He's out to get you, isn't he?"

"It would appear so." Lovejoy swallowed, his composure faltering slightly. "Look, forget about me. I blew the arrest. Violated the unwritten first rule of the FBI: Never embarrass the Bureau. If I'm lucky, they'll transfer me out of Denver, post me at a resident agency in the Ozarks or someplace equally out of the way. If I'm not lucky, they'll simply put me on unpaid administrative leave. Management's subtle way of suggesting that possibly I should consider another line of work."

"Maybe you're overreacting."

"Uh-uh. I understand bureaucracy, remember? I know how these people think. The higher-ups will hang me out to dry in order to save themselves." He showed her a half smile. "The simple fact is—in my estimation—I'm finished."

"Peter, I'm sorry. . . ."

He brushed off her sympathy. "Given my own penchant for rearguard action of the CYA variety, I can hardly criticize Drury for doing the same thing. But here's my real point, Tamara." He rarely used her first name; the sound of it was mildly startling to her. "As far as I can determine, you're pretty much okay so far. Not being the team leader, you can't be blamed for the screw-up in L.A. In all probability, you can maintain your Denver post and keep your career on track. Unless . . ."

"Unless"—Moore completed his thought—"we stay here in Islamorada and Dance surfaces in Fort Myers."

"Correct."

"Then I'm up shit creek. Without a paddle."

"Without even a canoe. Drury is certain to punish you for your bad judgment. Field duty in Alaska and a black mark next to your name in your personnel folder—something like that." He turned to her, his face blushing in the red glow of sunset. "So I'm not the one who should be deciding this. How do *you* want to play it? I'll leave it as your call."

Moore sat back in her seat, thinking first of her long climb from the Oakland slums to graduation day at Quantico, then of Jack Dance.

"Potato chips," she said finally.

Lovejoy nodded. "Lay's."

"And ice cream."

"Store brand. One quart."

"What flavor?"

"Vanilla."

"You're right. Doesn't sound like Jack. Jack's not a vanilla man."

Lovejoy studied her, caught the beginning of a smile at the corner of her mouth, and answered it with a grin of his own. "Not vanilla. Of course."

"More like rocky road."

"Extremely rocky." His smile faded. "You shouldn't feel obligated to do this. Under the circumstances, you're risking a great deal more than I am."

"We're partners. We share the risks."

"You're certain?"

"Just drive."

Low over the horizon, the sun was a crimson smear, garish in death, its long horizontal rays bloodying the blue-green shallows of Florida Bay.

# 27

Steve found Kirstie in the kitchen, peering into the oven, squinting against a wave of heat.

"Where's Jack?" she asked without looking up.

"Bathroom."

He leaned over her shoulder and breathed in dinner's spicy aroma, a blend of garlic, chicken, and cheese.

It occurred to him that after tonight he would never again taste his wife's cooking, set the table, help her clean up afterward. These mundanities of domestic life seemed suddenly more important than any grand romantic moments.

"Smells good," he said, holding his voice steady. "What is it?"

"Chicken breasts Parmesan."

"Fancy."

"Quite practical, actually." She shut the oven door. "There were a lot of odds and ends I needed to use up." She moved away from him, to the counter, and began serving a tossed salad into three porcelain bowls. Red sunlight, filtering through the bottle-glass windows, glimmered in her hair like a nimbus of fire. "And speaking of odds and ends . . ."

"Yes?"

"When is Jack leaving?"

"Tonight."

"After dinner. Right?"

"Dinner and . . . coffee." He fingered his pants pocket, feeling the shapes of six small capsules, then withdrew his hand with a stab of shame.

"He's not sleeping over," Kirstie said firmly.

"Of course not."

"I don't want him here when we're in bed."

"Why not?" Steve tried to be funny. "Afraid he might join us?"

Kirstie turned to him. "To be honest, I can't say what I'm afraid of. I just don't trust him." She held up a flour-stained palm. "And please don't tell me he's a great guy. I'm tired of hearing it."

Steve hadn't been planning to say it, anyway.

"He'll be gone soon," he replied simply. *We both will,* he added in his thoughts.

Her gaze flicked to the nylon jacket he still wore. "You're not worried about sunburn now, are you? It's nearly dark."

"Guess I just feel more comfortable with it on."

"You sure you're not coming down with something?"

"I'm fine."

"You keep saying that. How come I don't believe you?"

"Because you've got a suspicious nature."

Smiling, he kissed her lightly on the mouth. As their lips met, he wondered if he would ever again be this close to the woman he loved.

Jack left the bathroom quietly, checked to be sure he was unobserved, and crept down the loggia into the master bedroom.

The bundle of scuba gear had to be somewhere. Steve had hidden it after returning from the reef. This afternoon Jack had searched most of the house without success. But he hadn't looked here.

The bedspread was wrinkled, the bed still indented with the imprint of Steve's body; he had lain there for hours, dispirited and fearful. Jack smiled. Conscience was such a weakness. Fortunately, he had never suffered from it. To him, the moral sense he'd glimpsed in others was as utterly alien as the weather patterns of Jupiter, and as remote from his own concerns.

In the middle of the room, he stopped, quartering the area with his gaze. What was the most obvious hiding place? Under the bed? No, not enough clearance for the bulky carrying case.

The closet, then. He looked inside.

Clothes on hangers. Suitcases on the floor. Nothing else.

Wait.

A small pool of water ringed the largest suitcase.

He unclasped the latches and opened the lid.

The bundle of gear had been hastily crammed inside, wrapped in a towel in a futile attempt to prevent water leakage.

Jack removed the bag, rummaged in it, and found his Swiss Army knife.

There were other knives in the house, of course. Steak knives, carving knives. But those were difficult to conceal. And any of them, unlike this weapon, would be unfamiliar in his hand.

He practiced extracting and retracting the spear blade, pleased by the sharp snap it made with each release.

When he slipped the knife into his pocket, he felt complete again, revitalized. His old sense of power and control was back.

Sometime tonight he would find a way to feed this knife of his.

It was hungry now. Hungry for blood.

# 28

Silence around the dinner table.

Kirstie ate slowly, watching Jack Dance and her husband, who watched each other.

Strong violet light, the last glory of the sunset, flooded through the French doors, dimming the bulbs in the wrought-iron chandelier to a mere afterthought. The faces of the two men were murky and strange in the purple glow.

Jack, chewing industriously with his elbow on the table, delivering forkfuls of food to his mouth with conveyor-belt efficiency, was an engine single-mindedly stoking itself. Steve, barely nibbling at his portion, seemed lost in dark thoughts.

On the floor by Jack's feet, Anastasia whined. Absently, Jack offered her a bite of chicken.

"I wish you wouldn't feed her," Kirstie said. Her voice seemed loud and startling in the stillness. "I don't want her begging for table scraps."

Jack shrugged. "She's a good dog." His smile, meant to be ingratiating, was merely insolent. "Deserves a little attention now and then. Don't you, sweetheart?"

He ruffled Ana's fur. The wolfhound made a contented purring sound.

"She gets plenty of attention, but not at the table."

Kirstie looked at Steve, hoping for support. "Anyway, she's already eaten."

"Still seems to have an appetite," Jack said.

"Dogs always have an appetite."

"Well, that's why they should be fed." He gave Anastasia another scrap, then let her lick his fingers. "See how she loves her Uncle Jack?"

Kirstie studied his face, his hazel eyes, and saw no benevolence there, no fondness for the dog, no enjoyment other than malicious satisfaction.

*He's doing this only to get me upset,* she realized. *He doesn't even like Ana. He just . . . hates me.*

Hate. A strong word. Maybe too strong. Yet it seemed to fit.

And why not? She hated him, didn't she? She wasn't even sure why. The feeling was almost instinctual—the automatic response of two natural enemies—the lion and the hyena, the mongoose and the . . .

Snake.

They continued their meal without further conversation. The sun was gone, darkness total, by the time dinner was finished. From the garden droned the shrill buzz of cicadas. Somewhere a vireo sang.

"Delicious, Mrs. G." Jack wiped his mouth with a napkin.

"Delicious," Steve echoed emptily.

She acknowledged their compliments with a muted thank-you, then added perfunctorily, "Anyone for dessert?"

"Just coffee, please," Jack said, and Steve nodded.

She rose. "I'll put these dishes in the sink, then put on a pot of decaf. That okay, Jack?"

"Perfect." He stood also. "Let me help you clear the table."

"How thoughtful."

"The least I can do."

His politeness was grating in its artificiality, her own responses equally false.

*Isn't it funny how we're all pretending everything is normal when we know it's not?*

She gathered up the plates and carried them into the kitchen. Anastasia trailed her, hunting for more food.

"Quit it, Ana. You've had enough."

She filled the sink with soapy water and let the plates soak. Turning, she nearly stumbled over Ana, begging theatrically, her paws lifted, head cocked.

*"Damn."* She caught her breath. "All right, out of the kitchen. Go on. Out."

She shooed Ana into the dining room, then followed, passing Jack as he carried in the glasses.

"You've spoiled my dog," she said with a frozen smile.

"Hey, let her live a little. These go in the sink?"

She nodded. "Please."

Ana circled the table, sniffing the floor. She found Steve and nuzzled his leg.

"Get away, girl," Steve muttered as he collected napkins and place mats.

"He's leaving soon," Kirstie whispered close to his ear. "Or I am."

"Don't worry. Everything will be fine. . . . You, uh, you put on the coffee?"

"Not yet."

"You're having some, too, aren't you?"

"Sure. Why?"

He turned away. "Just wondered."

Jack returned and began to stack the salad bowls. Anastasia licked his pants leg industriously. Jack laughed.

"Hey, sweetheart, I love you, too."

"Ana," Kirstie snapped. "Stop that."

The dog obeyed with a hurt expression.

*At least she still listens to me,* Kirstie thought bitterly. *She hasn't completely forgotten where her loyalties lie.*

Steve came back from the kitchen, his hands empty, and looked for something to do.

"Looks like we're just about done here," Kirstie said. "If you'd like, you can start the coffee."

"I'll do that." He glanced at Jack. "In fact, why don't you two go sit on the patio, and I'll bring out the coffee when it's ready?"

The words were addressed to her, but at the margin of her vision she caught Jack's nearly imperceptible nod.

"Uh . . . fine," she answered.

"Okay." Steve half turned toward the kitchen doorway. "It'll take maybe five minutes—"

Ana, still seeking attention, reared up and planted both forepaws on Steve's side, sweeping her tongue across his face.

"Hey, hey, get *down.*"

He took a clumsy backward step. Ana scrabbled at his waist to hang on. Something shifted under Steve's jacket—Kirstie saw a flash of panic on his face, a jerk of his hand toward his side—too late—the jacket flapped open, and a metallic object, bulky and blue-black, tumbled out.

It hit the floor with a crack and skidded across the inlaid tiles, coming to rest against one leg of the table.

The Beretta.

Kirstie looked blankly, uncomprehendingly, at her husband.

Steve returned her stare, then shifted his focus to Jack.

Their gazes locked.

For a moment—it might have been a second or an hour—no one moved.

A splintering crash.

Shatter of porcelain.

The salad bowls Jack had been holding, now in pieces on the floor.

Jack on his knees, plunging under the table, groping for the gun.

Steve threw Anastasia aside, flung himself prostrate, right arm outstretched.

Jack's hand closed over the blued barrel. Steve seized the handle and wrenched the pistol free.

He scrambled backward and lurched upright, aiming the Beretta at Jack in a shaking hand.

Slowly, Jack got to his feet, panting raggedly, his hair in sweaty disarray.

From the doorway, Ana whined.

Kirstie stood motionless, her glance ticking from one man to the other.

This couldn't be happening. It was some kind of joke. She waited for Steve and Jack to burst out laughing.

But there was no laughter. Steve merely steadied his gun hand and wiped a strand of hair from his forehead. Jack watched the Beretta warily, a vein beating in his temple.

The slow, visible pulsation of that vein finally convinced Kirstie that all this was real.

"What the hell is going on?"

The voice startled her. She needed a heartbeat of time to recognize it as her own.

Jack smiled. A smile cleansed of any phony friendliness now. Pure malice, open and concentrated, frightening to see.

"Tell her, Stevie. Explain to your lovely wife exactly what's transpired here."

"I—I don't know where to start."

"Then I'll start for you," Jack said breezily. "Your husband and I share a secret, Mrs. G. See, I have a nasty habit. And he knows about it. He's known for seventeen years."

Steve interrupted. "I wasn't *sure*."

"You were sure enough. Especially when you began to hear about Mister Twister."

Mister Twister. Kirstie frowned. The name was vaguely familiar. Something she'd read in a news magazine months ago.

"Who . . . ?" She coughed, swallowed, found her voice. "Who's Mister Twister?"

Jack grinned at her. "I am."

"What does that mean?"

"Seven women in the last fourteen months. That's what it means."

"Seven women . . ."

The TV news reader's voice came back to her, the words sharp in her memory like shards of glass: *Nationally the manhunt continues for a serial killer now officially linked to the deaths of seven women in six western and southwestern states. . . .*

Her throat closed up. Breathing was suddenly difficult. She struggled for air.

"It was you," she whispered, staring mesmerized at Jack. "You're the one they're looking for."

He lifted an eyebrow. "You know that much?"

"I heard . . . on the TV . . . this afternoon." She shut her eyes. "I turned it off before they gave the details."

"Well, that was a mistake, Mrs. G. A bad mistake."

She turned to Steve. "Why haven't you told me? And why haven't you turned him in by now?"

Steve dropped his gaze. "Kirstie . . ." The word was a croak, followed by silence.

"I'll explain why," Jack said. "He hasn't turned me

in because we're working together. We're partners, your hubby and I."

She would not hear it, would not believe. "That's impossible."

"I already told you, we share a secret. All along Stevie's known exactly who and what I am. But he could never tell anyone because, you see, he helped me kill my first girl. He was my accomplice."

"It wasn't like that," Steve cut in.

"My accessory, then. After the fact. He covered for me."

"I didn't know what I was doing."

"You knew you were lying. You knew you were obstructing justice. You knew, Stevie. You knew."

Steve said nothing. Small muscles in his cheek and jaw twitched under the skin.

"Is that true?" Kirstie whispered, already knowing the answer.

Steve looked at her. Slowly he nodded.

Kirstie moaned. Her stomach dropped away. The floor listed dangerously under her feet. She grasped the edge of the dining table to keep her balance.

Suddenly the rest of her life was losing its reality, melting into a dream, a meticulously detailed delusion. The house in Danbury, her job, her marriage—all of it was dissolving like smoke before her eyes, leaving only this room and these two men and the gun in her husband's hand.

Her husband. But he wasn't, couldn't be. The man she had loved, had wed, was not the stranger facing her, this man who'd admitted to being an accessory to homicide.

The room began to spin. She thought she might pass out.

*No.*

She couldn't afford the luxury of helplessness, not

now. Now was when she had to be strong, stronger than she'd ever been in her life.

With trembling effort she forced down panic and light-headedness, mastered her emotions.

Later she would feel things about this. Later she would rage and grieve. Later, when it was over and she was safe.

Jack clapped his hands, the sound shocking in the stillness. "Okay," he said briskly, "let's not waste any more time. You have the pills?"

Steve wouldn't look at his wife. "I have them."

"How many?"

"Six."

"What's the usual dose?"

"Two."

"Okay. Six ought to do it."

Kirstie listened, her heart pounding, not rapidly but in a hard, steady beat. The screeching hum of the cicadas outside seemed louder than before, deafening, an external projection of the scream building in her own throat.

She tightened her grip on the table, needing the feel of something firm and solid, something that made sense.

"What pills?" she asked, holding her voice steady, betraying no lapse of control.

Jack answered. "Your husband's had some trouble sleeping lately. Guilty conscience. Too many secrets. Too many lies. So he brought along some sleeping pills. Did you know that?"

"No."

"You ever take a sleeping pill, Mrs Gardner?"

"Once or twice."

"Well, you're taking some tonight. Six. More, if necessary."

"The pills won't hurt you," Steve said hastily. "They'll just . . . knock you out."

Anger rose in her like a rush of heat, momentarily overriding fear and caution. "Oh, good. I'm so glad you don't want to hurt me. I can't imagine your ever doing anything to hurt me."

He flushed. "You'll be fine. Really."

"Fine. Sure. Of course I will. Why wouldn't I be just fine?" A new question struck her. She watched Steve's face. "Where will you be when I wake up?"

"You don't need to know that," Jack said.

She understood. The realization winded her. She had to catch her breath before she could speak.

"You're running away?" she whispered incredulously, her gaze still fixed on Steve. "With *him*?"

He averted his face, reluctant to look into her eyes. "I've got no choice."

"Of course you have a choice."

"They'll put me in jail."

"That would be better than this."

"No." She heard terror in his voice, a child's panicky tears. "I'm sorry, Kirstie. I'm sorry."

With his left hand he dug in his pocket and removed a crumpled plastic bag. Inside were six white capsules.

Kirstie studied the bag, then mentally stepped back, putting all her fears and hatreds on hold while calmly, logically, she assessed the situation from a distance.

Steve had a gun. But he wouldn't use it. Not on her.

Jack must be unarmed. That was why he'd lunged for the Beretta. He wasn't certain of his hold on Steve.

She wished Ana had been trained as an attack dog. One word of command, and the borzoi would be at Jack's throat.

Pointless to think about that. Ana would never hurt anyone, least of all her sugar daddy, Uncle Jack.

Was that why Jack had played fetch with her on the

beach, fed her at the table? Had he wanted to be certain the dog would see him as a friend?

Forget all that. The pills. Think about the pills.

If she offered no resistance, if she let the two men drug her . . . she would die. She was certain of it. Steve didn't want to kill her, but Jack did, and Jack was the stronger personality of the two, the more resourceful, the more ingenious. He would find a way to take her life.

Couldn't take the pills, then. Couldn't allow herself to be sedated.

What was her alternative?

To bluff. To gamble her life on Steve's basic decency.

She needed to get to the radio. To reach it she would have to pass through the kitchen. Steve blocked the doorway.

Boldly she took a step toward him.

"This is ridiculous," she heard herself say.

"Keep back." Steve waved the gun at her.

Ordinarily the Beretta would have scared her—she'd always been nervous in its presence—but here, now, it seemed to hold no menace. It was a toy, a prop, not even aimed at her but at some other woman she was observing from a secure vantage point.

She took another step. "Get out of my way."

A string of words ran through her mind, spoken in a stranger's voice, remote and wise: *She's being very brave.*

Steve licked his lips. "I said, get back."

She didn't listen. Another step, and now she was facing him from an arm's length away. Beads of golden fire, the reflected glow of the chandelier bulbs, glittered on the lenses of his glasses, masking his eyes.

"I don't know what you've gotten yourself involved in," she said, "but you're not a murderer."

He raised the gun, the muzzle pointed at her chest.

"And even if you are," she added, "you won't kill me."

She brushed past him, into the kitchen, and then she was walking swiftly toward the door to the radio room, refusing to look back.

Steve's shout rose after her. "Where are you going?"

"To contact the police."

There. It was said. Let him shoot her now, if he wanted to.

Nothing happened.

She stepped into the radio room, out of the gun's range, and then abruptly she lost the comforting perspective of distance and snapped back inside herself.

Her unreal composure shattered. Violent tremors radiated through her body. Her shoulders popped and jerked.

It took nearly all her remaining strength to turn on the overhead light, to slide the chair away from the table, to sit, to find the radio's power switch and flip it up.

Then the microphone was in her hand, and she was spinning the channel-selector dial, searching for a distress frequency, wishing she could stop her teeth from chattering so badly.

# 29

Steve felt as if someone had reached inside him and scooped out all his guts, leaving him eviscerated, hollow.

He stood in the doorway, staring across the length of the kitchen, and thought of horror movies, the dead roused to a shambling semblance of life. Those meandering zombies, glassy-eyed and stiff-limbed—he was one of them now, a walking corpse.

Jack moved to his side and followed his gaze.

"I can't shoot her," Steve said. "You know that."

"I know."

"So it's over." He wasn't sure whether to be frightened or relieved. He seemed past the point of feeling anything at all.

"No, it isn't."

"She's talking to the police right now."

"Don't count on it."

Steve turned to him. "Why not?"

"Because I think of everything, Stevie." Jack smiled. "Remember that." He went through the doorway. "Come on. Let's collect your wife. She's got a date with Mr. Sandman."

Steve took his arm roughly, animated by a brief spurt of living energy. "But not Mister Twister."

Jack shook himself free. Smiled again. A cold, reptilian smile. "Of course not."

He headed through the kitchen, sauntering with the lazy suppleness of a man in complete, unquestioned control.

Steve let a moment pass, then—reluctantly but inevitably—followed.

The radio was an old Kenwood model with separate transmitter and receiver components. Chester Pice had shown Kirstie how to use it two weeks ago, when she and Steve had arrived on Pelican Key.

In an emergency, Pice had said, all she had to do was dial either the UHF frequency 243.0 or the VHF frequency 121.5, then broadcast a request for help. Easy enough.

Except it wasn't working, dammit. It wasn't *working.*

She sat hunched over the transmitter, frantically twisting the channel-selector dial through a series of full rotations.

No frequency numbers appeared on the LED display. She couldn't tune in any channels. The thing was broken. Worthless.

She spun the dial once more with a savage jerk of her wrist.

Still nothing.

Desperately she fought to restrain her fear, to suppress it as she'd done earlier, but this time she couldn't overpower the crazed, wailing terror rising in her, shaking her as if with palsy, chopping her thoughts into witless fragments, reducing her nearly to screams and tears.

This was too much, too damn *much.* The radio had to work. For it to malfunction now was just no fair.

"No fair," she babbled, "no fair at all."

Dimly she was aware that she was talking—thinking—like a frightened child.

*No, don't. Stop it, stop it right now. Deal with this. And figure it out.*

She focused her thoughts, tried to think the problem through.

Were all the components connected? She couldn't find any loose wires.

How about the antenna feed line? Oh, hell, it looked okay, too.

One of the knobs on the transmitter's face was labeled POWER & WATTAGE. Maybe that was the problem. Not enough power.

She dialed the wattage higher, tried the channel selector again.

No luck.

She was out of options. There was nothing else she knew how to do.

"Come on," she whispered, furious at the radio for failing her when she needed it. "Damn you"—she banged her fist against the side of the transmitter—"*come on*!"

Behind her, soft laughter.

She whirled in her seat, and there was Jack, leaning against the wall just inside the doorway, chuckling mirthlessly. And a yard behind him—who else but his buddy, his ally, Steve, stiff and shell-shocked, his face unreadable.

Slowly Kirstie set down the microphone.

"What did you do to it?" she asked Jack, her voice dulled by a sudden crushing onset of despair.

"A little minor sabotage." His fixed smiled made his face a comic mask. "Simple actually. I lifted off the cover of the transmitter and found the VFO. Variable frequency oscillator, I mean. This one was a Colpitts circuit, wired to the tuning knob. I tore it apart. Just reached in with my fist and ripped out the circuitry. Not the most sophisticated way to attack the problem, but it worked. You can still pick up signals—I didn't mess with the receiver—but as for transmitting, forget it."

"I see."

"Bottom line: you're cut off from the outside world, Mrs. Gardner."

"I see," she said again.

"Where did you learn about radios?" Steve asked.

Jack answered without turning. "In prison. Shop class."

Kirstie wasn't listening anymore. She heard only the dull throb of the twin generators outside, the sound pulsing through the thin exterior wall like an echo of her own heartbeat.

Her gaze slid away from Jack, briefly exploring the room.

No back door. A window in the side wall—could she climb through? Not fast enough. Jack would grab her before she was halfway out.

The doorway to the kitchen was the only usable exit, then.

She took a breath, rose from the chair. "Well, it looks like I'll have to talk to the police in person."

Jack went on smiling. "Now, how do you plan to do that?"

"I'll take the motorboat."

"No chance."

"I'm going."

She moved toward him. He stepped up fast and slammed her backward with a sudden, vicious shove. The floor skidded out from under her, and she collapsed into the chair.

"Hey," Steve snapped. "Watch it."

"I didn't hurt her, Stevie. Now give me the pills." Steve hesitated. "Give them to me."

Kirstie could see Steve didn't want to. And she could see that he would.

Slowly he handed them over.

Jack rested his elbow on the arm of the chair and leaned close to her, the six white capsules in his palm filling her world. "Swallow these."

Lips sealed, she shook her head.

"They won't kill you. Put you to sleep for a while, that's all." He pressed his hand to her mouth. "Go on."

She averted her face. Jack grabbed her by the chin, made her look at him.

"Open your damn mouth."

She looked past Jack and saw Steve watching.

"I said, *open your mouth*."

Desperately she gazed into her husband's eyes, pleading voicelessly for help. She saw anguish in his face, but no resolve.

Jack's fingers crept up under her lips like burrowing beetles and peeled them back from her teeth.

"You're very stubborn, Kirsten Gardner," he breathed. "It's an unattractive trait in a woman."

If he tried to pry her jaws apart, she would bite off his fingers like a snapping turtle.

He seemed to guess her intention. "You won't cooperate?" He let go of her mouth and studied her coldly. "Well, maybe I can persuade you."

The first stinging slap caught her on the left side of her face. A backhanded slap: she felt the crack of his knuckles on her cheek.

*"Don't."* Steve stepped forward, lifting the gun.

Jack didn't even look at him. "Shut up, Stevie. This is business, not pleasure."

Past involuntary tears of pain, Kirstie saw Steve's face, still tormented, still irresolute.

"Will you take the pills?" Jack hissed.

She glared at him, projecting all the wordless defiance she could summon.

His right arm blurred. A second slap, harder than the first, rocked her sideways. She sagged, gasping, and Jack took advantage of her momentary weakness to force one of the capsules into her mouth.

Somewhere in the background, a clatter of footsteps and an angry woof. Anastasia had heard the slaps. She scampered into the room, casting bewildered looks at her master and mistress and her Uncle Jack.

Jack ignored the dog. "Swallow it," he ordered Kirstie. "Come on. *Swallow it*!"

Kirstie rallied her strength and spat the pill in his face.

*"Shit."* Jack raised his hand to strike again. Ana snarled.

"Cut it out, Jack." It was Steve who'd spoken, his voice abruptly firm and calm. "Right now."

Jack hesitated as if gauging Steve's seriousness, then drew back with a slow exhalation of breath. A meaningless smile twitched like a tic at the corner of his mouth.

"Sure. No problem." He pocketed the five remaining pills and circled behind the chair. "She doesn't have to take the damn things anyway." Kirstie watched him unhook the rubber-insulated wire linking receiver and transmitter. "I'll just skip ahead to part two of the procedure. If that's okay with you . . . buddy."

Kirstie looked at her husband. He swallowed.

"I don't know," he whispered. "Maybe we shouldn't. I mean . . . maybe it's not too late to work something out, some other plan. . . ."

"It *is* too late." Jack flicked the wire in his hand. "You're in deep now, Steve-o. You're committed."

The wire traced another arc, a slow-motion whip.

Kirstie stared at it, then at Steve, then at the wire again. Her mind seemed frozen; she couldn't think, couldn't imagine what Jack was about to do.

"If she'd taken the pills without realizing," Steve said, "it might have been different. She would have just gone to sleep. This way . . ."

"This way is harder." Jack nodded, and the wire swished again, slapping his open palm. "So? I've done hard things in my time. Now it's your turn. Unless you can't handle it. Unless you're too weak."

Kirstie spoke up. "Don't let him manipulate you—"

"Shut your damn mouth." The absence of emotion in Jack's voice made the command somehow more dangerous. "How about it, Stevie? You know what's necessary. Either let me go ahead, or start measuring yourself for prison blues. Your call."

Steve stared at Kirstie for a long moment, then slowly closed his eyes.

"Do it," he said thickly.

Jack seized her two arms, twisted them roughly behind her back. Agony screamed in her elbows and shoulders. She let out a small yelp of surprise and pain, and Anastasia barked twice.

"Sorry, Mrs. G." The tender skin of her wrists burned as he wound the wire around them. "But I'm afraid this is for your own good."

Panic clamped down on her. Bound, she would be helpless, more helpless than she'd ever been in her life. She couldn't fight back, couldn't run, couldn't protect herself in any way.

"Let go of me!" It was her own voice, pitched to a keening frenzy. *"Let go!"*

She kicked her legs wildly. The chair creaked, rocking under her. Anastasia's whine escalated to a ululant howl.

"Sit still, goddammit." Jack knotted the wire in place. "You're not helping yourself."

With the microphone cord he lashed her wrists to the chair's wooden back rail. Kirstie tugged desperately, needles of fire shooting through her shoulders, lancing her neck.

Steve still had not opened his eyes. His face was a tight mask.

Anastasia howled louder. She crouched on her haunches in a corner, head lifted, shrilling crazily like a wolf baying the moon.

"Shut her up," Jack snapped.

Steve blinked, unwillingly dragged back into the reality of this moment. He glanced down at the dog and seemed to notice her presence in the room for the first time.

"Ana. Be quiet, girl." The order, empty of force, fell listlessly from his mouth. There was no expression on his face. "Hey, quiet now. Quiet."

The borzoi didn't even hear him. She lifted her head and pitched another wild, piercing lament.

And then Jack was moving toward her, a gleam of silver in his hand.

The knife.

A flick of his thumbnail, and a wicked blade popped up.

He seized Anastasia by the ears, jerked her head back—one stroke of his wrist—the blade sliced her throat in a wide arc, choking off her next cry in a frothy gurgle of blood.

*"No!"* Kirstie was shrieking now, all dignity lost, shrieking not in fear but in blind fury and grief. *"No, no, no, no!"*

Steve stared as if hypnotized, eyes glassy, as Ana's elegant, angular snout whipsawed crazily back and forth, her white coat blushing scarlet, the floor under her feet awash in a sudden lake of blood.

Kirstie writhed helplessly in the chair, straining at the cords and screaming, screaming, screaming.

Jack pointed the red knife at her. "Hush. Or you're next."

Her screams trailed off into sobs and whimpers. She blinked to clear her vision, then looked at the two men who were her captors: Jack, grinning, manic, delirious with the ecstasy of the kill; and her husband, dazed, almost comatose, staring dumbstruck at the bloody harlequin still quivering on the floor.

"Steve"—her words were forced out between shuddering catch-and-gasp sobs—"you can't let him go on doing this. He's crazy. He's *insane*."

Steve's lips moved. He mouthed one word: *Insane*. He showed no other response.

Jack laughed. "No, I'm not." He crossed to the far side of the room. "I'm a realist, that's all. I'll do what's necessary to ensure my own survival."

The dripping blade hacked through the antenna feed line. He jerked the other end out of the radio.

"And your hubby's no different. Little Stevie may lack my dramatic flourish"—he knelt and looped the antenna wire around Kirstie's ankles, lashing them together, then secured her legs to the chair—"but he's equally committed to staying alive. At any cost."

That statement seemed to reach Steve at last. To reach him even though Ana's death had not. Slowly he shook his head in feeble protest.

"Not . . . *any* cost." He coughed, trying to clear his voice of its unnatural rasp, and focused his gaze on Kirstie. "I told him I wouldn't allow you to be harmed. And I won't. I swear."

She refused to permit him to get away with that. "I've been harmed already. In more ways than one."

He flinched as if struck. "I'm . . . sorry."

The words were so small, so obviously inadequate, that no reply was necessary.

Jack checked all the knots again, then nodded. "You're not going anywhere. Have a nice night, Mrs. Gardner. Hope you don't mind the smell of blood."

He walked out of the room, chuckling. Steve lingered a moment, seemed to consider saying something more, then turned and departed in silence.

Kirstie was left alone in the sudden stillness, her only companions a ruined radio and, on the floor a yard from her feet, the motionless body of Anastasia, sprawled in a slowly widening red stain.

# 30

No-see-um's Bar & Grill was perched like a ramshackle vulture on a wharf overlooking Tea Table Key Channel, southwest of Upper Matecumbe Key. Hot rods and pickup trucks cluttered the parking lot, their fenders nuzzling glittery rivulets of beer-bottle shards. A bored dalmatian, leashed to a post outside the bar, scratched itself monotonously as Lovejoy and Moore walked past.

"No-see-um's." Moore studied the buzzing neon sign, gaudily pink against the ink-black sky. "What could that mean?"

"I believe it's the name of a local pest. The no-see-um. Similar to a gnat, only somewhat smaller." Lovejoy swatted something invisible that had darted too near his face. "In all probability, I just killed one."

The bar was dimly lit, smoky, loud with conversation and country music. Two big men with pliers on their belts played pool in a corner of the room. Fishermen, probably, who wore the pliers to pry the fishhooks from their catches.

Lovejoy found himself liking No-see-um's instantly. It lacked the slick, touristy feel of the tiki-bars and hotel restaurants in the area. This was a real place.

The aroma of cooked fish reached him from the kitchen. His stomach gurgled.

He glanced at his partner. "Do you happen to recall the last time we ate?"

"This morning. Breakfast on the plane."

"It might be advisable to grab some dinner here."

They took a table with a view of the water, placed orders with a waitress named Dorothy, and gave her a look at Jack Dance's mug shot. She hadn't seen him.

While waiting for the food, Moore used the pay phone to check in with the sheriff's station, and Lovejoy showed Jack's picture to the bartender and assorted patrons. The two pool players were happy to interrupt their game for a chat with a fellow from the FBI.

"What's this bird done?" the nearest man asked, chalking his cue tip.

"We believe he's guilty of multiple homicide."

"Damn straight," his friend said. "I saw it on the news. Mister Twister. He here?"

"I can't answer that."

A rough elbow nudged him. "Come on, you can tell Bud and me."

"What I mean is, there's simply no way, at present, to ascertain his whereabouts."

"Aw, shoot. You must have some reason to be poking around in these parts."

"Actually, the search is by no means confined to this vicinity. Law enforcement officers are engaged in an extensive manhunt operation throughout the United States."

"Well"—the first man, Bud, lined up a shot—"if we eyeball him, we'll give a holler."

"I would advise you to call the sheriff's department or the state police."

"Will do." A flick of the cue, and Bud banked the six-ball off the cushion, into a corner pocket.

Lovejoy found Moore in the hallway near the

phone, looking at a collection of salvaged junk from local shipwrecks. A gold coin, a musket, a large pitted sphere identified as a cannonball.

"New Jersey faxed us that police report," she said. "Otherwise, nothing new."

"Apparently no one here has seen Jack."

"Any bars or restaurants left that we haven't checked?"

"As far as I can determine, no. And there are no more motels, either." Lovejoy pressed his fingertips against the glass surface of the display case. "Possibly we should have gone to Fort Myers, after all."

"Too late now."

He nodded, studying his reflection in the glass. "Too late."

Shortly after they returned to their table, dinner arrived. Moore had ordered the grilled shrimp, Lovejoy the fried fish basket. The portions were huge.

"I can't eat all this," Moore said, astonished.

"Certainly you can. Consider it a last meal for the condemned."

"What did you get, anyway?"

He hoisted a forkful. "Dolphin."

"You're eating Flipper?"

"Dolphin *fish*."

He sampled it, then nodded. Delicious.

Lovejoy thought he could get to like the Keys. Tasty meals, fiery sunsets, no allergens to trigger sinusitis.

*Perhaps I'll relocate here after I quit the Bureau,* he thought, then tried to decide whether or not he was being funny. He couldn't tell.

He and Moore passed up Dorothy's offer of key lime pie for dessert. Two new patrons had entered the bar separately in the last twenty minutes. To be thorough, Moore showed them Jack's mug shot while Lovejoy paid the tab.

A woman with bleached-blond hair and an armadillo purse squinted at the photo for a long moment, then turned to Moore and quipped, "Looks like my ex." A burst of raspy smoker's laughter followed.

The other new customer was a large, leathery man in his sixties, cutting into a turtle steak at the far end of the bar. He shook his head after a silent perusal of the mug shot. "Afraid not. Who is he?"

"Suspect in a homicide case."

"I might have guessed. Lord, what's this world coming to?"

Moore found him familiar. She searched her memory, then found the visual match she was seeking. Mr. Brundle. Of course. Wonderful old Mr. Brundle, who had managed the grocery store in her Oakland neighborhood for decades, giving away candy bars and comic books to the kids, until one summer night an angel-dusted punk had put three jacketed hollowpoints in his head.

Like Mr. Brundle, this man was big and mellow and tough, with the same salt-and-pepper hair, the same slightly paunchy, lived-in body, the same wise, knowing eyes.

He noticed that she was staring at him. Taking no offense, he extended his hand. "Chester Pice."

"Tamara Moore, FBI."

His brief smile was slightly sad. "When I was your age, a black woman couldn't sit in the front of a bus or eat at a lunch counter south of the Mason-Dixon. Now here you are—Miss Tamara Moore, a special agent of the FBI."

"Sometimes I almost wish I weren't."

"Like tonight?"

"Like tonight."

He traced his finger over the mug shot. "This fellow the reason?"

"Yes."

"Evil-looking man, all right. It's the eyes that give his soul away. Shark's eyes, flat and dead. What's his name?"

"Jack Dance."

Pice took another bite of turtle steak, then frowned. "Jack Dance. Funny."

"What?"

"I could swear I've heard that name somewhere."

"He's been in all the papers."

"I don't read 'em."

"And all over the TV."

"Don't own one. No radio, either, except for my communications gear."

"Then . . . how?"

"I can't say." He pondered the problem, then shrugged. "Conversation, maybe. Someone might've mentioned this news story to me. Sure. That must have been it."

"But you're not certain?"

"I'd like to be. But no." He glanced at the photo again. "Anyhow, I'm positive I've never met him."

"Well, if you think of anything that might help us, anything at all . . ."

"I'll get the sheriff's people on the horn. You bet I will, ma'am." Pice wagged his fork at her in a gentle warning. "In the meanwhile, you be careful hunting this fellow. He's a bad one."

Moore nodded. "That he is."

The night was still hot, the lonely dalmatian still tied to the post, when she and Lovejoy emerged from No-see-um's. They leaned against a salt-silvered railing and watched a motorboat cruise through the channel, leaving a wake of white foam.

"Jack's not here," Lovejoy whispered. "He never was."

Moore was inclined to agree. "So what do we do now?"

"We keep looking."

"I knew you were going to say that."

"Do you have any superior alternatives to propose?"

"None at all."

The water slopped lazily against the pilings, a strangely soothing sound. Moore looked out to sea. Near the eastern horizon sparkled a solitary light, motionless and faint.

"Boat?" she asked, pointing.

"House, I imagine. On some small island."

"Wish I were there."

"Me, too." Lovejoy shut his eyes and savored the fantasy. "Alone with the parrots and the palm trees, cut off from everything."

"Sounds like paradise."

"My estimation also. Personally, I must admit I envy them—whoever's on that island. They don't have to deal with any of this." He sighed. "They don't have a worry in the world."

# 31

Jack shifted uncomfortably on the sofa and looked across the living room at the high-backed chair where Steve sat rigid, the Beretta held stiffly in his hand.

The blued barrel gleamed in the lamplight. The room blazed, every bulb burning. Steve had insisted on that. He wished, apparently, to banish all shadows. He had not yet learned that some kinds of darkness could not be dispelled.

"You planning to stay up all night?" Jack asked, then instantly regretted it. The question was too obvious.

Steve smiled briefly. "Yes, Jack. I am."

"We'll need to be fresh in the morning."

"You sleep, then."

"I'm not tired."

"Neither am I."

"We've got to trust each other, Stevie."

A soft, derisive snort. "Oh, sure. You're a real trustworthy individual."

Another interval of silence between them. Outside, a boat purred past, one of many that had slipped through the night during the last three hours, reminders that Pelican Key was less isolated than it seemed.

When the boat was gone, there was nothing to hear but the crickets' monotonous chirping and, from the woods, rare spurts of birdsong. Though Jack was no naturalist, he had spent enough summer days on the island to recognize the peppery trills of a yellow-breasted chat and, farther off, the long, rising glissando of a parula.

He had always liked bird calls. It had taken him years to understand that the shrill, warbling cries reminded him of screams.

Reaching over to the end table, he took a last sip of his Coke, which had long ago gone flat. It was the third can he had drained.

The day's heat had not let up, and the humidity seemed to have actually increased with the approach of midnight. A warm paste of sweat bonded his shirt to his chest and back. Now and then a stray droplet rolled out of his hair and trickled down his neck like a tickling finger.

Through the patio doorway, a hot, sticky breeze carried the scent of night-blooming jasmine into the room, a breath of perfume, exotic and enticing. Jack thought of the woman he had killed in San Diego; she had worn a fragrance like that.

A good kill, San Diego, but not as good as what was waiting for him in the radio room, if only he could find some opportunity to make his move.

So far there had been no opportunities. Hell, he didn't even have his Swiss Army knife anymore. Steve had compelled him to stow it in a kitchen drawer. The blade had still been wet with Anastasia's blood.

Killing the dog had been a mistake, he decided. Or maybe his real error had been to get carried away when he'd slapped Kirstie around.

For one reason or another, Steve looked at him differently now. And he never stopped looking, never showed the slightest inclination to drop his guard. That cold gray gaze remained fixed on him, as did the muzzle of the gun.

*Should have been a hypnotist,* Jack thought moodily. *Then I could have put the bastard in a trance, lulled him to sleep. A smooth patter, soothing words—that's all it takes if you know the technique. Like those New Age relaxation tapes Sheila uses. Better than sleeping pills, she always says. . . .*

Sleeping pills.

Jesus, how could he have forgotten about that?

Steve had given him six pills. He'd fed one to Kirstie, who had spat it out.

The others . . .

Lightly, inconspicuously, he touched his pants pocket.

The others had gone in there.

Five capsules. More than twice the maximum dose. Easily enough to put Steve under.

Jack sat silently for a few minutes longer, working out the details of his plan.

Then he rose and stretched. "Captain, the first mate requests permission to use the head."

Steve got up. "I'm coming with you."

"Oh, fuck, Stevie. Not when I'm taking a crap." He showed a sheepish smile. "I don't even know if I can do it with somebody watching."

Steve hesitated, then yielded. "You can go in alone. But I'll be right outside."

"Great. My bodyguard."

They didn't speak again until they arrived at the bathroom. Jack reached for the door.

"Wait." Steve switched on the lights and went in first. Briskly he checked the drawers, the medicine cabinet, the storage area under the sink. "Okay."

"You afraid I stashed an Uzi behind the commode or something?"

"Just being careful."

"Paranoid, you mean."

"Around you, a little paranoia may be justified."

Alone, with the door shut, Jack felt safe and secretive. The bathroom was a private place, a refuge, where he could work his mischief unobserved.

Quickly he checked the medicine cabinet, hoping to find the rest of the sleeping pills. There were none. No surprise. Steve had said his insomnia was a secret; he'd kept the pills hidden from his wife. Well, five would be sufficient.

Jack took apart the capsules, pouring their contents into an unfolded Kleenex. A small heap of white powder formed. The tissue, neatly folded, went into his pocket, along with the empty gelatin casings. He would need those.

He removed the paper shade from a light fixture over the sink, then wrapped the bulb in bathroom tissue, being careful to wind the wrapping loosely so it would not ignite too soon.

Next he replaced the shade. In a carrying case on the counter he found an assortment of Kirstie's toiletries. He dug out a jar of nail-polish remover, then brushed the liquid liberally over the wall near the lamp, painting a diagonal trail that snaked down to a wastebasket. More toilet paper went in the basket, to be doused with the remaining alcohol in the jar.

A flush of the toilet for realism, and he stepped out into the hall. "Nothing like a successful dump to make Jack Dance a new man."

"You'll never be a new man, Jack. You're stuck with yourself."

"Wouldn't have it any other way."

They left together. Steve, still wary of shadows, did not turn off the bathroom lights.

In the living room, Jack shook his empty Coke can. "I'm up for another. How about you?"

"All right."

Steve watched as Jack retrieved two more cans from the fridge and popped the tabs. They resumed sitting, Jack on the sofa, Steve in the armchair, a precise re-creation of the original tableau. The only variation in detail was Steve's nylon jacket, which he had finally shed and draped over the back of the chair. His short-sleeve shirt was as limp and sweat-soaked as Jack's own.

A fly buzzed erratically around the room, alighting on the mantel, the globe, the arched window framing the garden. Its wings glittered.

Jack wondered how things were progressing in the bathroom. The toilet paper wrapped around the hot bulb must be smoldering nicely by now. How long would it take to flare up? How quickly would the flames spread, first to the lamp's paper shade, then to the trail of flammable liquid on the wall?

Not much longer, he figured. Another minute at most.

"Something occurred to me while you were in the bathroom." Steven sipped his soda. "Your boat. The little inflatable."

"What about it?"

"When Kirstie came in from the reef, she left it at the dock, alongside the motorboat. Pice will see it when he shows up tomorrow. He'll know there's someone on the island besides Kirstie and me. We'll lose the element of surprise."

"Hell." Jack hadn't thought of that. He was doubly annoyed—at himself for this lapse, at little Stevie for outthinking him.

"Besides," Steve added, "if the boat has been reported stolen, Pice might even recognize it and radio the police."

"It's got to be moved."

"Back to the cove?"

"No, that's not necessary. I can hide it in the brush on the beach. Cover it with fronds and sedges."

"You're not doing it alone. We'll go together."

"What are you, my freaking shadow?"

"No, Jack. I'm your partner. Partners do everything together. They . . ." Steve paused, sniffing the air. "What the hell?"

"Something wrong?"

Steve stood. "I think I smell . . ." He took a step toward the loggia, then froze. "Oh, *fuck*. What did you do? What the hell did you *do*?"

Looking past him, Jack could see a flickering reddish glow at the far end of the hall.

"Don't move!" Steve bolted for the kitchen, returned a moment later with a small fire extinguisher. "Don't you fucking *move*!"

Then he was racing down the hall, his footsteps banging like a drum roll, diminishing fast. A moment later, an angry dragon hiss: spray from the canister.

Jack unfolded the Kleenex and poured the granules into his own can of Coke.

The empty casings he scattered like seeds around Steve's armchair. Crouching down, he made a show of frantically collecting them

"Christ." Steve's voice, breathless and fluttery. "So you're an arsonist now. Is that it?"

Jack palmed the last casings and held them in a tight fist. He got to his feet as Steve approached.

"Hey, Stevie, don't get all bent out of shape. Just a minor practical joke to liven up a dull evening."

"What were you doing on the floor?"

"Killing a bug. One of those big Palmetto mothers."

The gun lifted ominously. "Another lie, and you're dead. What's in your hand?"

With feigned reluctance Jack spread his fingers.

Steve frowned, momentarily bewildered. Then he understood.

"You had some left," he whispered.

"Five."

"Enough to knock me out for hours. You son of a bitch."

"I wouldn't have hurt you, Stevie."

"Shut up. How did you think you'd get away with it, anyway? Didn't it occur to you that I'd know you set the fire as a diversion?"

Jack let his gaze slide away from Steve's face. "I intended to let you find me in the kitchen. You would have thought all I was after was my knife." He met Steve's eyes in a good imitation of childish defiance. "Would've worked, too—except after I put the stuff in your soda, I dropped the empties. Couldn't pick them all up in time."

"You just can't stop thinking about her, can you? You can't control these impulses of yours?"

"It's not like that."

"You're so fucking sick, Jack. And so fucking dangerous."

"I wasn't going to hurt her." He lifted his shoulders in a jerky, helpless shrug. "Really. You've been making me nervous with that gun. That's all."

Steve's mouth twitched. "Well, I'll tell you something, Jack. You're making me a little nervous, too." He waved the gun at the armchair. "Sit."

Jack sat.

"Now . . . drink it."

He looked at the soda. "Oh, hell, Stevie."

"Go on."

"You're going to need me alert tomorrow."

"The effects will wear off by then. In fact, a few hours' sleep will do you good. Aren't you the one who said we need to be fresh in the morning?"

Jack closed his hand over the soda can. "Shit," he muttered in angry acquiescence, and took a sip.

"All of it. Gulp it down."

Jack obeyed.

"Good boy." Steve sat on the sofa and lifted Jack's soda can. "You took your medicine. Daddy's very proud."

He drank Jack's Coca-Cola. Jack watched, keeping his face expressionless. He did not quite relax until Steve had drained the can.

"All right." Steve rose from the couch. "Let's move the runabout."

"We could wait awhile."

"No way. In an hour you'll be out cold. Then I'd have to go by myself. And to be honest, I don't trust you enough to leave you alone with my wife even if you're unconscious."

"Nice. Real friendly attitude."

"We stopped being friends awhile ago, Jack. I thought you would have figured that out by now."

*Yeah, buddy boy,* Jack thought as Steve marched him into the foyer, then out the door. *I figured it out. Now here's something for you to figure out.*

*One hour from now, I'll be the one with the gun.*

*And you and your lovely wife will be dead.*

# 32

The pain in Kirstie's shoulders had become a spread of tingling heat, draping her like a skin-tight shawl. Tendrils of agony shot down her arms, electrifying her elbows and wrists, as she went on raising and lowering her hands behind her with mechanical monotony.

Occasionally a string of whispered words punctuated her labor. The same words, always.

"Goddamn you, Steve."

Oddly, she felt no desire to curse Jack. Jack was hopeless, irredeemable. Curses would be wasted on him.

But for her husband to stand by and allow that smirking psychopath to tie her to this chair with electrical wires—for him to simply watch, his gun as useless as a toy, while his wife was reduced to helplessness—for him to have permitted that violation of her person was a betrayal so deep it could never be forgiven.

For a long time after she'd been left alone, she had given in to alternating paroxysms of grief and terror. Finally the tears had dried to salty tracks. And a new emotion, equally intense and far more healthy, had risen to her surface.

Rage.

How *dare* they do this to her? Steve, especially. How *dare* he?

She was a modern woman, college-educated, career-oriented. She worked for PBS, for Christ's sake. She wasn't some peasant prostitute in a snuff movie. She could *not* be treated this way.

Fury had revived her, made her strong. She'd begun to consider means of escape.

Craning her neck, she'd scrutinized the radio console behind her. The transmitter and receiver components were housed in metal cases with clever edges and sharp corners. If she could maneuver her chair a little closer to the table, then rub her wrists against the radio till the insulated wire had been sawed through . . .

That was her plan. For some immeasurable stretch of time—hours now—she'd been struggling to carry it out. By gently rocking her chair, she had inched within reach of the table; by repeatedly shrugging and dropping her shoulders, she had dragged the binding on her wrists vertically along the nearest edge of the receiver.

There was no way to gauge how quickly the wire was being worn. She thought she sensed a little more give in it, but that impression might be only her imagination.

One thing was certain: the muscles in her arms and shoulders were rapidly reaching a point beyond soreness, a point of total exhaustion that would make any subsequent movement impossible.

She had no idea what Steve and Jack were up to. For a long time there had been silence. Then a frantic clatter of activity—Steve yelling, rapid footsteps—she had thought the men were having a fight.

*Good,* she'd told herself. *Maybe Steve will shoot the son of a bitch.*

But she'd heard no gunshots. Only silence again.

And now . . . footsteps.

The two men walking through the living room, into the foyer. The front door opening. Then closing a moment later.

No further sounds.

They'd left together, via the front door. Why?

To sit on the porch, maybe. The house was hot. Outside, it might be cooler.

Whatever they were doing, at least they were gone for the moment. And the wires definitely did seem looser now.

Ignoring pain and fatigue, she rubbed harder.

Steve kept the Beretta trained on Jack as the runabout motored slowly away from the dock. Jack steered, easing the throttle arm to port, guiding the boat to the island's eastern shore. The motor, in low gear, burred softly.

Slowly the lights of the house receded, screened off by trees. Lifting his head, Steve saw no moon, only a blaze of stars, diamond bright. Their reflected brilliance shimmered on the water like whirling sparks of fire.

He supposed this would be the shape of his life from now on. Tropical nights, starlit waters, the rustle of palm fronds—and guilt and shame and fear.

Prison had always terrified him. His fear of incarceration with violent, conscienceless men, spurred by his own guilt and by Pete Creston's vivid stories, had become almost phobic in its intensity.

Yet now he wondered if his fears hadn't been misplaced. Prison was a waking nightmare, but to forfeit one's soul, become a man like Jack Dance—wasn't that a still grimmer version of hell?

*You're not turning into Jack,* he said to himself, disturbed by the thought. *That's ridiculous. He's a murderer, for God's sake.*

A comforting rebuttal, but hardly persuasive. He was aiding Jack. Helping him escape arrest, in order to kill again. He had already allowed his wife to be struck twice, each slap a hard crack of sound like a pistol's report. And afterward . . .

He remembered how she'd stared into his eyes, begging speechlessly for help. Help he had refused to give.

No, he wasn't as bad as Jack. But he was getting there. And the longer they stayed together, the more like Jack he would become.

Unless, of course, Jack killed him first.

Steve pondered that possibility as the runabout approached the white coral beach.

He didn't think Jack would continue to pose a threat to him once they were safely underway in the *Black Caesar*. It was Jack's obsession with Kirstie that was making him crazy now.

At least, Steve wanted to believe as much. But he could be wrong. Jack had never planned on having a partner. Probably he still didn't want one.

*And I'll have to sleep eventually. Hell, I'm . . . I'm starting to feel pretty damn drowsy now.*

The stress of the day's events must be catching up with him. There was a peculiar pins-and-needles tingling in his fingertips, a new heaviness in his eyelids.

*Better fix some coffee when I get back. A whole pot—and I'll drink it black.*

On Pice's boat he would have to risk sleep. But he did not dare close his eyes while he and Jack were on Pelican Key. Not with Kirstie a prisoner in the radio room.

The boat brushed the lip of the coral ledge. Jack looked up. "Okay if I get out and haul her in?"

Steve nodded. "We'll both do it."

They waded through the shallows, dragging the inflatable onto shore, then carried it farther up the beach into a tangle of brush.

The water revived Steve somewhat. "Cover it up," he ordered, pleased to be feeling slightly more alert.

"Wait a second." Jack reached into one of the grocery bags in the bow. "There's something I want to get."

Steve lifted the gun. If Jack had stowed a weapon on board . . .

Click, and a sudden yellow glare. A flashlight.

"Bought it in Florida City." Jack smiled. "We can use it to find our way back."

"Terrific. Now cover the goddamn boat."

Jack camouflaged the runabout with leaves and grasses while Steve watched over him, his finger resting lightly on the trigger. He wished he had the courage to shoot this man, put a bullet in his evil, calculating brain.

But he couldn't. He needed Jack. That was the hell of it. He'd made his bargain with the devil, and now their fates were inseparably joined.

Inseparably joined. A picture swam into his mind, a television image of Siamese twins, some random memory of a newscast he'd once seen. The infants' faces blurred, changed, became his own face and Jack's. Inseparably joined . . .

The image dissolved into a hallucinatory stream. He felt his eyes closing. It occurred to him that he was drifting toward sleep.

No, impossible. He was standing up. Nobody could sleep standing up. A person had to be in bed to sleep. Sleep and bed, two concepts inseparably joined.

He was . . . floating. . . .

Jack tossed a last pile of brush on the runabout and clapped his hands. "Done."

The harsh smack of sound shocked Steve awake. He shook his head to clear his thoughts.

What the hell had happened there? Christ, he'd nearly nodded off. It looked like wading to shore hadn't done much to revive him, after all. He needed coffee, whole pots of it.

Jack was the one who ought to be fighting drowsiness. He'd taken the sleeping pills.

That last thought—*Jack took the sleeping pills*—almost suggested an idea to him, some ugly trickery on Jack's part; but the idea was complicated, hard to grasp, and his mental processes seemed to be growing dangerously torpid.

Jack beamed the flash down the beach. "The trail starts there. We can come around the back way, reenter the house through the patio."

It was the same trail the three of them had taken early this morning. Steve thought of Ana romping with Jack, fetching sticks for him. His gut tightened, and a spurt of anger squeezed some of the fatigue out of his system.

"All right," he said brusquely. "Let's move."

They trudged along the beach. Jack, in the lead, swept the flashlight's pale circle across stretches of coral sand, pebbly and pitted and stark, a moonscape in miniature.

"You ever going to put down that gun, Stevie?"

"Not till I feel safe."

"When will that be?"

Steve frowned, once more blinking sleep out of his eyes.

"I don't know," he mumbled. The statement came out slightly slurred. "I don't know if . . . if I'll ever feel safe again."

# 33

Free.

A final jerk of her wrists snapped the worn wire, liberating her hands.

Kirstie stretched her arms, teeth gritted against the pops of pain in her joints, the aching soreness in every muscle.

"God," she whispered. "Oh, my God."

She leaned forward, intending to attack the antenna wire that secured her feet to the chair, then experienced a swooning sensation of vertigo. Head lowered, she shut her eyes and fought off rippling waves of faintness.

Her fingers were numb and clumsy. She fumbled with the knot Jack had tied to bind her ankles. It wouldn't yield. Wild frustration rose in her and nearly tore a scream out of her throat.

Finally she found the knot's weakness. It unraveled in her hands. The loop of antenna wire slipped to the floor.

Awkwardly she rose upright. Her knees fluttered. She took a rickety step, then another.

Steve and Jack had left via the front door. She hadn't heard them come back in. They must be still out front.

She'd have to leave via the back exit. Hidden in the woods, she could plan her next move.

She glanced around the radio room. The lone window was sealed shut by humidity; Steve had tried to pry it open shortly after their arrival, only to find that it resisted his best efforts. There was no chance she could succeed where he had failed.

The patio, then.

Anastasia lay before her, a mottled heap. Kirstie knew she had no time to waste; the men might return at any second, and her opportunity would be lost.

Still, she couldn't deny herself a last moment with her dog. Kneeling, she stroked the borzoi's fur, once so smooth and silken, now stiff, bristly, matted with drying blood.

Her hand came away red and tacky. A rather small hand, yet not long ago Anastasia had very nearly fit inside it. Kirstie remembered staying up with Ana on her first night in a new home, patiently waiting out the darkness, holding the tiny, shivering pup close enough to hear the comforting beat of her mistress's heart.

"You're a good dog, honey," she heard herself whisper now, though she knew the time was long since past when such words could matter. "A good, good dog."

Tears misted her vision. She was reminded, absurdly, of how peeling onions always made her cry.

Enough of this. Time to get moving. Come on, now.

She stood, wiped her eyes, and left the room without looking at Ana again.

Her sandals clicked on the kitchen floor, the faint noise loud as an alarm bell in her ears. Leaning against a counter, she removed the sandals, then held them in one hand and proceeded barefoot.

Not only her hearing but all her senses seemed heightened, unnaturally acute. She perceived every detail of the room: the hum-rattle-hum of the refrigerator, the smudges of grease on the stove's burners, the dinner dishes still soaking in the sink, where she had left them four hours and a lifetime ago.

In the middle of the kitchen she stopped, arrested by a thought.

Dinner dishes. Silverware.

Knives.

There were knives in the drawer near the sink. Some were steak knives, long-handled, with serrated blades. Good weapons.

She was by no means sure she could actually . . . stab someone. . . .

But it would be good to have the option.

She stepped up to the drawer, pulled it open.

Blood shouted at her. A small pool of blood, crusted over, nearly dry, and centered in it, Jack's Swiss Army knife, the wicked spear blade still extended, striped in red-brown streaks.

In her mind she saw it all again: the casual swipe of Jack's hand, the blade slitting Ana's throat like a letter opener, the dog's racking convulsions.

Shock propelled her backward. The drawer came with her, sliding out of its frame. It crashed on the floor. Knives, forks, spoons scattered across the tiles in a ringing spray of metal.

A loud noise. To her ears, deafening. It would have been easily heard outside the house.

If the men were on the front porch, as she assumed, then they must be coming for her now.

Get out. *Get out!*

She left the knives and broke into a run, streaking through the dining room, her heartbeat accelerating as time dilated into dreamlike slow motion.

The patio doors were just ahead, hanging ajar to let in the night breeze.

Outside. Through the patio and garden. Her bare feet padding on concrete, on grass, on dirt.

The gate was shut but not latched. She threw it open, slipped her sandals on, and then the path was unwinding before her, drained of color in the monochromatic starlight, as she sprinted away from the house.

Irrationally she was afraid to look back, afraid she would see Jack bearing down on her, the bloody knife in his fist.

She plunged ahead, veering drunkenly from side to side on the path, beating stray branches clear of her face. There was no sound in her world but her panting breath and the furious scuffing of her sandals. Around her, walls of clotted shadow, the dense foliage bordering the path. Ahead, only darkness. Darkness . . .

Light.

She rounded a curve and stumbled to a halt.

In front of her, perhaps twenty yards away, was the bobbing circle of a flashlight's beam.

The wan yellow glow illuminated Jack Dance's face from beneath, throwing his features into ghastly relief.

Directly behind him stood Steve, gun in hand.

But it wasn't possible. They had gone out the front door. She'd *heard* them. What were they doing *here*?

"Shit." That was Jack, his voice knifing through the madcap confusion of her thoughts. "How the hell did *you* get loose?"

The beam rose to dazzle her as he focused the flashlight on her face.

"Your wife is getting to be a real problem, Stevie." There was ugly relish in the words. "The kind of problem that cries out for a solution."

The beam brightened, the amber circle expanding. Jack was coming closer.

Steve stood motionless, his expression oddly dazed,

vacant. He looked—Jesus—he looked as if he were asleep on his feet.

She would get no help from him. And Jack knew it. The cold, feral gleam in his eyes told her as much.

*Back in the house. Dammit, go!*

She turned. Ran.

The flashlight's glare had temporarily wiped out her night vision, and she nearly blundered off the trail as she sprinted headlong for the garden gate. No need to look over her shoulder; she could gauge Jack's distance by the brightness of the beam tracking her.

The gate flew up fast and slammed into her midsection. She flung it wide, ran through, then shut it and gambled a precious second fumbling with the latch. It snicked into place, and then she was running again.

Hope lifted her. The flashlight no longer had her pinned in its beam. She seemed to have outdistanced her pursuit.

As she passed the wicker lounger chair, she tipped it on its side, blocking the portico. Anything to slow Jack down and give her time to get out the front door, to the dock, the boats—

Just inside the patio doorway, she whirled, intending to close and lock the French doors.

She froze. Hope died. A new surge of terror grabbed her by the throat.

Jack was there.

She had not outrun him. He must have discarded the flashlight somewhere along the trail, then vaulted the gate and the lounge chair without slowing down. Now he was a yard from the doors, closing in like an express train.

She tried to slam the doors—too late—he wedged an arm and leg into the opening and pushed with the weight of his body.

Kirstie pushed back, palms pressed to the frame,

her face inches from Jack's, divided from him only by a quarter-inch panel of glass.

No use. She wasn't strong enough to hold him back. The doors were easing open as he muscled his way inside.

She gave up and ran for the doorway to the living room, knowing she wouldn't make it.

Behind her, a tinkle of shattering glass as the doors were flung wide. Thudding footfalls, Jack's bobbing shadow on the wall.

Steely fingers clamped over her arm. The room spun like a carousel. She executed a half pirouette and came face to face with Jack from a foot away.

His teeth were white in the chandelier's glow. He looked like a hungry animal, ready to feed.

Someone was screaming. She realized the cries were her own.

A blur of motion. Her fists, beating wildly at his chest.

He let her go. For a heady instant she imagined she'd hurt him with her blows.

Then, laughing soundlessly, he hooked his foot behind her ankle and upended her. Briefly she was weightless, her body tumbling in space, arms and legs extended as if in an endless free fall. She brushed past the dining table, her head barely clearing the sharp corner, and then a square of inlaid floor tile flew up and socked her in the jaw. She groaned.

"Guess what, darling." Jack's mouth was still stretched wide in unvoiced laughter. "Your hubby isn't here this time. Which means I am going to have some major-league fun with you."

The dining table loomed over her. She crawled under it, blindly seeking shelter.

Jack's fist snagged a belt loop on her shorts. "Uh-

uh." He spoke to her in a chiding tone, heavy with mockery. "You're not going anywhere."

The floor began to slide, smooth tiles slipping past her, a moving sidewalk. He was dragging her out into the open.

Her fingers groped for a leg of the table, a niche in the tiles, anything to hold on to.

She touched something sharp.

Porcelain shards. The broken bits of the salad bowls Jack had dropped earlier, when he'd lunged for Steve's gun.

Her fist closed over a shard. She twisted free of Jack's grasp. Snap-rolled into a squat and came up fast, thrusting the weapon at him. She was snarling.

The arrow-sharp tip punched through Jack's blue jeans, penetrating the meat of his left thigh. He stumbled backward, the shard still embedded in his leg, and then Kirstie was scrambling past him, through the nearest doorway.

Too late she realized she'd entered the kitchen. This route led back to the radio room. Dead end.

She spun around, hoping to retrace her steps, but Jack was already charging in pursuit. His face was crazed, splotchy with fury. He ran limping, blood wet on his pants.

No choice now but to retreat into the radio room. She slammed the door, locked it.

The knob rattled. Jack's voice through the door, muffled: "Goddamn you, bitch!"

The room was narrow, low-ceilinged, the walls closing in. She had to get out of here, *had to get out of here.*

Through the thin gap between the door and the frame, just above the latch bolt, poked the edge of a credit card. It withdrew, then appeared again, an inch lower.

Jack was trying to slip the latch.

She glanced wildly around the room. The only exit was the window, swollen shut. She was sure she couldn't open it.

But smashing it—that was another story.

She ran to the chair where she'd been tied up, hefted it with a grunt of strain.

The latch slid momentarily, jostled loose by the card, then sprang back into its socket before Jack could open the door. He would be quicker next time.

Hurry, hurry.

She shoved the chair through the windowpane in a cascade of glass fragments. Climbed up on the sill, swung her legs out.

Behind her, the door creaked open like a casket lid.

She flung herself forward. Hit the ground on one knee and dived into a thicket of saw palmettos. Burrowed in deeper, thrusting the pointed, fan-shaped leaves out of her way, belly-crawling over the tangled, creeping stems that littered the ground like a nest of snakes.

A shout from the window: "Sorry, Mrs. Gardner! You're not getting away!"

Jack probably couldn't see her. But he could follow anyway. There was no way for her to move fast enough in the choking brush to evade his pursuit—not without making enough noise to draw his attention.

Had it all been for nothing, then? All her efforts, wasted?

Desperately she wriggled forward on elbows and knees, hot tears welling in her eyes.

# 34

Standing at the window of the radio room, blood pasting his pants leg to his thigh, Jack Dance smiled.

This was what he lived for. Con jobs were lucrative, and ordinary seductions could be briefly satisfying, but nothing could compare with the twitch and jerk of a woman's body, her chortling death rattle, the blank amazement that invariably lingered in her unseeing eyes.

A few yards from the house, thickets of underbrush rustled frantically. Kirstie was somewhere in that tangle of shadows.

Even without his flashlight he could pick up her trail. Soon he would pay her back for the red hole in his leg.

Still grinning, he gripped the edges of the window frame and began to hoist himself onto the sill.

*"Jack!"*

He froze. The voice was Steve's, and it came from inside the house.

"Goddammit, Jack, *don't you touch her*!"

Hell. Little Stevie had been fading fast on the trail; Jack had assumed the sedative had put him under by now. But apparently adrenaline, triggered by concern for his wife, had restored his flagging energy.

Jack lowered his feet to the floor and moved away from the window. Kirstie would have to wait. As long as Steve had the gun and remained alert and active, he took top priority.

Steve's footsteps pounded for the front door. No doubt he was expecting to find Kirstie on the dock. When he saw she wasn't there, he would search the rest of the house.

Jack had to move fast.

He crept into the kitchen. From the scatter of silverware on the floor he retrieved his Swiss Army knife.

In the foyer, the front door banged open.

"Kirstie! *Jack!*"

Steve must be standing on the porch, peering at the dock in the strong starlight. There was a new quality to his voice, a blend of desperation, anguish, and escalating hysteria.

He would shoot Jack when he saw him. Shoot to kill. Jack had no doubt of that.

*Got to take you out first, old buddy. And I think I know the way.*

He switched off the lights in the kitchen and dining room.

The front door thudded shut. Fast footsteps retreated down the loggia. Having failed to spot Kirstie on the dock, Steve was exploring the house's east wing.

Jack entered the living room. He grabbed the remote-control device for the color TV, stuck it in his shirt pocket.

The room was lit by two table lamps and a torchiere. He unplugged all three lights and cut the cords.

Darkness. The only remaining illumination, a faint glow from the loggia.

He crouched behind the sofa, the knife in one hand, the remote-control in the other. Waited, heart beating hard and steady in a rapid metronomic rhythm.

Never before had he gone up against armed prey.

Danger added a new, electrifying dimension to the sport.

One thrust of the knife. That was all the chance he would have.

And all he would need.

Steve needed every bit of his energy to keep his legs moving, his eyes open, his head clear.

He understood now. Understood what Jack had done to him. The sleeping pills. Jack had tricked him into drugging himself.

On the trail he'd been close to collapse when Kirstie blundered into view. The shock of seeing her—the spurt of terror at the prospect of what Jack would do when he caught her—had been enough to rouse him to one last effort.

He had to find Jack. Not to talk with him, not to bide time until morning. All of that was over. It should never have begun.

Once, years ago, Steve had read an article about dogs crossbred with wolves to produce half-breed pets. The domesticated wolves were friendly, loyal, capable of learning commands. In most respects they seemed indistinguishable from normal dogs.

But at any moment, unpredictably, the wild wolf in the animal's makeup could tear through the semi-civilized veneer to slash and kill. There had been ugly, horrific incidents.

Jack was like that. An untamed thing, wearing the gloss of civilized urbanity. Because he spoke well and dressed nicely, because he smiled and laughed, he disguised the snarling predator within.

On the boat at the reef, it had been almost possible to forget that this man killed for pleasure, cheated women of their lives for a fleeting sexual thrill.

But when he cut Anastasia's throat, he had been truly himself. Steve had seen his face then.

He had glimpsed the same look—the same savage appetite—as Jack took off after Kirstie on the forest trail.

Steve would not play the role of partner to a wild beast. To do so would be to surrender his humanity to the bestial side of himself.

There would be no more rationalizations, no more compromises, no more bargains. He would find Jack and march him out to the generator shed and lock him inside.

Then take Kirstie to Islamorada and confess everything to the authorities.

He would go to prison. Maybe for years. But he would survive. And through it all, he would hold clear title to his own soul.

The bedroom doorway expanded before him. Sudden vivid imagery crowded his brain—Kirstie cornered in the room, flung supine on the bed, beaten and molested by Jack. Nightmarish scenes, distorted and terrifying. He pushed them away. The sedative was playing with his head, blurring the borderline between sensory input and hallucination.

The pistol in his hand felt reassuringly real. Tightening his grip on the handle, he slipped into the bedroom.

Empty.

He checked out the bathroom next. Foam from the fire extinguisher still slimed the walls. An acrid odor, a memory of smoke, hung in the air like a dissipating ghost.

No one in here, either. The west wing of the house, then. The kitchen, the radio room. That was where he'd find them.

He doubled back, fighting the looseness of his knees, the icy numbness in his hands.

He wasn't sure he even had the strength to lead Jack to the shed.

"Then I'll shoot the son of a bitch," he muttered as a strange, savage hatred—Jack's kind of hate—swelled within him.

He could do it if he had to.

And if Jack had hurt Kirstie . . . or *killed* her . . .

Steve would empty the pistol into the motherfucker's loveless heart.

He reached the west end of the loggia, slowed his steps.

Ahead, the doorway to the living room was dark.

All the lights had been left on. Now they were extinguished.

Jack was in there.

Lying in wait? Preparing an ambush?

Careful. Careful.

With the gun, Steve had a decisive advantage, if he was alert enough to use it.

That was the problem. His reactions were sluggish, his thoughts increasingly confused.

At least he was still sufficiently self-aware to perceive the degree of his impairment. He was not walking with eyes closed into whatever snare Jack had laid.

Warily he entered the room, blinking to adjust his vision to the dark. Near him stood a lamp on an end table. He clicked the switch. Nothing.

Unplugged? He risked groping for the cord. It had been slashed.

Jack must have similarly sabotaged the other two lamps. The dining-room chandelier probably could be turned on, but to get to the wall switch Steve would have to cross yards of dangerous territory.

The room offered many hiding places. Armchairs, potted plants, TV set, sofa. Shadows everywhere.

Palms wet, mouth dry, Steve advanced deeper into the darkness. The gun led him, its barrel swinging restlessly from side to side like the snout of a stalking animal.

Now he was halfway across the room. One of the big arched windows loomed on his right; he saw no one hidden behind the drapes. To his left lay the armchair where he'd sat watching Jack for long, slow hours. A dark shape, lumpy and vague, distorted the back of the chair.

He hesitated. Jack? Hunkered down behind it?

No. Only his own nylon jacket, draped limply over the chair.

From the dining room, a soft banging noise. The patio doors. Still open, swinging in the breeze.

He was passing the sofa now. A good place for Jack to conceal himself. Almost imperceptibly, he increased the pressure of his index finger on the trigger.

The dining room was less than five feet away. If he could get through the doorway, he could slap the wall switch, light the chandelier, then flush Jack out of hiding.

Only a few more steps . . .

Behind him, a burst of white light. A female voice.

*"—never wash my car again?"*

The television. Sound blaring. Phosphorescent picture tube throwing a pale, inconstant glow over the room.

He spun toward the set. Jack must be hiding there, must have hit the on-off switch by accident, given himself away.

But where was he? Where the hell was he?

On the margin of his vision, a flicker of steel.

He lurched sideways, and the knife ripped past him,

the blade coruscating in the light as it tore hungrily at his sleeve.

Steve pivoted to face Jack, pointed the gun.

*"That's right."* A male voice now. *"With the patented Dirt Eater—"*

His forefinger flexed.

The Beretta bucked in his hand.

A crash of sound.

Jack, twisting forward.

*I shot him,* Steve thought as his ears rang and the room changed color from blue to red to magenta in the television's glow.

No. Wrong. Jack wasn't collapsing on the floor. He was lunging over the sofa, the knife stabbing wildly.

*"—you can say good-bye to expensive visits to the car wash—"*

Steve seized Jack's knife hand, held the blade at bay. He tried to shoot again, but powerful fingers were already clutching his wrist in a death grip. Jack's face filled his field of vision, surreal in the stroboscopic light.

*"—and wet, sloppy do-it-yourself jobs in the driveway!"*

Jack stretched his mouth in a voiceless roar. He fought to free his knife hand from Steve's grasp. Steve held on, the Beretta rendered useless, pointed at the ceiling. The two men danced a ragged, stumbling waltz.

*"Thanks to Dirt Eater's miracle technology—"*

Jack slammed Steve up against the wall. His glasses flew free, and the world lost focus.

*"—you'll keep your car looking showroom clean—"*

Jack drove Steve's gun hand into the wall—again—again—shocking his knuckles with jolts of pain.

*"—and it takes less than ten minutes a week!"*

The Beretta was slipping from Steve's slick fingers.

Jack rammed his arm against the wall, and a blaze of heat burst from his elbow to his wrist.

*"Dirt Eater works great on all kinds of finishes—"*

Helplessly, Steve let the pistol fall.

Jack released him, grabbed at it.

*"—and on fiberglass bodies, too!"*

Steve's foot blurred. He kicked the Beretta across the room. It skated noisily on the tiles.

Jack socked him hard in the gut, driving breath and strength out of him, then jerked his knife hand free.

The blade arrowed forward. Steve flung himself sideways, out of its reach, and snap-rolled onto the floor.

Too late he realized he'd dived in the wrong direction, *away* from the gun.

*"So if you want to give your car that fresh-from-the-dealer shine—"*

Jack saw his mistake, scrambled for the Beretta on the other side of the room.

Steve grabbed the TV stand, pulled himself to his feet. Backlit by the picture tube, he made a perfect target.

*"—try the new Dirt Eater—"*

Jack picked up the gun.

*"—the best thing to happen to the automobile—"*

Steve spun behind the television.

*"—since gasoline!"*

Jack fired.

The TV set exploded in a cascade of pinwheeling glitter.

Jack shielded his eyes as sparks swarmed over him like angry fireflies.

Steve darted into the dining room. Here darkness was total. The breeze on his face told him the direction of the patio doorway.

He ran outside into a mist of starlight filtering through the latticed roof of the pergola. Without his glasses he perceived objects more than a few feet away as watery smears. The wash of bone white before him was the upended lounge chair; he remembered skirting past it on his way into the house.

He'd had the gun then. He'd still had a chance against Jack. Now he was disarmed, and he and Kirstie were doomed.

Clambering over the chair, he risked a backward look. Jack wasn't following, not yet.

The garden gate was still locked; he'd climbed the low wall to get inside. Now he lost a handful of seconds groping blindly for the latch.

He was sure Jack was behind him. Probably had him in the Beretta's sights.

Again he glanced over his shoulder. Still nothing. No movement, no footsteps, no sign of pursuit.

Then he was sprinting down the trail, while around him the tropical night rustled and buzzed and shrilled, jungle-movie noises, the soundtrack of a nightmare, and suppose all of this was only a nightmare—yes—and soon he would wake, Kirstie beside him, Anastasia curled on the floor near the bed, everything fine and normal. He rises from bed, he turns on the morning news—Mister Twister has been nabbed by the FBI in Salt Lake City, and he's not Jack Dance, he's a different man entirely, Steve's fears were unfounded, silly—how could Jack have murdered Meredith or anyone else? Good old Jack? Ridiculous. He's no killer, and Steve hasn't been concealing a homicide all these years, and so there'll be no more awful dreams like the one had last night, the one where Jack was loose on Pelican Key and Steve was running, running. . . .

Falling.

The dirt path tore the tender skin of his palms as he sprawled on hands and knees. Pain shocked him back to the reality of this moment.

His mind had drifted off again, anchorless, rudderless. Drifted into fantasy and hallucination.

A new wave of the sedative was spreading through him. The capsules were the time-release variety; some of the granules had been absorbed immediately into his bloodstream, but others were still in his digestive tract, where they would be broken down in successive phases over the next several hours.

If he could prevent any further absorption of the sedative, the dose he'd already assimilated would wear off quickly enough.

He looked around him. Jack was nowhere in sight. For the moment, then, he was safe.

With a final effort he lurched to his feet and staggered down the trail, toward the beach.

He knew what he was looking for. He only hoped he could find it in a world of darkness and fog.

Steve was gone by the time Jack reopened his eyes and blinked away the blue retinal afterimages spotting his vision.

Must have left via the French doors in the dining room. No time to hunt him down now. Without the gun, he was no longer a serious threat or an urgent priority.

Kirstie was Jack's main concern at the moment.

She would almost certainly be making her way around the house, toward the dock. When she reached it, she could take the motorboat to Islamorada.

Fortunately, the dense brush would slow her progress. Jack still had time to intercept her.

Still, she would be wary about approaching the dock. Somehow he would have to get close enough to squeeze off a clean shot.

Or perhaps—he smiled with the beginning of a thought—perhaps he could make her come to him.

# 35

Kirstie's arms were red with scratches, her legs peppered with insect bites. She had no idea how long she'd been thrashing through the brush or how near she might be to the dock.

Jack hadn't come after her. She was quite sure of that. And twice she'd heard what had sounded like a gunshot from the direction of the house.

Had Steve shot Jack? Was it possible?

She was hardly planning to go back and ask.

The night was hot and wet, the moonless sky bright with stars. Around her stretched a tangled waste of wildflowers, creepers, and sporadic eruptions of slash pines, their glossy needles gleaming like bundled knives. Birds screeched and hooted in the dark, an unseen audience for the drama she was enacting on this spotlighted stage.

Mud soaked her sandaled feet. Several times she had stumbled into small water holes concealed by a scrim of plant life. Mosquitoes had become a constant presence; she no longer bothered to wave them away.

The house was somewhere off to her left, invisible now, masked by trees and scrub. To her right must be the island's western shore, a beachless skirt of mangroves. And ahead, perhaps a hundred feet or a thousand miles, lay the dock.

If she reached it, she could steal one of the two

boats moored there and escape. After that, let the police handle things.

They would arrive, make arrests. Steve would go to prison as Jack's accomplice. He deserved it, of course; yet she couldn't suppress a surge of sadness at the thought.

She had loved him. Still did. Or at least she'd loved the man she'd thought he was. The man who had driven her out to the Connecticut coast one summer night and, under a sky striped with Perseid meteors, slipped an engagement ring on her finger. The man who had stayed by her hospital bed every day throughout her two-week battle with blood poisoning, when more than once she'd been certain she would die. The man who had waded, fully clothed, into a pond in Rocky Hill to rescue Anastasia when the pup appeared to be in danger of drowning.

The same man who had watched unmoving as Anastasia was knifed to death a few hours ago.

*You never really know anybody,* she thought as she struggled through stiff patches of broomsedge choked by the strangling stems of morning glories. *You think you do, but what you see is mostly what they're willing to show. And then the real person comes out, and it's . . . horrible.*

If she survived this, she would never trust another human being, never leave herself vulnerable, never take any kind of risk. For the rest of her life she would be wary and lonely and safe.

"Goddamn you, Steve," she said again, the words her mantra now.

A thicket of waxmyrtle materialized before her. She blundered through it, and then miraculously the underbrush began to thin out, and the breeze freshened with a sharper accent of the sea.

She'd made it. Having circled around the house,

she'd arrived at the southern tip of Pelican Key, where she would find the dock.

Of course, the men might be waiting. Her plan was her most obvious course of action; they were likely to anticipate it. And maybe those distant percussive cracks she'd heard earlier hadn't been shots.

She could assume nothing. One mistake, and it was over.

A slow shiver caressed her. If someone had asked yesterday, she would have said she didn't particularly fear death. It was natural, inevitable, and college had left her too deeply secularized to fear punishment in an afterlife.

But now dying scared her. She had watched Ana die, had seen the bewildered panic in her face, had heard her whimpering moans as death shook her in its cold, fierce grip.

She didn't want to go like that. Didn't want to go at all. She felt the imperative of survival as an animal must feel it, not in her mind but in her blood, in the racing energy that contracted muscles and electrified nerves.

Elbowing her way through the last of the ground cover, she emerged on the lip of the coral beach.

A few casuarinas grew here, their trunks throwing long shadows across the sand in the starlight. She crouched behind the nearest tree and peered out.

From her vantage point, the dock was a thin, comb-like projection in silhouette against the glittery shallows. The shadows of the pilings wavered on the water like a web of wind-stirred gossamer. A single boat drifted at the end of a slack mooring line, hull creaking secretively.

Jack's runabout was gone. Odd.

She remembered hearing a brief motor noise shortly after the men had left the house, while she was still a prisoner. At the time she'd assumed it to be a passing boat, cruising near the island on the way to blue water.

She'd been wrong. What she had heard was the runabout. Steve and Jack had moved it.

If she'd been thinking more clearly, she could have guessed as much already. The men had left via the front door, yet she'd encountered them on the path at the rear of the house. The only logical explanation was that they'd transferred the boat to a new location, then walked back.

None of which mattered anyway, because the other boat, the motorboat provided by Pelican Key's owners, was still here.

In less than two minutes she would be on her way out of—

Wait.

Movement on the dock. The shadowy figure of a man.

His dark outline blended with the masses of tropical foliage at his back, and only his restless pacing revealed his presence. His pacing—and a glint of starshine, faint but perceptible, winking fitfully as he moved.

Eyeglasses. Catching the chancy light with each turn of his head.

Squinting, she dimly made out the nylon jacket Steve had worn for most of the day.

A sigh eased out of her. The dock was off limits as long as Steve was guarding it. She couldn't reach the boat.

Still, there was the runabout. Possibly she would find it at the cove, where Jack had beached it originally.

Even the thought of retracing her route through acres of almost impenetrable vegetation—sharp-edged saw-palmettos, creeping ground ivy, foul-smelling skunkbush—exhausted her. But she would have to do it. And hope that Jack wasn't lurking in ambush somewhere along the way.

She was retreating toward denser brush when a hoarse whisper stopped her.

*"Kirstie."*

Frozen, huddled behind a clump of groundsel-tree, she listened.

"Kirstie, are you out there?"

Steve didn't seem to see her. He was just calling her name at random.

She waited, afraid to move and possibly draw his attention. It was a strain to hear him; his rasping stage whisper was barely audible.

"I shot Jack. But he's not dead, only wounded. And . . . he's got the gun."

Could it be true? Had Steve rebelled against Jack, redeemed himself? Skepticism competed with a desperate desire to believe.

"Jack's looking for me. Thinks I went north. But I doubled back to find you. I know you've come for the boat."

A breeze kicked up, and she heard his jacket ripple like a sail. The sparkle of his glasses was the sole identifiable feature in the ink-blot enigma of his face.

"Show yourself. Please. I won't hurt you. I never wanted to hurt you. I'm not part of this anymore."

But how could she accept that statement, how could she risk believing anything he said, when this could so easily be a trap?

Still, she *had* heard gunshots. She was sure she had.

"Please, Kirstie." His whisper turned sibilant, a hiss. "You've got to trust me."

Trust him? Did she dare?

A few minutes ago, she'd vowed never to trust another person. Now she was being asked to trust Jack Dance's accomplice.

But he was something more than that. He was her husband.

And she did believe he hadn't wanted to see her hurt. He'd intervened when Jack was slapping her around. Saved her life, probably.

Whatever his weaknesses, whatever his sins, he must still care for her. Now, repentant, he was offering a chance at escape.

"Kirstie? Can you hear me?"

She had to give him the trust he asked for, this one last time.

*"Please."*

Had to.

Slowly she stood. She walked forward, out of the cover of the trees, onto the hard coral sand.

"Here I am," she said in an answering whisper.

The glint of his glasses swung in her direction. "Thank God. Hurry up, get over here."

She did not hurry. Her steps were slow and measured as she crossed the narrow strip of beach.

"Come on. *Come on.*"

The dock was less than fifty feet away. She wished there were a moon. She wanted to see Steve's face, study his expression. If she could look into his eyes . . .

Her sandals crunched on coral, a soft, gravelly sound. The sea breeze twined around her bare legs, groping like lascivious fingers. On the horizon burned the lights of Upper Matecumbe Key, distant as the stars, close as the boat that could take her to Islamorada and safety.

She had left cover behind. Here on the yards of bleached sand she was totally exposed, a slender target in a field of white.

Ahead, Steve waited on the dock, motionless, a

swatch of night cut out of the larger darkness around him.

A bad feeling, a premonition of some kind, bobbed to the surface of her consciousness. Perhaps because Steve was standing so still, so deathly still, not running to greet her as she might have expected—or perhaps because she was so terribly vulnerable now, and more vulnerable with every forward step—whatever the reason, she felt suddenly as if she were walking down the center lane of a turnpike, traffic rushing at her, horns blaring, a quick, grinding death under a tractor-trailer's giant tires only seconds away.

She slowed her steps.

*"Kirstie! Dammit, what's taking you so long?"*

His strained whisper—something was wrong about that, too. She wasn't sure quite what.

Time slipped into a lower gear. Seconds elongated, stretching like taffy. The world took on a fantastic clarity; every ripple of starshine on the water, every weave and pucker of the coral beach, every smallest detail of her environment was magnified, brightened, enhanced.

But still she could not see Steve's face.

*"Hurry up!"*

She stopped.

There was no reason for it, no logic to it, or at least none she could name; but abruptly her legs would advance her no farther.

On the dock, a blur of motion.

Steve's right hand peeling back the flap of his jacket. Something shiny in his fist, rising fast.

The gun.

Betrayal.

*Jesus, no.*

She pivoted, legs pumping.

Behind her: *crack.*

Puff of sand at her feet. Chips of coral stinging her ankles.

She ran for the brush, the trees. Just in time she remembered to zigzag.

*Crack.*

The second shot landed along the straight-line path she'd been running a heartbeat earlier.

Trees close now. Ten feet ahead.

*Crack.*

Brief rustle of leaves as the bullet whizzed past her head and struck one of the pines.

Near miss, that time. Inches.

She reached the trees, flung herself headlong into the brush.

*Crack.*

God, he was still shooting.

*"Stop it!"* she screamed. *"Stop it, you son of a bitch!"*

She scrambled wildly through the ground cover, plunging into a dense, concealing thicket of horse nettle, heedless of the plants' slashing thorns.

Huddled there, shuddering all over, she waited for the next shot.

None came.

Perhaps he was following her. Moving in close for a surer kill.

She dared a look.

Steve remained on the dock. As she watched, he leaned over the side, aimed the gun straight down, and fired a single shot at the motorboat, puncturing the hull.

He was scuttling the boat. Denying her that means of escape. So he and Jack could hunt her down at leisure, take her life at will.

Shivering, she retreated deeper into the brush. She

didn't stop crawling until the dock was lost to sight, the undergrowth around her a solid barricade.

On her knees, she leaned against a rotted log, the corpse of a fallen magnolia. Large black beetles crawled on it. Some detoured onto her hand, her arm. She didn't care.

"Goddamn you, Steve," she said for the hundredth time, but with even greater feeling now.

He was every bit as bad as Jack. No, he was worse.

Jack, at least, had not used her love and trust to lure her into a death trap. Only her husband had been capable of that.

*He's sick,* she thought in time with a confused rush of emotions: rage, grief, pity.

Then she shook her head. It wasn't sickness. Steve was suffering from no delusion; he knew who she was and what she ought to mean to him; and he had tried, repeatedly and cold-bloodedly, to put a bullet in her back.

Had it all been a lie, then? Every moment of their years together? Every smile, embrace, kiss? Every shared secret and whispered confession?

"God . . ." She began to say the familiar words of her private mantra, but strength failed her. The curse, unfinished, became a kind of desperate prayer.

Crying, she staggered on through weeds and scrub, lashed forward by one thought.

The runabout.

Hidden somewhere.

Perhaps at the cove.

Jack shrugged off Steve's nylon jacket and slung it into the water with an angry swing of his arm. The eyeglasses followed, vanishing with a splash.

His ruse had nearly worked. If Kirstie had advanced just a few steps nearer . . .

No point in thinking about that. He would have to try again, that was all.

He checked the Beretta's clip. Eight rounds left, plus another in the chamber. Plenty of ammo.

Though he hadn't handled a gun in years, he was confident enough of his ability to hit a stationary target at reasonably close range. As a teenager he had often borrowed his father's Heckler & Koch .45—well, taken it without permission, actually—and driven out to the woods, where he would practice for hours, unobserved.

He'd been a good marksman then. But now, when it mattered—when he'd meant to pay back that little bitch for the bloody hole in his leg—his every shot had gone wide of the mark.

The stab wound, at least, had almost stopped its painful throbbing. Before leaving the house, he'd inspected the injury, then wrapped his thigh in a strip of bedsheet to stanch the blood. He could walk without limping now.

He turned his attention to the motorboat, fully submerged at last, dragged to the bottom by the weight of the Evinrude outboard. Through the crystalline water its outline shimmered faintly, blurred and strange, a ghost vessel in a dream.

Kirstie wouldn't be getting away in that boat, anyhow.

Only the runabout was left. Steve, of course, knew where it was concealed, but Jack was unconcerned about him. His energy had been fading fast. By now the sedative in his system must have put him under.

And Kirstie had no idea where to find the runabout. Still, she was certain to try. Where would she look first?

The cove.

Obviously. The cove was where the boat had been

beached in the first place. Probably she was on her way there right now.

Waiting for the boat to founder had cost him time. She had a head start. But he could catch up.

And when he did, his next bullet would not miss.

# 36

Where the forest trail met the coral beach, Steve found what he was looking for.

He had spotted it ten days ago, on an aimless walk with Anastasia. The borzoi, like all dogs, had liked to sniff everything within reach; but when she'd started nosing a waist-high shrub with scarlet flowers and yellow fruits, Steve had pulled her hastily away.

*Jatropha multifada.* The physic-nut tree.

Easy enough to recognize the species. Jack, in fact, had first identified it to him when they vacationed on the island together. Varieties of *Jatropha* grew throughout south Florida; one of them, native to Key West, was known by locals as "the bellyache bush."

An appropriate name for any of the *Jatropha* species, which collectively were responsible for dozens of accidental poisonings every year. The tempting, candy-colored fruits were irresistible to children; the seeds within the fruits contained a purgative oil similar to the ricin found in castor beans.

As little as two seeds could produce symptoms of gastroenteritis within a few hours. The larger the quantity, the faster the onset and the more severe the effects. A large enough dose could prove fatal.

Crouching by the bush, Steve plucked a small yellow capsule of fruit from the nearest branch. With trembling fingers he tore it open, plucked three seeds from the cavities.

He raised them to his lips. Hesitated.

*You sure you want to do this, Stevie?*

The voice, strangely, was Jack's. But the thought was his own.

A ripple of tingling cold skittered up his forearms as if in answer. A new wave of the sedative kicking in.

Goddammit, he had to get that shit out of his system. Adrenaline wouldn't keep him going much longer.

Eyes closed, he thrust the seeds into his mouth.

They were tasteless, crunchy. He chewed briefly, swallowed, then picked another fruit and consumed its seeds as well. A total of six so far.

How many would it take to get quick action? If he overdid it, he would face a painful, writhing death. But if he was too cautious, he wouldn't feel the effects for hours. Hours he could hardly afford to waste, not with Jack undoubtedly hunting Kirstie at this moment, the Beretta hot in his hand.

He plucked a third fruit, ate the seeds.

Nine now. He'd heard of people dying from a dose of ten.

But other than a mild burning sensation at the back of the throat, he still felt fine.

Dammit to hell, this wasn't going to work. Maybe he'd misidentified the plant. This might be some harmless shrub that only looked like a physic-nut. In that case he could gorge himself on seeds without effect, until the damn sedative finally put him under.

He jerked another fruit free of the branch, began to pulp it in his fingers to find the seeds, then froze, listening.

From the south end of the island, a distant crack of sound, then another, and more.

Gunshots. Four in all.

Then, rising high and breathless in the night air, Kirstie's keening cry.

*"Stop it! Stop it, you son of a bitch!"*

Christ, Jack was killing her. Killing her right now.

"Hell with this." Steve threw aside the fruit and pushed himself to his feet.

He had to save her. Had to find the strength somehow. If the seeds wouldn't work, then he would fight off the sedative with sheer willpower. He could do it. He—

A sudden agonizing stomach cramp bent him double. Sparks of white glitter whirled before his eyes. They expanded, merged, bleaching his world to a spread of arctic snow.

The poison. Kicking in.

*Jesus. It hurts.*

He collapsed on his side, trembling violently, as pain clamped down harder on his guts and currents of nausea raced through him like fever chills.

*You ate too many of the damn things.* The groaning voice in his thoughts was nearly drowned out by the hum and sizzle that seemed to fill his skull. *You killed yourself, you asshole. And Kirstie, too.*

Somewhere far away, a fifth gunshot sounded. He barely heard it. The noise had no reality to him. Nothing had any reality but the spasms of agony knotting his bowels.

He twisted on his belly and vomited. Again. Again. His stomach emptied, and he was left rasping with dry heaves that shook his body.

"Oh, God," he whispered. "Oh, God. Oh, God. Oh, God."

Fire laced his throat. His heart pounded impossibly hard in his chest, each separate beat threatening to shake him apart. Sweat dripped from his face in a silent, steady rain.

"God. Oh, my God . . ."

Flies were already gathering at the foul-smelling puddle he had made. Weakly he crawled away from it, off the path into a patch of weeds, then buried his face in the dirt, tasting grit. For some immeasurable stretch of time he did not move again.

Gradually pain and sickness receded, leaving him with the limp, hollowed-out feeling of utter exhaustion.

*I think you're going to make it, old buddy.* The interior voice was still Jack's, the words accented with cold mockery. *Looks like you bought yourself a second chance.*

"Second chance . . ." Steve licked his lips. His tongue was sandpaper. "Yes, Jack. That's what I've got."

He lifted his head from the dirt and blinked, trying to clear his vision.

The world seemed murky. Had the poison damaged his eyesight somehow?

No, of course not. It was his glasses; he'd lost them in the fight with Jack. That was why he couldn't see.

*All right, then. How am I doing otherwise?*

Methodically he took inventory of his symptoms.

The numbness in his extremities was still present, but less obvious than before.

His limbs had lost their leaden heaviness.

He no longer had to fight a nagging impulse to shut his eyes and yield to sleep.

His thoughts seemed clear.

"It worked." A crooked smile ticked at the corner of his mouth. "Goddamn *worked*."

He had purged himself of the drug. He was clean.

Fighting light-headedness and a residue of nausea, he struggled to his knees. The effort was too much for him. He fell forward, panting.

For a bad moment he was sure he would be sick again. His stomach convulsed. But there was nothing left inside.

He lay unmoving, concentration focused on deepening each breath and slowing his hectic pulse.

When he felt ready, he tried again to stand.

This time he succeeded. His knees fluttered badly, and he had to grab a tree limb for support.

Holding tight to the branch, eyes shut, he waited for his strength to return while considering his next move.

He had to find Kirstie. That much was obvious. Track her down and take her to the boat. Either the motorboat at the dock or . . .

Or Jack's runabout.

His eyes flickered open with a thought.

He'd forgotten the runabout. It was camouflaged under fronds and sedges on the verge of the beach, only a short distance from this spot.

The most logical thing to do was to leave the island right now. Take the boat, speed to Islamorada.

Could he navigate the harbor waters without his glasses? Probably. He might nudge a few buoys along the way, but there would be few other obstacles this time of night.

Within twenty minutes he could be at the sheriff's station, reporting everything.

But if he did that, he would be abandoning his wife. Leaving her alone on Pelican Key with Jack.

He remembered her desperate shriek: *Stop it, you son of a bitch!*

Afterward, nothing except a final gunshot, some moments later.

The coup de grace? The bullet that had ended her life?

Or was she still alive, but a prisoner?

He pictured her, bleeding, helpless, Jack's toy. Not

hard to imagine the kind of games Jack would play with her.

If he went to the authorities, how much time would pass before they believed his story and agreed to send a patrol unit to the island? An hour? Longer?

He could not leave Kirstie for an hour. Not when she might be in agony, might be dying.

The boat would have to wait. He would find his wife first. Find her and save her life.

If she was not already dead.

The thought stabbed him, icicle-sharp. He blinked back a stinging eyewash of tears as he headed up the trail.

# 37

Thirty-one pages of documents had come over the fax line at the sheriff's station in Islamorada, to be produced as hard copy by an inkjet printer, then stapled together by a thoughtful deputy. A complete record of the Montclair Police Department's 1978 investigation into the death of Meredith Turner, preserved on forms filled out when Tamara Moore was still in grade school, forms typed on electric typewriters and doctored with correction fluid, forms that were artifacts of the pre-computer age.

The death investigation form was first, followed by a crime-scene log, press release, chronological record, victim and crime information form, suspect information form, multiple pages of signed statement forms, a master report information form, and the follow-up form that had closed the case. After that, a new sheaf of papers: autopsy protocols, lab reports, and miscellaneous crime-scene photos, sketches, and evidence-collection inventories.

Moore had scanned the file once, then had gone back to study the suspect information form and the signed statements. As she read, she smoothed the flimsy fax paper with her hand.

"Something interesting here, Peter," she said without looking up.

Lovejoy, distracted and half asleep, was fumbling with the controls of a Mr. Coffee machine. "Mmm?"

"Jack was a suspect."

That got his attention. "In the Turner case?"

"Right."

He stared at her across twenty feet of checkered linoleum. They were alone together in the station's squad room, surrounded by schoolroom trappings: front desk, fluorescent ceiling panels, comical or inspirational posters tacked to cinder-block walls. Moore sat at the desk like a teacher; Lovejoy was a misbehaving student being held after class.

The rest of the station was largely deserted now, at two A.M. In the lobby, a sergeant biding time until retirement manned the night-watch desk; nearby, in a tiny alcove labeled Communications, a sleepy deputy tapped at the keyboard of a computer terminal; in one of the holding cells at the rear of the building, a sun-blistered transient snored on a steel bench. Somewhere a dog was barking, and no one seemed to care.

"So what does it say?" Lovejoy asked finally. The coffee machine began to gurgle.

"Meredith suffered a skull fracture and subdural hematoma. Cause of death was drowning; her lungs were filled with chlorinated water that matched a sample from the swimming pool. The head injury was consistent with a diving accident. She could have struck her head on the edge of the diving board itself or on the bottom of the pool."

"Except . . . ?"

"Except the coroner's investigator found no blood or tissue on the diving board, and given the height of the board and the depth of the pool, she probably couldn't have hit bottom, at least not with any force."

"It's been my observation that people don't always use the board. They dive off the side of the pool, into the shallow end. In some instances they've been known to crack their skulls."

"But Meredith was an experienced diver, a lifeguard. Not the type to make that kind of mistake."

"Unless she was drunk, stoned, something like that."

"Serology tests all came back negative."

"All right. Let's concede for the sake of discussion that her death was something other than an accident. How does Jack fit in?"

"Meredith's friends told detectives that Jack had been openly hostile toward her for years, and that Meredith was afraid of him."

The last of the coffee dribbled into the pot. Lovejoy poured two cups. "But apparently the D.A. didn't file charges, or they would have shown up on Jack's rap sheet."

"That's because Jack had an alibi." She consulted the sixth page of the statement form. "On the evening of Meredith's death, he took a long car ride with a friend. Steven Gardner."

"Steve . . ."

Moore nodded. "The postcard. 'Jack and Steve and I took the boat out yesterday.' Same Steve, I'll bet."

"Presumably, yes. The skinny kid with the glasses." Lovejoy carried the coffee to Moore, a boy bringing his teacher an apple. "Why wouldn't the police see through a ruse like that? One friend lying to protect another. Hardly an unusual occurrence."

"According to the report, Steve Gardner had a good reputation in town. A real straight arrow. And he stuck to his story pretty convincingly. Besides, the coroner's office wasn't certain of foul play. Meredith could have slipped and fallen into the shallow end—or hit her head on the diving board without leaving any obvious mark—or suffered a seizure in the water and struck the side of the pool while thrashing around. A hundred possibilities."

"And of course, the authorities wanted the case closed." Lovejoy sipped his coffee. "Looks bad for a town—one kid killing another, friend covering up. Better if it was an accident. Neater that way."

"You're a cynical man, Peter."

"Just a bureaucrat at heart. I know how these things work. Getting to the truth tends to be seen as less important than sweeping a messy situation under the proverbial rug."

Moore pushed her chair away from the desk. "So what do we do now?"

"It seems to me it would be advisable to locate Steve Gardner and ask him a few probing questions."

"At two A.M.?"

"Sometimes that's when you get the best answers."

A rap on the door frame. The sleepy deputy was there.

" 'Scuse me, folks. Sergeant Banks'd like to see you."

Moore stood. "He say why?"

Yawn and shrug. "Something turned up on patrol."

The desk sergeant, Banks, was gray-haired, red-faced, and badly overweight. His uniform sagged in some places and clung to him skintight in others. Deep half moons of sweat had formed permanent discolorations under his arms.

He refused to talk fast. Leaning back in his chair, lording over the lobby desk, he seemed to savor each syllable as it passed, slow and sweet as molasses, through his lips.

"There's this condemned restaurant over on Blackwood Drive, west of Route One. Patrol unit checks it out nearly every night. Rousting transients, y'know."

He paused to clean his teeth with a ragged thumbnail. Moore had to step down hard on an urge to grab the man and shake the information out of him.

"So tonight Parker and Ross are cruising the area, and when they go around back of this place, what do you suppose they find?"

"A Pontiac Sunbird," Lovejoy whispered, then caught himself making a definitive statement and added reflexively, "in all probability."

Banks cocked an eyebrow. "Aw, now you've gone and spoiled my story."

"Sergeant"—Moore kept her tone cool and professional, fighting back a rush of excitement—"did the patrol unit give you a description of the car? Year, color, license plate?"

"No plates. They're gone. Vehicle identification number's missing, too. Car's pretty well junked. Not stripped, exactly, Parker says. More like . . . trashed."

"What color is it?"

"White exterior, blue interior. It's a four-door hardtop, relatively new. Could be a '92."

"That may quite possibly be the vehicle we're looking for," Lovejoy said.

Banks nodded heavily, multiplying his chins. "I know."

"Jack trashed the car so it would pass for an old wreck." Moore was thinking fast, her mind remarkably clear despite long hours without sleep. "Took the tags so we couldn't link it with the airport theft."

"Conceivably. On the other hand, the possibility exists that this is a different Sunbird altogether." Lovejoy turned to Banks. "Was that location checked last night?"

"Doubtful. Darby and Brint work patrol on the Thursday P.M. watch, and those two sumbitches never do jack. Oh, they're *supposed* to poke around behind the restaurant, sure, but more'n likely they were sawing lumber in their car somewhere out on Industrial Drive."

"How about the night before?"

"No Sunbird then. I make the rounds myself on Wednesdays."

"Time frame is right," Moore said.

Lovejoy pursed his lips. "It's generally inadvisable to jump to conclusions. We have no proof that this is the car from airport parking or, even if it is, that Jack was the one who lifted it."

"Well"—impatience struggled with Moore's frayed self-control—"let's quit yakking and find out. We need to contact Miami, get a search team down here, go over that damn car with a microscope and tweezers."

"My recommendation also." Lovejoy picked up the desk phone, then remembered courtesy. "Excuse me, Sergeant. Mind if I make a call?"

Banks moved his big shoulders. "At your service. Tell you true, though . . . you people sure do move fast."

# 38

The swamp was hot and fetid, choked with clouds of mosquitoes, the pests swarming thicker here than in any other part of the island. Kirstie had lost the strength even to wave them off. They battened greedily on her, leaving a rash of bumps on every inch of exposed skin. When she brushed sweat from her face, her fingers came away dabbed with blood.

The bites didn't matter. The heat and humidity, the sweat trickling from her hair, the aching exhaustion in every muscle of her body—none of that mattered, either. Nothing mattered except planting one foot in front of the other, pushing herself remorselessly forward, crossing the endless yards of the boardwalk plank by plank, and arriving, finally, at the northern tip of Pelican Key. Then she would be at the cove, where maybe—just maybe—she would find the runabout.

Unless Jack or Steve found her first.

This boardwalk scared her. It was narrow and crooked and dark, and it could so very easily be a death trap. While making her way along it, she was as badly unprotected as she'd been on the beach. And an ambush would be easy in the swamp—the swamp, with its countless hiding places, its croak and buzz of ambient noise to mask more furtive sounds, its canopy of waxen leaves that eclipsed the stars and hung the trees in shadows.

She had never been here at night. The labyrinth of contorted mangroves and crisscrossing channels was creepy enough by day. Darkness made it a nightmare, some fevered blend of known and imagined terrors.

Cottonmouths glided through the opaque, tannin-stained water under her feet. Corn snakes and rat snakes writhed among the fantastically gnarled roots and branches of the mangrove thickets. The foul odor of hydrogen sulfide, signature of decay, hovered over the place like an evil, miasmic cloud. Somewhere a heron cried; to her left, a clump of marsh grass stirred with unseen activity; behind her, wood creaked in a low, regular rhythm, the footsteps of a restless ghost treading the boards. . . .

She froze.

Footsteps.

Someone else was on the boardwalk. Whether it was Jack or Steve was unimportant. Both were killers now.

Was one of them shadowing her? Doubtful; the tread was heavy and quick, with no suggestion of stealth. It was the walk of a man in a hurry.

Most likely he didn't even know how near she was. If she could hide till he passed by . . .

The footsteps quickened, closing in.

She ducked under the low railing and silently lowered herself into the murk, then eased beneath the boardwalk. The water, only slightly less saline than the ocean, was warm and pungent. Her tank top and shorts, instantly soaked through, clung to her skin in wrinkled patches.

It was difficult to judge the swamp's depth. The tide was not yet in, the red mangroves' arching prop roots only partially submerged. Her feet kicked, searching for the muddy bottom, then sank into spongy ooze nearly up to the ankles.

Her collarbone was at the waterline. The underside of the boardwalk loomed perhaps ten inches above her head. Not much clearance, but more than there would be at high tide.

She waited.

The footsteps were closer now. Touching the boardwalk, she could feel vibrations through the planks.

How near was he? Thirty feet? Twenty?

The creaks became solid thumps. Loosened dirt fell from between the planks, showering her in a gritty rain.

He was directly overhead.

She willed him to keep going, pass her by.

He stopped.

The moan welling in her throat would be fatal if released. She bit down hard and held it in.

What the hell had he stopped for? There was no way he could know she was hiding here. No possible way.

A pale flicker of luminescence above her. The wavering beam of a flashlight. It swept over the water near the boardwalk, then stopped, a small floating object pinned its glare.

One of her sandals.

She drew a quick, silent gasp.

The sandal must have slipped free when she entered the water. Bobbing on the surface, it pointed out her hiding place like a traitorous hand.

*He's on to me. Oh, God, he knows I'm here.*

Abruptly the flashlight swung downward, shining on the boardwalk itself, the beam's splintered rays fanning through the gaps between the planks.

Could he see her through the cracks? She didn't think so.

Her teeth wanted badly to chatter. She ground her jaws.

The light inched toward her, arriving in successive waves of vertical bands, crawling over her face, her hair, then slowly moved on.

He hadn't seen her. She might be okay, then. If he decided to keep walking—

*Thunder.*

A yard from her head, the planks exploded in a hail of splintered wood.

Shock and terror nearly tore a scream from her lips. With a ragged remnant of self-control she swallowed it.

A gunshot. That was what the noise had been. He had the gun—must be Steve, then—and he'd fired directly at the boardwalk, hoping to either kill her with a lucky hit or drive her into the open.

Over the shrilling clamor in her ears, she faintly heard the creak-thump of another footstep.

Above her. Directly above.

Heedless of noise—*his* ears must be ringing, too—she flung herself backward, dog-paddling wildly.

*Thunder.*

A second bullet. Another yard of the boardwalk, shredded. Debris showered her. The blue muzzle flash lighted the swamp like a burst of fireworks.

She refused to be panicked into committing a suicidal error. What she needed was cover. Cover that would allow her to swim to a new hiding place without being seen.

Scanning the black water, she saw a thicket of red mangroves growing adjacent to the boardwalk perhaps twenty feet away.

Overhead, creak-thump.

Again he was above her, tracking her by luck or instinct.

She executed a clumsy breast stroke, using her arms only, afraid to kick because the churning water might draw his aim. She swam for the trees.

Behind her, *thunder*.

A third gunshot. Spray of splinters and nails. Was he planning to obliterate the entire boardwalk three feet at a time?

She kept swimming. The mangroves glided alongside her. Their exposed roots glistened in the patchy starlight, a cage of polished wicker. She kept the roots between her and the flashlight's glow as she circled around the mangrove cluster and took cover behind the trees.

From this position she couldn't see the boardwalk, couldn't know if Steve had glimpsed her escape. She could only wait for the next shot, and the next.

Nothing.

The gun was silent.

The flashlight beam swept slowly over the swamp, first on the far side, then nearer to her. She saw its silvery trail in the water, gleaming like a long finger of moonlight.

The dense mesh of roots hid her from the beam even when it prowled over the mangroves. Still, the funnel of light hesitated, as if studying the trees.

"Kirstie . . . !"

Jack's voice—not Steve's—raised in a mocking shout.

What was *he* doing with the gun? Had Steve given it to him? Or were there two guns somehow?

"I know you're hiding there. No other place for you to be."

The beam glided across the water near the trees, silent and supple as a snake.

"You can't stay hidden for long, darling. I can see in the dark. Got my flashlight back; picked it up on the trail while I was heading for the cove. Not hard to guess that you'd be on your way over there. I'm afraid your game plan has been entirely too predictable." His voice lilted, became laughter. "Come on out now. *Ollee-ollee-en-free . . . !*"

The childhood call of hide-'n'-seek. Did he expect her to obey it?

The flashlight bobbed, trembled. A soft splash.

The angle of the beam was suddenly flatter, its point of origin near her eye level.

Rippling-water sounds.

Oh, hell.

Jack had left the boardwalk. He was coming after her. Sloshing through the water toward the trees.

At her back was a narrow channel unspooling like a ribbon between walls of mangrove roots. She took it, paddling furiously, retreating deeper into the swamp.

Her beating legs and arms stirred up new eruptions of mosquitoes. Their frenzied whines pursued her like the screams of angry ghosts.

Steve was on his way to the dock at the south end of the island when three gunshots sounded from the north.

He turned back, heading up the trail at a run. From somewhere ahead rose Jack's voice, faint but audible.

*"Kirstie . . . ! I know you're hiding there. . . ."*

Other words, softer, unintelligible.

Quick tears misted his eyes.

She was *alive*.

Alive and hiding, apparently. Jack seemed confident enough of catching her.

But he hadn't succeeded yet.

At the boardwalk Steve paused to slip off his Nikes. He knotted the laces to his belt, letting the shoes swing at his hip, then crept onto the planks, hunched low to make a smaller target. Barefoot, he made almost no sound as he proceeded deep into the belly of the swamp.

The planks disappeared abruptly. Giant holes in the walkway gaped at him like mouths, rimmed with glistening fangs of splintered wood.

What the hell had happened here?

No time to think about it. In the trees, a yellowish flicker.

Robbed of his glasses, he saw it only as a tremulous blur, a blob of color shivering like a raindrop on a windowpane. He identified it anyway. Jack's flashlight.

The bastard was hunting her in the black swamp water, looking for a clean shot.

With the Beretta, the flash, and the knife, Jack enjoyed a triple advantage over either of his adversaries. Steve could think of only one possible point in his own favor.

*He doesn't know I'm here.*

A small consolation, but it was all he had.

Soundlessly he swung down off the boardwalk, into the inky water, and joined in the chase.

# 39

Dead end.

Kirstie had retreated at least thirty yards into the swamp before realizing that the creek had narrowed to the width of a sidewalk. Ahead, it vanished entirely in a drift of close-packed turtle grass bordered by a wall of trees.

She turned, intending to double back. No chance. Jack's flashlight beam crept out of the gloom fifty feet away.

He hadn't seen her yet. The channel was crooked, overhung with gnarled branches; a bend in the creek blocked her from his view.

Instinct moved her faster than conscious thought. Turning toward the nearest mangrove thicket, she grabbed hold of the dense skein of prop roots and hoisted herself out of the water.

The roots gave way to a confusion of intertwined branches, closely stitched. Thick leaves with the texture of leather and the gloss of wax hung in dense array, layers of green tapestry barring her path. Frantically her hands probed the branches in search of an opening wide enough to wriggle through. There was none. No space between the trees, either; not only their roots and branches but even their trunks were interlaced in a lunatic jumble.

*No way through.* The words beat like fists in her brain. *No way through.*

She glanced behind her. Jack was rounding the bend, the flashlight's beam slowly swinging in her direction.

*No way through.*

All right, then. She wouldn't go through. She would go over. Over the top.

The closest tree wasn't tall, no more than fifteen feet high. She climbed it, feet and hands moving from branch to branch with desperate speed, dislodging dozens of long tubular seedlings. They dropped into the water, their soft splashes sure to draw Jack's attention at any moment.

*Faster. Faster.*

She reached the crown and started down on the opposite side. Handhold, foothold, handhold, foothold. *Like climbing on the monkey bars,* she thought irrelevantly. In some strange way she had become a child again, playing in the summer night.

Jack must feel the tug of similar memories. She remembered his mocking call: *Ollee-ollee-en-free.*

Kids at play—was that all this was?

She half clambered, half slid down the mangrove's mossy roots, into the black water, and found herself in a new creek running parallel to the one she had left.

Jack's flashlight still searched the other channel. He didn't know where she had gone. Thank God.

With gentle strokes she swam along the waterway. The flashlight's glow receded. She advanced into a deepening darkness.

Black mangrove trees began to appear along the channel, encroaching on territory colonized by red mangroves years before. Steve had explained it all to her: how the red mangroves built soil out of shells, sand, and mud captured by their roots, blending it with the compost of their own rotted leaves. When the new land was firmly established, the black mangrove moved in and slowly wrested possession of it from the red.

All very interesting, and yesterday she would have expressed the appropriate wonderment at the adaptability of nature in the appropriate respectful tone, the kind of sentiment her colleagues at the PBS affiliate would understand.

Now she hated the swamp. She saw nothing in it worth preserving. The swamp was evil-smelling black water and hunched, spidery trees and pools of sucking mud. The swamp was mosquitoes and sand flies and unseen slippery things that brushed past her in the murk, briefly nuzzling her bare legs. The swamp was everything hostile to human life, and human life—her own life—was all she cared about right now; and as for what her coworkers might say about that particular observation while they sipped their mineral water and sliced their Brie and tuned in *MacNeil-Lehrer*—well, she simply didn't give a shit.

*Drain it,* she thought with a kind of savage hysteria. *Just drain the goddamn thing and pour concrete and put up condos. Condos and a shopping center, and to hell with the ecosystem.*

She realized she was losing control. Not terribly surprising; she was neck-deep in slime, hemmed in by contorted caricatures of trees, pursued by a killer, and lost. Yes, lost. The maze of zigzag channels had left her hopelessly disoriented. She no longer had any clue where the boardwalk was or how to find dry land.

Well, maybe Jack was lost, too. Maybe she could find her way out of here and leave him wandering in the swamp till the mosquitoes sucked him dry.

Gazing over her shoulder, she saw no hint of the flashlight. No sign of movement—

*There.*

Spreading ripples in the water. A low, dark form perhaps a hundred feet away, moving toward her.

An alligator? Steve had said there were none on the island. But suppose he'd been wrong.

Didn't look like a 'gator, though. It looked . . .

Human.

A man's head and upper body. Ripples radiating from his arms as they cut the water in quick scissor-like strokes.

Was it Jack, his flashlight off? Or Steve?

She didn't know or care. What mattered was only to get away, lose her pursuer down some side channel.

She swam faster, each jerk of her arms tearing a new ache out of muscles still sore from her ordeal in the radio room.

Ahead, the channel forked into two narrower passageways. Both routes receded into blackness. She went to her right.

A backward glance eased her tension slightly. Her pursuer was no longer visible. For the moment she had outpaced him, and he would have no way to know which route she'd taken at the point where the channel divided.

The creek led her past stands of dead mangroves, the ravaged victims of some recent fire perhaps sparked by a lightning strike. Their jungles of roots remained intact, forming the banks of the waterway, but their trunks were rotting, the branches leafless and splintered.

She swam on. The creek widened, deepening. Her toes tried to touch bottom, couldn't.

Around her, more dead trees. Fire had gutted this entire pocket of the swamp. Even here, though, there was life. Orb weavers had webbed the sagging branches in gossamer; hermit crabs scuttled busily among the roots. In the water, tiny mangrove seedlings already had sprouted, promising renewal.

Though she had no love of spiders, crabs, or mangroves, life's refusal to accept defeat heartened her. If the smallest living things went on fighting for survival against every obstacle, she could do no less.

A noble thought, rich with inspiration, but she had no time to savor it.

The creek had dead-ended.

A breath of angry sibilance: *"Shit."*

She'd blundered down another blind alley. The wide, deep pool was hemmed in on almost every side by withered and toppled mangroves, the only opening the narrow passageway she'd taken a minute earlier.

Double back? Or wait here and hope her pursuer had gone the wrong way?

Neither.

He was coming.

She saw the glitter of ripples that announced his approach.

No way to get past him. And no time to climb through the trees and escape as she had before.

Motionless in the water, she was less easy to spot than he was. But he would see her soon enough.

She sank lower, the waterline rising to her chin.

From the far end of the pool, a whisper: "Kirstie?"

She breathed through gritted teeth.

"It's me, Steve. I want to help you."

Christ, the same line he used before. Did he think she was enough of an idiot to fall for it twice?

"If you're here, answer me. Please."

*Fat chance, you son of a bitch.*

She prayed for him to turn and leave, continue his search in the other channel.

"Kirstie . . . ?"

He swam closer. Hell, he would be right on top of her in a minute. Couldn't help but see her then.

Unless . . .

She drew a deep, slow breath, filling her lungs, then closed her eyes and gradually lowered her head beneath the surface.

Submerged, she was invisible. The turgid water, the color of dark tea, would conceal her as completely as a bath of ink.

The only question was how long she could stay under.

She waited, eyes squeezed shut, fighting the incipient panic prompted by the cutoff of breathing. Bubbles of air escaped her pursed lips and rose past her face to pucker the surface of the swamp. She could only hope Steve wouldn't notice.

Seconds ticked past. She counted heartbeats, gave up after fifty.

There was no way to know if he was still nearby. She simply had to stay down as long as possible, then pray he would be gone when she finally surfaced.

Faintly she was conscious of a burning sensation in her chest. Her lungs were beginning to cry out for oxygen.

She ignored the warning, concentrated on staying calm. It was easier than she had expected. The warm salt water was the amniotic fluid of a second womb; suspended in it, she was an unborn child again.

An unborn child . . . with no umbilical cord.

The distress signals broadcast by her body became more urgent. Her extremities tingled. Her head pounded. She pictured her face turning blue, eyes bulging behind closed lids.

*Better surface.*

*But what if he's still here?*

She could hold out a little longer. She was sure of it.

Arms folded, she hugged herself. No more air bubbles dribbled from her mouth. Her lungs were empty.

Irrelevant images began popping on and off in her mind like flashcubes. A birthday party, the children's laughing mouths smeared with cake frosting. A clumsy kiss in a grade-school stairwell. Bleeding knees, scraped in a rough fall on a gravel path. The green campus of Amherst College. A golden retriever named Lancelot plunging into a field of summer dandelions. Steve, stiff in his tuxedo, guiding his bride's hand as she cut the wedding cake.

Random memories, fragments of her life. She wondered why she so often visualized herself as viewed from a distance in those scenes, as if she had not lived her life at all, but had merely observed a story unfolding.

Lungs bursting now. Fire in her throat. Hands and feet numb. Freight-train roaring in her ears.

Oddly she no longer felt the desperate need to relieve these symptoms. Though her body was starving for oxygen, her mind seemed curiously detached, her thoughts drifting, drifting. . . .

*No. Snap out of it. And get oxygen—now.*

She surfaced. Instantly her unreal calm was shredded as breath flooded her lungs. Shaking all over, fighting waves of light-headedness, she swallowed great gulps of air. The fire in her chest died down to embers, then to ashes. Her fingers and toes returned to life.

Only when she'd filled her lungs for the third time did she remember Steve. Dizzily she scanned the area.

He was gone.

She'd outlasted him. And nearly outlasted herself.

Jack paused, listening.

From a parallel channel, soft noises had risen a moment earlier: a muffled splash, an almost inaudible whisper. Sounds so faint he was hardly sure he'd heard them at all.

It made no sense anyway. Why would Kirstie whisper? She was alone.

Unless Steve was with her, had found her somehow.

Impossible. Steve was unconscious. He had to be.

Well, perhaps there had been no whisper. Perhaps he'd misinterpreted the sigh of the wind or the buzz of an insect.

One way or the other, he would find out.

He turned back, hunting for a passageway to the parallel creek. Yards of muddy water glided past, lined with misshapen trees. Somewhere a barred owl released a feline screech, its harsh cry scraping the night, fingernails on a blackboard.

Jack supposed most people would hate the swamp, would recoil from this place as if from a stinking carcass. Rot and mire, shadows and mist—nothing beautiful here.

But he felt a peculiar kinship with the swamp. Its comforting darkness concealed secretive, predatory things, hungry things that fed on weakness, things not unlike himself.

The swamp's natural predators had eyes that saw in the dark. He had a flashlight. They had fangs. He had a knife, a gun.

How many rounds left now? Six, he calculated.

It would take only one shot to stop Kirstie's heart.

Only one.

Kirstie pedaled water, catching her breath and clearing her thoughts.

Having failed to find her here, Steve must be retracing the route he'd taken, intending to explore the other branch of the channel. But at any moment he might return. She had to move on.

Still, returning the way she had come was too risky. Suppose she ran into him in the dark.

There was another option. The dead mangroves were largely stripped of branches; she could muscle her way between the trunks easily enough.

Briskly she swam for the nearest thicket of trees. Their roots, grayish-white and slimed with algae, broke the waterline in a jumble of knots and creases, like the folded gray matter of the brain. Topping the mound, a copse of fire-blasted trees sketched a tracery of coal-black lines against the sky.

At the skirt of roots she paused, catching her breath. She heard no sound to signal Steve's reappearance. No sound at all except the ambient croak and hiss that formed the swamp's perpetual background noise.

It occurred to her, for no particular reason, that this was one hell of a way to spend her summer vacation.

The thought made her smile. The upward curl of her lips felt shockingly strange, an unnatural action.

There were so many things she'd taken for granted. Smiles. Laughter. Clean clothes. Shelter and food. Physical safety—even with all the craziness in the news, she had rarely felt endangered.

Now all of that was gone, and she was no more than an animal, hunted in the wild, struggling desperately for survival.

She shook free of those thoughts. Later she would muse on what she'd lost and what she'd learned. Later.

Grunting with strain, she grabbed hold of a thick root, hauled herself partway up, then found a foothold and reached higher. Her right hand closed over another, larger root. . . .

It came alive in her grasp.

Her next split second of awareness was a blur of fragmentary images: the shuddering, convulsive movement of something long and black and grotesquely twisted; a smear of pinkish-white describing a looping trajectory toward her right arm.

Her mind had time to form one word: *snake.*

Then—pain.

A shock wave of glassy, wrenching pain in her forearm just below the elbow.

Her fingers splayed. She let go of the snake and slid a foot lower on the mass of roots. Somewhere a siren started wailing, its cry high and ululant, ripping the night air.

Thrashing wildly, the snake whipsawed its head and bit again, fangs drilling into the meat of her right shoulder.

The siren climbed in pitch, whooping breathlessly.

Another roiling twist of its body, and the snake clamped down on the tender skin above her left breast.

She threw back her head, dazzled by pain. The siren, oddly, had taken on the quality of a human voice, or nearly human, a voice shrilling with the outraged, plaintive terror of a child.

*"Get it off me, get it off me, get it off!"*

Its fangs were twin syringes sinking deep. She beat at the long writhing body with her fists. The snake lashed backward, and in a frozen instant she saw it clearly: the broad, flat head, the lidless eyes bisected by vertical pupils, the mouth stretched wide to expose shining fangs and surreal pinkish-white lips.

*White mouth.* The thought floated like a bubble just at the level of consciousness. *It has a white mouth.*

Then the bubble popped, the idea was lost, as the snake lunged again.

She dodged it. Her sudden sideways movement sent her tumbling backward into the water with a splash.

It showed its fangs once more, challenging her, then slowly unpacked itself from the jungle of roots where it had lain in ambush. Coil by coil its ponderous, impossibly long body unkinked, while its head nosed languidly toward the water.

She watched, numb with trauma, wondering blankly if it meant to come after her and finish the job.

Finally the snake's full extension was presented to her like an unrolled carpet. How long was the goddamned thing? Five feet? No, six. Thick, too—not ropelike—an undulating cylinder of muscle, nearly as large in diameter as her lower leg.

The snake slipped into the water, lung inflated, head and neck lifted above the surface. For an eerie moment it seemed to regard her out of one cool, unwinking eye.

Then it glided off into the murk. She followed it with her gaze until it had merged with black water and vaporous air, like some evil spirit of the swamp that had briefly materialized out of mud and rot and miasma, only to surrender its form and return, ghostlike, to its essence.

In the near distance, violent splashing.

Turning, she saw a faint yellowish glow.

Jack's flashlight.

She remembered the siren's wail that had split the night.

No siren, of course. Screams. Her own voice raised in cries of blind panic. She'd given away her position without even knowing it.

And now Jack was coming for her. Coming fast.

He was swimming like a maniac, chopping the water with wild, vigorous strokes. Already his flashlight's beam tickled the branches of dead mangroves at the other end of the channel.

She clawed at the roots, trying again to find a handhold, but her fingers wouldn't work right—they were spastic and uncoordinated, her muscles still fluttering with the aftereffects of trauma—the roots kept slipping from her grasp.

Light dazzled her.

Turning her head, she looked blinking into a yellow glare.

" 'Evening, Mrs. Gardner!" Jack called cheerfully. "Funny meeting you here."

He was wading in the shallower part of the creek, flashlight in one hand, gun in the other. Black water retreated from him in lazy ripples as he took a final step toward her.

Then slowly he lifted the gun, taking aim.

Kirstie waited, breath stopped. No way out for her, not now. She wondered how the bullet would feel as it chewed through muscle and bone.

"Count of three, sweetheart!" He was laughing. "One! *Two*!"

The flashlight jerked sideways.

A splash—Jack facedown in the water—a muffled crack as the gun discharged into the muddy bottom, launching a geyser of sediment.

In the moment before he'd meant to shoot her, he'd lost his balance somehow. Slipped on the wet mud, maybe. Or had the snake gotten him, too?

She didn't know, couldn't guess. Some kind of miracle had taken place, and she was in no position to argue with it.

This time her hands found purchase in the roots. She hauled herself out of the water.

Ducking under the mangroves' leafless branches, she kicked a deadfall of rotted timber out of her way and plunged blindly into the night.

# 40

For a confused moment Jack had no idea what was happening.

He'd been prepared to fire when a sudden impact from behind had hurled him headfirst into the water.

The gun had punched a hole in the creek's thick sediment and gone off. Recoil and the spray of mud and water kicked up by the shot had shocked him into releasing both pistol and flashlight.

Now he groped for the Beretta, half buried in the mire.

*Slam.*

Another collision, and he was shoved sideways, out of reach of the gun.

He spun around, twisting free of whatever shapeless thing was trying to get him in its grasp, then surfaced, gasping.

A yard away, Steve surfaced also.

Wet hair was plastered to his forehead. His eyes squinted comically to compensate for the loss of his glasses. In his hand was the Beretta, caked with black muck.

The two men faced each other, hip-deep in the shallows.

"Goddamn," Jack breathed. "Thought you'd be out of action by now."

Steve shook his head. "I'm still in the game."

Jack glanced toward the thicket of mangroves where Kirstie had been cornered. She was gone.

"Well, congratulations, Stevie. Looks like you rescued your precious wife from certain doom. I wouldn't have missed her at that range."

"I know."

"So what now? You plan to shoot me?"

"Yes."

"Just like that? In cold blood?" He raised both arms, displaying his empty hands. "When I'm no threat to you?"

"You're always a threat, Jack. To me and Kirstie and everybody else you come in contact with. Remember that coral snake we found in the bathtub of the plantation house when we were teenagers? It was dead, but it could still bite. That's you. You never give up."

"Tough talk." Jack forced a smile. "But you won't shoot me. You can't. Not like this. In a fight, sure; you nearly nailed me back at the house. But now that I'm disarmed and willing to surrender, you're not going to gun me down. Your conscience won't let you."

"Wrong, Jack," Steve whispered, and looking into his eyes, Jack was suddenly cold, chilled by what he saw there, the pitiless intensity of that gaze. "My conscience won't allow a thing like you to live."

The Beretta steadied, its muzzle focusing like a lidless eye on Jack's chest from three feet away.

Jack gazed into that small black hole and saw eternity.

*So this is it,* he thought numbly. *Well, fuck it. I've had my fun.*

Steve's finger flexed, squeezing the trigger.

A dull, muffled click.

Misfire.

Jack allowed himself no time to think or feel. Instinct drove him.

He snapped his leg out, pistoned a kick at Steve's midsection, felt a thud of solid contact. Steve doubled over, and the gun sailed free, vanishing with a splash.

Instantly the Swiss Army knife was in Jack's hand, spear blade extracted with a flick of his thumbnail.

*Now. Go for the kill.*

With a ululant war whoop, the cry of a predatory animal, he flung himself on Steve and thrust the blade between his ribs.

Steve stretched his mouth in the shape of a scream. Only blood came out. It stained the water in coiling purplish swirls.

Jack wrenched the knife free and stabbed again, sticking Steve in the abdomen, then jerked the blade clockwise, turning it like a screwdriver.

"You son of a *bitch,*" Jack hissed. "Why'd you make me kill you, you stupid son of a bitch?" He rammed the knife in deeper, burying it up to the handle. "We could have been partners if you hadn't fucked it up!"

Dimly he was aware of an acid burn in his eyes, which might have been tears.

Steve tried once more to release the scream caught inside him. Racking convulsions choked it off.

Jack hung on to the knife, riding Steve in the choppy water as his body bucked and thrashed.

Then abruptly Steve went limp, breath sighing out of him.

Jack thought of Anastasia dying in the radio room just a few hours ago. It seemed strange that this man he had known, this man who had been the best friend of his adolescence, should die no differently from a dog.

He waited, but there was no further movement, no hint of life.

Panting hard, coughing up salt water, Jack dragged Steve's body onto a mound of mangrove roots and deposited it there like a sack of trash.

His hands closed over the knife handle. He pulled, trying to work the knife loose. The job was unexpectedly difficult. For some reason his strength seemed to have left him, and the burn in his eyes was more painful than before.

In fits and starts the blade inched free. Jack dipped it in the swamp water, then washed his bloody hands.

"Hell, Stevie." The croak of his own voice surprised him. "You asshole. You stupid fuck. I didn't really want to. You made me. I had no choice. You stupid, stupid bastard."

He had never experienced remorse over the other lives he'd taken. Grief and regret were weaknesses. Empathy, personal feelings of any kind toward another human being—a crippling handicap.

Steve, though . . . Good old Stevie . . .

*Quit it. Cut it out.*

There was no point in blaming himself. Steve could have lived if he hadn't been so obsessively concerned about his wife. He'd let love warp his judgment, jeopardize his own safety. Now he was dead, and soon Kirstie would join him. His quixotic self-sacrifice had accomplished nothing.

Jack squared his shoulders, blinked away the moisture in his eyes.

Strength, cunning, and viciousness ruled this world. Love and loyalty purchased only death. Steve should have learned that lesson. Instead he'd clung to his comforting delusions, his ridiculous romantic self-aggrandizement, and finally paid for his stupidity with his life, as he'd deserved.

Yes. As he had deserved.

Reassured, his personal code reconfirmed, Jack turned his back on the cat's-cradle webbing of the mangroves' stiltlike roots and the motionless figure lying there.

Submerging, he recovered the Beretta, then manually retracted the slide. The chamber was clogged with thick, gluey mud; an empty shell casing was lodged inside.

Jack shook his head slowly, a thin smile printed on his lips. Such a little thing, the casing of an expended round, and yet it had saved his life—and ended Steve's.

Easy enough to see why the gun had misfired. The Beretta had been mired in mud when it accidentally discharged. Recoil had opened the breech, and instantly mud had flooded the chamber, preventing ejection of the shell case. While the casing was still in place, another round could not be fed into the chamber, and no shot could be fired.

Jack dug out the shell case and, after a moment's hesitation, pocketed it; an ounce of metal that had saved his life ought to serve nicely as a good luck charm.

With a fingernail he scraped the chamber, then closed the breech and cocked the gun.

There was nothing else to salvage. The flashlight was useless now, its internal parts corroded by water, the bulb dead. Well, he could do without it. Dawn was near.

He waded in the direction of the boardwalk, intending to find Kirstie and finish his night's work.

At a bend in the channel he looked back. Steve was

a dark, unmoving shape almost lost amid the meshwork of shadows and the snarled net of roots.

"So long, old buddy," Jack whispered.

Then he turned away, vaguely annoyed with himself for this last nostalgic indulgence, and moved on, becoming one with the dark.

# 41

Kirstie had almost given up hope of escaping from the swamp. The maze of waterways was bewildering, incomprehensible. She might be swimming in circles for all she knew. The boardwalk had vanished; perhaps it had never existed. Perhaps all this was a dream, a fever dream; or perhaps she was dead already—killed by Steve on the beach or by Jack in the swamp—dead and sentenced to an endless prison term in hell.

She swam on, aimlessly, hopelessly, limbs flailing in ragged, uncoördinated strokes that churned up a foamy wake.

God, there *had* to be a way out of here. The swamp wasn't even big; swimming in a straight-line path, she could traverse it in a few minutes. But there were no straight lines here. Every channel was insanely contorted, bent and folded and turned back on itself, impossible to navigate.

*I'll die here,* she thought with a thrill of gooseflesh. *I'll die, and no one will ever find my body. And the mangroves will build new root systems over my bones.*

She could picture it—a skeleton woven into the web of roots—a skeleton with her face.

*Don't.*

With a shudder she rejected the image. No point in thinking like that. Defeatism was wrong—perversely ungrateful, in fact—after the inexplicable miracle that had saved her life only a short time ago.

She kept going. The water seemed thicker now, heavily clouded with silt. Beating her way through it was like swimming in mud.

Her right arm curved forward in another breaststroke, and her fingers sank into something soft and oozy. A bank of wet clay.

Another dead end? No. Not this time.

She let out a sound midway between a sigh and a chuckle, a sound expressive of all the relief she had ever felt.

She'd made it. She'd reached the shallows at the border of the swamp. Dry land ahead.

"Oh, thank God," she mumbled in a blurred sleepwalker's voice. "Thank God, thank God, thank God."

Struggling through the thick, viscid mire, she half staggered, half crawled out of the water.

Around her, a few buttonwood trees formed a transitional zone between the red and black mangroves and the live oaks and mahoganies that grew in drier soil.

She shambled a dozen yards from the swamp, hoping to escape the worst of the mosquitoes, then collapsed, exhausted, at the base of a mahogany. She lay there, coughing weakly, her head in her arms.

*Rest,* she thought vaguely. *Just for a little while.*

Her whole body hurt. She had more aches than muscles.

If she lived through this, she was going to get fat and lazy. She never would work out again.

The thought made her smile.

Then slowly the smile faded as she became aware of a new kind of pain, throbbing throughout her right side.

The bite wounds in her arm, shoulder, and chest burned like splashes of acid.

Shaking herself alert, she examined the twin punctures in her forearm. The site was swelling noticeably, the surrounding flesh turning an ugly purple.

An infection? No, this was something different. Something worse.

*White mouth.*

The thought startled her, words from nowhere.

*The snake had a white mouth. Yes. I remember that.*

*And it swam with its head out of the water.*

Those details held some significance her dazed mind could not quite grasp. She struggled to make herself see.

*White mouth . . .*

*Cottonmouth.*

*The cottonmouth swims like that.*

*Oh, dear Jesus.*

The snake was a cottonmouth, a water moccasin, and it had bitten her. Bitten her three times, with each bite burying its fangs deep.

Its hollow, venom-injecting fangs.

Poisoned. She had been *poisoned.*

And even while she struggled so desperately to live, she was slowly dying inside.

# 42

It was four A.M. when the big Bell 204B chopper, a commercial variant of the UH-1 Huey, touched down on Blackwood Drive.

Lovejoy and Moore stood outside the condemned restaurant, squinting against the rush of wind from the twenty-foot rotor blades. A few yards behind them, the two deputies, Parker and Ross, leaned on the hood of their patrol car and watched also.

The helicopter squatted like an immense insect on the asphalt, blocking both lanes. There was no traffic at this hour anyway.

Before the blades had finished spinning, the side door slid open, and five men and two women disembarked. They wore FBI jackets and carried equipment cases. The search team.

"Judging by its markings, I would say that's a Miami P.D. chopper," Lovejoy remarked as he and Moore led the group to the rear of the restaurant, where the junked Sunbird sat forlornly on its rims.

The team leader nodded. "Field office keeps a Bell Jet Ranger at the heliport on MacArthur Causeway, but that bird doesn't have sufficient passenger capacity for the eight of us. Miami P.D. uses the Huey for utility work. We borrowed it, with pilot, for the trip to Fort Myers."

"I assume Jack's presence there has still not been absolutely confirmed."

"Haven't you heard? The news isn't even that good. The whole Fort Myers angle turned out to be a dead end."

Lovejoy glanced at Moore and raised an eyebrow. "Is that so?"

"Our Prints people found clean latents on the Dynasty's door handles, matched them with two juveniles in the Miami area. Repeat offenders, real losers; must've lifted the car for a joyride, and they were too stupid—or too wasted—to wear gloves."

"From what I understand, Dance was reported to have been seen in a convenience store."

"Another red herring. The local cops got a little overexcited on the basis of a very preliminary report. When one of our street agents showed the so-called eyewitnesses a photo six-pack, they failed to select Jack's mug shot. The upshot is, there's no longer any reason to believe he was ever near Fort Myers. I hope this lead will pay off."

"My feeling also," Lovejoy allowed, imagining how nice it would be to inform Deputy Associate Director Drury of that particular turn of events.

While the two latent-prints technicians dusted the Pontiac and the photographer popped flashcubes, the team leader, recorder, and two finders began searching the area for discarded license plates or any other item that could plausibly be linked to the car. Having found nothing in the immediate vicinity, the team leader conscripted the deputies, split up the group into two-person squads, and expanded the search to cover Blackwood Drive, a half mile of Route 1 in either direction, and all intersecting streets within that perimeter.

By five-thirty, the prints technicians were thoroughly

frustrated. The Sunbird, they informed Lovejoy and Moore, had been wiped clean. Dashboard, door handles, steering wheel, gear selector, trunk lid, hood—all polished and immaculate. The only items not yet dusted were the ashtray and rearview mirror, both of which had been removed at the start of the procedure for close inspection later.

Nothing in the ashtray. "Jack doesn't smoke," Moore observed in an undertone.

Lovejoy frowned. "According to the statistical data I've seen, neither do approximately a hundred million other Americans."

Liberal application of gray fingerprint powder to the rearview mirror revealed a partial latent in the lower left-hand corner. Enough of the pattern area was intact to permit a comparison.

The first technician photographed the impression with a Folmer-Graflex fingerprint camera, shooting a roll of 120 Tri-X and carefully bracketing the exposures. His partner lifted the print on a strip of Scotch tape and smoothed it onto a glossy white card. Together they examined it in the glare of a portable arc lamp, then compared it with a faxed copy of Jack's prints.

"Right index," the first technician said.

His partner nodded. "Central pocket loop, eleven ridges from delta to core."

"He must have adjusted the mirror when he started driving. Wiped it later, but missed a spot."

The second technician remembered Lovejoy and Moore. "It's a match," he reported in the tone of an afterthought.

Lovejoy wanted to turn handstands. The thrill of vindication was intoxicating, an electric charge. Looking at Moore, he saw the same heavy exhilaration in her eyes.

They were still wordlessly congratulating each other with smiles and traded glances when the searchers returned. The team leader carried three plastic evidence bags filled with what looked like trash.

"It *is* trash," he said in response to Moore's question. "At least that's where Parker found it. In a dumper outside a warehouse half a mile south of here, on a side street called Industrial Drive."

Parker, the deputy, was trying hard not to look smug.

The recorder read off the items on the evidence inventory. Auto registration form, proof-of-insurance form, and other glove-compartment documents consistent with the Pontiac Sunbird stolen from Miami International. A vehicle identification number matching that of the stolen Sunbird. And a single license plate—not from the Sunbird but from some other car.

"He switched plates." The team leader shrugged. "Probably saved him from being pulled over. We can locate the other vehicle easily enough to confirm that part of the story. For identification purposes the VIN is all we really need."

Lovejoy consulted with Moore while the search team packed up their equipment and the deputies made arrangements to have the car towed. In the east the sky was brightening, the long night at an end.

"It seems to me . . . that is . . . I really do feel justified in saying we've almost got him." Lovejoy felt himself shaking, literally shaking, with excitement. "He would appear to be . . . very close."

"Close." Moore ran her hands over her hair, a nervous, distracted gesture. "But still one step ahead. Where's that map we borrowed from the sheriff's station?"

"I believe it's in the car."

They turned on the sedan's reading light and studied the map of Upper Matecumbe Key.

"He walked to that trash bin from here." Moore traced Jack's probable route with her finger. "A half mile south, just off Route One. Industrial Drive's a dead end. Let's assume he returned to the highway and continued south. . . ."

Her fingernail reached a narrow inlet labeled MARINA. She raised her head to look at Lovejoy.

Both of them were thinking of Albert Dance's trips to Florida in the *Light Fantastic,* the postcard that began, "Jack and Steve and I took the boat out yesterday," the snapshot of young Jack and his friend posed casually at the end of a dock.

"Boats," Moore whispered.

Lovejoy nodded, his hands closing slowly into fists. "Boats."

# 43

Deep in the tropical hammock, amid blooms of orchids and bursts of bromeliads like frozen fireworks displays, under a canopy of leaves allowing glimpses of pale pink sky, Jack Dance hunted.

Throughout the night he had been bitten by mosquitoes, stung by centipedes, jabbed by thorns and briers, scraped by poisonwood and manchineel. His shirt was speckled with burs, his pants shredded; dried mud crusted the insides of his shoes.

Acre by acre he quartered Pelican Key. He had explored the cove and the salt ponds, where roseate spoonbills sifted the fine silt for a breakfast of shellfish, and now he prowled the forest south of the swamp, moving slowly toward the island's eastern shore.

His prey was here somewhere. He would find her. He would not be denied.

He was no longer quite sure why it was necessary to kill Kirstie Gardner. The boat would arrive in a few hours. All he had to do was ambush the captain, then race for the Bahamas. Kirstie could do him little harm after that.

Still, he wanted her. She was precisely his type. Another Meredith.

His eyes narrowed at the memory of Meredith Turner. Bitch. Evil, emasculating bitch.

The songs of cardinals and yellow-throated warblers whistled giddily through the clear, fragrant air. Morning glories opened tremulous blue petals to receive the day's first light. Fastened to the bark of a gumbo-limbo, a tree snail gleamed like a gemstone, its porcelain-smooth shell a rainbow in miniature.

Beauty. Beauty everywhere.

Jack saw none of it.

"Bitch," he breathed, the word low and susurrant, scratchy in his throat.

He was eleven years old. Sleepless in the dark, listening to faint noises from the living room.

His parents were out. He was alone in the house with his baby-sitter.

Or perhaps not alone.

Silently he crept to the top of the staircase, peered out from under the banister.

In the flickering glow of a lava lamp, two pale figures twisting on the sofa. Meredith's white breasts flopping as she groaned. The man with long hair grinding his hips in the slow, measured rhythm of a dance.

Jack watched though the bars of the balustrade till both bodies shuddered in mutual release.

The man left shortly afterward. Jack, in bed once more, touching his penis and thinking, heard the back door swing shut.

Soft footsteps on the stairs. Meredith checking on him, leaning through the doorway, her face limned by the dim light from the hall.

Lying still, eyes half closed, Jack whispered, "I saw what you did."

"What, Jack? You say something?"

"I saw it. You let that guy fuck you. Did it feel good?"

"I . . . You had a dream, that's all. I didn't—"

"Felt good, didn't it?"

"Go to sleep, Jack."

"I could do it. I'm old enough."

"Jack, please . . ."

"I've got a dick, too. See?"

He snapped on the bedside light, kicked off the covers. He'd removed his pajama bottoms. His penis was stiff and red from rubbing.

"Oh, God, put on your p.j.'s—"

"P.j.'s are for little kids. I'm not little. I'm eleven. You're really pretty, Meredith."

"Cut it out—"

"I'll tell. I'll tell what you did. I'll tell my folks, and they'll tell yours."

"Christ, what are you trying to do, get me *killed*?"

Jack liked her sudden panic. Enjoyed the sense of power it gave him. Meredith's parents were devoutly religious, fanatically strict; she had to be terrified of what would happen if they found out about the long-haired boy.

"Let me put it in you," he said softly, "and I won't tell."

"Are you *crazy*?"

"I can do it as good as that guy. I'm old enough."

"You are *not* old enough—Christ—you're in the sixth grade!"

"Let me do it to you, or I tell."

*"No."*

"Let me, or else."

*"Stop it."*

"Let me."

"Oh, God, this is sick, you can't mean this—"

"Let me."

"Jesus. Jesus . . ."

"Let me."

Sobbing, she turned away from him and tugged at her skirt. Jack watched, pleased with the control he now exercised over this girl who was in high school, nearly an adult, taller and stronger than he was, yet a captive to his will.

*Guilt makes people do things.* It was a lesson he meant to remember.

Meredith's skirt was a wrinkled rag on the floor, her panties dangling from one ankle. She sat on the bed and spread her legs.

"What are you waiting for?" Her voice had thickened like paste. Tears glistened on her cheeks; Jack thought of slug tracks. "Do it. Get it over with."

"Aren't you supposed to kiss me and stuff?"

"Just goddamn *do* it."

He eased himself inside her, slowly, slowly.

And his erection died.

"What's the matter?" Fury and shame made her cruel. "Can't you even get it up?"

"I'm trying."

"You little asshole. You twisted fuck."

"Hey, shut up."

"You can't do it 'cause you're queer."

"I'm *not.*"

"Maybe you could do it with a boy. You want me to find you a boy?"

"I *hate* you."

"Faggot."

*"Bitch."*

"Fag, fag, *fag*!"

She escaped from his bed. For long minutes he heard water running in the bathroom pipes.

Meredith never baby-sat for him again. He told his parents he was too old for a sitter, and they agreed.

He no longer touched his penis. He had no more erections. It was as if a switch had been thrown, shutting off his sexuality.

Until his freshman year of high school, when a dark-haired, green-eyed girl who looked nothing like Meredith seduced him, almost against his will.

No humiliation this time. He was not a queer, not a faggot. Meredith had lied.

The sudden revelation of his sexual potency was the explosive rupture of a dam. Years of suppressed urges burst like floodwaters through the levees and restraining walls he'd built. He needed sex; he could not get enough.

Speedily he acquired expertise in the game of seduction. He possessed all the requisite assets: good looks, skill at manipulation, and a chilly brazenness that passed for charm.

He kept score of his conquests. In one memorable year he bedded thirteen of his classmates, two girls from other schools, and his young math teacher, Miss Chamberlain.

He had redheads, brunettes, girls with raven hair. No blondes, however. No Merediths.

Blondes, he told his envious friends with a shrug, were not his type.

In a deeper sense, though, they *were* his type, his only type. It was Meredith who obsessed him as he lay in bed in the unforgiving dark. It was Meredith he could not forget. Meredith, who had deceived and insulted him. Meredith, who had tried to make him less than a man.

He waited until August of 1978 before taking revenge.

"Bitch," he whispered as he held her underwater and let chlorinated water flood her lungs. "Fucking bitch."

Though he had killed her, she'd never truly died. She survived in every woman who reminded him of her. In Laura Westlake of San Antonio and Dorothy Beerbaum of Dallas and Veronica Tyler of Phoenix and all the others.

And now, Kirsten Gardner.

The others had paid for Meredith's crime. Kirstie would pay also. And after the hell she had put him through tonight, he would savor her death, draw it out with a connoisseur's relish. She would be his best Meredith yet.

The trees thinned out. The dense hammock gave way to a clearing speckled with darting swallowtails. An oval of open sky spread a pale lucent wash over thickets of bottlebrush and rustling stargrass.

Half hidden in the grass, almost lost amid the star-shaped blossoms, lay Kirstie's other sandal.

"Well," Jack said aloud. "Well, well, well."

He knelt and picked it up. The sole was caked with mud. She had been here after leaving the swamp.

Carefully he examined the grass. Tufts of green leaves, trampled by hasty footsteps, had not yet sprung upright.

Couldn't have been very long ago when she passed through.

She was close.

His gaze traveled slowly over the clearing. A thin streak of glitter—something fine, threadlike—was strung along the garish spikes of a bottlebrush plant.

Spider web? No.

A strand of fabric, snared by the shrub.

He plucked the thread free, held it taut between two fists. Though it was ragged and flecked with dirt, its original color was still recognizable.

Yellow. The color of Kirstie's tank top.

He followed the line of flattened patches in the grass. At the edge of the clearing he found a second yellow thread, fluttering in the beaklike flowers of a bird-of-paradise. Just beyond it, a third.

The tank top, unraveling, had left a loose strand every couple of yards. Even outside the clearing, in the comparative gloom of the canopied forest, he could pick out new threads now that he knew what to look for.

The hunt was nearly over.

He would have her soon.

# 44

Kirstie lay supine on the bunk in the musty darkness, fighting hard for breath.

The poison had done something to her respiratory system. She couldn't seem to get enough air. Twice in the woods she'd sunk to her knees in a swoon; only by lowering her head had she saved herself from a blackout.

She lifted her hand to her throat and felt for the carotid artery. Her pulse had been frighteningly weak and fluttery the last time she'd checked. Now she detected no pulse at all.

*Dead, then. I must be dead.*

The thought was meant as a joke, but she didn't smile.

Thirst choked her. She wished she had water.

There was water in the house, and the house was not terribly far away. The old Kirstie could have walked there in five minutes. But this was the new, pathetically debilitated Kirstie, the Kirstie locked in a losing battle with whatever witches' brew of toxins had been unleashed on her system; and this Kirstie could not walk another five feet.

It had required all her energy merely to take refuge in this one-room shack, part of a line of ramshackle row houses on the eastern end of the island. The shacks, she recalled Steve telling her, had been erected in the early part of the century, when a lime tree plantation had flourished on Pelican Key.

Two bunks, upper and lower, were built into one wall. There was no furniture, no lighting, no kitchen or bath; the one window long ago had been boarded up. The plantation workers had been housed like prisoners, two to a cell, without even a toilet of their own.

Hard to imagine how anyone could have lived in this filthy hole. But dying here—that was a different story. She was beginning to develop a disturbingly vivid picture of what that would be like.

Something whined in the dark. Mosquito, shut in with her. A tickle on her shoulder; the bug had alighted to feed. She was too weak to brush it away.

Well, let the goddamn thing drink its fill. Maybe the snake venom would kill it. Maybe—

Distantly, the slam of a door.

She stiffened.

Had it been the wind? Had one of the row-house doors blown open and shut?

Another slam. Closer.

A brief pause, time enough for her to realize that she could feel her heartbeat now, its rhythm strong and fast, and then a third door banged shut, nearer still.

Someone was methodically checking the shacks, one at a time.

Absurdly she was seized with the impulse to fight. Crazy; she had no weapons, no strength.

But to lie here immobile and let death take her—to put up no final resistance, simply cower like a beaten animal . . .

Her right arm hurt too much to move. Reaching down with her left hand, she groped on the floor. Her fingers brushed past the dried carapaces of dead insects, brittle as bits of eggshell.

What did she think she was looking for, anyway? A shotgun conveniently left under the bunk? Or maybe a hand grenade or a bundle of dynamite sticks? Hopeless.

*Slam.* Closer.

She punched through a gummy meshwork of cobwebs under the bunk. Feeling along the wall, she touched something small and hard and slender, sharply pointed at one end. She withdrew it carefully.

A nail.

Some workman must have dropped it while boarding up the window. A good, long nail—three or four inches.

*Slam.* Very close now.

A ripple of light-headedness passed through her as she struggled upright. She took a slow step, then another, treading lightly to prevent the loose floorboards from squealing.

*Slam.* The next door down.

She found the door frame, leaned against the wall, the nail clutched tight in her fist.

Hardly a lethal weapon. But if she put it in his neck, she might disable him long enough to grab his gun—assuming he had a gun—and shoot him, shoot to kill.

She could kill now. Kill either of them. Yes, even Steve. He was not her husband anymore.

Outside, a crunch of footsteps.

There was a very good chance she would be dead within a few seconds. Oddly the thought did not frighten her. She had done her best. She could not have done more.

The door swung open. Pallid light streamed into the gloom. The emaciated shadow of a man stretched along the floor.

Kirstie raised the nail, holding it parallel with her line of vision.

The shadow wavered. The man leaned forward, his face in profile sliding into view.

At first she didn't even recognize him. Mud streaked the bird's-nest tangle of his hair. His eyes, sunk deep in the sockets, were underscored by dull crescents the color of dead flesh. Beard stubble dusted his cheeks, fringing cracked and swollen lips, the parched lips of a wanderer in the desert.

And his shirt—God—it was crusted with blood.

He didn't see her. Though she had hesitated, though she ought to have forfeited the advantage of surprise, his glazed eyes, blinking vapidly, appeared to focus on nothing at all.

Against such a badly weakened adversary, even a three-inch nail wielded by a woman on the verge of collapse might prove as effective as a bayonet in a soldier's hand.

But somehow she couldn't make her arm lash out in a deadly thrust. It would be like . . . like killing a dead man.

Instead, almost involuntarily, she breathed his name.

"Steve . . ."

The sound of her voice took a second to register with him. He turned in her direction, eyes narrowed, lips pursed.

She couldn't interpret the look on his face. Warily she lifted the nail in her clenched fist.

"Stay where you are. Don't try anything."

He didn't seem to hear. With dreamlike slowness he reached out to touch her left hand, then gently pried open her unresisting fingers. The nail clattered onto the floor.

"Kirstie . . ." he whispered in a voice like death.

The sudden violence of his embrace shocked her. The press of his mouth against hers seemed to capture and condense every kiss they had ever shared into a frenzy of desperate, hurried intimacy.

She didn't understand—it made no sense, none of it—yet she found herself holding him tight, stroking his matted, brier-strewn hair, as his mouth brushed her neck and he spoke her name again and again, each separate moan a new, agonized confession of remorse.

If this was another trick, another trap, then she would let him deceive her, let him win.

# 45

The guardhouse at the marina was manned by an elderly wharf rat in a security guard's jacket and cap. His name, he told Lovejoy and Moore, was Mickey Cotter, and he worked the night shift, from midnight to seven A.M.

Lovejoy showed him the mug shot. "The gist of the situation is that we're looking for this man. His name is Jack Dance."

Cotter put on a pair of reading glasses and held the photo under the lamp on his desk. "Face don't look familiar. What's he called again?"

"John Dance. Often called Jack."

"I'm no damn good at remembering people. Boats I know. Never forget a boat."

Moore saw an opportunity. Cotter looked as if he'd hung around this boatyard for decades, a permanent fixture.

"In the seventies," she said, "Jack used to visit Islamorada with his father. They had a twenty-five-foot flybridge cruiser, the *Light Fantastic*."

*"Light Fantastic?"* Cotter's glasses slipped down, and he thumbed them back onto the bridge of his nose. "Oh, sure. I knew her. She tied up here every August. Unusual design—semi-displacement hull. She could be trimmed with flaps; you don't normally see that feature on a canyon runner. I remember one time

there was a problem with the flaps. She was riding high—"

Lovejoy cut short the reminiscence. "So, from what I understand, you're saying that you did meet Jack?"

"I surely did. 'Course, he was just a kid back then. Smooth talker, though. Never entirely trusted him. Had a friend, nice boy, came with him every time."

"Could his friend's name, by any chance, have been Steve Gardner?"

"Why, yes. That was him. Stevie Gardner. Wait a minute. Pretty sure I heard something about that young man only recently." He lifted his cap and scratched his sun-browned scalp, frowning hard. "I got it. Chet told me. He's on Pelican Key."

Moore was lost. "Who is?"

"Steve Gardner and his missis—they're taking a vacation there."

A startled glance passed like a spark of static electricity between Moore and Lovejoy.

"Pelican Key," Lovejoy said. "Would that happen to be close-by?"

"Three miles due east. Why? You interested in finding Steve, too?"

"As a matter of fact, yes." Lovejoy nodded grimly. "I think it's fair to state that we would be extremely interested in having a conversation with Mr. Gardner."

"Well, heck, Chet's about to head out there right now. He showed up a few minutes before you did, in a real sweat. Seemed peculiar to me; a little early for him to do one of his milk runs—"

Moore interrupted. "Where can we find him?"

"Basin C. Boat's the *Black Caesar*. The man you want is Chester Pice. Better hurry, though."

Lovejoy slid behind the wheel of the sedan. By the time Moore jumped into the passenger seat, Cotter had raised the gate. Lovejoy gunned the motor, and the car shot forward.

"Chester Pice," Moore said as Lovejoy tore through the empty parking lot. "I talked to him at the restaurant last night. He'd heard of Jack, but he wasn't sure where."

"In all probability, it came back to him."

They left the car illegally parked near a battered pickup truck—Pice's, presumably—and pounded down a flight of rickety steps onto the wharf. At the far end of the third basin, a thirty-foot sportfisher was easing out of its berth.

Pice stood at the controls on the flying bridge. Behind him, the sky burned with the promise of the still hidden sun.

Moore hailed him with a shout, barely audible over the engine roar. "Mr. Pice!"

"Miss Tamara Moore! Want a lift?" She nodded. "Well, hop aboard!"

A yard of water separated the dock from the moving boat. Lovejoy hesitated, muttered a quiet scatological protest, and sprang nimbly onto the gunwale. Moore took a breath and followed. She was grateful to land without a sprained ankle.

"Why don't you talk to him, see what prompts this early-morning excursion?" Lovejoy fumbled his walkie-talkie out of his pocket. "I've got a call to make."

Moore climbed the ladder to the flying bridge. She waited until Pice had maneuvered the *Black Caesar* clear of the dock, then asked, "You remembered something about Jack Dance, didn't you?"

He grunted an affirmative. "Woke up an hour ago, and it was clear as glass. Fellow by the name of Steve Gardner mentioned Jack to me. He and his wife are finishing up a two-week stay in the old Larson house."

"Are they the only people on Pelican Key?"

"Yes. Or at least . . . I hope they are." Pice throttled forward, guiding the sportfisher between the buoys that marked the harbor entrance. "I got on my radio at home, tried to raise them. No answer."

"Why didn't you call the sheriff's department?"

"Prefer not to trouble them till I'm sure there's a good reason. This could be a false alarm. The radio room in the Larson place is nowhere near the bedroom. If the Gardners were asleep—and most folks are, at six A.M.—they wouldn't hear it. Figured I'd check things out for myself."

"Alone? That would have been dangerous."

"Not quite alone." He pointed to a Winchester Model 70 carbine laid carelessly on the bench behind the helm seat. "Brought a friend."

"Well, now it appears you'll have a whole crowd of friends." The voice belonged to Lovejoy, joining them on the bridge. He turned to Moore. "I radioed the search-team leader, requested a flyover of Pelican Key."

"They know which island it is?"

"Chopper pilot seems to. He says that he fishes these waters when he's not flying."

"A Huey can do more than a hundred miles an hour. It'll get there before we do."

"In my estimation, the sooner, the better."

Pice left the harbor and steered southwest, chased by a strong breeze out of the north that raised a heavy chop on the water. The straits would be rough.

Watching the shoreline blur past, Moore wondered if this was the same route Pice had taken when he delivered the Gardners to Pelican Key two weeks ago.

Had the couple stood on this bridge, where she and Lovejoy were standing now? Had Steve Gardner thought of his earlier visits to the Florida Keys, the carefree times he'd spent with his friend Jack? Jack, whom he'd lied for, under oath. Jack, who'd made his first kill at age eighteen and had gone on killing ever since.

The real question was how well Steve really knew Jack, how many of Jack's secrets he'd learned or guessed, and what secrets of his own he'd kept hidden from the world—perhaps even from his wife.

His wife . . .

Moore turned to Pice, leaning over the control console, his face lit by dawn's ambient glow and the lighted dials and gauges. "Describe Mrs. Gardner to me."

Pice opened the throttle a little further, and the tach needles climbed. "Attractive woman. Blond. Nice smile, pleasant way about her. Kirstie's her name."

"What color are her eyes?"

"Her eyes? Blue, I think. Yes. Blue."

Moore gripped the handrail tight, blinking against a fine mist of spray. She had no idea what was going on, how Steve and Kirstie Gardner fit into this puzzle now so nearly pieced together. But suddenly she was afraid.

Seven women had died. Eight, counting poor Meredith Turner. There could not be another.

Please, God. There could not.

As the *Black Caesar* swung east into Tea Table Channel, the red-orange rim of the sun burst through the horizon, setting the sea aflame.

# 46

Their embrace might have lasted a minute, an hour. They clung to each other, swaying slowly like dancers.

"It's all right, Steve," Kirstie murmured in a soothing tone. "Everything is all right."

His breath was damp on her neck. "Forgive me."

"I do. I do."

The words felt like a second marriage vow.

Abruptly his knees weakened; he sagged in her arms. She helped him to the bunk and sat him down like a weary child. He slumped against the wall, eyes half shut.

Under the ragged remnants of his shirt, a faint trickle of fresh blood was visible. Droplets pattered on the bunk, red rain.

She looked him over more carefully. Blood had soaked not only his shirt but his pants, even staining the Nikes tied incongruously to a belt loop. His feet, bare like her own, were raw with lacerations.

He was not a dead man, as she'd thought. But he was close. So close.

She touched his cheek. His eyelids fluttered. He blinked at her, then noticed the incisions in her arm and shoulder, ugly and swollen and ringed with purplish vesicles.

"What . . . what happened?" he croaked.

"Snake bit me."

He nodded. His mouth curved into a brief, rueful smile. "Me, too."

She knew which snake he meant. "Have you been ... shot?"

"Stabbed." The word was a hoarse rasp. "Jack left me for dead. In the swamp."

The swamp.

In her mind she saw it again: Jack plunging forward, the gun firing harmlessly.

At the time she had attributed her survival to some sort of miracle. And now it appeared she'd been right—only it had been a different order of miracle from what she'd imagined.

It had been Steve. Risking his life to knock Jack off his feet and prevent the fatal shot from reaching its target.

But if Steve had saved her—if he had been willing even to die for her—then why ... ?

"Why did you try to shoot me?" she whispered.

"Shoot you?" He lifted his head, honest bewilderment in his eyes.

"On the dock."

"I was never near the dock."

"Dammit, I *saw* you."

"It must have been Jack."

She almost made some sharp reply, then hesitated. What had she seen, exactly? Steve's nylon jacket, the glint of his eyeglasses, the gun.

He was wearing neither the jacket nor the glasses now. And the Beretta—Jack had that, didn't he? He'd had it in the swamp.

"Oh, God," she whispered. "It *was* him." And she had hidden in the black waters as Steve pleaded for her to answer. So much blood and pain could have been saved, so much horror. "If I'd known ..."

"Doesn't matter now. Listen." Every word, every

breath, cost him an obvious effort. "We can still get away."

"How?"

"Jack's runabout. I helped him hide it. I was on my way to it when . . . when I saw your footprints in the dirt."

"Is it far?"

He coughed. A spray of vivid red bearded his chin. "Just beyond these shacks. Maybe . . . fifty yards north . . . Edge of the beach . . ."

She took his hand. "Then let's go."

He struggled to rise, pushed himself halfway to his feet, and then his legs folded and he sank to the floor, head lowered, gasping.

"Can't," he whispered, "No more . . . strength."

She gripped his shoulders and helped him up. He reclined on the bunk. Another sputtering cough brought fresh blood to his lips.

"Boat is . . . camouflaged." His voice was fading, barely audible. "Palm fronds."

"I'm not going without you."

"You have to. Get to shore. Tell the police. Tell them"—his eyes squeezed shut—"everything."

She hesitated, then nodded. It was the only way. "I'll tell them. And they'll come for you. You'll be all right."

His labored breathing was more regular, his features smooth. He did not answer.

Unconscious. Perhaps slipping into a coma. The blood on his mouth—it signaled a hemorrhage, didn't it?

She had to hurry. She'd gotten her husband back. She would not lose him again.

A last caress of his matted hair, and then she was moving toward the doorway. Distantly she was aware of new energy surging through her, a fresh release of adrenaline combating the poison's effects.

She left the shack, shutting the door softly behind her, and headed down the line of row houses.

Fifty yards north, he'd said. Not far.

She reached the end of the line, turned the corner—and stopped.

"Out for your morning stroll, Mrs. G?"

Kirstie felt no shock, no fear. She felt nothing. The only words in her mind were a simple acknowledgment of the obvious: *Well, of course.*

She stared at Jack Dance, standing less than six feet from her, limned by a haze of morning light.

No longer was he the neatly dressed, suavely smiling figure she had seen on the beach twenty-four hours ago. The crisp lines of his jeans and denim shirt had been chewed to ragged tatters. His hair, formerly combed and styled, was a disheveled horror flecked with black crumbs of earth.

And his smile—it was still there, stubbornly ineradicable, as if pasted on his face, but it held no humor now, not even the cruel humor of mockery. It was the frozen smirk of a madman.

Civilization had dressed him up in clothes and manners, concealing his essential self under a gloss of style. A night in swamp and jungle had scraped off that disguise. Now he was naked in her sight, a thing subhuman and despicable. She wondered if all his victims had seen him that way in their last moments.

*So close,* a voice in her mind whispered. *I was so close to making it.*

A hurtful, piercing sliver of regret was the only emotion she had the strength to feel.

"Nice day for a walk," Jack went on pleasantly, trying for a light, bantering tone, the glib insouciance of the man he had spent his life pretending to be. "But an even better day for you to die."

The Beretta in his hand slowly lifted, the muzzle targeting her chest.

She waited, safely past the final extremity of fear, at a point of surreal calm.

Though she was unafraid, she heard her heart pounding. Louder. Louder. The hard, steady throb unnaturally audible.

No. Not her heartbeat.

The *whop-whop-whop* of rotor blades.

Jack frowned. "What the hell . . . ?"

He glanced up, and his face froze.

*"Shit."*

Kirstie followed his gaze, glimpsed a metallic glint in the western sky, brightening as it expanded.

Fingers clamped on her arm. Jack pulled her to the front of the building, kicked open the door of the nearest shack. A rough shove, and she stumbled through the doorway and fell sprawling on the floor.

He hugged the door frame, watching the sky as the chopper swung directly overhead.

"Miami P.D.," he muttered. "Goddammit."

She couldn't quite understand. The police? Was he saying the police were here? It seemed like a dream. Everything was a dream.

Slowly the helicopter moved on, its rotor noise diminishing as it explored the north end of the island.

When he turned to her, his face was flushed and wild, his eyes unnaturally wide. "Looks like you get to live a little longer, Meredith. If I were you, I'd savor every moment."

"My name's not—"

The door slammed behind him. Darkness closed over her like a smothering embrace.

Outside, brief rattle of the doorknob. A thud, shaking the wall. Then, running footsteps.

Kirstie crawled across yards of bare floorboards till the wall bumped up against her groping hands. She pulled herself upright, crabbed along the wall to the door, and tugged at the knob.

The door wouldn't yield. Jack had secured it somehow, though there was no lock.

The only other exit was the window, boarded up. She had no tools with which to work the nails free.

Trapped, then. She was trapped.

Her brief burst of energy was over. Her thoughts swam giddily; she could make sense of nothing. The police were here, but how? She hadn't reached Islamorada, hadn't even found the boat . . .

It didn't matter. Nothing mattered. Despair and fatigue overwhelmed her.

She slumped against the door. The only desire left to her was a feeble, plaintive wish to see the sunrise.

Almost certainly the last sunrise of her life.

# 47

Jack had a plan, of course. He always had a plan.

The copter was well to the north now, hovering over the lagoon. An observer on board was unlikely to see him from that distance; but to further reduce the risk of being spotted, he kept off the road, jogging through the woods, as he headed south to the plantation house.

Almost two days ago he had escaped from the strip mall in North Hollywood while another helicopter buzzed overhead, quartering the area like a hungry hawk. Now after crossing three thousand miles, here he was again, hiding from his enemies, a field mouse scrambling for cover in the brush.

But still free. Still capable of action. As long as he could move and think, he had a chance.

Kirstie was one card he held. If necessary, he could use her as a hostage to buy himself time, convert a siege into a standoff. A desperate option, which he would exercise only as a last resort.

Better by far to get away. There was a chance of that, too. He saw a possibility of performing another magic trick, a second vanishing act. To slip free of his pursuers' talons for a second time—sweet, if he could manage it. Very sweet.

And if all his hopes failed, if he faced capture and the unendurable prospect of life imprisonment . . . well, the Beretta tucked inside the waistband of his pants still held three rounds, by his count. Enough to finish Kirstie—and himself.

He found the garden and skirted the wall till he reached the western side of the house. Twin diesel generators rumbled there, in a shed outside the radio room. Ten-gallon drums of fuel were stacked in a corner.

Lugging one heavy drum by the handle, Jack climbed through the window Kirstie had smashed. Flies swarmed over the floor near Anastasia's spread-eagled body, drawn by a pool of congealing blood.

He uncapped the drum. Fuel gurgled out, leaving a wet trail behind him as he made his way through the kitchen and dining room. The can was nearly empty when he reached the living room, awash in virgin daylight slanting through the big arched windows. He kicked scraps of kindling out of the fireplace and baptized them in the last drops of fuel.

Near the fireplace was a bundle of long matches used for lighting tinder. He retreated to the patio, struck a match, and tossed it inside.

The bright wisp of flame descended in a slow-motion loop, graceful as a dying firefly, and dropped into a puddle of fuel at the foot of the mahogany table.

*Whoosh.*

The eruption of yellow-orange flame was a second sunrise. Jack stumbled backward, overcome by a rush of intense heat.

Instantly the table was crawling with angry snakes of flame. The paper shades of the chandelier caught fire. The ceiling smoked.

From the center of the garden Jack watched, briefly mesmerized, as the fire spread. Through the living room windows, the sofa and leather armchairs were visible, spitting flame like dragons. Pots burst, flowers crackled. The globe tipped over, a planet ablaze, some nightmarish vision of Armageddon. The miniature schooner on the mantel died in a fury of flame-lashed rigging.

Distant percussive noises like the pops of a cap pistol signaled the explosion of the kitchen's bottle-glass windows. The floral-print curtains over the French doors flashed out of existence in sheets of whirling sparks. Webworks of filigreed iron decorating the doors and windows began to melt and bend, twisting the artists' designs into grotesque Rorschach blots.

Jack went on watching, fascinated by the brisk, energetic destruction rampant before him, the triumph of chaos over order, entropy's last word. It pleased him to have been the agent and midwife of the fire. He liked its mindless hunger, its gleeful rapacity; and he relished, as always, the violent death of beauty.

Turning away at last, he hurried out the garden gate. He pounded down the trail, then veered into the woods when he heard the helicopter's approach.

Behind him, the Larson house threw off a black column of smoke, spiraling slowly, a tornado garlanded in embers.

The copter was closer now, drawn to the flames like some giant moth. Jack huddled by a royal poinciana, concealed beneath an umbrella of feathery leaves and scarlet blossoms, while overhead the rotor blades whacked the air like giant paddles and the Huey's turboshaft engine screamed. Wind from the blades gusted through the forest, shaking thickets of shell ginger and kicking up lazy streamers of dust.

Then the chopper passed on, and Jack started moving again.

The row houses were less than a hundred feet away. He dared a breathless sprint under the open sky, gambling that the copter crew would have their attention focused on the blaze.

The door to the shack was still secured. Before leaving, he had removed his belt, looped it around the knob, and nailed it to the door frame with his pocketknife.

He wrenched the blade loose, kicked open the door, and found Kirstie slumped on the floor.

"Get up," he snapped. "Move."

She groaned.

"Dammit, *move*!"

He yanked her to her feet and brandished the knife in her face.

"Do what I say, or I'll cut you. Understand?"

The threat had no effect. She seemed to be beyond fear.

"Give it up," she whispered. "It's over."

"Uh-uh, sweetheart. I've only just begun." He slipped the knife into the vest pocket of his shirt and hustled her out the door. "Now let's get going."

They stumbled away from the shacks. Looking south, Jack saw the chopper descending, its gleaming fuselage gradually eclipsed by smoke and flame.

The cops were landing to explore the house, save anyone inside. Perfect.

He guided Kirstie into a tangle of scrub on the verge of the beach. Together they staggered through the prickly brush, scaring birds and butterflies out of their path. The orange sun, fiercely bright, stabbed at their eyes through breaks in the foliage.

"Where . . ." A gasp stole her question. "Where are we going?"

"My runabout. Then the open water. By the time anyone figures out we're gone, I'll be cruising down Highway One in another stolen car."

Kirstie didn't ask where she would be. Jack imagined she already knew.

# 48

Lovejoy squinted at the red radiance of the sun, furnace-hot on the horizon. Pelican Key was concealed somewhere in the sheet of glare.

"Smoke." Pice stabbed a finger at the spray-flecked venturi windshield.

A dark plume bisected the spread of crimson light.

Lovejoy thumbed the transmit button on his walkie-talkie and asked the team leader to report.

"House on the south end of the key just went up like a Roman candle. Pilot already radioed for fireboats. We're setting down to perform a search-and-rescue."

"I would advise you to maintain your alertness. You could be walking into a trap."

"How bad *is* this s.o.b., anyway?"

"He's the devil. And it appears he's not through raising hell."

A stiff wind beat at the water. The *Black Caesar* panted on the swells. Curtains of spray burst over the port bow, soaking the foredeck; water gurgled in the scuppers.

Pelican Key materialized slowly out of the sun's candescence. On a level stretch of ground between the dock and the house's flagstone court, amid beds of flowers, the Huey crouched on its skid, rotor blades still spinning. A line of tiny figures in dark blue jackets, hunched low, sprinted up the path toward the gate with revolvers drawn.

"Want us to tie up at the dock?" Pice asked.

"No." Moore scanned the shoreline, using a pair of binoculars borrowed from the control console. "The fire's a diversion. Like the locked storeroom in the CSGI office."

Lovejoy had been thinking the same thing. "It would be preferable to circle the island," he told Pice. "Is there another dock?"

Pice manhandled the wheel, swinging the *Black Caesar* to the northeast. "No. You could drop anchor in the cove, though. Or drag a dinghy aground—"

Moore interrupted. *"Look."*

Perhaps half a mile ahead, a small boat glided away from the beach, trailing a white vee of foam.

"Two persons on board." Moore adjusted the focus on the binoculars. "Man and woman, I think. Woman is seated in the bow. Blond Caucasian, must be Mrs. Gardner. The man . . ."

She strained to get a clear view of him through a rainbowed mist of spray.

"It's Jack," she said finally.

"What's his heading?" Lovejoy asked Pice.

"'Due north. Probably means to turn west eventually and come ashore on Windley or Plantation Key."

"If we give chase, things are likely to get dangerous. I can't order you—"

Pice brushed aside Lovejoy's politeness. "No need for orders. I volunteer."

He slammed the throttles open. The sportfisher plunged ahead.

"He sees us," Moore said, staring through the binoculars, her voice taut.

The runabout hooked east, into the sun.

"It's no use, Jack," Lovejoy whispered. "In my considered opinion, your luck has finally run out."

# 49

Kirstie sat on the runabout's sailing thwart and stared blankly at the water rushing past. Flecks of turquoise checkered the swells, dancing amid a flotsam of orange sun-sparkles. Pretty. So pretty . . .

"Son of a *bitch*."

Glancing up, she saw Jack twisted in his seat, his gaze fixed on a sportfisher half a mile astern.

The *Black Caesar*? She thought it was.

He turned toward her. A child's petulant fury distorted his face—helpless, shaking rage at a world that would not let him have his way.

"First a chopper, now a boat. Got a whole fucking armada on my ass." He yanked the outboard motor's throttle arm, and the runabout fetched east. "But I'll beat 'em anyway. You hear me, Meredith?"

"I'm not Meredith!" she protested hoarsely over the buzz of the engine.

"Yes, you are." The glittery malice in his eyes hinted at a deeper craziness, an insane obsession rooted at the base of his soul. "For me, you are."

Behind them, the sportfisher altered its heading. It ran east, accelerating to twenty knots, rapidly narrowing the gap. The lurid light of sunrise smoldered on the choppy water. On the retreating horizon a wide fan of smoke unfolded slowly from Pelican Key.

Jack gathered up the three bags of supplies in the

bow and hurled them overboard, lightening the boat. The sportfisher continued to close in.

"You can't outrun them," Kirstie said.

"Yes, I can."

"Their boat's faster than yours."

"But not as maneuverable. You know the nursery rhyme: *Jack, be nimble; Jack, be quick . . .*" He flashed a smile at her, a weird simulacrum of the cocky grin that had defined his earlier persona. "That's me. Nimble and quick. I can slip through the reef, easy as threading a needle. That big mother will run aground if she tries it."

Kirstie looked past him at the cruiser expanding with a roar of diesel engines. "You won't even get to the reef."

"Hey, show a little faith." That smile again. "I've got a way of making them back off."

He withdrew the Beretta from his waistband.

Leaning over the safety rail for a better view, training the binoculars on the runabout, Moore saw the pistol come up fast.

Instinctively she pulled back, a split second late.

The bullet caught her left arm below the elbow, shattering her radius and ulna.

Pain walloped her, knocked her reeling to the deck of the bridge.

Blur of action to her right. Pice seizing his Winchester.

What came out of her mouth was one long unpunctuated cry of distress: *"No don't you'll hit the hostage!"*

"Warning shot," Pice snapped. He poked the gun barrel past the windshield and squeezed off a round, aiming high.

* * *

The rifle's report cracked like a stinging hand clap over the water. Reflexively Kirstie ducked.

A strong hand closed over her shoulder and wrenched her roughly off the thwart. Jack thrust her in front of him and screamed.

"Shoot me now, you assholes!" Frenzied exhilaration shredded his voice. "Come on, *shoot me now*!"

He pistoned out his arm, the Beretta pointed like an accusing finger, and fired again.

Lovejoy was on his way across the bridge to help his partner when the venturi windshield exploded in a cloud of shards.

Pice shielded his face with his arm. Lovejoy, caught off balance, had no chance to protect himself. Crumbs of glass chewed through his face like rodent teeth.

*"Jesus."*

He stumbled, blinking blood out of his eyes. For a heart-stopping moment he thought he had been blinded. No. Cuts scored his forehead and cheeks; blood had dampened his eyes only as it spattered.

At the steering console, Pice fired a second warning shot.

Lovejoy ran a handkerchief over his face and crouched beside Moore. He tore off the sleeve of her jacket, then removed his necktie and wound it around her arm at the elbow, making a tourniquet.

"This no-account mother's gonna kill us both," Moore said with a twitchy attempt at a smile.

"Probability of that is zero. We've got him on the run."

At least, he hoped they did.

The reef wavered on the horizon, a crooked line against a brassy smear of sun.

Jack had hoped the sportfisher would cut her speed,

giving him time to find some narrow channel between the rocks.

No such luck. The cruiser was hard astern, bearing down on him like a runaway train.

Well, there was an alternate way of crossing the reef.

He gunned the motor, pushing the runabout to full throttle. The bow lifted. The boat bounced crazily, skimming the water and shooting up fans of spray, as the Yamaha outboard shrilled.

"Some fun, huh?" he asked Kirstie with a bark of laughter.

Her eyes, wide and strangely vacant, stared out from behind a foam-drenched net of hair.

Clutching her closer, ignoring her feeble moan of protest, Jack fired another shot at the sportfisher's bridge.

The third bullet blasted a smoking hole in the control console, showering Pice with sparks.

"You okay?" Lovejoy yelled.

"Bastard missed me. Knocked out my oil gauges, is all."

Lovejoy finished knotting the tourniquet in place. "It would be advisable to lie still," he told Moore.

"Like hell." She fumbled her .38 out of her shoulder holster with her good hand. "Where I grew up, a flesh wound is about as serious as a paper cut. We've got to give Pice some protection."

"All right, cover him from here—but stay down. I'll attempt to draw Jack's fire."

He swung onto the ladder and descended to the weather deck, awash in spray. A sliding door admitted him to the galley. Lurching from handhold to handhold, he advanced to the main cabin, where a companionway ladder lowered him to the forward stateroom.

V-berths were built into the bulkheads. He stood on a berth and opened the overhead hatch, then hauled himself up onto the foredeck. On elbows and knees he wriggled to the stem of the prow.

The runabout was fifty feet away, a speeding arrowhead on a feathery shaft of wake, launched at the red bull's-eye of the sun.

Lovejoy fired a round well wide of the mark, hoping simply to get Jack's attention and prevent another shot at the bridge.

Jack heard the bullet whiz past and caught a glimpse of the man prone on the foredeck, intermittently visible as the sportfisher's bow lifted and plunged.

The reef was less than a minute ahead. He could afford no further distractions.

Next time the bow swung down, he would take the fucker out.

The cruiser's bow rose on a swell, then dipped as the wave passed. For an instant the gunman bobbed into view, a perfect target.

Jack pulled the trigger.

Nothing.

The Beretta was empty, the sixteen-round clip finally exhausted.

"Shit." Jack pitched the gun overboard.

It didn't matter anyway. If he cleared the reef, the sportfisher couldn't follow. Either she would be forced into a hopelessly time-consuming detour, or she would founder on the rocks.

The *Black Caesar* shook with the twin diesels' vibrations. Glass shards clinging to the windshield frame shivered and fell like melting icicles.

Moore saw the reef and yelled a warning to Pice. "Coral ahead!"

"I know it." The captain's voice was calm. "He's trying to wreck us."

"Won't he wreck himself, too?"

"He doesn't think so. He's got a daredevil stunt in mind."

"What have *you* got in mind?"

Pice showed her a grim smile. "Just hang onto that rail when I tell you to. And tell your partner to get below deck."

The reef was close now. Thirty seconds.

Jack scanned the line of rocks and saw a short stretch of coral flatter than the main line of the ridge. He jerked the throttle arm sideways, aiming for that spot.

A lightweight craft running at top speed on a rough sea was capable of hydroplaning over a reef, skimming the jagged outcrops without being caught and torn.

It could be done. He'd heard stories of such maneuvers while hanging around boatyards in the Keys many summers ago.

The trick was in the timing. You had to catch a wave, ride it like a surfer, let the rolling carpet of water sweep you over the rocks to safety on the other side.

Ten seconds.

*Jack, be nimble . . .*

"Peter! Get below!"

Lovejoy heard Moore's shout in the same moment when the reef appeared out of a whirl of spray, dead ahead.

He scrambled away from the stem and dropped down the hatch.

Through the bulkheads, the big diesels howled like

tortured beasts. He gripped the companionway ladder, lacing his fingers between the treads.

*What's Pice up to? It would appear, to put it bluntly, that he's about to get us all killed.*

Five seconds.

Jack released Kirstie and pushed her into the bow. He nudged the throttle stick to the right, correcting for a few degrees of leeward drift.

*Jack, be quick . . .*

"Hang on!" Pice shouted.

Moore grabbed the safety rail with her good hand. The reef was terrifyingly close. No way they could stop in time. She braced for impact.

Pice rammed the paired throttles into neutral and spun the wheel to starboard.

Lovejoy heard the sudden drop in engine noise, felt the boat's shuddering turn. In the main cabin, something tipped over with a crash.

He tightened his grip on the ladder, knuckles squeezed white.

Silently he prayed.

Two seconds.

*Jack, jump over . . .*

One second.

*. . . the candlestick.*

The runabout reached the reef on a crest of surging water and rose, propelled by momentum, lifted on the blanket of spray thrown up by the rocks and rising higher, higher, sailing over the reef in a graceful slow-motion curve.

Somewhere Kirstie was screaming. Jack ignored her. He had done it. He was flying. *Flying.*

The boat's nose tipped down.

The reef flew up.

He had time to realize he hadn't cleared the rocks—

Crack-up.

The runabout slammed headfirst into the coral ridge and blew apart in a hail of shattered floorboards and hissing Hypalon tubes.

Moore clung to the handrail as the *Black Caesar* heeled to starboard, scraping the reef on the port side.

Dimly she was aware that Jack's boat had broken up.

She hoped Mrs. Gardner was all right.

No more victims. Please.

The force of the collision catapulted Kirstie out of the runabout. Her world turned somersaults, reef and sky exchanging places, and then the reef was behind her, water rushing up in a kaleidoscopic glitter, cold shock of immersion, and she floundered, gasping, fists slapping the green swells.

Around her bobbed scraps of the runabout, pushed by the wind. Inflation compartments, their seams burst, shriveled slowly like punctured balloons. Splintered driftwood scraped the rocks. The severed stern slowly foundered, buoyancy chambers deflating, the weight of the outboard motor bolted to the transom dragging it down.

On the far side of the reef, the *Black Caesar* hove to. The brawny figure on the bridge was Captain Pice, pointing at her, while beside him a woman in a dark suit jacket shouted for someone named Peter.

It all seemed distant, unreal, an out-of-body experience. Perhaps she hadn't survived the crash, after all. Perhaps she'd died with Jack.

Jack . . .

*Had* he died?

And if not—where was he?

Sudden urgency stabbed through her unnatural calm. She turned, scanning the water, and abruptly a huge dark shape filled her field of vision.

Jack rising up, mouth twisted in a snarl, hands reaching out like an animal's claws.

Kirstie almost found the strength to scream, and then those hands closed off her throat, fingers squeezing, and she was plunged under the waves.

In his mind, Jack was eighteen again, alone with Meredith Turner in the swimming pavilion, holding her underwater, drowning her, drowning the bitch.

"Fuck you, Meredith," he rasped as her blond hair fanned and rippled, graceful as a sea anemone. "*Fuck you.*"

Something tugged his right leg.

What the hell?

Another tug, and he was yanked below the surface.

Through the crystalline water he saw a taut cable extending from his foot to the submerging mass of the runabout's stern.

The mooring line. He must have gotten tangled in it when he tumbled free of the boat. One end was cleated to the transom; as the stern descended, the rope was pulling him along.

If he released his hold on Kirstie, he might be able to free himself.

Yes, he might. But he would not try.

*We die together, Meredith. I'll never let you go.*

Sinking deeper. Sunlight fading. The need for air a searing ache in her lungs.

She pummeled Jack, battering his shoulders, delivering weak blows to his head.

No use. His hands still wrapped her neck, a python's coils, constricting tighter, tighter.

In desperation she raked her ragged nails across his chest, clawing his shirt to tatters.

Buttons popped loose. His vest pocket flapped open. Something compact and shiny spilled out and cartwheeled slowly through the water.

A knife. His Swiss Army knife.

She seized it. Fumbled the spear blade out of its slot.

Instantly the choking pressure on her neck was gone. Jack grabbed her knife hand, held the blade at bay. It glittered between them, silvery in the dimming light.

She struggled to break free of his grip. Impossible. His fingers were iron bars, unyielding.

Slowly he pushed her hand back, driving the knife toward her own throat.

He meant to savage her with the blade, kill her with the same knife that had ripped open Steve's belly in the swamp.

Steve . . .

Probably dead by now. Or dying, alone in the dark. Because of this man in the water with her, this predator, this venomous snake.

Fury made her strong.

She stiffened her arm, stopping the blade only inches from her neck, and then with a final, wrenching effort she forced the knife forward, overpowering Jack as he fought to hold her back, and thrust the needle-sharp point into the soft skin below his jaw.

Blood erupted in a black spume. He released her arm, twisted free of the knife, and she stabbed again, gouging his face—again, slicing through his lips—again, grooving a horizontal slash across his forehead—again and again, her arm swinging wildly, while his hands flailed in a useless attempt at self-defense.

Air bubbled from his mouth, mixing with fluttery ribbons of blood. His eyes were wide and confused, and in them she could read his thoughts, his terrified, plaintive protest: *This can't be happening to me*!

She thought once more of Steve, then of poor Ana, then of the seven women Jack had bragged of killing, and the knife hacked yet again, butchering his face, the blade carving savagely as fierce ecstasy swelled in her, a frenzied, orgiastic exultation that craved blood and pain.

In that moment she understood the dark passions that had moved Jack through his days and nights of death. The thrill of slaughter, the giddy joy of havoc. She knew how he'd felt when he claimed each victim's life.

And she knew that there was a small part of him in her, in everyone. A part that must be resisted if it was not to be released.

Agony.

His face torn, a dozen new mouths opening to lick the water with tongues of blood.

He gave up trying to fend off the knife's attacks. The hungry blade would not be denied.

Spasms shook his body. His legs kicked, arms thrashed; he jerked and twitched and flailed, convulsions hammering him out of shape.

His women had died this way. He'd relished their furious contortions, their final shuddering exit from this life.

But now he was the one dying in a frenetic tangle of limbs, he was the one going down alone into the dark; and it was no fun at all.

The rope dragged him lower. Kirstie began to slip

away. He made a last attempt to haul her with him to oblivion. His bleeding hands found her leg; his fingers closed over her ankle. She kicked free. And then she was above him, out of reach, and he went on dropping like an anchor, cheated of his prize.

Looking up, he saw her in silhouette against the sunstruck surface of the sea. She seemed to hover there, limned in an aureole of sun. He thought irrationally of those near-death experiences people reported, the angel beckoning to the liberated spirit at the entrance to a tunnel of light.

But this angel wasn't beckoning. She retreated from him, cruel in her indifference. The light faded. And he was plunging down in an endless, weightless fall, into a pit of night.

Kirstie watched Jack vanish into the gloom. The last she saw of him was his upturned face, incised with a crosshatched intaglio of scars, his eyes wide and staring, mouth stretched in a voiceless scream.

Then he was gone, lost somewhere within a rising cloud of blood; and with him went her anger and her strength.

A wave of weariness passed over her. Her fingers splayed; the knife fell from her grasp to join its master in the depths.

She had almost no energy left. But enough, perhaps, to reach the surface before her last residues of air seeped away. Enough to live.

Kicking hard, she climbed toward daylight.

# 50

The search-team leader and the chopper pilot were first to reach the row of shacks on the east end of Pelican Key.

To the south, palm trees writhed and twisted like damned souls in the fire's hot breath. Flames had consumed the Larson house with astonishing rapidity. The smell of gasoline had hung in the air throughout the search team's brief, dangerous reconnaissance.

When it had become obvious that no one could be left alive in the inferno, the team leader had ordered a retreat from the house, then paired off his people and sent them to search the rest of the island.

He and the pilot approached the first shack in line, service revolvers drawn. They positioned themselves on both sides of the door frame. Silent count of three, and the team leader kicked open the door and pivoted across the threshold.

The shack was empty.

Next door down, same procedure, same result.

Next door, same procedure—

He froze in the doorway.

Someone was there. Lying motionless on the lower bunk.

"FBI, hands up!"

The figure did not stir.

"I said, *put your goddamned hands up*!"

Nothing.

He beamed his flashlight at the bunk.

"Oh, Christ." That was the pilot.

The team leader thought it had been a long time since he'd seen that much blood from just one man.

The two of them moved toward the bunk, less warily now, with nothing to fear. The man they had found was unmistakably dead. His eyes were shut, mouth open, skin bleached of color. Blood had run freely from a wound in his abdomen. It dripped on the floor, monotonous as water torture. A few somnolent, fat flies crawled lazily over the vivid red stains.

"Nice smell, huh?" the team leader observed, sniffing the copperish reek.

The chopper pilot didn't answer. For six years he had seen duty as a street cop before taking to the air. The lesson had been drilled into him that his first priority in a situation of this kind was to confirm that the subject was deceased.

Conscientiously he pressed his thumb against the dead man's carotid artery.

He felt a pulse.

"Hey. We've got a live one here."

The team leader took a moment to register this information. "Jesus," he said softly, staring at the parched mouth and sunken cheeks. "What could keep him going?"

"Willpower."

"We'll need a paramedic crew to medevac him off the island—"

"Medical chopper will take twenty minutes just to get here. We can airlift him ourselves in my Huey."

"This guy needs plasma, oxygen. You don't stow life-support gear on board."

"If he's survived this long, he may hang on till we get him to the mainland. It's our best shot."

The team leader nodded. "Point taken. Let's move."

Together they lifted the unconscious man off the bunk.

A groan, a flutter of eyelids. The bloodless lips moved, forming a barely audible word.

"Forgive . . ."

The team leader grunted, backing out of the gloom into the blossoming day. "You don't need to worry about forgiveness, pal. Whatever it is you've done, nobody will say you haven't suffered enough."

Lovejoy, swimming in suit pants and button-down shirt, had just made it over the reef to the scattered flotsam of the runabout when Kirstie surfaced in a spreading slick of blood.

"Mrs. Gardner!" He was already reaching for his gun, hoping water hadn't damaged the cartridges. "Where is he? *Where's Jack*?"

Her words dribbled out between breathless gasps. "I . . . killed . . . him."

"You *killed* him?"

"Yes." She regarded Lovejoy with blank, innocent eyes. "He deserved it."

Lovejoy shook his head slowly, a smile—his first smile in what seemed like a long time—teasing the edges of his mouth. "On that particular point, I wouldn't venture to disagree."

She let him lead her through a narrow gap in the reef to the *Black Caesar*'s dive step. Pice assisted her on board, then winced as he noticed the swollen puncture marks on her arm.

"Cottonmouth, eh? Lord, he nipped you something nasty—"

Kirstie cut him off. "My husband . . . you've got to

help him. He's in a shack on the island, near the main house. Dying . . . or dead."

Lovejoy took out his walkie-talkie. "I'll tell the search team." In a lower voice he asked Pice, "Do you carry antivenin?"

"No, but they'll have plenty at the hospital. Meantime, there's a first-aid kit in the aft cabin. It's already been put to good use." Moore's arm, Lovejoy noted, had been bandaged and secured in a makeshift sling. "She'll need water and painkillers, and a dab of antibiotic on those open sores."

"I'll take care of that, Captain," Moore said. "You just get us to Islamorada."

"In record time."

Moore escorted Kirstie into the cabin. Pice hurried up to the bridge, and a moment later the diesels roared as the *Black Caesar* swung toward land.

Alone in the cockpit, Lovejoy radioed the search-team leader. "Dance is dead. Tried to flee the island, and his boat broke up on the reef. There's more to the story, but it can wait."

"Congratulations." The other man's voice crackled over the speaker. "Sounds like you beat the devil."

Lovejoy felt no triumph, only exhaustion. "We recovered the hostage. She says her husband is in a shack, dying—"

"We already found him. Getting set to fly him out of here. A Code Blue team might pull him through, but I don't know. He's in bad shape. I wouldn't give the wife any false hopes."

"In my judgment, she's in no condition to be informed at all."

As he pocketed the radio, Lovejoy released a wet, noisy sneeze. His sinuses, miraculously unclogged since his arrival in the Keys, were clear no longer. Sea spray and chilly water had done their worst. He'd caught a cold.

He sneezed again, miserably, then turned toward the cabin and saw Kirstie standing in the doorway, Moore at her side.

"I heard," Kirstie said simply. "He's alive."

Lovejoy hesitated. "It's touch and go."

"He'll make it."

"In my view, it would be inadvisable to—"

"Look."

Head lifted, she pointed toward a distant spark rising slowly from the sooty haze that was Pelican Key.

The helicopter.

It climbed higher, higher, then seemed to hang suspended in the sky, a morning star.

"He'll make it," Kirstie said again, dampness in her eyes. "I know he will."

She watched the point of light until drifting smoke wiped it from view. Then she stepped to the railing and stared at Pelican Key, gliding past.

The Larson house was a roofless shell. Out of the spread of churning vapors, one long tendril of red leaped up to slash the sky like a flaming sword. The sun, swollen on the horizon, flooded the world with a febrile, apocalyptic light.

Lovejoy gave Moore a nod. Together they joined Kirstie at the handrail. She gazed at the distant fire, tears wet on her cheeks.

Moore took her hand. "Don't be afraid."

"I'm not." Kirstie shook her head slowly. "Not anymore. It's just that Steve always loved that house. He'll be so sorry it's gone." Her voice dropped lower, hushed and contemplative. "Or maybe he won't. Maybe he's ready to let it go, now that he's found what he was looking for."

"What, Mrs. Gardner?" Lovejoy asked. "What did your husband find?"

Kirstie turned to him, and he was startled to see that through her tears she was smiling, a smile clean of grief or pain. Her voice was a whisper.

"Redemption."

The boat moved on, and Pelican Key receded, melting in a crucible of sun, dissolving like the last wisps of a dream.

Don't miss the next exciting thriller by Brian Harper ...

# BLIND PURSUIT

Erin Reilly was shocked out of sleep by the urgent buzzing of her intercom.

She leaned on one elbow and studied her bedside clock's digital display, red against the dark.

2:16 A.M.

From the living room came another prolonged buzz, insistent as a stabbing finger.

One of her patients? At this hour?

Like any psychologist, she occasionally received post-midnight phone calls and beeper messages from anxious or depressed people in need of help. But an unscheduled visit to her apartment was something new.

She'd never even released her home address, and she wasn't listed in the phone book. So how . . . ?

As the intercom blared again, she kicked aside two layers of blankets and swung out of bed.

The hardwood floor was cold. Her toes curled reflexively.

A pair of slippers lay somewhere nearby, but she didn't take the time to hunt them down.

Barefoot, she hurried into the living room. Carpet in there, thank God. Warmer.

Again and again the intercom blatted at her, bursts of angry noise, distressing as a baby's wail. She groped for the controls. "Hello?"

The voice that crackled over the speaker was familiar, the most familiar voice in her world, but startling now: "This is Annie."

*"Annie?"* Not a patient with a problem. Her sister, and her best friend. "It's after two A.M. What are you doing here?"

"I'm in trouble. Please. Need to . . . talk."

In the oddly halting quality of her speech, Erin thought she heard suppressed sobs.

"Of course," she said instantly. "Come on up."

She was already holding down the ENTER button to release the lock on the lobby's security door. After a count of eight, she let go.

Agitated, she unlocked her own door and flipped the wall switch. A brass torchère and two end-table lamps threw crisp ovals of light on the white walls.

She drew a breath of comfort from the pristine orderliness of her home and, by extension, her life. No muss and clutter, no untidy loose ends.

The white sofa, glass coffee table, and teakwood entertainment center were objects of minimalist design and spare, elegant simplicity. They mirrored her soul no less exactly than the careful notations in her appointment book, the crisp lines of her signature, her manicured hands, the styling of her hair: swept back from her forehead, trimmed short at the nape.

She returned to her bedroom and, without switching on a light, found her slippers and robe.

Her apartment was on the top floor of a four-story building, a high-rise by local standards. The bedroom windows framed miles of moonlit rooftops and brush-choked vacant lots. In the distance the lights of downtown Tucson flickered faintly, cupped by the dark humps of mountains and canopied with stars.

Beyond the rows of carports at the side of the building, traffic hummed past on Pantano Road, and a dry wind shivered through the fronds of palm trees.

Erin shivered, too, as she left the bedroom. Forty-five degrees tonight—chilly for southern Arizona—though the temperature would climb to eighty by midafternoon.

The desert in springtime was an environment of extremes—cold nights and hot days, long stretches of aridity punctuated by brief bursts of punishing rain, spiny beavertail cacti and spindly ocotillo costumed overnight in garish floral blooms.

Living here in this season ought to teach a person to be prepared for abrupt changes, for the constant certainty of surprise.

But Erin had not been prepared to hear her sister's voice over the intercom.

Admittedly, Annie did tend to get emotional about things. But she'd never disturbed Erin so late at night, not even with a phone call.

Something must be really wrong.

*I'm in trouble,* she'd said.

Whatever trouble it was, it must have just come up. Annie had sounded fine on the phone a few hours ago, when Erin had called her to make a lunch date for tomorrow.

*Not tomorrow,* she corrected herself, remembering the time. *Later today.*

She paced the living room, running through a mental checklist of possible crises.

Pregnancy? Unlikely. Her sister knew enough to take precautions, and she hadn't dated seriously in a while.

Illness? She'd given no hint of any problems.

Death in the family? Impossible; they had no family left except each other now that Lydia was gone.

Annie ran her own business, so she couldn't have been fired; and her shop was doing well, so she wasn't bankrupt.

Drugs, alcohol, something criminal? No chance.

Well, Erin would find out as soon as Annie arrived at her door.

It was taking her a long time, though. The elevator was slow, but not this slow.

What if Annie was afraid to face her for some reason? Afraid to disclose this secret of hers?

Unthinkable. The two of them had been close—more

than close, inseparable—for their whole lives. Holding something back would be completely out of character for Annie, wouldn't be like her at all.

But coming to Erin's place at this hour, desperate and mysterious—that wasn't like her, either.

And she still wasn't here.

"Damn," Erin murmured to the stillness around her. "I'd better see if she's downstairs."

She found her purse, the shoulder strap looped over the back of a dining-room chair, and took out her keys. Briefly she wondered if she ought to slip on some clothes. It would be embarrassing to be caught roaming the building in her robe.

Oh, forget about it. At this hour no one else would be up.

She scanned the hallway—deserted—then shut and locked the apartment door behind her. Rows of closed doors passed by as she walked quickly to the elevator, her slippered feet padding on the short-nap carpet, the terry-cloth robe gently scraping her bare legs below her pajama bottoms. She punched the call button.

Hum of cable. Squeak of gears. The doors rattled open.

No Annie inside.

Erin got in, pressed LOBBY. The elevator descended, groaning.

Third floor. Second. She jangled her keys nervously.

Lobby.

The doors parted. She stepped into the building manager's fantasy of potted ferns and saltillo tile.

The exterior door was closed. A glass door: Annie was not visible outside it.

Near the elevator was the manager's glassed-in office, dark. No one there, either.

But it made no sense. There was only one elevator, and Annie hadn't been on it.

Had she taken the stairs? Why would she?

More likely she'd lost her nerve, gone away. God, she must be badly upset. Must be—

Behind her, a rustle of movement.

Erin turned. "Annie?"

Froze.

Not Annie.

Her heart kicked. Breath stopped.

The man was tall and heavyset, red-bearded, an uncombed shock of scarlet hair spilling out from under a baseball cap, the bill cocked low over his eyes. On the fur collar of his winter coat lay a bristle-toothed leaf, deposited there by the sword fern in the alcove where he had lain in wait.

His hands were gloved. In his right fist, a gleam of metal.

She almost screamed, and then his left hand shot out, seized her shoulder, slammed her up against the elevator doors.

The impact winded her. She had no breath, no voice.

Thrust of his right arm, the metallic thing digging into her stomach below the breastbone, two sharp prongs pinching her skin through the robe and pajama top.

From a yard away she stared into his eyes. They were empty of emotion, flat and coppery, expressionless as coins.

She had time to think that she had never seen a pure sociopath before.

His forefinger flexed.

Pain exploded in her. Her jaws clicked shut and her vision blurred as the pain went on and on, singing in every nerve ending, a single high note held unwavering at its peak.

Blindly she lashed out with her fists, trying to drive him back. The blows fell like flower petals on his chest.

Whistling static rose in her brain. She wanted to cry out, shout for help, but her mouth wouldn't work.

Her knees loosened. Her arms flapped spastically.

The static rose to a steady, hissing roar, and Erin was gone.

Everything was gone.

## 2

Annie Reilly, sleepless in the dark.

Her bed creaked with each restless change of position. She lay on her left side, her right, prostrate, supine, under the covers, on top of the covers, the pillows pressed to her cheek, mashed against her breasts, flattened under her stomach, discarded on the floor.

Hell.

She couldn't sleep.

Beyond her windows, higher in the foothills, a choir of coyotes lifted their voices in piping, ululant wails. A ghostly serenade.

Normally, Annie liked hearing those distant cries, the leitmotif of a desert night. She appreciated the reminder of her distance from the city, her closeness to the weathered peaks of the Santa Catalina range, rising like stone spires and broken battlements against the expansive sky.

But tonight the songs disturbed her. She pictured a coyote band, lean and scruffy and ravenous, heads lifted as they sang of strange hungers and gnawing needs.

Blood songs. That was what they were. Songs that were the prelude to a kill.

A slow current of dread rippled through her like a fever chill.

She'd never envied Erin's apartment over on the east side of town. Never wanted to live amid the strip malls and the auto lots. Preferred her town house in the lap of the Catalinas, remote from traffic and distraction.

But in town, at least, the desert's wildness was held at bay.

Erin must be sleeping soundly now. No nocturnal predators sang to her.

Erin. Predators.

Her foreboding sharpened. It was less a thought than a taste, the bitter flavor of fear at the back of her mouth.

Her hand fumbled for the nightstand. She didn't know what she was reaching for until her fingers closed over the plastic shell of the telephone.

Call Erin? In the middle of the night?

Crazy.

She released the phone, climbing unsteadily out of bed. In the kitchen she poured a glass of milk.

There was a phone in the kitchen. Again she felt the irrational impulse to call.

*What are you going to say? That you had a premonition of danger, so you decided to wake her up at two-thirty?*

Too bizarre.

The milk was cold and foamy. It relaxed her. A little.

Funny how she couldn't shake her unease, though.

Of course, insomnia was nothing new to her. For most of her life, she'd suffered occasional nights when she couldn't sleep at all. More frequent were the nights of interrupted sleep, when nightmares would startle her awake; she often spent an hour or more chasing away their ugly afterimages before she dared shut her eyes again.

The bad dreams were always the same, always a replay of the worst night of her life, the pivotal trauma of her childhood.

Tonight, however, was different. Tonight her anxieties were not focused on the past.

It was Erin she was afraid for, though she had no idea why.

Well, they would laugh about it at lunch. Maybe Erin would offer some Freudian interpretation of her anxiety attack. Something to do with sex. It all had to do with sex.

Annie smiled, but the smile faded as another coyote call split the night.

She became aware of eyes watching her. Green eyes like her own, but unlike hers, these were luminous in the moonlight. They studied her with an owl's unblinking attentiveness.

"Can't sleep either, huh, Stink?"

The colorpoint shorthair wound sinuously around her ankles, his fur ermine soft.

"Those mean old coyotes keeping you up? They're not after *you.*"

Stink didn't answer.

"Maybe you want some milk. That it? Does Annie have milk and you don't? Unfair, you say? You have a keen sense of justice, Stink."

Stink did not really stink. His malodorous appellation commemorated a kittenish habit, fortunately now outgrown, of throwing up at the least excuse.

Annie fixed a saucer of milk for the cat. Stink sniffed it, sniffed again, almost declined the offering, reconsidered (perhaps out of politeness), and lapped the bowl dry.

Finished, he nuzzled her leg in gratitude. She bent to caress his neck, his back. When he purred, he sounded like a very small person snoring.

Stroking him, Annie thought about the animals outside in the night, not safely sheltered like Stink, but huddling in dark burrows or flitting anxiously from one brushy hiding place to the next.

Bad to be alone and unprotected in the dark, with the coyotes keening.

Again she thought of Erin, though there was no reason for it.

Erin . . . and nocturnal hunters, stalking prey.

# 3

Sprawled on the lobby floor, she twitches and flops.

He peels off a glove, thumbs her carotid artery.

Heartbeat weak but regular.

She'll live. For now.

The Ultron stun gun goes in his coat pocket. A top-of-the-line model, complete with safety trigger and double-shock plates. The battery will produce 150,000 volts when the trigger is squeezed.

Normally he strikes from behind. Curls a gloved hand over the victim's mouth, rams the gun into the nerve center at the base of the spine, and discharges the current. For some technical reason, explained by the Ultron's manual but incomprehensible to him, the voltage cannot pass into his own body even when he's grappling with his victim.

This time he had no chance to grab her until after she spun around. Then he delivered a five-second pulse directly to her solar plexus. The resulting disruption of her nervous system should keep her immobilized for at least ten minutes.

It was his first face-to-face encounter. He found it interesting to watch her eyes roll up white in their sockets.

He enjoys this phase of his activities. Using the stun gun, then exploring a woman's body with his hand while she lies unconscious and unresisting. . . . It gives him a shameful, furtive thrill of pleasure, makes him feel—for once—fully alive.

What comes later . . .

No pleasure then, only a compulsion he can't override.

He pushes aside these thoughts. Has to get moving. Someone may enter the lobby at any moment and find him here.

He kneels by her, scanning the tiled floor. A key ring lies near her jerking hand. Car keys are included in the set. Good.

The keys disappear into another pocket. Then he lifts her in his arms. She's reasonably tall, perhaps five-eight, but slender, no more than 125. Slung over his shoulder, she's easy to carry; and the reflexive spasms trembling through her muscles create the pleasing illusion of a futile, panicky struggle against his superior strength.

He catches the scent of her hair as he lugs her to the side door. Faint fragrance. Not perfume. Bath salts.

The door opens on the parking lot that serves the complex. Rows of automobiles, pickup trucks, and motorcycles are arrayed under metal carports. Fluorescent bars cast a pale, glareless glow on steel and fiberglass.

In the doorway he pauses, scanning the area.

The moon, a waning crescent, hangs low over the horizon, hooked in a mountain's clawlike peak. It washes the asphalt in milky light. Anyone watching from a window or balcony will see him once he exits.

Fortunately the blue Taurus is parked in one of the more desirable assigned spaces, only a short distance from the door.

He takes a breath and carries her there, staying clear of floodlights. Behind him, the apartment building looms dark against an icy spray of stars. On Pantano Road, safely screened off from the parking lot by colonnades of oleanders in white bloom, cars shoot by like comets, and a motorcycle whines past, mosquito quick.

If a car should turn into the lot . . . if he should be pinned in the headlights . . .

He walks faster. His breath becomes hoarse and ragged, loud over the whistling buzz of cicadas.

Only once he is under the carport roof, concealed from any likely observer, does he again feel safe.

Fumbling the key ring out of his pocket, he unlocks the trunk and pops the lid. Gently he deposits her inside, laying her on her back.

From a utility pouch clipped to his belt, he removes cut lengths of rope. Binds her ankles first, then her wrists. To further restrict her movements, he lashes her wrists to her right thigh.

Good. Very good.

A roll of heavy electrician's tape is also among the contents of the pouch. He tears off a six-inch strip, prepares to seal her mouth. Hesitates, studying her face. His first opportunity to look at her, really look at her, up close, in the flesh.

Dangerous to indulge himself this way, under these circumstances. Still, he cannot turn away. She holds him fascinated.

Of the women he has taken, she is by far the most beautiful. By far.

He admires her as a connoisseur of art would admire a fine painting, attentive to every detail. It is an undiluted pleasure to study her lovely face as minutely as he likes, with no risk that she will return his gaze or challenge his absolute control.

She is thirty years old, balanced at that delicate equilibrium point between youthfulness and full maturity. Her skin is smooth, powdered with faint freckles; a light suntan endows her with a pink, scrubbed look, wholesome somehow. Offsetting these girlish features are her strong cheekbones and blunt jaw, which give her face a squarish shape, and her wide, serious mouth, not a child's mouth at all.

Her auburn hair, combed away from her forehead, shines even in the carport's wan fluorescence. A stray lock lies along her temple like a spiral of sewing thread, reddish-gold.

Peeling back her eyelids, he stares into gray eyes, smoky and mysterious.

He parts the flaps of her robe. Removes one of his gloves so he can stroke her white pajama top, feel its softness. Satin.

The clean lines of her neck, the bare skin stretched

taut over her thin collarbones, the scatter of reddish freckles on the margin of her cleavage, cupped in the buttoned neckband. . . .

He reaches for the top button. Wants to see her breasts—

*No.*

He jerks his head away as if slapped.

His mouth twists. A noise that is both grunt and gasp hiccups out of him. Its echo hops like a frog among the metal stanchions of the carports.

Dirty. Unclean. Corrupt.

He will not . . . touch her. Not that way. She has another purpose.

Quickly he tapes her mouth, then digs a blindfold out of his pants' pocket and snugs it over her eyes. Knots it tight in the back of her head.

Helpless now. Deprived of mobility, speech, sight. She is a free agent no longer. She is his.

Erin Reilly is his.

The Ford's trunk thumps shut like a coffin lid.

ALSO AVAILABLE FROM

# BRIAN HARPER

## SHIVER

## SHUDDER

## SHATTER

Available in Signet paperback.

**The perfect killer . . . the ideal victim . . .**

# SHIVER

LAPD homicide detective Sebastian Delgado thought he'd seen it all. Until the killer Gryphon began stalking the streets of Los Angeles, his M.O. an intricate puzzle. Delgado had no suspects, no leads, no clues. . . .

A new woman has become an unwilling contestant in the Gryphon's deadly game. Wendy Allen—lovely, innocent, living alone. Such sweet, easy prey . . . or is she? It will take all of Delgado's experience and Wendy's hidden reserves of strength to win this terrifying game of death.

**"Scary, riveting . . . brings real depths to the serial killer novel."**
**—*Mystery Scene***

**The ultimate innocent becomes the sweetest prey. . . .**

# SHUDDER

One little boy was dead. That was bad.

The killer was still on the loose. That was worse.

But for LAPD homicide detective Robert Card, the nightmare was even closer to home. He already has made one mistake in his hunt for the serial killer—a mistake which filled him with guilt and terror. He could not afford another as he moved through a labyrinth of masked madness and lethal lust. For Card has a little boy of his own—a little boy who was the prime target of a murderer who craved innocent blood. . . .

**"An absorbing thriller."**
***—Publishers Weekly***